About the Author

Christie Barlow is the author of *A Year in the Life of a Playground Mother*, *The Misadventures of a Playground Mother*, *Kitty's Countryside Dream*, *Lizzie's Christmas Escape*, *Evie's Year of Taking Chances* and *The Cosy Canal Boat Dream*. She lives in Staffordshire with her husband, four kids, horses, chickens and a mad cocker spaniel.

Her writing career came as somewhat a surprise when she decided to write a book to teach her children a valuable life lesson and show them that they are capable of achieving their dreams. The book she wrote to prove a point is now a #1 bestseller in the UK, USA and Australia.

Christie is an ambassador for @ZuriProject raising money and awareness and engaging with communities in Uganda through organisations to improve their well-being. She is also Literary Editor for www.mamalifemagazine.co.uk, bringing you all the latest news and reviews from the book world.

She loves to hear from her readers and you can get in touch via her website, Twitter and Facebook page.

@ChristieJBarlow
facebook.com/ChristieJBarlow
www.christiebarlow.com

Also by Christie Barlow

A Year in the Life of a Playground Mother
The Misadventures of a Playground Mother
Kitty's Countryside Dream
Lizzie's Christmas Escape
Evie's Year of Taking Chances

The Cosy Canal Boat Dream

CHRISTIE BARLOW

A division of HarperCollins*Publishers*
www.harpercollins.co.uk

HarperImpulse an imprint of
HarperCollinsPublishers
The News Building
1 London Bridge Street
London SE1 9GF

www.harpercollins.co.uk

This paperback edition 2017

First published in Great Britain in ebook format by
HarperCollinsPublishers 2017

Copyright © Christie Barlow 2017

Christie Barlow asserts the moral right to
be identified as the author of this work

A catalogue record for this book
is available from the British Library

ISBN: 9780008240905

This novel is entirely a work of fiction.
The names, characters and incidents portrayed in it are
the work of the author's imagination. Any resemblance to
actual persons, living or dead, events or localities is
entirely coincidental.

All rights reserved. No part of this publication may be
reproduced, stored in a retrieval system, or transmitted,
in any form or by any means, electronic, mechanical,
photocopying, recording or otherwise, without the prior
permission of the publishers.

For Agnes Barlow,
The brightest star shining in the sky.

Prologue

Little Rock Marina was a beautiful place to live; linked to the Trent and Mersey Canal it was home to two hundred narrowboats and set in a ninety-acre woodland. Small boutiques, coffee shops and all things crafty adorned the jetty. Nell Andrews' narrowboat was moored in a fantastic spot on jetty number ten, right in the heart of the marina, overlooking the popular deli. To the right of the deli was the butcher's and to the left, a gift shop, which could only be described as an explosion of all things floral and shabby chic.

Just a little way up the towpath was The Waterfront, an historic-looking pub with its reclaimed timber and brick, and a beautiful place to sit in the summer, overlooking the water, when the whole place became a hive of activity with dog-walkers and narrowboat enthusiasts.

But Nell and Ollie's favourite time of the year had always been winter. Once December arrived they'd enjoyed early-morning frosty walks around the marina, finding the twinkly lights that were decked on the roofs of the boats magical. In the dark evenings, they'd loved battening down the hatches and cosying up in front of the log burner, feeling content inside the 'Nollie', a name Ollie had come up with for their floating home.

Nell and Ollie's boat had been moored at Little Rock Marina for all of their married life. They'd met at college, aged seventeen, and the moment Nell had clapped eyes on Ollie, with his blonde corkscrew curls and infectious smile, she'd fallen in love. At the time, he'd been training to be a mechanic and she was studying business. Ollie's passion was to tinker with engines; he was always at his happiest when covered head to toe in greasy oil, with his head under a car bonnet, and he'd opened a small mechanic's yard on the edge of Heron's Reach, a picturesque village, which was a stone's throw away from the marina. It didn't make a lot of money, but it had been enough to keep their little home afloat.

In the past five years there had been nothing more appealing than waking up, throwing open the doors of their little narrowboat and watching the world float by. But recently things had changed for Nell. Now, as she clambered up on to the deck and stared vacantly at the clouds sporadically dotted in the sky, she allowed her mind to drift along with them. With one hand she clutched tightly at the grey woollen blanket draped around her shoulders and with the other held a steaming mug of tea. As she blinked back the tears and stared out over the tranquil marina, Nell knew that today was going to be one of the most difficult of her life.

Two hours later, Nell flicked up and down her clothes rail trying to decide on an outfit. She knew it was silly to worry about what she was going to wear; Ollie wouldn't mind what

The Cosy Canal Boat Dream

she was wearing when she said goodbye. She took a deep breath, smiled and glanced over at his overalls hanging on the back of the door. Once his yard had finally been sold, his overalls were all she'd kept. She couldn't bear to part with them.

Finally, she set off up the towpath, her bag slung over her shoulder and her hands buried deep inside her coat pockets. She knew that the perfect place to lay Ollie to rest was on the other side of the marina, just by the lake. Over the wooden bridge there was a huge willow tree that adorned the bank and underneath its graceful foliage of arching branches was a bench where Nell and Ollie would sit talking for hours, watching the world go by.

Everywhere was peaceful, the ancient oak trees that flanked the gravel path swayed and the colourful daffodils danced in the light breeze as Nell dabbed her eyes with a tissue. She was struggling to accept that Ollie had truly left her, but she knew that however hard it was, it was time to move on.

She was on her way to meet her mum, Gilly, who she'd spotted in the distance standing on the little wooden bridge, throwing bread to the mallards below.

'Come on, Nell Andrews, be brave! You can do this,' the words whirled around inside her head.

Her mum swung round and smiled warmly towards her daughter, 'Morning, you okay?' she asked, throwing her arms open wide and giving her a hug.

'Not really,' Nell answered shakily, her eyes finally unleashing the tears she'd bravely been trying to hold back.

Gilly rubbed her arm, 'It's going to be alright, you know, in time. Come on,' she encouraged.

Nell could only manage a nod, not trusting herself to speak. They linked arms and slowly walked over the bridge towards the huge willow tree and perched on the wooden bench underneath it. Nell clutched her bag against her chest, feeling close to Ollie for one last time. For a moment neither spoke; they just stared out over the tranquil water of the lake, Nell lost in her own memories.

It had been six months since the decision was made to switch off Ollie's life-support machine, and she still missed him dreadfully. The pain twisted in her heart; it was still raw and never went away.

Every time Nell thought of Ollie, her eyes brimmed with instant tears. She remembered the night of the accident as though it was yesterday, and could still hear Ollie's voice swirling around inside her head, 'Gherkins, you want gherkins? Are you sure you aren't pregnant?' He'd joked.

'Of course I'm not, it's just that I've picked up some of those fancy biscuits from the deli and I could murder a slab of Stilton and pickles to go with them.'

'Your wish is my command,' he'd laughed, picking up his keys and kissing Nell lightly on top of her head.

'I'll be ten minutes max.'

He'd climbed on to his motorbike and pulled on his helmet. Nell had watched him disappear into the foggy night from the window of the boat. Once the roar of his bike had petered out she'd switched on the TV and thrown some more logs on to the fire. She'd drifted off to sleep and the next thing she knew she'd heard footsteps and a rap on the door.

The Cosy Canal Boat Dream

Ollie hadn't been gone nearly ten minutes; in fact he'd been away for over two hours.

The moment she opened the door her heart had sank and she knew Ollie wasn't coming back. There, standing on the deck of their narrowboat were a couple of policeman, who'd informed her that Ollie had been knocked off his bike by a lorry. From that moment on, Nell's life had descended into complete darkness.

Nell turned towards her mum, 'I can still smell him at times,' she said, her voice barely a whisper, 'Is that madness?'

'No,' Gilly answered softly, feeling her daughter's pain.

'Sometimes, I wake up and I actually think he's still there, lying next to me and then I remember – he's never coming home. My life feels so dark all the time.'

'You will get through this and be happy again,' Gilly rested her arm around her daughter's shoulders and pulled her in close, 'I promise.'

'When?' Nell's voice faltered.

'One day,' was the only comfort Gilly could offer. Her own heart was breaking seeing her daughter in so much pain. 'Are you ready?' she asked tentatively.

Nell nodded and bit down on her lip before looking up at the sky.

'I love you, Ollie Andrews, with all my heart. The love we shared was so special,' she paused, 'Thank you for choosing to marry me and loving me so unconditionally,' the words tumbled out of her mouth.

Nell's eyes glistened with tears as she reached inside her

bag and took out the urn. She stood up and clutched it to her chest, her hands visibly shaking and her legs trembling as she slowly walked towards the water's edge.

'This is our special place and I promise I'll visit all the time. You just try and keep me away,' smiled Nell through her tears.

She unscrewed the lid and scattered Ollie's ashes into the air, 'Goodbye, Ollie. I'll love you forever.'

'Goodbye, Ollie,' Gilly whispered, standing by her daughter's side.

They clung to each other as the tears freely flowed down their cheeks. Nell wished with her heart that Ollie was still here but that was one wish that would never come true.

Chapter 1

Two years later...

Nell heard the creak of the door and looked up, startled, 'Hey, I can't believe you're up so early. I noticed the light on.'

Bea was standing in the doorway of the Nollie, her breath misting. She was wrapped up tightly in her duffel coat, sporting a warm smile and clasping a white paper bag.

'Come on in and shut the door, it's freezing out there.' Nell smiled up at her best friend.

Bea unbuttoned her coat and scooted over to the seat next to her.

'I couldn't sleep, I've had a bit of a restless night,' admitted Nell.

Bea touched her hand affectionately, 'Ollie's birthday?' Her voice was suddenly wobbly.

Nell met her gaze and they shared a sad smile.

'Yes, Ollie's birthday. The first of February.'

For a moment, they sat in silence, 'Cuppa?' Nell asked. 'I think I can squeeze a couple more cups out of the tank and have a shower before the water needs filling up this morning.'

'Yes please, and in there is a couple of warm croissants,' Bea slid the paper bag over the table towards her.

'Have you already been to the deli?'

She nodded, 'I couldn't sleep much either. I'm way ahead of schedule today.'

Bea owned the delicatessen in the hub of the marina called The Melting Pot, which was famous for its hot chocolate, savouries and scrumptious homemade cakes. Nell used to work for her part time, taking care of the accounts, but since Ollie had passed away Bea had taken her under her wing and she now worked for her full time behind the counter of the deli, serving customers, which was a welcomed distraction.

From the first day of high school Nell and Bea's friendship had been cemented over a pair of laddered tights. Bea had saved Nell with a spare pair she'd whipped out of her bag and from that moment they'd become best friends. They'd sat next to each other for the next five years, then from the age of eighteen frequented the local pubs together. Bea had attended catering college and spent most of time testing out new recipes on Nell. Her work ethic was faultless and she'd soon landed a job alongside a well-known chef in the city of Lichfield. This had been Bea's ticket to freedom, and she had escaped her suffocating parents, flown the nest and rented a flat above the delicatessen at the marina.

When the owners of The Melting Pot had decided to sell the business, Bea had immediately snapped it up for herself, whipping it into shape with counter array of cakes, speciality cheeses and flapjacks to die for.

The Cosy Canal Boat Dream

Nell had beamed with such pride for her friend on her first day of opening – the deli was a dream come true for Bea.

Bea was married to Nathan and they had one five-year-old son called Jacob, who was the cutest thing Nell had ever set eyes on. But as his godmother, Nell knew she was biased.

When Ollie had been alive, the four of them had been firm friends and had enjoyed most weekends in each other's company, rambling around the marina and eating Sunday lunches at The Waterfront. Life had been perfect.

'What are you doing after work today?' asked Bea, 'Would you like to come over to the cottage for your tea? Jacob would love to see you.'

'I'd love to see him too, but I'm having tea with Mum, after we've visited the lake.'

Bea nodded, 'How is Gilly? I've not seen her for a couple of weeks.'

Gilly lived down the lane from Bea in Bluebell Cottage, the same property in which Nell had lived for the whole of her life. Gilly was the proud owner of a vintage bicycle with a basket and a bell and could often be seen cycling around the marina.

Nell rolled her eyes and smiled, 'She has her hands full at the moment!'

'Intriguing. What's she up to this time?'

Gilly, who was in her mid-fifties, but appeared much younger than her age, had been drowning in her own grief. Her husband, Nell's father, Benny, had unexpectedly passed away from pneumonia five years ago – an event that had rocked their world. Since then Gilly had thrown herself wholeheartedly into every local crafty organisation in the village, from basket weaving, painting antique furniture and had even joined the pottery club.

'Last week she was ferreting around in the greenhouse at the bottom of the garden when she found a tabby cat curled up in an old blanket on top of a bag of compost. She took it into the cottage and made it up a bed in front of the Aga. She thought it seemed a little unwell and a little plump and decided to make it an appointment at the vets for the following morning. There was no collar or tag. She didn't even know its name, but by the time next morning arrived Mum found three extra bundles of fluff curled up next to the mother.'

'Kittens?'

Nell nodded.

'How wonderful!'

'The little mews made my heart melt; utterly gorgeous to say the least.'

'What's Gilly going to do with them?'

'She's placed a notice in the vets and the local post office, but as yet no one has come forward to claim her. At the moment she's named her Rosie, because she was lying on the bag of compost she uses to plant her roses, and knowing Mum I think she would be quite happy to keep them all!'

'Maybe I could talk Nathan into homing one. I just need to make him think it's his idea and we'd be on to a winner,' she grinned. 'Jacob would love a kitten.'

Nell smiled at Bea. She pictured her curled up in front of the fire after a long hard day at the deli with a kitten snoozing on her lap.

The Cosy Canal Boat Dream

They both finished their tea, then Bea glanced at her watch, 'The scones are due out any minute; I'd best nip back to the shop.'

'What time is it? I feel like I've been up for hours.'

'Just gone 6.45.'

'I have been up for hours.'

'I can easily sort out some cover if you don't feel up to coming in.'

Nell shook her head, 'Thanks, but I need to keep busy. I'll be along as soon as I'm ready.'

Bea gave her a quick hug before flicking the latch and stooping down to climb through the door. Her footsteps echoed on the plank that connected the towpath to the boat as she ambled across towards the deli.

'Right, Nell Andrews, it's time to paint a smile on your face, life must go on,' she murmured to herself, unconvinced, standing up and running her hand over Ollie's photograph while she blinked away the tears. Birthdays and anniversaries always hit her hard.

Five minutes later, she stared at her reflection in the bathroom mirror. 'Jeez, Andrews,' she said out loud, smoothing down her wild hair and washing away the smudged eyeliner.

'I really need to learn to take my mascara off before climbing into bed,' she muttered, reaching for her wash bag. Then, just like every morning, she took out her pack of contraceptive pills. She stared down at Tuesday's pill in the palm of her hand and suddenly had no idea why she was still taking these little pills after all this time. Everything had carried on in the same routine for the last two years. Her life had been on auto-pilot and she'd never wanted to completely let go of it, up until now. Even though Ollie wasn't coming back, she felt strong enough to look towards the future. Nell switched on the tap and made the decision to swill the pill down the sink.

After a quick shower, she twisted her blonde hair up into a bun, threw on her favourite jumper and dabbed on a smidgen of lipgloss. She was ready to face the world. Once outside, the cool morning breeze whispered around her ears as Nell stood on the deck of the 'Nollie' and breathed in the early morning fresh air.

She glanced across towards the blue and gold lettering of a neighbouring boat, 'The Old Geezer'. Fred Bramley had been their neighbour since they'd moved on to the 'Nollie'. Nell found him an interesting character with his grey bushy eyebrows and matching beard. He always wore a flat cap and a nattily kempt white cable knit that resembled a cricket jumper. He was retired and spent most of his days sitting on the deck of the boat fishing, even though in all these years she'd never actually seen him catch anything. For a brief moment the doors of the flagship opened and Fred appeared on the deck clutching a mug of tea.

'Good morning,' chirped Nell, catching his eye.

He tipped his cap in acknowledgement. He was a man of few words but always gave a nod and a smile.

'Have a good day,' Nell called cheerfully before he disappeared back inside his boat. She gazed across at the other narrowboats with their brightly coloured names and flowerpots scattered on the roofs. Even in winter the marina was arrayed with colours that glistened in the early morning frost.

The Cosy Canal Boat Dream

This morning there was a chill in the air and, according to the weather forecast on the radio, it threatened snow.

'Happy birthday, Ollie. I miss you so much,' she whispered up into the grey sky.

As she stepped down onto the towpath she stumbled, then heard a loud yelp as she was knocked clean off her feet and landed with a bump.

'Ouch.'

'You okay?'

Startled, she looked up and then was yanked to her feet by two strapping arms.

'Down boy, sit still.' The man's voice was firm. He clipped a lead on to an excited red setter, whose front paws excitedly danced.

Feeling like a fool, Nell swallowed, 'Handsome dog.' She had no idea where either of them had sprung from. A second ago, there'd been no one even in sight.

'Killer dog this one. Not one for making friends,' the man replied, with a massive smile etched on his face.

'Really?' she answered slightly bewildered. The dog looked harmless enough to her, in fact kind of dopey.

'Yep, really, trained to kill, this one.'

Nell took a step back but didn't take her eyes off the dog.

'Watch this,' the man cleared his throat. 'Roll over.'

Immediately the dog dropped to the ground and swiftly rolled on to his back and waved his gangly legs into the air.

'Killer dog, indeed,' she chuckled.

'Daft as a brush,' the man replied with a playful grin. 'I'm sorry, we weren't looking where we were going.'

'No harm done,' replied Nell, brushing down her coat.

'Are you sure?'

She nodded, 'No broken bones, this time.'

The man was of average height, and as he raked his hand through his dark floppy fringe and pushed it to one side, Nell noticed his glistening hazel eyes. 'Let's hope there isn't a next time,' he smiled.

They held each other's gaze for a moment longer than necessary and for the first time in a long time Nell felt a strange sensation, her heart gave a little flutter.

'Your accent, Irish?'

He gave her a lop-sided grin, 'It sure is.'

'Not one you often hear around here.'

Nell was just about to introduce herself properly when his phone rang and he delved into his jacket pocket. 'Excuse me,' he smiled, glancing at his screen, then answered the call. Nell watched as he strolled up the path towards the boathouse. He flicked a glance over his shoulder and caught Nell's eye, then waved his hand above his head. Who was that handsome stranger? She hadn't seen him around these parts before.

She was just about to make her way to the deli when she remembered she needed to refill the water tank.

Damn.

If she didn't fill it up now she'd be kicking herself later, especially if the weather turned any colder today. Unravelling the hosepipe from outside the marina shower block she stretched it towards the water tank of the 'Nollie'. After hooking up the pipe to the tap and dangling the hose inside the tank, she switched it on, then stood and waited.

The Cosy Canal Boat Dream

'Aunty Nellie!' She heard a squeal.

Spinning around she spotted her five-year-old godson in a pair of bright-yellow wellies clomping up the wharf, with Nathan quickly following behind him.

'Aunty Nellie, look at my new wellies,' Jacob screeched to a halt in front of her.

'Wow!' She squatted in front of him for a closer look. 'Two questions, Jacob Green. Have you grown and do you think I can borrow those wellies?' asked Nell beaming.

Jacob giggled, 'Don't be silly, Aunty Nellie, they'll be too small for you!' His eyes sparkled, then he giggled as Nell scooped him up in her arms and hugged him tight.

'Daddy said you may need extra hugs today,' Jacob said, and that familiar feeling of grief rushed to the surface as she placed Jacob firmly back on the ground.

'Jacob,' Nathan interrupted.

'Are you sad today, Aunty Nellie?' Jacob asked, pulling at her scarf and ignoring his dad.

'A little,' she murmured, pinching her thumb and forefinger together, 'But all the better for seeing you,' throwing her arms open for another hug and burying her face in his mousy locks. As he pulled away, tears threatened in Nell's eyes. Nathan leant forward, squeezed her arm and pressed a swift kiss to her cheek.

'We all miss him,' he whispered softly in Nell's ear.

She nodded and smiled. 'So, Jacob, where are you off to this bright and early?'

'Before-school club. It's the only time Daddy can take me today.'

'Day off work. I'm off to a trade show,' Nathan answered. 'I'm still searching for the parts to the ...' he hesitated.

'Motorbike,' Nell's voice faltered. She had a sudden flashback of Ollie and Nathan stooped over the lump of metal, building the old machine.

'I'm sorry, I didn't mean to upset you,' Nathan said, gently touching her arm.

Over four years ago, Ollie and Nathan had decided to build a motorbike from scratch. The pair of them had spent hours in the shed at the bottom of Nathan's garden working on the machine together. It was at times like this Nell missed washing his greasy overalls and hearing all about the mechanical parts that they needed next, even though she'd no idea what any of them did or what they were for.

'You haven't upset me. I'm doing just fine. Good memories are what I need to cling on to, especially on days like today,' she said suddenly, swinging her head around and remembering that the hosepipe was still attached to the water tank.

'I think the tank's full. Jacob, are you strong enough to switch off the water?' she asked raising her eyebrows in the direction of the tap.

'I am, Aunty Nellie,' he saluted heartily.

Bea spotted them from the deli window and joined them outside. Everyone smiled as Jacob clumped towards the tap. He grasped it with both hands and spun it around until the water stopped.

'All done!' He shouted triumphantly.

Nell gave him the thumbs-up and pulled the hose from the tank.

The Cosy Canal Boat Dream

'Will you ever live in a proper house, Aunty Nellie?' he asked her and she cupped her hands around Jacob's bright-red chubby cheeks.

'I love my floating home,' she answered, planting an enthusiastic kiss on top of his head.

Tears threatened again, thinking of Ollie and how proud he would be of Jacob, who was such a bundle of fun and growing into a remarkable young boy.

'Right, young man, say goodbye to Mummy and Aunty Nellie. Let's get you off to school.'

Bea kissed his cheek then swung him round before planting his feet firmly back on the floor.

'See you later, alligator,' Nell smiled, holding up her hand for a high-five.

They both stood outside the deli and watched Nathan and Jacob walk hand and hand up the wharf until they disappeared.

Nell felt a pang of sadness, 'I only have one regret in life so far,' she said sadly.

'Which is?' Bea answered softly.

'That we never got round to having children,' she replied, wiping away a tear. 'I always hoped to be a mother.'

Bea placed her hand in the small of Nell's back as they walked inside the deli. 'You'll make the perfect mother one day.'

'Maybe one day.'

'Definitely one day,' Nell reassured her.

Chapter 2

The morning had passed quickly and by lunchtime the deli was pleasingly heaving with customers. There were the regulars who lived on the canal boats who placed frequent orders and those folks who were just passing by. Today everyone seemed in good spirits despite the miserable grey February weather outside.

Nell heard a clonk on the deli window and looked up to see her mum sliding from the saddle of her bike. She balanced the handlebars against the window and grabbed her purse from the basket. Catching Nell's eye, she waved.

'You've got to love the smell of freshly baked bread,' she beamed, swinging open the door to the deli and sniffing the air. 'Pop one of those bloomers in a bag for me, love.'

'Good afternoon, Mum,' said Nell, smiling, reaching for a lightly baked loaf. 'Not too dark,' she added quickly.

'Are you trying to suggest my bloomers are burnt,' Bea chuckled, scooting towards Gilly and kissing her on both cheeks.

'Absolutely not, wouldn't dream of it. Oh and one of those iced buns too.'

The Cosy Canal Boat Dream

Nell reached into the glass cabinet, which was bursting with mouth-watering cakes and pasties while Gilly rummaged around in her purse.

'They are on the house today, Gilly!'

'Very kind of you, Bea, thank you.'

'You're welcome. I hear you've gone and gotten yourself some very cute additions to your household.'

'Indeed, you must bring Jacob over, he'll love them!'

'I will!' Bea touched Gilly's arm before disappearing back into the kitchen.

'You look tired,' Gilly said, lowering her voice as she spoke to Nell.

'Honestly, I'm okay.'

'My guess is you barely slept,' she narrowed her eyes and gave Nell her 'she knows best' look.

Nell gave her a weak smile, 'A little bit of a restless night, that's all, Mum.'

'Understandable. Christmas, birthdays and anniversaries are always the hardest,' Gilly raised her eyebrows knowingly.

Ollie's first birthday without him flashed through Nell's mind. She'd spent the day a blubbering wreck up at Bluebell Cottage, with only her mum for company. They'd been on a long walk, visited the lake and after dinner they'd curled up on the settee with a bottle of wine, a box of chocolates and watched a marathon of rom-com films. That day had felt hollow, but despite all the heartbreak, Nell knew she'd come a long way in the last two years; those feelings weren't as painfully raw as they had once been and that was all down to the love and support of her mum and Bea.

Nell slid the bag over the counter towards her mum.

'I'll see you later,' Gilly said warmly, before grabbing her bread and walking out of the deli.

Nell took a breather for the first time today as the deli began to quieten down. She wandered into the kitchen and quickly loaded up the dishwasher before washing her hands and hanging the tea towel over the rail of the stainless-steel oven. Bea was glazing a tray of sausage rolls.

'I could murder a cuppa,' said Nell, 'Shall I put the kettle on?'

'No need, I've read your mind. I was just about to bring you through a skinny cappuccino,' she nodded towards the two steaming mugs.

'Skinny, are you trying to tell me something?' Nell brought her hand up to her chest in mock outrage, pretending to look hurt. 'Do I need to go on a diet?' she joked.

'Ha no! It was my new year's resolution to try and cut down, but you know what, sod that,' she said taking hold of the mugs, 'Wait there! Two luxury hot chocolates with the works coming right up!'

'Now you're talking!'

Five minutes later Bea and Nell were leaning against the counter, holding the most scrumptious-looking drinks, laced with marshmallows, cream and chocolate flakes.

'Wow, I'm going to need an afternoon kip after this!'

Bea chuckled, 'It's calorific but, my gosh, it tastes good,' she said, scooping up the cream with a spoon.

'Look at this place,' Bea flicked her eyes around the small café. 'It looks like a bomb's hit it after that mad rush.'

The Cosy Canal Boat Dream

There were half a dozen empty tables that were littered with crumbs. 'I'll brush up after this and wipe the tables down,' offered Nell.

'You are a superstar. What would I do without you?'

The pair of them both cupped their mugs and sipped their hot chocolates while staring out over the marina through the window of the deli.

Suddenly, Bea placed her mug down on the counter with a clatter and hit Nell's arm. She nodded towards the window.

'Who's that? I've not seen him around these parts before.'

Nell's eyes darted over to where Bea was looking and smiled at her friend's sudden enthusiasm. The man standing in front of the deli window was the same man whose dog had knocked her clean off her feet this morning.

'Put your tongue back in, Bea, you're physically panting,' she ordered, but not admitting to her that her own stomach had done a slight flip at the sight of him again.

'The hot chocolate's too hot. Well, that's my story and I'm sticking to it,' Bea giggled.

'You're married,' grinned Nell.

For a second they both watched the handsome stranger, taking in his navy-blue jumper that clung to his toned abs, his overalls tied around his waist and wild, dark hair, which he constantly raked away from his eyes.

He flicked his head up and down the jetty and seemed quite anxious before spinning round and locking eyes with Nell for a split second.

Damn, he'd caught her staring.

'It doesn't stop me from looking, though. He's ...' Bea grabbed Nell's arm and gave it a squeeze.

'Coming in,' she smiled.

All eyes were on the man as they watched him push open the deli door, letting in a blast of cool air. 'Hello again, I thought it was you,' he said, in his soft Irish accent.

'Hello again?' Instantly Bea swung towards Nell, raising her eyebrows. She was itching to know who the stranger was.

'This is ...'

The man smiled and acknowledged Nell's hesitation, 'Guy,' he said, thrusting his hand towards her. 'Guy Cornish. I don't think we introduced ourselves properly this morning.'

'This morning?' Bea queried.

'Nell, Nell Andrews. Pleased to meet you,' she beamed, shaking his proffered hand 'And this is ...'

'Bea,' Bea chirped, with a wicked glint in her eye, 'So come on, what am I missing? How do you two know each other?'

'This morning Guy swept me off my feet.'

'He did, did he? And how come I know nothing about this?' Bea enquired playfully.

'Well not Guy, technically, but his dog.'

'And he's the very reason I'm pacing up and down the marina like a mad man. The lolloping hound has run off. We've only been here a couple of days and I've no clue where to start looking for him.'

'How long ago was this?'

'About five minutes,' he glanced at his watch anxiously.

'Don't worry. He can't have gone far. I bet he's headed up

The Cosy Canal Boat Dream

the path near the woodlands. He'll have sniffed out a rabbit or something.'

'I don't think he's that intelligent,' he joked, but there was no mistaking the worried expression firmly planted on his face.

Nell stood motionless for a moment wondering what to do, then taking a deep, calming breath she said, 'I'll help you look. That's okay isn't it, Bea? We're over the dinner-time rush now.'

'Yes, of course. You go. This time of day it's always quiet.'

He gave Nell a grateful smile, 'You will?'

Nell nodded, 'I know the back paths,' she answered, thrusting her arms into the sleeves of her coat and quickly zipping it up. 'Come on, I'm sure it won't take long to find him.'

Once outside the deli they headed towards the far end of the marina and strolled past all the shops, before hitting the trail that led to the woodlands.

'What's his name?'

'Sam,' Guy replied, and began to shout the dog's name and rattle his lead.

Speedily, they carried on walking along the path, 'So I take it you aren't from around these parts, then?'

'With an accent like this?' he laughed. 'No, it's my brother who owns the boatyard here. I'm helping him out for a while.'

'Ed's your brother?' Nell said astounded.

'He is indeed.'

'Ahh, you're helping him out because of his operation?'

'Yes, he's laid up for six weeks after a hernia operation, so

I offered to come and give him a hand at the boatyard he's always raving on about.'

Ed had owned the boatyard at the marina for as long as Ollie and Nell had moored the 'Nollie' there. He seemed a little older than Guy and, as far as Nell was aware he had no wife or children. He was always a happy-go-lucky fellow, nothing was ever too much trouble. During the past year, Nell had often noticed his light on in the boat shed until the early hours of the morning when she couldn't sleep. He was always beavering away, restoring and painting boats and was well thought of at the marina.

'What do you think about the place so far?' Nell asked, while Guy carried on beckoning for Sam in between chatting to her.

'I can see the attraction,' he snagged her eye and she didn't know why but she felt herself instantly blush. He paused for a second, 'Ed was always what my mum would call a tinkerer. Always up to his armpits in grease and oil.'

'Just like my Ollie.'

'Ollie?'

'My husband,' she answered, traipsing alongside Guy. 'Was my husband,' she exhaled.

'Was?' Guy commented, not making eye contact but looking up ahead for Sam. 'Divorced?'

'Widowed. He passed away. In fact it's his birthday today.'

Immediately Guy stopped in his tracks and swung towards her. 'I don't know what to say. Are you okay?' he asked kindly.

Nell offered him a warm smile, 'What can you say? Life

The Cosy Canal Boat Dream

was difficult for a while but it's becoming more bearable. I'm getting there, as they say.'

'What happened? Do you mind me asking?'

Nell shook her head, 'Ollie was involved in a motorbike accident, and eventually his life-support machine was switched off and you know what?' she touched his elbow, 'This is the first time I've spoken about it without bursting into tears.'

'It sounds like it's been a very difficult time for you.'

They carried on walking in silence before stopping a little further up and leaning against an old rickety fence. The pair of them stared at the stunning scenery. The fields stretched for miles and miles.

In the last twenty minutes or so the temperature had dropped dramatically and Nell shivered.

'It looks like it's threatening snow,' said Nell, 'Let's hope we find Sam soon.'

Guy nodded, 'You're cold,' he said, ruffling a hand through his hair before slipping off his scarf and handing it to her.

'Thanks,' she replied, wrapping it tightly around her neck. 'It doesn't look like he's come this way. Let's head back towards the marina.'

They both turned around and began to quickly walk back up the path, 'I can't help but ask,' she said, curiosity getting the better of her, 'about your accent.'

'Irish.'

She nodded, 'Ed doesn't have an Irish accent.'

'That's very true. We have different fathers. He's ten years older than me. My mum and his dad split up years ago and then she met my father, Niall.'

'Whose name sounds very Irish!'

'Yep, hence the accent. Ed moved across here some time ago after meeting a girl at work. She was on a short-term contract at a firm he used to be employed at over in Ireland, but she was from around these parts and when her contract was up, she moved back home and he followed her.'

'I didn't even know Ed had a girlfriend.'

'He doesn't now. They split up a couple of months later, but he liked the place that much he never came home and has been here ever since.'

'What about you?'

'Me?'

'Yes, have you got any family of your own?'

His eyes seemed to harden for a moment, 'Only my dog, who seems to have done a complete runner on me.'

'Don't worry, he can't have gone far, we'll find him.'

They hurried back towards the marina and the whole place looked deserted on this cold grey day except for a van parked up at the far end of the towpath. Then, out of the blue, all they could hear was a sudden continuous banging that seemed to echo all around them.

'What's that noise?' Nell asked, glancing up the wharf.

'That man over there. He's hammering a sign on to the front of that building.'

She squinted ahead to see the man throw his tools into the back of the van, start the engine and drive off.

'What's that place?' Guy asked as they carried on walking towards it.

Nell paused outside the building and a small wave of

sadness washed over her. She was rooted to the spot and stared up at the sign. 'For Sale,' she murmured despondently.

'It looks like it's been empty for a while. Shame, it looks like it was a beautiful building.'

Nell had forgotten how much she adored this place. Some of her favourite memories were made right there, inside that building.

'It was. It's the Old Picture House.'

'Picture house?'

She nodded, 'A cinema with a difference. In it's heyday, on a Friday night, it used to be packed to the rafters. It really was the place to go. Ollie and me had our very first date there, must be over twelve years ago now, and when I was a kid I'd spend my Sunday mornings here with my dad watching films. This place was the heart of the community for years.'

'I bet you were a cute kid,' he smiled at her.

Nell laughed, his words taking her a little by surprise. 'Adorable my dad said, but he was biased.'

They both stared up at the building. The roof looked worn and the grimy bricks were streaked by the rainwater that had dripped from the broken gutters. Half of the windows had panes of glass missing and the other half were boarded up. Worn heavy velvet curtains still hung in the upstairs windows, but they looked as if they were clinging on for dear life. What was once a magical building was now badly in need of some tender loving care.

Out of every inch of Nell's body poured the memories of her early dates with Ollie. They were good memories and magical moments she'd never forget. She could still remember the thousands of anxious fireflies dancing around in her stomach on their very first date, the smell of his aftershave and the feeling that surged through her body when he had held her hand for the very first time. That night he'd offered to pick her up from Bluebell Cottage and just before seven o'clock there'd been a rap on the door. Nell had waited a moment at the top of the stairs, not wanting to appear too keen, until her dad shouted 'I'll get the door.'

How embarrassing.

She'd sprinted down the stairs quicker than an Olympian and threw open the door to find Ollie standing on the doorstep, timidly smiling back at her. It was early autumn and the sun was still shining in the early evening sky. He'd stood shyly, with his hands in the back pocket of his jeans, and she couldn't help but notice his tanned muscly arms on show.

'Hi,' he'd said, then nervously raked a hand through his unruly hair. They'd walked to the marina, and she could remember looking back over her shoulder as they wandered up the garden path, only to notice her mum and dad peeping from behind the curtain. At that time of year the walk to the marina was a pleasant one, along the towpath. Honeysuckle still festooned the hedgerows and the narrowboats slowly glided past them up the canal. They'd ambled side by side, their elbows banging against each other's. Her heart was thumping and she forced herself to breathe calmly. Feeling his presence so close to her had made every ounce of her body tingle. His eyes sparkled and met hers, then, finally, he'd stretched out his hand and their fingers had entwined. They'd strolled hand in hand for the rest of the way.

The Cosy Canal Boat Dream

At the end of the evening he'd walked her home. They'd lingered on the doorstep for what seemed like hours before he'd taken her hands in his. She'd shivered in anticipation as he tilted her chin up and lowered his head towards her and kissed her gently. Her heart had been beating so fast that she honestly thought it was going to explode and that was the moment she knew, she wanted to be Ollie Andrews' girlfriend.

A sigh escaped her and she met Guy's eyes.

'Are you okay?' he asked.

'Sometimes I wish I could turn back time and have my life again,' but Nell knew standing there looking up at the building she couldn't turn back the clock. She'd lovely memories of the Old Picture House and ones she would cherish forever.

'What happened to this place? Why did it close down?'

'I'm assuming financial difficulty. I suppose these days people watch films online and less and less people began to use the place. It never really moved into the digital age, it continued to run exactly how it had done since the day it opened, with its projectors and ice-cream sellers in the foyer.'

'There was a little place like that in Ireland. It kept going and going and soon it was all the rage again. The Vintage Cinema, you even had waitress service to your seat.'

'That sounds just like this place. When you walked inside the foyer it felt like you were a Hollywood film actor. There was a beautiful chandelier and floor-to-ceiling posters of the latest films as well as the old classics. You should have seen it. Then there was … Gladys, I think that was her name. She was the woman who sat behind the wooden box taking your money. Oh and I can't forget the plush velvet red bucket seats, once you sank into them there was no getting out, well not with much dignity, anyway. It was a very sad day when the doors closed for the final time.'

'Such a shame the magic can't live on.' Guy added, 'And now it's up for sale.'

Nell felt saddened by the 'for sale' sign, but it was only a matter of time before the property was sold on. 'I'm surprised it's not been sold sooner.'

'It'll be more than likely snapped up by a builder, then flattened for houses.'

She felt a sudden pang in her heart at the mere mention of Guy's words.

They stared for a moment longer until they were interrupted by a distant yelp, then a bark.

'Sam,' Guy shouted, 'Sam, where are you, boy?'

They both stood rooted to the spot, waiting for him to bark again.

'Sam,' he boomed again.

The next bark came from somewhere behind them. They both spun round. 'Over there, I think,' said Nell, hurrying towards the water's edge.

She strained to look between the moored canal boats. 'There, over there,' she pointed.

In the distance, standing to attention on the bow of a boat, was Sam. As soon as he spotted them, his tail swished madly and he began to woof excitedly.

The Cosy Canal Boat Dream

'How the hell has he managed to get himself all the way out there? I didn't even know he could swim.'

'It's instinct. All dogs can usually swim.'

'Come on and mind your head,' Nell said, squeezing between the rails at the end of the jetty, then jumping down on to a small rowing boat that was tied up.

'Grab an oar.'

Guy dithered, 'Who does this boat belong to?'

'Fred Bramley. He's my neighbour, lived on the marina for years. That's his boat there. The one next to mine, "The Old Geezer."'

'Will he mind us pinching his boat?'

'Needs must! We're only borrowing it. I'm sure it'll be fine.'

Rubbing her hands vigorously in an attempt to warm them up Nell untied the rope and grabbed an oar.

'Jump in, what are you waiting for?'

Guy hesitated for a second, 'I have to admit, I'm not too keen on water.'

She glanced back up in his direction and tried to read his expression. With the anxious look on his face she realised that he wasn't joking and looked absolutely terrified.

Nell wondered how to put it tactfully. 'Guy, you need to get in. I can't rescue your dog by myself, I need help lowering him into the boat.'

'Is the only way to get there by boat?'

'There's the long walk round to the far jetty but it'll take about ten minutes.'

'I'm being silly, aren't I?' he said, but still didn't move.

'See that box on the bow of the "Nollie",' she nodded

towards her narrowboat, 'There's a life jacket in there. Go and grab it quickly.'

There was a look of slight relief on Guy's face as he turned and hurried towards the box. Watching Guy slide the life jacket over his head, her heart hammered against her chest. She felt a little saddened. That was Ollie's life jacket and she hadn't set eyes on it for a while, but it was the perfect fit for Guy.

He made his way back to the boat. The colour actually drained from his face as he grabbed the sides of the rickety old thing and began to lower himself in.

'Whoa,' he exclaimed as the boat began to rock.

'Try and steady yourself and sit still, it can be a little daunting when you first climb in.'

Once Guy was safely perched on the edge of the seat she noticed his knuckles turning white as he clung on for dear life.

'You really don't like water, do you?'

He shook his head and stared out towards Sam.

Nell immersed the spoon of the blades into the water and began to row gently.

'No holidaying on a cruise ship for you, then,' she joked, trying to lighten the mood and put Guy at ease.

He shuddered, 'I can't think of anything worse. I think it's safe to say I'm petrified of water.'

'I hadn't noticed,' she said, cocking an eyebrow and offering him a warm smile.

'I know it's pathetic, a man of my age ...'

'About thirty?'

The Cosy Canal Boat Dream

'Twenty-nine actually.'

'Good guess.'

'But ...'

He squeezed his eyes shut as they glided smoothly towards the barge.

'But?'

'It happened a long time ago, I was only seven years old.'

'A very long time ago then,' she said, playfully.

He peered through one eye, 'Cheeky. Near to where I live in Ireland there was a lake. Every school holiday, I used to hang out there with my mate Dan and build dens in the forest near by, but this one day we came across a small rowing boat that had been abandoned near the water's edge. It was Dan's idea to see if we could row it to the other side of the lake. Unfortunately, halfway across, the boat began to leak and it capsized and I couldn't swim. In no time at all we were both clinging to a sinking boat and the water was getting higher and higher around us. I clamped my mouth shut while Dan screamed for dear life. Dan could swim but didn't want to leave me. Luckily for us, a dog-walker heard him, jumped into the water and rescued us both. That was the last time I ever went near open water, until now.'

'Sounds very traumatic,' exclaimed Nell.

'If I close my eyes I can still remember the stench of the water,' Guy shuddered.

She manoeuvred the rowing boat as calmly as possible through the icy cold water. As they approached Sam, he rocked excitedly from one paw to another. His tail was wagging and he began to woof.

'Look at him, he's soaking wet,' Guy exclaimed. 'Without a doubt he's been in the water.'

'Okay, here's what I'm going to do. I need to steer closer to the boat and tie it onto that wrought-iron ring over there. I need to make sure you don't float away when I climb out.'

Guy looked awful, his face was ghastly white, he clenched his cheeks and the fear in his eyes said it all.

'Don't worry, I'm not going to let anything happen to you.'

He nodded, soothed by Nell's words, then looked wistfully towards Sam and gave an exasperated sigh.

'Don't move!' Nell joked, smiling.

'I've no intention of going anywhere,' Guy said, folding his arms.

Nell took the oars out of the rowlocks, dug the blades in the water and stopped the boat. She reached and grabbed the rope then slowly tilted herself towards the wrought-iron ring and tied the little rowing boat securely to the side of the canal boat.

'It doesn't look like anyone's home,' she murmured, hurling herself on to the deck.

'Who owns this boat?' Guy questioned.

'Much Ado About Nothing,' she read the bright lettering on the side of the boat, 'I've no idea. It's only been moored here a couple of days, it's probably someone just passing through.'

As soon as Nell was standing on the boat, Sam sprang at her, leaving her covered in wet, stinky paw prints. She grabbed his collar and patted the top of his head. 'Good boy.'

The Cosy Canal Boat Dream

'He's definitely been in the water,' she claimed, wrinkling her nose at the stench. 'Throw me his lead.'

Guy reached inside his coat pocket then gently threw the lead towards Nell, who caught it and clipped it on to Sam's collar. Nell peered through the glass window, 'No sign of anyone,' she said, carefully lowering herself back into the boat, then encouraging Sam to jump, however he was sitting firmly on the deck of the canal boat and refusing to move. Nell glanced earnestly at Guy.

'Any ideas how I can get him to move?'

Once more Guy rummaged inside his pocket and produced a treat and passed it to Nell. 'Try this.'

She swallowed hard then exhaled, 'Okay boy, come on, let's get you on board so we can all get home.' She held the treat towards Sam, who immediately leapt into action and propelled himself on to the boat, Nell's smile drooped slightly as the boat began to rock.

Guy squirmed, closed his eyes and clasped tightly onto the wooden slacks he was sitting on.

Nell coaxed Sam to lie between her legs and patted Guy's knee, 'Here take this.' He opened his eyes and she passed him the lead. 'Keep him still. We will be back on dry land in no time at all.'

Nell placed the oars back into the rowlocks, grasped one in each hand then placed the blades in the water and began to row gently back towards the quayside. They both sat in silence until finally the little rowing boat bumped lightly against the jetty.

'We are here, safe and sound.'

Guy's eyes met with Nell's.

'Phew,' he said as she tied up the boat, then held out her hand towards Guy.

'Let's get you off this boat and on to dry land.'

'Yes captain,' he answered, relieved.

As he placed his hand in hers, Nell felt him tense up, then he slid one foot in front of the other and slowly manoeuvred his way off the boat. Once his feet were firmly on the ground he heaved a huge sigh of relief. Sam trotted happily off the boat behind him.

'Are you okay?' asked Nell gently.

'I feel an idiot, but I am now I'm back on dry land,' he laughed nervously, 'Even though I still feel like I'm swaying!' He gripped on to the railings, steadied himself and began to take deep breaths before exhaling sharply.

'You're not going to have a panic attack on me, are you?'

He shook his head warily. 'I think I'm ready to move.'

'Good,' Nell answered, seeing a slight smile spread across Guy's face. She couldn't help but beam at Sam, who sat patiently at the side of Guy, his tail thumping on the ground.

'You go first.'

Guy bent down and began to squeeze back through the railings, pulling Sam behind him.

'Do you fancy a ...?'

Before Nell could finish her sentence, Guy gave her a mischievous grin over his shoulder then cocked an eyebrow.

'I was going to say coffee,' she declared, feeling her face turn a dark shade of crimson.

The Cosy Canal Boat Dream

'Of course you were,' he beamed, standing up and poking his hand back over the top of the railings.

'I was!' protested Nell, knowing a huge smile had crept across her face.

'You protest too much,' he teased.

'I see you're already on top form,' Nell joked, placing her hand on top of the railing and deciding to hurl herself over the top. As she swung her leg over, Guy firmly gripped her arm to help steady her.

'Thank you,' she said, flashing a grateful smile. Her heart swelled at how gorgeous he was.

'I was only teasing you, you know.' He nudged her jokingly in the ribs.

'I know! Anyway, how are you feeling now?'

'A little light-headed and a right wimp, if I'm honest,' he muttered embarrassedly.

'Don't be daft. For the first time in years you've been back on the water, you're bound to feel panicky. How about that coffee to steady your nerves?'

Guy flicked his eyes between Sam and the 'Nollie'. His smile faded slightly and Nell sensed his hesitation.

'I know it's another boat, but it's a different type of boat, very steady. You won't even feel like you're on water. You can sit in your life jacket if that helps.'

'Oh very funny!' he cocked his head with the most gorgeous smile.

Nell had instantly warmed towards Guy; he put her at ease and was easy to talk to. It was nice to have a little male company once more.

'Do you need to be somewhere else?' He glanced towards the deli.

'Wait there a second.'

She quickly strolled towards the deli and spotted Bea cleaning the empty bread shelves behind the counter. She spun round when she heard the bell above the shop door tinkle.

'Hello, you. Have you found him?' she asked, with a worried look on her face.

Nell smiled and nodded. 'All safe and sound. Somehow he'd managed to get himself stuck on a barge at the back of the marina. We borrowed Fred's boat to rescue him.'

'Thank God, even though it sounds like you've both been on quite an adventure.'

'Do you need me? I was going to grab a quick coffee with Guy?'

Bea stole a look at the clock, 'Let's call it a day. You get off. It's quiet now and if you need me later, just text.'

Nell smiled a grateful smile at her friend, 'Will do, but I'm absolutely fine. See you in the morning.'

'Here, take these,' Bea scooped up a couple of cream doughnuts into a box, then slid them over the counter.

'Me working here is no good for my diet, you know!' she laughed, knowing full well that in the last six months the weight had begun to pile on.

'You working here is no good for my profits either,' she giggled, shooing Nell out of the shop, 'Now go and enjoy your coffee.'

Nell closed the door behind her to find Guy waiting patiently outside and Sam lying at his feet.

The Cosy Canal Boat Dream

'I have to say, he does stink a little.' Nell looked towards Sam, 'Why don't you hose him down while I nip on board and find some towels? He can dry off in front of the fire.'

'Sounds like a plan,' Guy said, sounding more cheerful than he did ten minutes ago.

'The hose is just over there outside the shower block.'

'Great, see you in five,' he added cheerily, holding her gaze.

'See you in five,' Nell bit down on her lip to suppress her smile as she jumped on to the 'Nollie'. What was it about that handsome Irish charmer that made her stomach flip so easily?

Chapter 3

Once inside the cabin Nell placed some old towels on the rug in front of the fire. For a second, she watched Guy through the small porthole before placing the kettle on the gas and the cakes on the table.

A few minutes later, the latch lifted and his bright smile beamed around the door.

'Is it okay to bring Sam inside?'

'It is, come on in, he can sit by the fire.'

Guy stooped down and walked on to the boat with Sam following behind. He swung his head round and took in his surroundings. 'Wow! Look at this place. It's like a proper house inside,' he said in amazement.

'It is a proper house, just on the water!' Nell exclaimed, laughing.

'I have to admit, that's the part I'm not keen on.'

'Come on through, you'll be surprised. There's a kitchen and everything, all mod cons in here, you know.'

'I've popped your life jacket back in the box.'

'Great, thanks, and you know where it is if you ever need it again and thanks for the loan of your scarf,' she said, handing it back to Guy.

The Cosy Canal Boat Dream

'I've no intention of ever needing a life jacket again in my lifetime, but thanks anyway,' he grinned. 'Do you know, this is the first time I've ever been inside a barge?'

'I'm surprised you've taken over Ed's job if you're scared of water and never been inside a narrowboat,' Nell mused, passing him a towel to dry off Sam, who was standing at Guy's side and wafting his long snout in the air.

'I surprised myself by accepting his offer but he promised me faithfully that all the boats that needed restoring and painting would be firmly on dry land inside the yard, but I am beginning to doubt he's told me the whole truth.' He rolled his eyes in jest.

Suddenly, Sam began to shake violently, spraying water everywhere.

'Whoa! Sam stop,' Guy commanded in a stern tone, quickly throwing a towel over his back and rubbing him down frantically. 'I'm so sorry!'

Sam looked up with his dopey eyes, 'How could anyone resist those puppy-dog eyes,' Nell giggled, wiping away droplets from her face.

'He has his moments. There, that's better, he's all done.' Nell took the towel from Guy while they both watched Sam in amusement as he circled round and round, chasing his tail until he finally lay down in front of the burning embers of the fire.

'Make yourself at home, why don't you?' Guy laughed.

'He's a gorgeous looking dog.'

'But a bit scatty!'

Sam was now fully stretched out on the rug. 'And definitely has bagged the best place on the boat.'

'There's something quite enchanting about a real fire,' Guy said watching the flames crackle and burn.

'There is. I do love this time of year. Take a seat,' Nell gestured towards the bench, 'Oh and welcome to the Nollie!' she flung her arms open wide.

'Nollie?' She met Guy's gaze as he raised an eyebrow.

'Nell and Ollie: Nollie.'

'Aw I see!' he exclaimed, loosening his coat and sliding between the table and the seat, he settled next to the window.

'It was Ollie's idea,' said Nell proudly of their little floating home.

'And a very good one.'

'Coffee?' she asked, reaching for the mugs just as the kettle began to whistle.

'Perfect,' he answered rubbing his fingers together, 'I think I'm finally beginning to thaw out. It's bitter out there today.'

A flutter of white caught Nell's eye and she peered towards the tiny porthole, 'Look, it's beginning to snow. I could watch the flakes fall for hours.'

Guy turned towards the window and Nell slid into the space next to him. They both watched the tiny snowflakes flurrying to the ground from the grey sky.

For a moment there was comfortable silence until Nell jumped, 'I've forgotten your drink, what a rubbish host I am,' she said, standing up, 'and these are courtesy of Bea,' she slid the cream cakes towards him.'

'They look divine.'

The Cosy Canal Boat Dream

'I'm lucky to have first dibs on all the leftovers each day but it's no good for the figure.' She patted her tummy in jest.

'You look fine to me.'

Nell quickly turned away to make the coffee, a perfect excuse to the hide the corners of her mouth that had lifted. She could feel his solid warm gaze watching her before she settled back down next to him.

'This is the first time it's snowed in over a year,' Guy said, his gaze turned back to the window.

'It is,' Nell answered softly, with a sudden memory of Ollie flooding her mind. It was their first Christmas on the 'Nollie' and they had spent Christmas Eve entwined in each other's arms in front of the fire sipping mulled wine while watching *Scrooge* when Nell had uttered the words: 'I wish it would snow, that would complete Christmas.' She remembered Ollie's mischievous wink, 'You never know,' he replied. The next morning, Ollie had woken her up from her slumber by kissing her tenderly on the lips, 'Merry Christmas, Nell,' he'd whispered, as he took her by her hand. A trail of paper snowflakes led her to the door of the 'Nollie'. 'Go on, open the door,' he pressed, kissing the tip of her nose.

'What are you up to, Ollie Andrews?' His eyes twinkled, 'Close your eyes, Nell.' Ollie flicked the latch, grasped her hand, then led her carefully up the steps on to the deck of the boat. 'You can open your eyes now.'

The second Nell had opened her eyes she gasped: the whole 'Nollie' had been covered in pretend snow, just like a magical winter wonderland. Their first Christmas had been perfect:

dinner at the 'Nollie' and the evening spent at Bluebell Cottage with her parents.

Nell turned towards Guy and smiled. There was something about Guy she was easily drawn to and she felt at ease talking to him. 'There's something hypnotic about watching the snow fall.'

'I agree,' he said, 'Even better when you're with beautiful company.' His eyes sparkled and Nell's pulse began to race.

'I'll take that compliment,' she smiled shyly at him, knowing it had been a long while since anyone had paid her a compliment and she liked it.

'Thanks for rescuing Sam today,' he flashed Nell a grateful smile before cupping his hands around the mug of steaming coffee and taking a sip.

'It was my pleasure.'

Guy and Nell turned towards Sam, who was whimpering in his sleep while his front paw twitched.

'He's exhausted and dreaming. I think his little adventure has tired him out.'

'And me!' Nell laughed, stretching her arms, 'Rowing that boat has certainly given my arm muscles a workout.'

'I was useless, pathetic in fact. I'm sorry.'

'You were! You can make it up to me, but no apology needed,' she teased.

Guy laughed. 'We will never know how he got out there, but everything happens for a reason.'

'A reason?'

'Yes, a reason.' Guy stretched out his legs under the table and Nell felt them brushing against hers.

The Cosy Canal Boat Dream

'I wouldn't be sat here now with you if it wasn't for Sam. I'm a strong believer in fate.'

Nell smiled up at him.

'How are you bearing up?' He asked cautiously.

'My arms are fine.'

'I didn't mean your arms,' he laughed, bumping his shoulder playfully against hers, 'I meant with your husband's birthday.'

She swallowed hard and held his gaze, 'I've learnt to take one day at a time but those days are certainly getting easier.'

'There's a brightness in your eyes, time to start living again,' he observed.

She nodded, 'Time to start living again.'

Guy leant across the table and covered Nell's hand; he squeezed it tight, she felt her body tremble a little.

'That fire is making me feel sleepy,' she murmured, 'and the snow is coming down thick and fast.'

'Have you any plans for tonight?' he asked.

'Mum's expecting me for tea, but with the weather like this she'd understand if I didn't venture out.'

'Do you fancy some company?'

Nell's face flushed as she glanced upwards at him and all of a sudden felt a little shy, 'Are you sure?'

'There's nowhere else I'd rather be' and he was surprised just how much he meant it after everything he'd been through recently.

'Well, in that case. That'll be lovely.'

'Have you ever lost anyone close?' Nell asked, suddenly curious about the man sitting next to her.

'Not in the sense you have but ...' he paused.

Nell could tell by the sudden glistening of his eyes that he'd lost someone who had meant the world to him.

'My granddad, Hector.' His mood dipped a little, swallowing down a lump in his throat. 'Look at me getting all emotional, it always happens when I speak about him.'

'He must have been very special,' said Nell softly.

He gathered himself together and lifted his eyes towards her. A smile spread across Guy's face as he remembered his granddad. 'Without a doubt, he was my rock and taught me everything I know.'

'Sounds ominous,' Nell said lightening the mood a little.

'Ha, not at all, great memories. He bought me the best present ever when I was a kid.'

'Which was?'

'A box of Lego.'

'I think Bea would disagree with you there – if she stands on one more bit of Lego,' Nell chuckled while picturing Bea hobbling across the floor holding her foot and swearing profusely, 'She's threatened to throw Jacob's in the bin.'

Guy laughed, 'My mum used to moan when it jammed the Hoover.'

'So why was a box of Lego the best present in the world?'

'Because Granddad showed me how to build everything from a bog-standard house to the Empire State Building and when I was older he let me go onto the site with him and taught me how to lay bricks, plaster and get my hands really dirty.'

'So he was a builder?'

The Cosy Canal Boat Dream

'Yes, even though Granny wasn't impressed when he came home covered head to toe in dust every night. She used to shoo him straight upstairs into the shower. He died a while ago now but he and Granny clocked up over fifty years of marriage.'

'That's fantastic!'

Guy shook his head, 'She's no longer with us, sadly passed away six months after him. I know it sounds daft, but I honestly believe she died of a broken heart. She couldn't bear to be apart from him.' He closed his eyes for a brief moment and Nell noticed the sadness in his voice.

'It's not daft at all.' Her own eyes brimmed with tears at the thought of his grandma too sad to carry on.

Guy leant forward and wiped a tear from her cheek that had escaped.

'I didn't mean to make you cry,' his voice faltered and he gave Nell a weak smile. 'Here,' he said, taking a tissue from his pocket.

'Sorry I was lost in the moment there. That's so sad and romantic.'

'I was sure he was going to live forever and now they are no doubt rocking the heavens together. I miss them both dearly. Even though I knew Granddad had been ill for a while, his death was still like a kick in the stomach. It felt like my whole world had collapsed.'

This was a situation Nell could wholeheartedly relate to; first her dad and then Ollie.

'Were your family supportive?' Tears threatened again as Nell thought of her mum and Bea, her heart swelled with love for them both, she could never have got through the tough times without them.

Guy turned towards her, 'Hey, I'm meant to be cheering you up and look at us getting all maudlin.'

For a split second his fingers entwined around hers, Nell squeezed them, then smiled up at him.

'I know,' she said, throwing caution to the wind while glancing down at her now-empty coffee mug, 'I think we are both in need of something a little stronger, even if it's a school night.'

'Oh why not. You've talked me into it.'

'It didn't need much persuasion,' she laughed, standing up and grasping a bottle of wine from the rack at the side of the fridge before pouring two large glasses.

The pair of them sipped at their wine thoughtfully, both tinged with sadness over the loss of their loved ones.

'Hug?' Guy asked softly, reaching towards her and taking her hand. The feel of his touch sent shivers downs Nell's spine and her skin prickled with goose bumps. A feeling she had missed for such a long time.

'That would be nice.'

'How's that? Comfy?' He rested his arm around her shoulder. It had been a while since she'd felt the comforting weight of an arm draped around her and she nestled into him as if it was the most natural thing in the world. Hearing the thump of his heart, 'Perfect,' she murmured, startled by her own feelings. The feeling of being close to someone again made her tingle all over as she wrapped her arm across his stomach and inhaled the gorgeous aroma of his after-

The Cosy Canal Boat Dream

shave. She could feel the intense heat radiating from his touch and wondered if he could feel it too as her heart skipped a beat.

'So tell me about Guy Cornish,' she asked. 'Who is this Irish man who's turned up at Little Rock?'

'There's not a lot to tell. I'm twenty-nine and owner of a scatty dog ...' he paused.

'Job?'

Guy exhaled, 'A suit, work in the city, dealing with financial stuff.'

'You don't sound too chuffed about that?' Nell said, detecting the change in the tone of his voice.

'It pays the bills.'

Nell lifted her head and gazed towards him, 'Single?' she asked calmly, even though her heart was hammering in anticipation of the answer.

For a brief second the question hung in the air and he rested his chin of the top of Nell's head while she reminded herself to breathe normally.

'I'm single,' he replied.

Goose bumps prickled over every inch of her body, 'That's good, then,' the words left her mouth before she could stop herself.

Looking Nell in the eyes, he smiled. She noticed the gentle lift of his mouth and for a brief moment she thought he was going to kiss her. She'd no idea what had come over her – she'd only just met the man. Her heart was beating wildly and it was then Nell had felt it: raw chemistry, an attraction, a feeling she'd not felt for a long time.

'It's the wine, makes me brave,' she giggled, tearing her gaze away.

'You've only had one sip,' he laughed. He nudged her playfully with his elbow.

Nell felt the corners of her mouth lift, 'When are you due back in Ireland?'

'In a few weeks' time when Ed is back up on his feet.'

Suddenly, Nell felt a tiny pang. It was daft really, she barely knew the man but there was something inside her that didn't like the thought of him returning to Ireland anytime soon.

They sat in a peaceful silence, watching the snowflakes settling on the roofs of the pretty barges through the porthole of the 'Nollie'. Smoke from neighbouring boats spiralled into the grey sky.

Guy turned towards Nell, there was a sudden brightness in his eyes, 'Let's raise a toast,'

'What are we toasting?'

'Ollie's birthday, my grandparents and to life.'

'That sounds like a great toast.'

They both clinked their glasses against each other's. 'Cheers, life.'

'Life,' Nell smiled, taking a sip of her wine.

Nell felt content and happy and even though Guy had only just come into her life, she didn't like the thought of him disappearing out of it anytime soon.

Chapter 4

'Aunty Nellie, Aunty Nellie, you are living in a floating igloo.'
Nell looked up to see Nathan pulling an excited Jacob along on a bright-red sledge towards her.

'Daddy stop!' Jacob shouted as he hurled himself out of the sledge and crunched through the snow towards Nell.

'Those wellies came in handy.'

Jacob's face beamed.

'Does Aunty Nellie get a huge hug?'

'Absolutely,' Jacob flung his arms wide open.

Nell stooped to wrap her arms around him and planted a kiss on the tip of his cold nose. She smiled at Nathan, 'Morning. Did you have a successful day yesterday and find the part for the motorbike you needed?'

He shook his head regretfully, 'No, but I managed to purchase a whole lot of other junk that I'm not entirely sure I needed. Well, according to Bea anyway. The second she heard the key in the door she shooed me to the back of the house and demanded I deposit my scrap in the shed because she wasn't having any more half-built motorbikes in her kitchen.'

'And rightly so – boys and their toys,' Nell grinned, turning back towards Jacob, who currently had a mischievous smile on his face while scooping up the snow and patting it into a ball.

'I hope you aren't ...' Too late! Jacob launched the snowball straight at Nell, who promptly chased him, squealing, towards the deli. As Jacob pushed open the door Nell bundled him into her arms and blew a raspberry on his neck as he tried to wriggle free.

'What's all this noise?' Bea appeared from behind the counter, smiling at her son.

'Aunty Nellie is chasing me,' Jacob giggled as Nell lowered him to the ground.

Bea pecked Nathan on his cheek then touched Nell's arm. Nell met her gaze. 'You didn't text me last night, everything okay? I was worried about you.'

Nell nodded. Last night she'd spoken to her mum soon after Guy had left. Her mum had understood with the heavy snowfall that she hadn't wanted to walk out in the bitter chill of the February air.

'Yes, I'm all good.' Bea pressed a swift kiss to her cheek and gave her a quick hug.

'So, young man.' Bea crouched down in front of him. 'You've had a quick play on your sledge before school.'

Jacob grinned.

'Just remember to wrap up well at school today if you go outside to play,' she pulled up the lapels of his coat and his bobble hat down over his eyes.

'Mummy!' he giggled, pushing his hat back up on his head.

The Cosy Canal Boat Dream

Bea grasped his scarf and pulled Jacob towards her, then kissed his forehead.

'Some of the supplies haven't been delivered yet; they must be having some difficulties getting through the lanes with the weather. We're low on milk so I've rung ahead to The Waterfront who are going to lend us a few pints. I'll nip over and grab them now you're here,' she said, standing up and turning towards Nell.

'No need, I'll collect them. I've still got my coat on and it gives me a chance to pull my favourite godson on his sledge through the snow for five minutes.'

'Aunty Nellie, I'm your only godson! You're silly.'

'But it doesn't stop you from being my favourite, though, does it?'

'When I pick Jacob up from school I'll start the tea,' Nathan smiled at Bea then gave her a quick peck on the cheek.

'And that's why I love you so much.'

The door to the deli swung open and a blast of cold air hit them, 'Good morning,' the postman chirped, handing Bea a handful of letters from his sack before disappearing as quickly as he appeared.

'I won't be long.' Nell said, following the postman outside.

Nell and Nathan crunched through the snow in their boots, pulling a giggling Jacob behind them on his sledge. The Waterfront pub was situated at the far end of the marina and was a place Ollie and Nell would often frequent on a Friday night.

Nathan abruptly stopped outside the Old Picture House. He mustered a smile, 'Well, that's that, then. The place has finally gone up for sale.' They both stared up at the for sale sign.

'It's so sad,' Nell's voice suddenly wobbled. 'Guy mentioned it would probably be knocked down and no doubt houses built in its place.'

'Guy?'

'Ed's brother, he's come over from Ireland to help out at the Boathouse while Ed recovers from his operation.'

'Ah, Bea did mention something about him yesterday, and you know what, unfortunately he's probably right.'

Nell's heart plummeted; she could still visualise herself as a child sat next to her dad in the bucket seats with her legs dangling towards the floor, then years later cuddled up with Ollie waiting for the lights to dim so she could pinch a fizzy cola bottle from his pick 'n mix.

Nell drew in a deep breath and her heart twisted. 'Ollie would be devastated to see this place demolished, especially for houses.'

Nathan draped his arm around her shoulders and gave her a quick squeeze before they carried on walking towards the pub, 'I miss him too you know.'

Nell nodded, 'I know.'

'Especially yesterday. I knew what day it was and that's why I took myself off to the motorbike convention. I wanted to do something that we enjoyed doing together. It made me feel a little bit closer to him. Does that sound daft?'

'Not at all.'

'How did you cope with yesterday?'

'Actually, quite well. Time does make things a little easier.

The Cosy Canal Boat Dream

It's nice to actually talk about him without bursting into tears. I've come a long way.'

'I'm glad,' Nathan smiled at her.

'Right, here's my stop.'

Nell swung around towards Jacob, 'You have a good day at school, young man, and tell Mrs Smith I think it's time I had a new painting for my fridge,' she gave him the thumbs-up.

'I'm on it, Aunty Nellie. I'll draw you a picture of Oreo.'

Nell raised her eyebrow, then glanced towards Nathan, 'Who's Oreo?'

'I've no idea … Jacob?'

'One of Gilly's kittens, but Mummy said I've got to keep it a secret from …' Jacob cupped his hand to his mouth and gasped.

'Daddy,' Nathan interrupted.

'Mummy said if we convinced you it was your idea, it was a no-brainer,' he scratched his head, not quite understanding what the word meant, 'We could have one of the kittens.'

'Did she now?'

'Am I in trouble?'

Nathan grinned, 'No, not at all, but hopefully the name is negotiable.'

'Good call,' Nell whispered to Nathan before waving her hand in the air and disappearing up the steps of the pub to collect the milk.

Chapter 5

When Nell returned to The Melting Pot, Bea was huddled over the computer in the corner of the office, shuffling various bits of paper and staring at the screen.

'Just checking the emails before we open up, and shifting through this post.'

'Anything interesting?'

'No, just the usual new suppliers offering deals of various produce, but I'd rather stick with the devils we know.'

'Absolutely, Mark from The Waterfront said not to worry about the milk, no doubt one day you will return the favour.'

'That's lovely of him and, yes, of course I will.'

Nell shivered, 'At least it's warmer in here than out there today. She shrugged off her coat and hung it over the chair. 'I've got a feeling we may be a little busy today. There won't be many boats moving in that icy water.'

'I think you may be right,' Bea answered, flicking the cursor up and down the screen.

'Erm, is that a bacon bap you're secretly scoffing in the corner? What happened to let's eat sensibly after Christmas?' Nell mused, putting the milk in the fridge.

The Cosy Canal Boat Dream

Bea grinned before taking another generous mouthful, the brown sauce oozing all over her plate.

'Busted! But, my God, I needed that! I feel hungry all the time. I'm blaming the weather. How can anyone think about eating lettuce leaves and dieting at this time of year? I need comfort food, good old stodge.'

'Summer bodies are made in winter you know,' Nell laughed, 'And where's mine?'

'Bottom oven and there's a mug of tea for you over there.'

'Superstar,' Nell plonked herself in the chair opposite Bea and glanced up at the clock, 'Another fifteen minutes until we open.'

'Listen out for the oven timer, there's sausage rolls in the bottom oven and scones in the top.'

Nell nodded and began to devour her sandwich. 'You didn't fill me in on yesterday, what happened to the dog?' Bea said looking up from the computer and meeting Nell's gaze.

'Somehow, Sam managed to get himself all the way over to the boat moored right at the back of the marina.'

'I noticed that boat the other day. It's not a regular, is it? What's its name?'

'If I remember rightly, 'Much Ado About Nothing,' I've not seen it before and, come to think of it, haven't seen any movement on it either. I'd say it's been here a few days max.'

'And it won't be going anywhere soon in this weather. Did you manage to coax Sam back on to the rowing boat okay?'

'After a little persuasion. It didn't help with Guy, who happens to be scared stiff of water, being rooted to the spot.'

'What's the story there, then?'

'A near-death experience with water when he was a kid. God knows how's he's going to manage the boatyard!' Nell chuckled.

Hearing the tinkle of the bell above the shop door they both quickly glanced at the clock.

'It's not time yet, we've another five minutes.' Nell said, taking another swift bite of her sandwich before standing up.

'Shop.' They heard a voice shout. 'Anyone there?'

'I recognise that voice,' Nell whispered, 'It's Guy.'

'Gorgeous Guy?' Bea said, while Nell rolled her eyes at her.

'I don't mind dragging my weary body off the chair to serve him,' Bea grinned, scraping her seat back.

'You stay there, I'll go!'

'Not a chance!'

Bea noticed Nell taking a tentative look in the mirror before smoothing down her hair and following her on to the shop floor.

'Good morning,' Bea sang with Nell looking over her shoulder.

Guy's face beamed back at them both. There was no denying he was looking very handsome standing on the other side of the counter with his tousled hair, slight stubble and dressed in a pair of olive-green overalls.

'Tom Cruise eat your heart out – all that's missing is the shades,' Bea muttered under her breath.

'Good morning to the pair of you.'

Guy's eyes twinkled towards Nell. He gestured to his mouth then raised an eyebrow at her.

The Cosy Canal Boat Dream

Nell smiled, 'What?' she asked, amused.

'You've got brown ...' he pointed towards her mouth.

Nell couldn't help but feel a teeny bit embarrassed as she quickly wiped her mouth with the back of her hand.

'Brown sauce,' she rolled her eyes, 'As you can see the diet didn't start today!'

'Wrong time of year for that dieting malarkey. I need something warm and stodgy before I take on the mammoth task of stripping out the inside of a boat.'

'Bacon, sausage and egg barm?' Nell suggested.

'Sounds perfect and a coffee to take out.'

'Give me two minutes,' she said, disappearing into the kitchen, leaving Bea chatting to Guy.

'How's Ed?' Bea asked, pressing the button on the coffee machine, which immediately began to whirl, quickly followed by a blast of steam, then complete silence. Bea looked at it, mystified, before wiping her flushed cheeks on her pinny.

'I think it's being a little temperamental this morning.'

'Best have a cup of tea, I think,' he grinned, leaning on the counter and staring at the array of cakes. 'The operation went well and he's recovering nicely.'

Nell could hear their conversation while she bustled about in the kitchen preparing his sandwich.

'That's good to hear. Are you staying with him up at Little End Cottage?'

'Sort of, I'm in the annexe attached to the cottage, which gives me and Sam our own space, but I can keep a close eye on Ed too when he arrives back from hospital. The nurse said he shouldn't be in too much pain, but it's the usual no stretching and lots of rest and I'm not sure Ed is one for sitting still. I'll be on hand to make his meals and generally be at his beck and call.'

'He'll love being waited on hand and foot,' Bea said, 'Pass on our best wishes and I'll take him up his favourite steak and ale pie when he's home.'

Guy smiled, 'I hope there'll be enough for two!'

'Of course.'

Nell walked back into the shop and placed the sandwich down on the counter. 'How's Sam today?'

'He slept like a baby last night after his little adventure but so did I after that bottle of wine.'

Nell could feel Bea's stare burning into the side of her face. 'Wine?'

'Yes, you know the drink that comes in a bottle, usually with a cork.' Nell replied with a sarcastic grin.

'Mmm,' Bea eyed Nell doubtfully as she turned back towards Guy, 'I'm glad you both slept well. Here, have the sandwich on the house. I'm sure Bea won't mind.'

'Not at all,' Bea answered with a look that said to Nell that this conversation was far from over.

Guy's face lit up, 'Thank you, that's very generous of you both. I'll see you every morning with this kind of service. Nell, you are the best and now I know why Ed raves about this place so much.'

Bea coughed and folded her arms.

'And you too, dear Bea, you both are simply the best.' Guy grinned cheekily before disappearing through the deli door.

As soon as the door was shut, Nell turned to Bea, 'I can't

The Cosy Canal Boat Dream

believe you let me come out here with brown sauce dripping from the corner of my mouth!'

Bea leaned in closer towards Nell, 'Hmm, and I can't believe you missed out the part about drinking wine with a handsome stranger,' she teased.

'Don't be daft, I rescued his dog and he was very grateful,' she answered, chewing her lip while watching Guy stroll towards the boat yard with Sam trotting at his side. He looked back over his shoulder and snagged Nell's eye.

'He likes you, mark my words.' Bea pulled her I-know-best look while Nell kept her poker face.

'You heard it here first, Nell Andrews, you just remember that.'

Nell flapped her hand at Bea, 'Get back to work, Bea, you are driving me insane!'

As soon as Bea's back was turned, Nell felt the corners of her mouth lift and her face blush. There was something about that Irish charmer that made her stomach instantly flutter.

Chapter 6

By mid-morning Nell and Bea had been run off their feet. The beef and horseradish rolls were a hit and had sold out in no time at all. There were a couple of loaves of bread left and Nell was already baking her third batch of scones.

'I'd a feeling today was going to be busy,' Nell said, wiping her hands on her pinny and exhaling sharply.

'Where did all those people come from? You'd think there was going to be a food shortage with the amount everyone has bought,' Bea exclaimed, leaning against the counter and taking a breather. 'We've not even had a tea break yet.'

'It's the weather. It's difficult for the boats to move so I think everyone is panic-buying, just in case the snow fall gets heavier.'

'Let's just hope our supplies get through okay, but I think we have enough ingredients in the pantry to keep us going for a few days at least.'

'According to the weather,' Nell flicked on to her phone, 'It's forecast rain from this afternoon, so hopefully the panic buying will settle down.'

'Here's hoping. Did you remember to take the last batch of

The Cosy Canal Boat Dream

scones out of the oven? I'm not sure I heard the timer buzz in the mad rush?'

'Oh shoot,' Nell replied, quickly grabbing the oven gloves before hurrying to the back of the kitchen and flinging open the oven door.

'Double shoot,' she pulled out the baking tray and stared. 'Well and truly cremated,' she looked aghast, 'That's my fault. I forgot to set the timer with it being so busy.'

'Not to worry, it's just one of those things,' Bea answered, leaning against the door frame, 'Pop them on the side and once they've cooled down I'll throw them out to the birds. They are probably in need of a good feed in this weather.'

They both whipped their heads round as they heard the shop bell tinkle, 'No rest for the wicked,' Bea rolled her eyes.

They hurried back behind the counter to find the postman standing there for the second time today.

'Sorry Nell, I missed this one before,' he smiled, handing over an envelope to her. As soon as the postman left the shop Nell put the envelope down on the counter.

'Anything important?'

'Bank savings, annual statement. Ollie's life insurance.'

Nell had had no idea that Ollie even had any life insurance until she'd had to sell the yard.

'I'll put the kettle on, come on. Oh and I'm putting the closed sign up for ten minutes, we deserve a break.' Bea announced, walking towards the door and pulling the latch down.

'Here comes the rain now too.' Both of them looked up to see to see the sleety rain drumming against the glass and boat owners quickly pulling their windows shut.

Nell moved into the kitchen and clutched the bank statement while Bea switched on the kettle and ferreted around in the cupboard for a couple of mugs.

'I never knew what to do with this money, it was just never important in the grand scheme of things.'

'You did the right thing bunging it into a savings account, it'll have gained a little interest,' Bea said, perching on the table waiting for the kettle to boil. 'Any ideas what to do with it now?'

'Not got a clue,' answered Nell, watching Bea make the drinks and settling in the chair opposite her. Nell hadn't really given the money a second thought up until now. 'I don't particularly need anything, maybe in time I could invest it in property or a business.'

'Are you going to open it?'

Nell nodded, then carefully opened the envelope. Her eyes flitted over the numbers on the page and exhaled, 'Sixty-five thousand pounds.'

Bea gave a low whistle.

'Why did I ever ask him to go out that night, Bea? If only ...'

'Oh Nell, I don't know what to say, we all miss him and I know it's not the same but we are always here for you.'

'I know.' Nell flashed Bea a grateful smile. 'No amount of money will ever replace him.'

'It won't and look ...' Bea paused, 'you don't have to do anything with the money, leave it where it is for now.'

Both of them sipped on their tea before Nell pushed the letter to one side, then skimmed over the pages of the local newspaper.

The Cosy Canal Boat Dream

'What you need is a little company,' Bea suggested, thinking that one of Gilly's kittens might just be the thing for Nell.

'Mmm, I believe you are going to have a new addition to the family very soon,' Nell lifted an eyebrow and gave Bea a knowing look.

Bea sat up straight in her chair, 'Wait, how do you know about that?'

'Call it my psychic powers.' Nell grinned, remembering Jacob's little face when this morning he literally let the cat out of the bag.

'You saw it, didn't you?'

'Saw what?' Nell eyed Bea suspiciously.

They held each other's gaze and no one spoke for a second.

'Saw what?' Nell repeated with a confused look on her face. She leaned forward and folded her arms on the newspaper and stared straight at Bea, who promptly blushed.

Bea opened her mouth and closed it again.

'Spill Bea Green,' Nell insisted, nodding encouragingly. 'All eyes are on you!'

Bea looked suitably composed, 'I think we may be talking about two different things.'

Nell lifted an eyebrow, 'What are you talking about, then? Come on.' Nell drummed her fingers on the desk in jest.

Bea swallowed and managed a nod, 'At this moment in time I'm trying to ignore the queasiness in the pit of my stomach.'

It took a second for the penny to drop, 'Sweet Jesus, you're pregnant! You are, aren't you?'

A huge beam spread across Bea's face, 'I am.'

Nell squealed, 'Come here, let me give you a hug,' she said as she squeezed her friend tight.

'I thought you'd spotted the test I left in the toilet the other day.'

'Ha no, but congratulations!'

'Thank you, we are both delighted, but we've not told Jacob yet as it's still early days.'

'Mum's the word!' exclaimed Nell.

'For the time being anyway,' Bea grinned, 'Now what was it you were on about?' She sat back down on the chair.

'Oreo!'

Bea gasped, 'Has Gilly spilt the beans? I've not run it past Nathan yet.' A worried look flashed over Bea's face.

'Don't panic, Nathan took it all in his stride.'

'Nathan? Oh God, how does he know?'

'Well he's about this big,' Nell gestured with her hands, 'cute chubby cheeks, clomps around in the brightest pair of wellies and is not very good at keeping secrets!'

'Jacob, the little monkey.' Bea rolled her eyes and shook her head laughing.

'Anyway, back to Baby Green, how far gone are you?'

'Early days, only eight weeks or so. I'm feeling so-so, a little queasy at times, but I seem to be eating my body weight in anything and everything.'

'Well don't overdo it, you know I can help with the early morning baking if you don't feel up to it.'

'I promise I will ask if I need any help.'

'Good,' Nell replied, skimming the newspaper once more and turning the page.

The Cosy Canal Boat Dream

'Anything interesting?'

Nell sighed, twisting the paper towards Bea. 'Now this is what makes me sad.'

'Nathan and I were only talking about this last night.' Bea glanced at the paper.

There on the property page of the local newspaper were the details of the old derelict picture house.

'Such a shame,' Nell said sadly, a wave of nostalgia washing over her.

'They could easily throw up a few houses on that plot. How much is it up for?'

Nell stared at the page and then Bea.

'It's up for auction. Ollie and I always talked about doing something together, a project that would benefit the community and bring the kids and the older generation back together. Everyone these days spends their life tapping not speaking.'

Nell's mind began to whirl and she wriggled in her chair excitedly as she read aloud the reserve figure. Nell had a sudden sparkle in her eyes. Bea knew that look on Nell's face – she was mulling something over.

'What if? ...' Nell hesitated for a second.

'Go on, what are you thinking?'

'No, I can't, I'm just being daft.'

'Come on, say what you're thinking,' urged Bea.

Nell swallowed and took a deep breath, 'What if I bought the place?' Once the words left her mouth her thoughts became reality.

'What would you do with it?'

Nell bit down on her lip, gazed out of the window then

turned back towards Bea, 'Use Ollie's money to restore it, turn it back into a picture house in his memory.'

It took Bea a second for Nell's words to sink in.

'Are you serious?' Bea shot her a sideways glance.

'How much do you think a project like this would cost?'

'You are serious!'

Nell nodded, 'I think I am.'

The excitement rose inside Nell. She'd often talked with Ollie about undertaking a project that would bring the community back together and this could be it. Not only would it benefit the whole marina, but it would stop new houses being built.

'You'll need to ask someone in the know. Shall I ask Nathan? He might know someone.'

Nell's eyes grew wide then her face broke into a smile. 'Would you?'

'Of course.'

'I just need to know how much a project like this would cost. I could co-ordinate it myself.' Nell's routine had been the same day in, and day out in the last couple of years, this project would be the perfect opportunity to get her teeth into something new which would benefit the whole community.

'That'll keep you busy,' Bea mused, finishing her drink.

'It would, wouldn't it. There's no harm in looking into it.'

'No harm at all.'

Chapter 7

It was Friday evening and Nell stood nervously on the steps of the annexe to Little End Cottage. She rapped on the door then dug her hands into her pockets to shield them from the frosty temperature of the night air. As she waited she shuffled her feet from side to side and snuggled deep inside her coat to keep warm.

She knocked again and still nothing.

'Damn,' she muttered to herself. She'd ventured out into the cold night on a whim. She'd never even considered there wouldn't be any answer. She'd lain awake last night and had barely slept a wink, thoughts of restoring the Old Picture House had her pacing the length of the 'Nollie' in the early hours of the morning.

She'd had many honest conversations with herself, was she just running away with some romantic notion or could this be a possibility, was she even capable of renovating the Old Picture House back to its original state and make it into a viable business?

The previous evening, after seeing the property in the newspaper Nell had visited her mum at Bluebell Cottage. She'd sat in the kitchen tucking into homemade cottage pie and shared her aspirations for the abandoned building. While Nell enthused about the plans that were whizzing around in her head, she noticed a shift in mood in her mum.

'The thing is, Nell, that place closed down for a reason. If a proper business person can't keep it afloat, what chance do you have? Projects like that can be draining mentally and run way over budget. Who's going to manage the place?'

'Well, me of course.'

'Abandon Bea after she gave you a job, a lifeline after everything that happened?' Gilly tutted.

Feeling deflated, Nell had sunk back in her chair with three gorgeous kittens on her lap. She'd never considered Bea in any of this. Once the picture house was up and running would she need to leave her job? It was something she hadn't even considered and now here was her mum putting a kibosh on the whole thing with zilch enthusiasm before it had even begun.

'Ollie and I had always talked about a project, something that would benefit the community and bring a new zest for life into the area.'

'And Ollie wouldn't want you to run yourself into the ground. How will this project be funded?'

Nell hesitated, 'With his life insurance and our savings.'

Gilly had dismissed the subject almost immediately, leaving Nell feeling confused and squashed. It wasn't quite the reaction she'd expected or wanted.

That was the reason she was here now, knocking on Guy's cottage door. She couldn't get the notion of the renovation

The Cosy Canal Boat Dream

out of her head, despite her mum's opinion. She wanted an outsider's opinion, someone who didn't have any emotional attachment to the situation.

Nell stared up at Little End Cottage, the place was still picturesque even in the midst of February with the ivy entwined around it's oak-beam porch and the smoke swirling out of the chimney pot above the thatched roof. There was still no answer; she hesitated then followed the pebble path around the side of the property.

She stood on her tiptoes and peered through the window and caught sight of Guy walking into the living room, then she spotted Sam curled up on the chair by the side of the log burner.

Guy looked as if he'd just come out of the shower, wearing just a pair of grey lounge pants as he stood in front of the TV towel-drying his hair.

Nell found herself gazing at him, rooted to the spot, and couldn't help but admire his toned, tanned torso. And there it was again, that tingle, goose bumps and flutters in her stomach that had been missing for so long.

Suddenly, Guy jumped up in the air, flung the towel and began to play an imaginary guitar. As Nell watched his exaggerated strumming and lip-synching she couldn't help but giggle. Just as he was about to jump off the settee she lifted her hand to knock on the window, catching Sam's eye, who promptly leapt out of the chair and launched himself barking straight at the window.

Startled, Guy stopped in his tracks, whipped his head round and locked eyes with Nell. He casually stepped down from the settee as if it was the most normal thing in the world and his face broke into a smile. Two seconds later, he opened the door to the annexe. Leaning against the doorframe he folded his arms and beamed, 'Sorry, I didn't hear you knock, I was just ...' His eyes twinkled. 'I was just ...'

'You were just what?' Nell cocked her head to one side and grinned.

'You can't beat a bit of Jimi Hendrix. That's all I'm saying!'

'If you say so,' Nell bit down on her lip to quash her smile and secretly wishing Sam hadn't spotted her at that precise moment. They stared at each other for a brief second before Guy remembered his manners and stepped to one side.

'Forgive me, come on in. It's freezing out there.'

'Thank you,' Nell brushed past Guy and stepped into the hallway while taking in his divine spicy masculine fragrance, which sent a tingle down her spine.

She heard Sam sniffing at the bottom of the door, which he soon managed to nudge open before he excitedly came bounding towards her.

'Hello boy,' Nell said, crouching down and ruffling his ears. He thumped his tail and scampered down the hallway, then promptly returned with a ball that he dropped at Nell's feet.

'You have a friend there.'

She smiled cheerfully, 'That's good to hear.'

A wooden staircase adorned the hallway, 'Here, let me take your coat,' Guy said, hanging it over the banister.

The hallway was lit by a lamp. Stripped wooden beams ran the length of the ceiling and it was extremely quaint and cosy.

The Cosy Canal Boat Dream

'Make yourself comfy in the living room. It's probably best if I go and pop some clothes on.' Guy gestured towards the solid oak door.

Nell blushed slightly but couldn't stop her eyes flitting over his body one more time before he disappeared into the bedroom.

Sam followed Nell into the living room. It was just how she imagined it, the furniture was sparse and simple, a chesterfield, an antique dresser and a roaring log fire. She settled on the chair next to the wood burner and Sam lay on the rug at her feet, wagging his tail, his tongue hanging out whilst staring at his ball. She could hear Guy humming to himself, then he popped his head around the doorway.

'Cup of tea before I sit down?'

'Only if you have time?'

'I'm sure Jimi Hendrix won't mind, I can jump off the sofa anytime,' he winked before disappearing into the kitchen.

Nell gazed around the room. She noticed numerous photographs on the dresser and wandered over to them. She instantly recognised Guy as a young boy, sitting on a man's lap in the front seat of a digger. 'My granddad,' Guy appeared, placing a tray of tea and biscuits down on the coffee table.

Nell swung round startled, 'Sorry, I wasn't being nosey.'

'Don't worry, that's one of my favourite photographs. Sugar?' asked Guy.

Nell nodded, 'Just the one, please.'

He passed her a mug of tea and she sank back into the chair by the fire. 'So what can I do for you?'

She looked up and met his gaze, 'I've got a mad idea spinning round in my head and I've no idea what to do about it or whether it's even doable. I've tried to talk it over with Mum but she seemed ...' Nell paused, 'I think reluctant is the word I'm looking for.'

Guy leaned forward and cupped his hands around his drink, 'Sounds very intriguing.' He joked, and stared at her with a curious expression.

'So, I wanted to run it past someone ...'

'Independent,' he finished off her sentence.

'Exactly,' Nell took a deep breath, 'Okay, here goes,' she exhaled, placing her mug on the coffee table, sitting up straight and tucking her hands between her thighs.

'You know the old building on the wharf, the one we stood outside.'

'The picture house?'

She nodded, 'That's the one. If I said to you I was thinking of buying it and renovating it back to its original state, how bonkers would you think I was?'

'On a scale of one to ten?' he grinned.

'I'm being serious.'

Guy's eyes widened, 'Well, I wasn't expecting that, but if I'm truly honest I'd no idea what I was expecting you to say.'

'You think it's a daft idea, don't you?' Nell sighed, picking up her mug of tea.

He popped a biscuit into his mouth, then slid the plate over towards her. She eyed him nervously, waiting for him to answer.

'I never said that! With what intention?' he asked.

The Cosy Canal Boat Dream

'What do you mean?'

'With the intention of selling it on to make a profit, or with the intention of trying to make a living out of it? What is your reasoning behind it?'

'A romantic notion,' she answered, as thoughts of Ollie flooded her mind.

'I'm not sure a romantic notion is going to pay the bills.' Guy's eyebrows lifted a notch and he jolted Nell back to the here and now.

'Ollie and I always talked about putting something back into the community, working on a project together and I think this it is. He wouldn't want to see the place bulldozed for houses. That old place has history. I loved spending time quality family time there, happy memories. Do you think it would be flattened for houses?'

'That's where the money is.' Guy admitted reluctantly thinking about all the times his granddad had scanned the paper looking for opportunities, to renovate spare land to build new properties.

'I can imagine,' she took a breath, 'but I want to turn back time, I want everyone flocking back to the Old Picture House for their first dates and creating memories like I have.'

'I think I said my granddad was in the building trade and in my experience a plot like that has loads of potential but there will already be numerous interested parties. Someone may have already put in an offer.'

'According to the paper, it's up for auction.'

'Okay, so that's a little different.'

'What do you mean?'

'Auctions are all about ready cash. Once the auction is won you usually have about fourteen days to complete the transaction, and you'll have to take the property in whatever state it's in. The local builders will have the means to snap up projects like this quite easily and the workforce to carry out any work.'

'What if I had the ready cash?'

He held her gaze and from the look in her eyes knew she meant business.

'Then I would say if you held your nerve at auction you would be in with a good chance of winning, depending on the reserve, your budget and the money needed to actually furnish it too.'

'So, you're saying I need the money to win the auction and then a little bit more.'

'A hell of a lot more. Okay, if your bid was successful and you renovate the Old Picture House, what are you going to do with it then? Are you going to run it as a business, film museum? What's the plan? Are you in it to make a profit? A project like this could cost you even more in the long run. The place closed down for a reason.'

So many questions. Guy sounded just like her mum now and Nell had to admit she hadn't really thought that far in advance, but one thing she did know, she had fire in her belly and something was telling her to do this. Nell sucked in a breath, 'It sounds all very expensive now you are throwing these types of scenarios at me,' she said.

Guy placed his cup down on the table, 'Hey, I'm not trying to put a dampener on it all.'

The Cosy Canal Boat Dream

'Like my mother,' she interrupted and couldn't get her head round why her mum was so dismissive of the idea.

'All I'm saying is don't go into this with your eyes shut. It will be a hell of a lot of money to lose if it doesn't go to plan and I've spent a lot of time with my granddad and have seen many a project unfinished due to lack of funds.'

Nell's eyes began to prick with tears and she came over all emotional, 'I think I was dreaming there for a minute,' a tear rolled down her cheek.

'Hey, don't knock dreams. Anyone's dreams can come true; you have to believe in yourself.' Guy caught Nell's eye. 'You have to budget for costs that you may never have even thought of. Here,' he fished inside his pocket and handed her a tissue.

'Thank you,' she said dabbing her eyes. 'I just feel I have to do this. Something in Ollie's memory.'

Nell hadn't really thought about the whole project in that much depth. She'd on many occasions watched re-runs of *Homes Under the Hammer* on a Saturday afternoon and admired anyone who took on a mammoth task of knocking down and building houses. She cast her mind back to her childhood and remembered the stress of her parents replacing their kitchen. But surely this project would be different: she wouldn't be living in it, she could manage everything from the safe haven of the 'Nollie'.

Guy smiled then nodded encouragingly, 'It's definitely achievable, but do your homework first.'

Nell knew Guy was right. When Bea had taken over the deli everything had gone wrong initially. The boiler had packed in, the ovens were on their last legs, the roof had leaked and the whole place had needed bringing into this century. But she had done it, and she had an amazing business now.

'So ...' she smiled over at Guy, 'Your granddad, did he have his own construction business?'

Guy nodded, 'He was a very successful, very reputable man over in Ireland. He never had to advertise, all his work came about by word of mouth. Back in the day, he gave me a Saturday job: I was his lackey, at his beck and call,' he smiled, 'the tea boy.'

'You have to start at the bottom,' Nell chipped in.

'That's exactly what he said! But I loved working alongside him and had visions of Cornish and Sons becoming a building phenomenon. I loved the dirt on my hands, the muck in my hair, working outside in the fresh air.'

'But you became a suit? Stiff collars and ties.'

'I did,' he rolled his eyes, 'but that's a story for another day.'

Nell didn't press him any further, but peered up at Guy through her fringe and grinned, 'So you like getting your hands dirty?'

'I do,' his eyes danced playfully. 'What is going on in that little mind of yours, Nell Andrews?' he gave her a lopsided grin that sent her heart into a spin.

'Maybe you could help me, guide me and point me in the right direction. If I decided to go ahead with the picture house?'

'I suppose I could be your right-hand man.'

'Would you? Are you absolutely sure?' she spluttered happily.

'One hundred per cent. I'm already quite excited about

The Cosy Canal Boat Dream

the project, but that auction needs to be won first. And you need to think seriously about your plans for the place.'

Nell didn't know exactly what that entailed but she liked the thought of Guy being her right-hand man, guiding her through the project. She liked the thought of spending more time with him, full stop.

'The more I think about it the more excited I am about the whole thing.'

'Have you any other plans for tonight? We could talk figures, come up with some ideas.' He gave her a cheeky smile.

Nell felt her cheeks flush a little as she held his gaze.

'My only plans tonight involved a bottle of wine and then I'd probably curl up with a book. I know ... I sound so old!'

'I can open a bottle. I owe you one of those,' he stood up waiting for Nell to answer, 'and maybe a take-away. I've not eaten yet.'

Nell nodded, 'That sounds perfect and an offer I can't refuse, but as long as you don't mind me gate-crashing your Friday night.'

They both stared at Sam, who was lying flat out on the sheepskin rug.

'Look at him, he's not going to be much company, you win hands down,' Guy softened his words, 'Even if you are bending my ear about properties.'

Nell felt her whole body prickle with goose bumps. She'd begun to feel alive again, something she hadn't felt for a long time. And thanks to Guy Cornish she couldn't think of a better place she'd rather be at this moment in time.

Chapter 8

Nell watched Guy disappear into the kitchen and glanced at her mobile phone screen, which lit up with Bea's name.

She swiped the screen to read a text, 'Fancy a girls' night at mine tomorrow. You know you want to!'

Nell smiled at Bea's playful goading. 'Absolutely! See you tomorrow,' she replied.

Nell heard two glasses clonk on the kitchen table and the fridge door open, then a couple of seconds later Guy appeared in the doorway holding the wine, 'Pinot?'

'My favourite, thank you.'

Guy gave Nell a soft smile as he poured them both a glass.

'I hope you don't mind but I've made myself comfortable near the fire.' Nell was sitting on the rug next to the wood-burner with her legs stretched out before her.

'I don't mind at all, curry or Chinese?' He asked handing the menus to Nell before poking the embers and adding more logs to the fire. He settled on the floor opposite Nell.

'Chinese – this is a lovely one and it delivers,' she thumbed the menu.

The Cosy Canal Boat Dream

Guy phoned the order through and they chatted about anything and everything while waiting for the food to arrive. It didn't take long to be delivered and Guy scooted to the door and returned clutching a bulging white carrier bag that smelt delicious.

'Well, this is the moment of truth,' Guy grinned, plating up the food.

'What do you mean?'

'Let's see if this is as good as the Chinese back home.'

He gave a low whistle, 'Actually, not bad,' he nodded with approval while taking another mouthful.

'I told you it was good!'

Just at that moment, a buzzing noise forced them both to glance towards the sideboard, where Guy's phone was vibrating. He placed his knife and fork on the plate and wandered across to answer it.

For a brief moment, he stared at the screen. Nell wasn't actually sure if he was going to answer the call, but after a couple more rings he cleared his throat and swiped the screen.

'Yes,' he said rather abruptly, which took Nell a little by surprise. She noticed he shifted uneasily from one foot to another before snorting quietly under his breath listening to the caller and looking agitated. Nell studied his profile. She couldn't deny, with his dark hair and hazel eyes he was looking very handsome standing there in his grey lounge pants and tight-fitting white t-shirt.

He caught Nell's eye, then looked away.

'I'm not getting into a conversation about this now, I have company.'

Nell had no idea who the other person was on the other end of the line but Guy couldn't seem to get rid of them fast enough.

'Enjoy your trip.' His voice was flat and he ended the call sharply, then crouched back down opposite Nell to finish his food.

'You okay? That sounded a little fraught.'

For the first time this evening Guy was silent. Nell continued to eat her food and waited for him to speak.

'Just work issues,' he mumbled.

Nell shot him a quizzical look. 'Any work issues in particular?'

'Nothing I want to worry you about.'

'Do you need to go back home?'

'Maybe,' he said.

Nell pressed her lips together and felt her insides suddenly tremble. She wasn't sure why, but she didn't like the thought of Guy returning to Ireland any time soon. She was already used to him hanging around Little Rock Marina; it felt as if he'd always been here, part of the furniture.

They both sat silently for a moment while they finished their food. Sam was still stretched out fast asleep.

'Do you like living in Ireland. It's a place I've never visited,' asked Nell bracingly. A surge of emotion ran through her body.

'That's where my home and job is.'

'You never answered the question,' she said tentatively, 'You seem to lose that spark in your eyes when you talk about work. Are you happy in your job?'

His shoulders slumped and he shrugged, 'It pays the bills.'

The Cosy Canal Boat Dream

'If you're not enjoying something, just change it.'

'Ever thought of becoming a counsellor, an agony aunt?' he said, laughing. 'If you're not enjoying something, just change it.' He mimicked Nell's words.

Gazing up at him, he was grinning at her, 'Are you making fun of me?' She swiped his leg playfully, 'I was only saying!'

'Sometimes you just get stuck in a rut.'

Nell scrunched her face up, 'I know that feeling. For the last couple of years, I've felt like I've been stuck in the same routine and existed on a day-to-day basis but I've finally come out the other side. Only you can change it.'

'I know, I know, maybe I've had no reason to change it before.'

Nell could feel his eyes clamped on her. She sipped her wine to hide her smile. Was he flirting with her? She was sure he was flirting with her. Nell was conscious of her heart pounding.

'What's stopping you from staying?'

'A home, a job.'

Nell could see Guy's point. 'If you're enjoying it here, surely Ed would have enough work for you at the boatyard and, look at this place, he's not going to kick you out of here in a hurry.'

'He's already agreed to rent this place out, in principle, to a young couple who are moving into the area.'

'Oh,' Nell replied.

'Anyway, let's change the subject. The last thing I want to be doing is talking about my boring job.'

'So what shall we talk about?'

'You know that boat? There's something strange about it,' said Guy, standing up and piling the plates on top of each other.

'Which boat?' Nell quizzed.

'The one that Sam was stuck on. What was it called again?'

Nell racked her brains for a second, 'Much Ado About Nothing,' she recalled.

'When I took Sam for a walk after work he was standing on the edge of the jetty and barking towards it.'

'He'd probably spotted a bird or something?'

'Maybe, but I had to yank him away.' Guy stood up, 'I'll clear these plates away.' He gathered them up and then hovered in the doorway, 'This is what I actually miss,' he said locking eyes with Nell.

Nell tilted her head, 'Miss?'

'Proper adult conversation,' he said, before turning around and disappearing towards the kitchen.

Nell acknowledged what he was saying. For the past couple of years, she'd missed her late-night chats with Ollie, grabbing a take-away whenever the mood suited and drinking a bottle of wine together.

'Sat here with you, it just feels natural. I feel relaxed for the first time in a long time,' Guy admitted, walking back into the room and settling back down. 'More wine?' he asked holding up the bottle.

'That'll be lovely.'

'If you want, why don't we book an appointment to view the Old Picture House? At least then I can have a look around and give you some idea of how much you may need to spend? I used to quote for the majority of Granddad's jobs.'

The Cosy Canal Boat Dream

'Would you do that for me?'

'Of course. Like I said, I'll be your right-hand man,' he smiled.

Nell felt a bubble of happiness rise inside.

'Let's book an appointment for next week.'

'Leave it with me,' Guy said, opening the door to the dresser and handing her a pile of DVDs. 'Fancy watching one of these?'

She glanced at the films, 'You like chic flicks?'

He laughed, 'I found them in here this morning but I'm prepared to give one a go if it means ...'

Nell met his gaze, 'If it means ...?'

'You'll stay a bit longer,' he said slowly.

Nell chewed on her lip for a second, '*Notting Hill* it is, then. Guy Cornish, prepare yourself. You're going to love this.'

'What have I let myself in for?' he grinned, inserting the DVD into the machine. When Guy turned round Nell had plumped up the cushions and made herself comfy on the rug. He settled next to her. Gently his fingers reached for hers. Her eyes sparkled as he wrapped his arm around her shoulder and she nestled into his chest.

'You okay?' he said softly.

'More than okay,' she replied contently, feeling happiness for the first time in a long time.

Chapter 9

Bea scraped her hair back into an untidy ponytail and bent her head over the toilet. She'd lost count of how many times she'd thrown up in the last couple of hours alone.

Last night she'd spent the evening curled up on the settee with a bowl balanced on her lap. She'd felt sorry for Nathan, who'd pulled out all the stops and taken care of dinner.

But as soon as Nathan had placed the food on the table her senses had gone into overdrive and her body had surged with instant nausea. She'd pushed her chair back and raced to the bathroom, leaving a bewildered Nathan sitting at the dinner table all by himself.

It was six o'clock in the morning when Nathan knocked on the bathroom door. 'Have you been in here all night? I've just woken up and you were gone,' he asked, poking his head around the bathroom door.

'I hope I didn't keep you awake last night.'

'Slept like a log, but I'm assuming that's not what you want to hear,' he smiled warmly towards his wife.

'Yes, I've been here all night.' She answered, barely able to

The Cosy Canal Boat Dream

keep her eyes open. Bea's face was ghastly white; she was on the verge of tears and already at her wits' end.

'I'm not sure how much more I can take of this. I think I'm here for the foreseeable,' she whimpered wearily. 'I'm already fed up of this pregnancy lark.' She wiped her mouth with a tissue then heaved a sigh.

'Can I get you anything? A cup of tea, maybe?'

Bea shook her head. She'd gone right off tea and couldn't stomach the thought of it.

'Have we got any ginger biscuits? I need to try and nibble at something and maybe some iced water.'

'I'll have a look,' he answered, disappearing on to the landing.

'Nathan,' she shouted, who promptly appeared again, 'The deli ... I'm not sure I can manage it today, or maybe I could mid-afternoon if this sickness subsides a little. Could you possibly go and begin the baking?'

Nathan raised his eyes, 'Me in a kitchen? I'm not really into baking, Bea.'

'Time of need, Nathan. Nancy and Isabel work on a Saturday, they'll cover the tables and take the orders. Don't worry, it won't be that hard. Text Nell. I bet she's up. She'll give you a hand or go and knock on the "Nollie's" door.' His face look terrified, 'I'm fed up of this pregnancy lark too.'

Of course, Nathan was only joking but as tiredness washed through Bea's body she'd lost her sense of humour.

'You try sitting here.'

'I was joking,' he hurried over and kissed the top of her

head. 'Will you be alright if I leave Jacob here or shall I get him up and take him with me?'

'He's sleeping, leave him here. I'll try and get a little sleep too. If things get too much I can always give Gilly a call,' she said, vomiting once more as Nathen screwed up his face 'Eww, I'm out of here.'

Thirty minutes later, Nathan had left for the deli with a whole bunch of keys, instructions and a promise from Nell that she would be there the minute she spotted him walking up the towpath. Bea was grateful to them both. This morning she didn't even feel as if she could manage to get changed or even brush her hair. It had crossed Bea's mind that she might need to lean on Nell more and more if the nausea didn't settle down soon, but with Nell's new project on the horizon she didn't want to become a burden.

She peered around Jacob's door and smiled. He was tucked up and still sound asleep. He looked so peaceful lying there. She couldn't believe she would soon be going through all those sleepless nights again and then there was the dreaded potty-training – that was something she didn't relish, but looking at Jacob she knew it was worth it.

Bea walked downstairs and shivered. Usually first thing in the morning Nathan would light the log burner but with a change to his routine it was stone cold in the living room. She grabbed a throw from the settee and clutched it tightly around her shoulders. She stood and stared around the living room. They'd bought Driftwood Cottage before Bea had fallen pregnant with Jacob and she was excited to bring another little person into it very soon. She wandered into

The Cosy Canal Boat Dream

the kitchen, being careful not to step on the numerous trucks and fire engines that Jacob had been playing with yesterday. After kicking a piece of Lego to the side of the room she tossed a teddy bear on to the settee and opened the kitchen door.

Nathan may have prepared dinner last night but the dirty plates, glasses and mugs caught her eye, all still piled up by the Belfast sink. He hadn't even loaded the dishwasher. Bea sighed. She didn't have the energy or inclination to deal with it now. She risked a tentative look in the mirror at the bottom of the stairs, her face was pale and her eyes were tired. She wished she'd hadn't even bothered to look as she trudged back up the stairs to the safe haven of her bedroom.

The next thing Bea knew she was being shaken. She opened her eyes to see a smiley Jacob peering at her. 'Mummy I'm ready for my breakfast.'

'Good morning, my little man, do you want to climb inside for a cuddle first?' She threw back the duvet as a blast of cold air brushed against her body. Jacob snuggled up against Bea and she squeezed him tight.

'Where's Daddy?' he asked.

'He's gone to work at the deli for me today.'

'Why?'

Bea smiled down at Jacob, 'Because Mummy has been feeling a little unwell.'

'Was it Daddy's cooking?'

Bea chuckled.

'I prefer it when you make my tea. Daddy doesn't get it right sometimes.'

'Let's hope Aunty Nellie does all the baking in the deli today, then!'

'Have you got that bug that Ellie Hale has got from school? She was sick all over the beanbags. Eww,' Jacob held his nose.

'You are funny,' Bea answered, tickling his tummy. 'Not quite, but Mummy may be feeling poorly for a little while longer yet.'

'Why?'

'Because Mummy has got a baby in her tummy,' she said softly, waiting for the news to register on Jacob's face.

He looked directly at Bea's tummy then cupped his hands around his mouth and shouted, 'Hello in there.'

Bea giggled.

'Do you think he can hear me?'

Bea gave a theatrical nod, 'Absolutely, but of course it could be a girl.'

For a second Jacob looked horrified, 'A girl?' he said slowly.

Bea pushed his hair back out of his eyes and smiled.

'Can we send it back if it's a girl? They will want to play with dolls not fire engines,' Jacob said, with a very serious look on his face.

'I'm not sure that would be possible!' she grinned.

Jacob shrugged, 'How long do they have to stay in your tummy for?'

'They have to stay warm in here,' she patted her tummy, 'for nine months.'

'Is it like one of your ovens at work?'

'A little. When they are fully cooked they will come out and join our family. What do you think?'

The Cosy Canal Boat Dream

'I think it will be okay if they don't pinch my toys, and Mummy?'

'Yes.'

'Can I have my breakfast now? I'm starving.'

She grinned at him, 'You can, come on.' She replied, throwing back the covers and grabbing her dressing gown. On the whole Bea thought that conversation had gone very well.

Chapter 10

It was six o'clock when Bea heard the key in the door and the excited chatter spilling into the hallway.

Jacob swung his head round, 'Aunty Nellie, what are you doing here?' he squealed, launching himself straight into her arms.

'Wow, you are getting heavy,' she smiled, planting a kiss on the top of his head.

'No wellies today?'

'I'm inside Aunty Nellie, you're silly!'

She steadied him back on the carpet and rattled a white paper bag.

His eyes grew wide like flying saucers.

'Doughnuts!'

'Not before tea,' Bea shot a warning glance towards them both.

'Not before tea,' Nell repeated, giving the bag to Jacob, 'Go and put them in the kitchen.'

He saluted, grabbed the bag and ran off, pretending to be an aeroplane, towards the kitchen.

'I wish I had his energy,' Nell said, kicking off her shoes and sinking into the chair next to Bea.

The Cosy Canal Boat Dream

'Busy day?'

'You could say that!'

Nathan hung up his coat then popped a swift kiss on to his wife's cheek, 'How're you feeling?' he asked, inhaling the faint smell of sickness.

'Exhausted and queasy but I've managed to clear up all the pots in the kitchen.'

Nathan looked sheepish, 'Sorry, I fell asleep last night watching the TV and was going to clean up this morning but then ...'

'It's fine,' Bea interrupted, grateful that the pair of them had worked in the deli all day. 'Put the kettle on and make Nell a drink. Did you both cope today?'

Nell nodded, 'Nancy and Isabel organised Nathan while I baked and we even roped Mum in for a couple of hours. She was riding past on her bike and stopped when she saw the queue filtering out of the door. Before we knew it, she was behind the counter with your pinny on and had a whale of a time!'

Nathan walked back into the room, 'She was worth her weight in gold today, and you too, Nell,' he said, handing her a glass of wine, 'Thought you might be in need of this more than a cuppa,' he smiled, snapping open the ring pull on the can of beer before placing it on the coffee table.

Nell's eyes lit up, 'You know me so well.'

'Can I get you anything?' he twisted his head towards Bea.

'Just a glass of water would be good.'

He nodded before disappearing once more towards the kitchen, 'What's for tea?' he shouted.

The thought of food made Bea's stomach turn, 'I haven't started tea. Every time I stand up I feel dizzy,' she looked at him warily as he came back in the room and handed her a glass of water.

'I'm not sure I can even face any food,' she sighed.

'You have to try and keep your strength up,' Nell said, sipping her wine while balancing Jacob on one knee.

'Mummy's cooking a baby in her tummy,' Jacob suddenly announced, jumping from Nell's knee and kneeling on the floor to drive his cars around the play mat.

'How did he take it?' Nell mouthed to Bea.

'All good.'

'Will you still have lots of kisses for me, Aunty Nellie, when the baby comes?' Jacob cocked his head to one side.

'You'd better believe it!'

He gave her a cheeky smile and carried on playing with his cars.

'So I'm assuming you aren't up for a girly night tonight?' Nell asked Bea.

'I'm not much use to anyone,' she smiled, 'But you are more than welcome to veg out on the sofa with me and watch a film.'

'And read me a story at bedtime,' Jacob piped up.

'Deal!' Nell winked at him, 'If that's okay with you, Nathan?'

'Of course. Shall I nip out and grab a couple of pizzas? To be honest, after slaving over the ovens all day I don't feel much like cooking either.'

'Welcome to my world!' Bea grinned.

'Sounds like a perfect plan,' Nell answered, 'The diet starts on Monday.'

The Cosy Canal Boat Dream

'Again!' Both Nell and Bea bellowed at the same time.

Nathan stood up and grabbed his coat from the hallway. He fished around in his pocket and pulled out his wallet.

'Any toppings in particular?'

'Surprise us,' Bea answered, knowing full well she would barely be able to manage a slice.

'Oh, I nearly forgot,' Nathan said, pulling out a crumpled letter from his pocket and handing it to Bea.

'What's this?' she asked, flicking the envelope over.

'No idea, but it had to be signed for.'

She lowered her gaze to the envelope and tore it open. Her eyes scanned the words on the embellished cream paper, then she gasped. Both Nathen and Nell saw a wide beam spread across her face and her eyes danced with excitement.

'Come on, don't leave us in suspense,' Nathan hovered.

'I think we need a drum roll,' she paused, 'The Melting Pot, my little melting pot, has only been nominated for Delicatessen of the Year!' she shrieked.

'No way! That's bloody brilliant!' Nathan walked across the room and planted a huge kiss on Bea's lips. I'm so proud of you.'

'Fantastic news! It couldn't happen to a more deserved person, even though I may be a teeny bit biased!' Nell grinned, pinching her thumb and forefinger together.

'We need to celebrate when I get back!' Nathan said.

'Typical! The strongest drink I can have is blackcurrant squash.'

'Don't worry, we'll make up for it,' Nell winked at Nathan and Bea rolled her eyes.

As Nathan disappeared out of the door, Bea came over all emotional, 'Nell, I'm beginning to get a little worried.'

'About the competition?' Nell looked at Bea.

'That and how awful I'm feeling at the minute with the sickness and then when the baby comes along. How am I going to manage?'

'You are a wonderful mother!' exclaimed Nell.

'But how am I going to manage with the deli?'

'You may need to advertise for help.'

'What about you? Would you think of taking it over for me while I'm on maternity?'

Nell paused. She'd been thinking about this in the last couple of days. As much as she would help her friend as much as she could, her head was filled with her own dreams of the picture house and she didn't know how much time she would have to spare.

'Let's not worry about that now – one day at a time,' said Nell.

But Bea was worried. She always thought that Nell would run the deli when she wasn't there, but now things had changed and she had no idea what to do.

Chapter 11

It was Sunday morning and Nell had been up since the crack of dawn scrutinising her bank accounts, savings and generally looking over her outgoings, which were next to nothing these days.

The sale of the picture house had got her excited about life again. There was nothing stopping her from making an offer on the place; the funds were accessible, with the added bonus of her own savings – all she had to do was win that auction. Nell knew she'd been sitting on Ollie's insurance for a while, waiting for something meaningful to come along, and in her heart she knew this was it. If she managed to pull this off, it was an opportunity to make something of her life as well as honouring Ollie's memory.

Forty minutes later, with her bag swung over her shoulder, she'd decided to go for a walk and call in on her mum for a cup of tea. She was surprised to see Guy already pottering about in the boat shed, especially this early on a Sunday. The huge doors were pulled back and he was happily blacking the hull of one of the narrowboats, which had come in for painting. She could hear him whistling along to the radio and Sam was quite happily sniffing around the boatyard. Guy stood back to admire his work and wiped his brow. He must have sensed that someone was watching him because suddenly he swung round and locked eyes with Nell. He smiled, wiped his hands on a rag and strolled over towards her.

'Good morning, you're looking lovely,'

'You sound genuinely surprised,' she teased.

'Ha, you always look lovely. Are you off anywhere nice this bright and early?'

It was the first time Nell had bothered to put on a full face of make-up for as long as she could remember. She'd decided it was time to make the effort with herself and she'd definitely felt a spring in her step since Guy had come on to the scene.

'Why, thank you,' she answered, stuffing her hands deep in her pocket, 'Just off to Mum's. I've been going through all my finances, looking at every scenario and generally squealing with excitement into my morning cuppa. Just look at that place,' she swung her head towards the picture house. 'I'm going to do everything in my power to win that auction and re-open that place. Eek!' Aware that she was babbling, she smiled and snapped her mouth shut, 'Look at me going on and on.'

Guy looked mildly amused.

'Fire in your belly, that's what that is!' he grinned.

'Forgive me, I've not even asked, how's Ed?'

'Home, driving me insane. This morning, would you believe, he wanted to come into the yard and sit in the office, for

The Cosy Canal Boat Dream

company, he said, but I know he just wanted to keep a close eye on me and his yard.'

'And you told him …'

'No! He needs to take it easy. That's what I'm here for, to take away the stress until he fully recuperates. I have to say, though, I'm quite enjoying it. It's very therapeutic painting boats and generally getting my hands dirty.'

'Once Little Rock is under your skin, it's definitely hard to shake it off.'

They both stared out across the marina.

'I can't imagine living anywhere else, I mean, look at that view, it's like something out of a romance novel, tranquil, peaceful, great ambience, shops and, not forgetting, great people. I've always loved it here.'

'It rather does, doesn't it?' Guy agreed with a smile.

'It rather does what?' Nell asked in wonderment, losing the thread of the conversation.

'Have great people.' Guy's eyes locked with hers and Nell felt the beam creep over her face. 'Don't you forget that, Mr Cornish.'

'I've no intention of forgetting that,' he said with a twinkle in his eye.

At that particular moment, Nell leant forward, her eyes briefly lowered to his lips but she swiftly kissed him on his cheek, leaving Guy taken by surprise. His skin had felt soft and she smiled to herself. Her heart was fluttering as she turned and strolled up the wharf.

Nell could feel Guy watching her as she walked away and she smiled at him over her shoulder. Once she was out of sight her nerves sprang back into action as she carried on walking towards Bluebell Cottage. Her mind flitted back to her mother's reaction regarding the picture house, which the more she thought about it, the odder it seemed. Her mum had always supported her in everything she did, so why was this time different? It was almost as if her mum had got something against the renovation of the Old Picture House? Maybe it was just concern about taking on such a big project so soon after Ollie's death. But, after the unbearable sense of loss in her life, Nell felt that this was the way forward, a project she could really get her teeth into. The excitement made her body surge just thinking about. She just hoped her mum would get behind her once she realised how serious she was and then Nell would know that this was the right thing to do.

Chapter 12

Guy stood with a goofy grin on his face and watched Nell walk up the wharf and disappear out of sight before he turned back towards the boat shed. Her words were ringing in his ears, 'Once Little Rock gets under your skin.'

Since the night Nell had shared the Chinese with him, he'd found himself thinking about her more and more and he couldn't deny she was on his mind the second he woke up, and the moment he fell asleep.

In the past week alone Guy had felt happier than he'd been in a long while. Perhaps the change of scenery was doing him good. He made himself a brew, cupped his hands around the mug and stared out over the peaceful marina. Sam came and sat by his side, thumping his tail on the ground. 'What are we going to do, Sam? I think I'm falling in love with this place. I mean how can anyone not? Everything is just more laid back and there's no shirt and tie throttling my neck every day. What exactly have we got waiting back for us in Ireland?'

Sam cocked his head to one side and Guy laughed, 'Jeez, dog, it looked like you were actually listening to me there for a minute.'

Christie Barlow

Sam gave a woof and stayed by Guy's side.

'Right then, Sam, we've a couple of options,' Guy continued to speak, 'We could find a job and a house to rent here and hopefully live with Ed in the meantime or we could go back to Ireland for a life of misery in the financial world. What do you reckon?' he laughed to himself.

Sam began to whimper, 'I take it you're not keen on going back either? I'm not sure if I want to go back to that situation we left behind.' Sam woofed again.

Guy turned to him and raised his eyebrows, 'You neither? Are you actually answering me?' He ruffled the top of his head. 'I think I know why Ed loves this place so much. It certainly does have a good feel.'

Guy turned his thoughts to Nell. Even though he knew he'd only known her for a short space of time, he didn't like the thought of returning to his old life, one he wanted to escape from so much, leaving her behind. He found himself thinking of Nell more and more. She was so different to anyone he knew and he felt a sense of belonging and calmness when he was around her, something that had been missing from his life for a long time.

Guy glanced towards the moored narrowboats. They were pretty, with their brightly coloured flowerpots and bicycles strapped to their roofs.

'Back to work,' he said, fishing in his pocket and throwing Sam a treat. He placed the mug down on the bench and began to black the hull once more. 'Yep, that's looking good,' he said, talking to himself again. Then his face softened into a smile

The Cosy Canal Boat Dream

as he jigged away to his favourite tune on the radio.

As he began to paint the boat he began to think about Nell's idea, the restoration of the Old Picture House. He was more than happy to view the property with her – in fact he was delighted to.

If they made an appointment to view the inside of the dilapidated building he could certainly gauge how much money she'd have to set aside for the project. He took a moment and gazed towards the old building. It was definitely in a prime position, such a beautiful spot, and he could actually imagine it being restored to all its glory, even though he was sure Nell would be up against some stiff competition. He stared at the for-sale board and took out his mobile phone, punching in the number for the estate agents.

He waited patiently for them to answer, 'John German Estate Agents, Jennifer speaking, how can I help you?'

'I'm enquiring about the Old Picture House that's up for auction at Little Rock Marina, is there any possibility I could arrange an appointment to view inside ahead of the auction?'

'Certainly, sir. When would be best for you?'

He took the bull by the horns and provisionally booked an appointment for tomorrow lunchtime.

He hung up the call and surfed the estate agent's website from his phone for the property details and pressed print. The printer began to whirl and spat out the details of the property in the office. He'd have a good read over them later on tonight. After sliding his phone back in his pocket he looked around for Sam.

'Here boy, come here,' he patted his thigh a couple of times,

'Don't you be wandering off on me.' Guy looked around the boatyard but he couldn't spot him anywhere. Panic began to rise inside as he hurried to the office to see whether he'd curled up on the old battered armchair in the corner of the room, but still there was no Sam.

'Sam, where are you Sam?' Guy bellowed and walked to the front of the yard and stood by the huge wooden doors. 'You couldn't have gone far, you were only here a second a go,' he muttered to himself. He swung his head up and down the marina, but there was no sign of him anywhere. Guy noticed a shop assistant propping up a blackboard outside the boutique.

'Excuse me,' Guy shouted across the path towards her.

The woman looked up and smiled. 'You haven't by any chance seen a red setter? He's about this big ... and red,' he gestured with his hands, 'He was here a moment ago and now he's completely disappeared.'

She shook her head, 'I'm sorry, I haven't.'

'Thanks anyway.'

Guy walked over to the railings and anxiously glanced towards the jetty. He peered towards the water and his heart sank. 'Sam,' Guy shouted with all his might. There was Sam struggling to swim in the freezing-cold water. Guy knew the recent icy weather would make the water even more dangerous.

Guy had no idea what to do. He couldn't see any movement on the narrowboats moored nearby. People were probably enjoying a lazy Sunday morning lie-in. He looked up and down the wharf, praying that Nell would miraculously appear on her way back, but she'd only been gone five minutes and

The Cosy Canal Boat Dream

of course wasn't in sight. His whole body was trembling as he watched Sam struggling to swim near the same narrowboat that they'd rescued him from last time.

Before Guy knew what he was doing, instinct took over and he powered his legs towards the 'Nollie'. He jumped off the jetty on to the deck of the boat and flung open the lid to the box of life jackets. As he slipped his arms into the jacket and pulled the toggles tighter, he felt physically sick and heaved.

'Deep breaths, deep breaths, you can do this, it's only water,' he muttered to himself but wasn't convinced as his head pounded with absolute fear.

After ducking under the railings he hovered in front of the same little rowing boat that Nell had borrowed last time. He flicked a glance over towards Sam, who was scrambling up a small ramp on the water's edge. His back legs slipped and he fell into the cold water once more. Guy winced. With one more attempt he saw Sam clamber again and this time he made it on to the bank and immediately scrambled on to the deck of the same boat as last time, then collapsed. At least if nothing else, he was safe for the time being.

Guy exhaled and rubbed his hands in his face, 'Hang on in there, boy. I'm coming to get you.'

His fingers fumbled trying to untie the rowing boat. Finally the rope loosened and he grasped the side of the boat and pulled it towards him.

Stay calm, stay calm.

The little rowing boat bobbed on top of the water and Guy steadied himself as much as he could. He perched on the end

Christie Barlow

of the wooden slacks and rubbed his sweaty hands on his knees. His heart was hammering against his chest as he pushed the oars through the rowlocks, placed the blades in the water and pulled. At first, he found it difficult to manoeuvre the boat. Nell had made it look so easy, but he soon got into a rhythm and the little boat began to glide through the water, thankfully in the right direction.

He anxiously stared across towards Sam, who was now standing on all fours barking at the closed door of the narrowboat. Guy gritted his teeth and pushed the oars harder through the water. In no time at all Guy was at the side of the boat and Sam had mustered up some energy and was scratching furiously at the door.

'Sam, here boy.'

Sam cocked a look towards his master but he didn't stop. Guy remembered to tie the boat to the wrought-iron ring, just like Nell had done before so it didn't float away, before jumping on to the deck.

He heaved a huge sigh of relief before crouching down and pulling Sam towards him by his collar.

Sam was shivering but his eyes were bright, 'Let me look at you – what are you doing? We've got to get you back now,' he said, relieved that Sam didn't seem too traumatised by the freezing waters.

Despite Nell's previous assurances that the little boat was safe the very thought of climbing back into the rowing boat sent shivers down Guy's spine, especially without Nell to help steady Sam. He didn't quite know how he was going to manage it. But as soon as Guy let go of Sam's collar he ran straight

The Cosy Canal Boat Dream

back towards the door, his nose to the ground, sniffing a scent on the deck. He began to dig at the door once more.

'What is it, boy?' Guy cupped his hands around his eyes and peered through the glass of the door. He was mystified, 'There's no one home, Sam. What the heavens has got into you?'

Sam sat down and his front paws danced while he continued to bark. Guy tried to calm him down and with one last glance through the door something caught his eye. He gasped. There, lying on the floor of the canal boat, was a body. He knew the body hadn't been there a couple of days ago but didn't have a clue how long it had been there. His stomach performed a double somersault as Guy immediately yanked down the handle of the door to try and get inside, but it was locked. He took a deep breath, stepped back and tried to barge his whole body weight against it, but the door wouldn't budge. Quickly, he peered around the boat. Apart from the brightly coloured flowerpots and logs tied up on the roof, he spotted two very large painted rocks on the deck. He picked one up and smashed it through the glass pane of the door and then carefully bashed the splintered shards away. After reaching inside he felt for the key and promptly twisted it.

In a matter of seconds Guy was by the man's side. He grabbed his wrist and felt for a pulse, 'Yes thankfully,' he whispered to himself. It was weak but it was there.

'I'll get help.'

He reached for his mobile and rang for an ambulance, explaining he was on a narrowboat at the Little Rock Marina. He couldn't even give any details about the man lying there except that he looked approximately in his mid-sixties. He didn't even know his name. Guy placed a cushion under the man's head and quickly grabbed a blanket from the sofa.

Suddenly, he heard the man gasp for breath, 'Stay with me, please stay.' Guy murmured, 'Help is on its way.'

Sam began to bark again and Guy prayed it was the paramedics. He quickly stood out on the deck and looked towards the jetty and couldn't believe his eyes, there was Nell bobbing in a canoe at the foot of the narrowboat.

Guy heaved a huge sigh of relief, 'Am I glad to see you. I thought you were at your mum's.'

Nell looked confused, 'She wasn't in. What the heck is going on? I spotted the rowing boat tied up over here and heard Sam barking on the deck,' she said, grasping Guy's hand as he hauled her onto the narrowboat.

'It's a long story,'

'You're shaking,' Nell said.

'I'm not surprised, probably shock, fear and I'm just waiting for an ambulance but have no idea how that's going to work.

'Ambulance?' she asked, bewildered.

'There's a man collapsed on the floor inside.'

She glanced earnestly into the boat. 'Oh no, is he okay?'

'He's barely got a pulse but he's still with us.'

Nell quickly rushed to the man's side and held his hand. 'How on earth did you find him?'

He nodded towards Sam, 'Well that's all down to this clever boy, except I didn't think he was clever at the time, launching himself back into the icy cold water. He disappeared and I spotted him swimming across to this boat again.'

The Cosy Canal Boat Dream

'He must have sensed there was something wrong. How long do you think he's been here like this? Fingers crossed help arrives soon.' Nell swung her head around the boat, 'Wow, look at this place, it's like a shrine to the West End.'

The walls were littered with posters and memorabilia of stage and theatre productions.

'Obviously a fan of the theatre,' mused Guy, taking in his surroundings. 'There are plays on these posters that go back years.'

In no time at all, two paramedics appeared in the doorway and Nell moved out of the way. Guy provided as much detail as he could, then moved aside to the deck of the boat.

'Good boy,' Nell praised Sam, 'And you ...' she turned back towards Guy, 'You did amazingly well to row across here all by yourself.'

Guy nodded and smiled, 'I think I've surprised myself but am now in need of a stiff drink.'

'Firstly, I think you are in need of a hug.'

Nell took him in her arms. She could feel him trembling as she kissed him lightly on the cheek.

'I'm proud of you,' she whispered softly.

'Thank you, replied Guy rather coyly, 'But it's this boy that's the hero.'

'You are both heroes in my eyes,' said Nell, leaning forward and brushing her lips against his for a split second. 'Come on, let's get you back to the Nollie.'

Chapter 13

'This feels like déjà vu,' Nell chuckled, handing Guy a mug of sweet tea and nodding towards Sam, who had been hosed down yet again and was fast asleep on the 'Nollie' floor in front of the fire.

'I'd always imagined the inside of narrowboats to be full of plates hanging from the walls and those brass ornament thingies, but you've got this place looking very cosy with your duck egg blue interior, rosebud cushions and floral bunting draped everywhere. It's so very ...'

'Cath Kidston.'

'I was going to say homely!'

Nell smiled, 'I love it. Ollie was never that keen on all the flowery stuff but it was his idea to live on a boat so I got to choose and make most of the soft furnishings myself.'

'So why a boat?' Guy asked, sipping his tea.

'Because if you don't like your neighbours you can just go out and get yourself some new ones!'

They both laughed.

'Very true,' he grinned. 'Do you ever take the "Nollie" out?'

'Not since Ollie passed away. We used to spend weekends

The Cosy Canal Boat Dream

in the summer taking the boat further up the canal to the next pub, but when the weather gets a little warmer, it would be great to take the boat out once more.' Nell slid on the seat next to him and offered him a biscuit, 'How are you feeling now?' 'I just keep thinking how surreal it all was. What he did today is like something you read in a newspaper. How did Sam even know that man was in trouble?'

They both gazed towards him, 'Animal instinct,' said Nell. 'I read an article once about a dog that all of a sudden began to snuggle up to its owner's chest and whimper. She started to feel unwell and was later diagnosed with breast cancer.'

Guy raised his eyebrows, 'That wouldn't surprise me. I have to say that dog there,' he nodded towards Sam, 'Is definitely a keeper.'

'I think so too.' Nell said, softly locking eyes with Guy for a moment longer than necessary. The moment sent a thrill through her body.

'There's never a dull moment around this place is there?' Guy smiled.

'The paramedic said if it wasn't for Sam that man would have surely died.'

'It's unbelievable, isn't it?'

'All signs pointed to some sort of seizure. I suppose we'll never know. It doesn't bear thinking about, lying there thinking you are going to die and not being able to shout for help.'

'I did do something else today besides rescuing dogs ... again,' he laughed, 'Oh and saving an old man's life.'

'Which is?'

'I booked us an appointment to view the Old Picture House.'

'Us?' she smiled.

'Us,' he said. 'I did say I'd come with you.'

With a huge beam on her face she clapped her hands together then squeezed his arm.

'Don't get too excited. I may burst your bubble when I do a calculation of how much it could all possibly cost.'

'I'll cross that bridge when I get there. It'll be just good to have some idea. When's the viewing?'

'Tomorrow lunchtime, but I can change it if it's not convenient for you, with work and everything.'

'Bea won't mind. We shouldn't be too long, but I could get my mum to cover me.'

'How does Bea feel about your idea?'

'You mean the Picture House?'

He nodded.

'She's a little worried about the deli at the moment because of the pregnancy and the general day-to-day running of the place when she goes off on maternity leave, but I know she'll support me every step of the way, unlike others who seemed very ...'

'You mean your mum.'

'Yep. The more I think about it, the stranger it seems. It was like she didn't want to hear another word about it. That's why this morning I went over to talk to her, but she wasn't home.'

'She'll come round, even I can see how passionate you are about it.'

'Maybe she thinks I'm going to physically do the work myself, rebuild it and plaster it.'

The Cosy Canal Boat Dream

'You might have to if you run out of funds! I've seen that happen many a time.'

'Ha, very funny, but I'm determined that she doesn't put a dampener on it.'

'I think you'd look very attractive dressed in dungarees, hard hat on, ordering everyone about. You'd make a good gaffer!' Guy grinned, lightening the mood.

'You do now, do you? Let's just see if I win the auction first and then we can all take it from there.'

'All?'

'Yes all, you, Guy Cornish, are now my right-hand man. Don't think you are going anywhere!' she wagged her finger at him in jest.

He snaked his arm around Nell's shoulder and gave her a quick squeeze. Little Rock Marina was getting more appealing every day.

'Let's get that auction won,' he grinned.

Chapter 14

On Monday morning Bea marched over to the ovens muttering to herself and Nell glanced over in her friend's direction. She stood and watched as Bea flung open the door, slid in the baking tray and slammed the door shut.

Bea caught the look of amusement on Nell's face and huffed. She threw her hands up in the air, 'Okay, so I'm in a bad mood.'

'No shit, Sherlock, what's eating you?' For as long as Nell could remember she'd never witnessed Bea in a bad mood.

'No sleep again and then I discovered the dishwasher hadn't been unloaded, a pile of shirts was slung on the utility room floor, the toilet seat left up and the lid left off the toothpaste, so it's gone crusty. Urghh.'

'No sleep due to the sickness?' Nell probed.

Bea shook her head, 'No sleep due to his snoring. At three o'clock, I'd had enough and decided to curl up downstairs on the settee and I could still hear him rattling the roof.'

'Oh dear.'

'I could honestly see myself up on a murder charge and what's with leaving his shirts on the floor of the utility room by the washing machine? Why not open the door, put them in and switch it on? It's not rocket science. I just can't do everything all the time, especially feeling this nauseous.'

'Have you told Nathan?'

'I think it's safe to say he got it well and truly in the neck just before he took Jacob to school.'

'Hopefully, he'll get the message then, but in the meantime don't get worked up. It's not going to help your blood pressure. We need everything to be calm.'

Bea nodded, 'I know, and the pressure is on for the next week or so too.'

'What do you mean?' Nell asked, running the hot water and piling the dirty cups and saucers in the sink because the dishwasher was full.

'Delicatessen of the year competition. It's not as though we'd probably spot the judge either. It could be anyone and they won't be making themselves known.'

'So the judge will be posing as a normal customer and marking us for our presentation, customer service and baking?' Nell said, plunging her hands in the sink and washing up the dishes before hanging the sodden tea towel over the rail of the stainless steel oven. 'So we just need to ensure we are brilliant in every area!'

'Yes,' Bea answered, painting a smile on her face, 'We can do this.'

'We can indeed. For the next week or so we will smile wider than ever before and be extra polite to everyone who walks through that door, even if they are demanding or impolite.'

'Do you think I should become a little more adventurous with the take-away menu?'

Nell shook her head, 'Why fix something that isn't broken? We have a tempting selection of cakes, savouries and bakes. We offer, salads, soup, jacket potatoes, sandwiches, baguettes and deli bowls and not forgetting hot chocolate to die for and homemade lemonade. Need I go on?' she laughed, taking a breath.

'I think you've just about covered everything,' laughed Bea.

'And not forgetting a warm, friendly service every time. Just do what you normally do and you will shine brightly.'

'Yes, you're right, I was panicking there a little. Who do you think nominated me? Was it you?' she narrowed her eyes at Nell while icing the tray of cupcakes in front of her.

'I didn't, but if I'd have known about it I would have one hundred per cent. Maybe it's a happy customer who thought you deserved a little recognition for all your hard work?' Nell smiled warmly at her friend. 'You'll always get my vote.'

'And that's why you are my best friend, no matter how low and tired I feel, you always say the right things.'

'Ditto.'

Bea and Nell smoothed down their pinnies as they heard the bell tinkle over the shop door. 'Right let's get this show on the road,' Nell said, her face breaking into a huge smile while she high-fived Bea. 'Let's win this competition.'

'Absolutely. Oh and Nell, I'm sorry if I was in a bad mood just now.'

'Nothing to forgive,' said Nell, noticing that her friend was

The Cosy Canal Boat Dream

looking tired. Maybe she could offer to do some of the early mornings in the meantime, to lighten Bea's load, Nell thought to herself. It wasn't as though she'd even won the Old Picture House yet.

Chapter 15

It was one o'clock when Nell glanced up at the clock. Her stomach flipped when she saw Guy locking up the boat shed and ambling over towards the deli with Sam by his side. It was nearly time to view the Old Picture House and she felt a sudden surge of excitement rise inside her, knowing, in a few minutes time, she would be back inside the building once more.

Bea had been glazing the pastries before she wandered back behind the counter, 'You're smiling,' she teased, noticing Nell watching Guy's every move. 'There seems to be a little spark of excitement in the air.'

'Guy's on his way over.'

'So I can see and you seem to have gone all doe-eyed.'

'I have not,' Nell protested.

'Are you sure about that? You two seem to be spending a lot of time together – Chinese take-aways and bottles of wine.'

'One Chinese take-away and maybe three bottles of wine,' Nell quickly counted in her head. 'We were talking shop and then yesterday there was the dramatic rescue too,' Nell stated.

'Very convenient,' Bea joked, piling up a batch of freshly

baked sausage rolls on the tray inside the counter. 'But I don't blame you, you know. If I were single and not pregnant,' she patted her stomach, 'Cover your ears little baby – then I'd be having a little flirt myself.'

'You wouldn't?' Nell asked suddenly, feeling a little put out, which was silly because she knew Bea was only joking.

'I would.'

'Sshh, he's going to hear you,' Nell shushed her friend as the door of the deli burst open and Guy smiled at them both.

'You two look like you're up to mischief.'

'Who? Us?' Bea grinned, placing her hand on her chest in mock outrage. 'The most mischief I've been up to this morning is pinching a cupcake. What about you Nell?'

'Me? My halo always shines.'

'Mmm, why am I not convinced?' Guy teased, 'Are you ready?'

Nell looked across at Bea. 'Are you going to be alright on your own for ten minutes or so?'

'Yes, you two go. For some reason it's very quiet today and I want to hear all about it when you get back.'

Feeling nervous and excited Nell grabbed her coat and was soon walking towards the old cinema building with Guy and Sam at her side.

'Oh no,' Nell muttered under her breath.

'What's up with you? Second thoughts?' asked Guy, stopping in his tracks.

Nell nodded towards the towpath.

'Hi, Mum,' chirped Nell, as Gilly pulled on the brakes and halted the bike right in front of them.

'I'm coming to check you are okay.' Her voice sounded worried.

'Me, yes, why wouldn't I be?'

'Because I've just been to the butcher's and Alan tells me you've been involved in some dramatic rescue.'

'The joys of living in a small village. Rumours circulate quickly. Have you met Guy? This is Ed's brother.'

'Pleased to meet you,' they both said in unison.

'It was actually Guy who rescued the old man. It was that boat there – "Much Ado about Nothing".' Nell gesticulated with her arm in the right direction, 'Very apt name – you should have seen inside the boat.'

'Did you see the man?'

'Yes, but he was barely conscious.'

'Do you know his name?'

Nell shook her head, 'No, the paramedics arrived and took over.'

'The inside of his boat was quite an eye opener, definitely a huge film fanatic. His walls were covered with memorabilia spanning forty years, from what I could see,' chipped in Guy.

'When he's out of hospital we should go across and see how he is?' Nell turned towards Guy.

'You keep wanting to get me on that water, don't you?' He rolled his eyes at Nell.

'It's probably best not to go bothering the poor man when he's only just come out of hospital,' said Gilly in a very firm tone.

'Why? He'll probably like to see a friendly face and anyway it would be nice to see how he is.'

The Cosy Canal Boat Dream

'If he recovers at all?' Guy added. 'He looked in a very bad way to me.'

'At least he's in the best possible hands. Anyway, where are you off to now, Mum?'

Gilly looked ahead and didn't make eye contact with Nell, 'Just some errands,' she said, putting her foot on the pedal and riding off towards the shops.

Nell waited till her mum was safely out of earshot, 'She is acting stranger by the minute. Did you ring the hospital to see how the man was?' asked Nell, spotting the estate agent milling about outside the entrance to the Old Picture House looking at her clipboard.

Guy shook his head, 'Yes, but they wouldn't give me any details because I'm not a relative.'

'Hopefully, he's on the road to recovery. Despite what Mum says I think I will go and say hello when he's back on the boat. I'm intrigued about all that film paraphernalia, especially with opening up this place.'

'That's very confident, you've not even won the auction yet!'

'It's only a matter of time,' she grinned.

They looked up to see the estate agent walking towards them, checking her paperwork she thrust her hand forward, 'Mr and Mrs Cornish?' she smiled.

Nell flicked a curious glance at Guy who grinned, 'I should be so lucky,' he joked.

Nell felt herself blush and smiled.

'I'm Guy Cornish and this is my ...'

'Friend,' Nell interrupted shaking the estate agent's hand, 'Nell Andrews.'

'And I'm Jennifer, Jennifer Chambers,' she said, handing each of them a business card.

'Are you both from the area?'

'I am,' Nell answered, 'I live on the Nollie,' she glanced over her shoulder towards her floating home.

'Wow, that's cool! How do you cope in winter?' she asked, making polite conversation.

'As long as I remember to fill up the water tank and heat the water, I cope.'

'Do you live on a boat too?' She turned towards Guy.

He shook his head, 'I'm over from Ireland visiting my brother. He owns the boatyard here.'

For a moment, all three of them stood and stared at the Old Picture House. The pretty plot was in definite need of some tender loving care and Nell was hoping she was the woman to do this.

'Are you ready for a look around?' Jennifer asked.

'I'll just tie Sam up here,' said Guy, clipping a lead to the dog, who immediately sat down and whimpered in their direction.

'We won't be long,' Guy ruffled the top of his head.

'Do we need hard hats?' Nell turned towards Jennifer.

'Yes, there's a couple inside for you,' she said, 'Even though, on the whole, the place is actually structurally sound, it's more cosmetic restoration. A few broken windows, damp patches etc. What are your plans for this place? Are you looking for planning permission to build a couple of houses?' Jennifer

The Cosy Canal Boat Dream

asked, placing the key in the lock and pushing open the old heavy oak door.

Nell grimaced, 'I am not.'

'I think that was a definite no,' Guy said, laughing at Nell's disgust.

Before Nell divulged her plans they both followed Jennifer into an impressive foyer, 'Wow! Look at this place,' Guy exclaimed, spinning his head around, 'Just wow. It's like something out of the 1960s.'

It was as if time had stood still.

Huge framed posters of the old classic films adorned the walls and a crystal chandelier still hung on for dear life from the high ceiling. The worn red carpet stretched through the foyer to a regally arching balcony. Even though the wallpaper was torn, damp and flapping in the draft of the broken windows, it was still completely awe-inspiring.

Nell shivered, 'I knew it was magnificent but I'd completely forgotten how magnificent.'

'I think I'll have to agree with you there.' Guy exclaimed, taking in his surroundings.

'I've had some fantastic times in here,' she said, reminiscing before crouching down to the floor and picking up a small pink ticket, 'Look at this.' She held up the paper stub, 'Here's one of the old tickets.'

'There is certainly a magical feel about the place.'

'The owner kept all the original features.'

'Where do those stairs go to?' Guy asked.

Jennifer rustled through her paperwork searching for the floor plan.

Christie Barlow

'Up there was the big screen,' Nell remembered, glancing up towards the staircase, where glistening cobwebs decked the broken windows, which were in need of some major repair.

'The big screen?'

'Yes, that's where the latest films were always shown, the hot new releases. Once you bought your ticket from over there ...' everyone glanced towards the dated wooden booth, which still had a list of prices attached to the wall behind the glass. 'That's where Gladys used to sit. She was part of the furniture, and then you would purchase your ice-cream from an usherette, who was standing at the bottom of those stairs, before queuing up to see the film. Then downstairs, through that door and along the ramp, was the smaller screen, which either showed black and white movies or older films.'

'It's all very lights, camera, action.' Guy said, 'I can see why it was busy in its day.'

'Shall we carry on?' Jennifer asked, glancing at her watch, 'I do have a developer coming to look around this place shortly after you.'

Nell and Guy nodded.

'There must be quite a lot of interest in this place,' Nell probed, walking through the foyer towards the grand staircase.

'I'd be lying if I said there wasn't. I've never known such interest in a building before, but it's a prime location here at the marina, fantastic views across the water, fabulous facilities and we knew as soon as the owner wanted to sell the property that the phone wouldn't stop ringing.'

'Why sell it now when it's been stood still for so long?' Guy queried.

The Cosy Canal Boat Dream

'The owner was originally an actor. He retired abroad a good few years back. He'd bought it when the Old Picture House had actually closed its doors for the last time. He'd had visions of turning it into a film museum or even opening it up again as a cinema but I think his health isn't the best now and as far as we know he has no family, as such, to pass it on to. What is it you want to do with it? I don't think you said.'

'Exactly that.'

'Come again?' asked Jennifer.

'I too have visions of turning it back into a working picture house.'

Jennifer nodded with approval, 'I think you and the owner would get on like a house on fire, then.'

'Why an auction, though?' Guy queried as they walked through the foyer towards the door with a sign hanging off it, 'Little Screen,' Nell read. Guy held the door open and they walked into the old film room.

'The owner decided on an auction so everything is all over and done with quickly. He'd had sales in the past that had fallen through and this way whoever wins the auction has fourteen days to complete the transaction and then it's off his hands.'

'It's obviously not been in use for some time.' Guy held the door wide open so a little light could seep into the room. It was another glorious room but in need of a major re-vamp. There were rows and rows of old plush red-velvet bucket seats.

Nell sank down into one of them, 'I can remember sitting here, just like it was yesterday.'

'Let me show you the rest of the building,' Jennifer said, giving Nell a helping hand out of the chair.

They spent the next ten minutes wandering around and found a popcorn machine, cans of fizzy pop and sweets that were years out of date and a room full of cinema memorabilia.

'What's behind that door?' Guy probed.

'I've no idea, this part was always out of bounds to the public,' Nell answered as Jennifer propped open the door and a faint musty smell seeped out, 'This looks like the old projector room.'

Nell glanced out of the window on to the cinema room below before flitting her eyes around the room, 'What are those?' she asked, pointing to shelves and shelves of boxes at the back of the room. Guy wandered over towards them and flipped open one of the boxes. 'Oh my God, they are the old film reels. There are rows and rows of them. I bet they are worth a small fortune.'

'Do you think it's still working?' Nell asked, staring towards the huge black contraption standing in the middle of the room, which had a seat either side of it.

'Maybe, but at the minute there's no electricity,' Jennifer answered.

Nell sat in one of the chairs at the side of the projector, 'I can picture them sat here, loading up the film. It's amazing to think how it all worked before the days of digital and, whoa, look at that!' Nell shrieked, jumping out of the chair, 'I remember this,' she held up the hinged clapstick, 'Ladies and gentleman, please take your seats. The film will begin in one, two, and three.' Nell then snapped it shut and giggled.

The Cosy Canal Boat Dream

'You're kidding me, clapperboards! Gosh they haven't been around for donkey's years except in Hollywood,' Guy said in amazement.

'Is there anything you'd like to see again?' Jennifer asked nervously, glancing at her watch, knowing that the developer would be arriving anytime soon.

'I think we've seen everything we need to. Have you got an idea of costings?' Nell looked hopeful towards Guy.

'Yes, I've got a fair idea of how much this would cost to restore it to its former glory. It's not too bad, mainly cosmetic.'

Nell gave Guy an upbeat smile before turning towards Jennifer, 'What do you think my chances are of winning the auction?'

She flicked through a list on her clipboard and gave Nell a weary smile, 'You will be up against some tough competition. I really wouldn't like to say.'

Nell's heart sank but she wasn't going to be beaten. As Jennifer walked them back through the tattered but stunning foyer they shook her hand and thanked her for her time.

Once they were outside and the estate agent was out of sight, a sensation of excitement fizzed in Nell's stomach.

'I'm going to bid for this and I'm going to win,' she squealed, turning towards Guy and grabbing both of his hands, taking him by surprise and squeezing them tight.

Sam began to bark and thump his tail on the ground, excited by Nell's sudden outburst.

They both laughed. 'Glad to see you're still here Sam and not off swimming the English Channel,' Guy joked, untying his lead before turning back towards Nell. She beamed into his eyes and Guy smiled at her enthusiasm. Suddenly, Nell launched herself at him, pressing a swift kiss to his cheek she threw her arms around his neck and hugged him tight.

Guy could see the look of determination in her eyes. He had no doubt whatsoever that Nell was going to do everything in her power to win that auction. And he was going to help her...

Chapter 16

'Aunty Nellie, Aunty Nellie are you home?'

Nell heard footsteps and spotted Jacob through the porthole clomping up the jetty towards the 'Nollie', quickly followed by Nathan and her mum. She loved how he called her Aunty Nellie and hoped he'd never grow out of it.

Nell shouted. 'I'm home, come on in Captain Green.'

The door swung open and she was greeted by Jacobs's huge beam. He kicked off his boots and slid on to the seat next to her.

'What do I owe this honour? Even though I'm not complaining, it's a very nice unexpected surprise indeed.' Nell ruffled his hair then looked up to see her mum smiling and Nathan holding up a white plastic bag that smelled simply divine.

'Fish and chips.' Nathan said.

'Yes please!'

'I told you Aunty Nellie wasn't on a diet.'

Nell flicked her eyes between her mum and Nathan, 'Who said Aunty Nellie should be on a diet?' she narrowed her eyes at Jacob.

'Daddy said you and Mummy are always on a diet.'

'But he didn't say we needed to be on a diet?' Nell jokingly raised her eyebrows at Jacob and wagged her finger.

Jacob quickly snagged his dad's eye. He was shaking his head slowly. Jacob mirrored his move.

Nathan swiftly wiped his brow, 'Phew!'

'Mmm, I think you boys are sticking together,' Nell grinned, standing up and taking the bag from Nathan.

'Daddy said you should never joke about a woman's weight if you know what's good for you,' Jacob added and everyone laughed,

'That, Jacob Green, is a very sound piece of advice and one you should take note of for future reference.'

Nell reached up to the plate rack and began passing them to her mum, 'How many plates and where's Bea?'

'She's currently cleaning the display cabinets ... again.'

'Are you sure she should be doing that? She'll be exhausted standing on her feet all day. I only left her ten minutes ago and she was ready for home.'

'It's this competition. She wants everywhere to be spick and span.'

'Everywhere is always spick and span,' she answered, passing Jacob a cup of juice. 'Is she having any of this food?'

'No, but she's coming over when she's finished.'

They all sat around the table and there was silence as everyone began tucking into their fish and chips.

'As much as I love to see you all, and I'm not complaining, what are you all doing here?' Nell asked, swirling a chip in the tomato ketchup on her plate before popping it into her mouth.

The Cosy Canal Boat Dream

'Some guy called Guy,' Nathan grinned, 'just introduced himself to me as I was on the way to the deli to meet Bea ... Ed's brother?'

'That's the one,' answered Nell.

'Apparently, he'd recognised me from working in the deli on Saturday and mentioned he'd been to view the Old Picture House with you at lunchtime.'

'And I was on my way to the deli to catch you, see if you wanted to grab some food, but you'd just left, which was when Jacob suggested fish and chips,' Gilly answered.

Nell stuck her thumbs-up towards Jacob, 'Good call!'

Jacob giggled.

'You never said you were going to view the Old Picture House,' Gilly was staring straight towards Nell.

'You cycled off before I got a chance.' Nell knew that wasn't strictly true.

'You went with ... Guy, did you say? How come you took a stranger to view the place? I'd have gone with you.'

'I just wanted an independent opinion; anyway, he's not a stranger as such, he's Ed's brother, helping him out for a few weeks while he recuperates after his operation.' Nell could feel herself getting a little annoyed towards her mum.

'So the Old Picture House. Come on, what's your gut feeling Nell? I think it's a fantastic idea,' said Nathan oblivious to any tension between Nell and her mum.

Nell couldn't be sure, but she thought her mum seemed to make a funny sound and bristled when Nathan said he thought it was a good idea.

She paused. 'Guy has pointed the main areas for concern

and he's run some very rough figures past me, and I mean very rough. The only obstacle at this moment is winning the auction.' Nell was driven not only by ambition but her enthusiasm filled the 'Nollie'.

'So, he's an expert in this field is he then, this Guy?'

There was no mistaking the dismissive tone to Gilly's voice.

Nell's annoyance grew. 'Well, he's more of an expert than any of us. His granddad was a builder and he used to quote for his jobs.'

'So he knows what he's talking about, then,' Nathan added, which Nell was grateful for.

'I think it was just meant to be. Call it fate, call it what you want but in my opinion the timing of that place coming on to the market is perfect. It's something I can get my teeth into, something to remember Ollie by.' Nell wasn't going to let her mum dampen her mood.

'You don't need a building to remember Ollie by,' Gilly said and Nell shot her mum a scathing look.

'No, I don't, but Ollie and I always spoke about doing something like this and I know he would have approved. And I've got such fond memories of that place, Sunday mornings with Dad ... it just feels right.'

Gilly's mood seemed to soften at the mention of Nell's dad.

Nell smiled. 'Father and daughter time. I loved it especially when Dad bought me those penny chews that stuck to the roof of my mouth.'

'And blackened your teeth,' Gilly pointed out.

'The good old days. That's when going to the cinema used

The Cosy Canal Boat Dream

to be a reasonable price too,' Nathan said finishing the last of his chips. 'That could be our safe haven, Jacob,' Nathan winked at him. 'We could watch films on a Sunday morning and eat sweets.'

'But don't tell Mum.' Jacob brought his fingers to his lips and everyone laughed.

'That's it, us boys have to stick together.'

'The estate agent said the current owner, apparently an actor, had visions of turning it back into a picture house or a film museum but he retired abroad.'

'Any idea which actor?' queried Nathan.

Nell's eyes darted towards Gilly, who'd immediately stood up and begun to clear away the empty dishes. It was becoming quite obvious to Nell that Gilly had some sort of issue with the Old Picture House.

'No, the estate agent didn't say. Are you okay, Mum?' The words had escaped before Nell could stop them. 'I kind of get the impression you aren't bowled over by my idea.'

All eyes were on Gilly, who placed the last of the washed plates on the draining board, hung the tea towel on the oven door and sat back down.

'No, not at all,' Gilly said defensively, 'I just don't want you to rush into anything, get yourself in a financial mess and be disappointed. I'm just a little worried, that's all.'

'Well, don't be, I'm a big girl and won't do anything daft. Let's just see what happens. I'm going to weigh up all the pros and cons and what'll be will be,' Nell said, sensibly.

Gilly nodded. She smiled and for the moment it seemed her mind was put at rest.

'And what's this about you rescuing a man on a boat? It's all the talk in the butcher's this morning,' Nathan said, changing the subject.

'There's never a dull moment around here is there? It was Guy's dog, Sam, who swam across the water to raise the alarm. A man had collapsed on the floor of his boat.'

'Which boat?' Nathan asked, 'A regular or one that's passing through?'

'Much Ado About Nothing. It's not been moored long at the marina, probably passing through. In fact, Bea and I were only saying the other day we hadn't seen any life on it.'

'What were we only saying the other day?' Bea appeared around the doorway of the 'Nollie' looking exhausted.

'Come in and sit down. Budge up, Nathan,' Nell smiled up at her friend.

'We were chatting about Guy and his heroic rescue of the man on the boat. Cup of tea?'

Bea shook her head, 'I'm in one of those moods. I can't decide what I feel like. It's driving me insane. Maybe a blackcurrant cordial.'

'Coming right up.' Nell made Bea a drink and sat back down. 'Have you finished cleaning now? Again!'

'I have,' she smiled. 'I've even cleaned out the drinks display unit and re-stocked it. That's one less job for the morning, but that's the least of my worries,' she sighed.

'What's up now?' Nathan gave Bea a worried look.

'It's Nancy, our Saturday girl. She's just telephoned me to say she's moving to London. I knew she was unhappy with her studies and I was about to offer her a full-time job but

The Cosy Canal Boat Dream

she's decided to move to be nearer her parents. You can't blame her, really.'

'That's such a shame for us,' Nell said, offering Jacob a biscuit. He'd made a makeshift car track out of the place mats and was sitting quietly pushing his car around the table. Nell couldn't help thinking that if she won the auction this was going to put more pressure on her friend – she was already losing one member of staff and if she went too...

'Financially, I can afford another member of staff and with me being pregnant ...'

'Pregnant?' Gilly squealed, 'Why has nobody told me?' she shot a glance between Nell, Bea and Nathan. 'You said she had a stomach bug on Saturday,' Gilly swiped Nathan's hand playfully then scooted off her seat and hugged Bea. 'Congratulations to you both, all,' she said shaking Nathan's and Jacob's hands – who were both sitting there looking as pleased as punch.

'It wasn't my secret to tell,' Nell said, feeling a little guilty she hadn't told her mother.

'What about Isabel? Could she do more hours in the week?' Nathan asked, thinking of suggestions.

Bea shook her head, 'She's studying for her A-levels. Maybe I just need to advertise.'

'Ooh,' Gilly said, her voice in a thespian tone, 'Look no further!'

'Master of chocolate brownies and flapjack,' Nell grinned at Bea and winked in her mum's direction.

Bea felt a smile tug at her lips, 'Now why didn't I think of that? Are you serious?'

'Absolutely, all I'm doing is pottering around and I loved helping out on Saturday.'

'Full time is a lot to take on,' Bea said as she looked towards Nell.

'I'm sure we will make a fantastic team!' Nell nodded with approval. She was already feeling torn between leaving Bea in the lurch and bidding on the Old Picture House. Her friend needed her now, especially with being pregnant, to help out at the deli, but winning the Old Picture House would give Nell something to focus on, something that was for her and her own business for the future. Nell felt relieved that her mum was coming on board; it meant she felt less guilty about abandoning Bea if she was successful in winning the Old Picture House.

'In that case, then,' Bea thrust her hand forward, 'Welcome to The Melting Pot and we'll see you bright and early, eight o'clock sharp.'

'Can I start at nine? Only joking!' Gilly laughed, shaking Bea's hand. 'I'll see you both bright and early!'

Chapter 17

By ten o'clock the next morning Gilly had baked her first batch of chocolate brownies and was already getting into the swing of things. She hummed away around the kitchen of The Melting Pot without a care in the world. Her face flushed and her hair limp with the heat from the ovens, but clearly loving every minute of it. Today, Bea and Nell were both manning the front of the shop while she worked the kitchen.

Gilly stared out on to the lake at the back of the deli and took a second to admire the magnificent view. This morning everything seemed a lot brighter, the rain had stopped, the sky was blue and small purple crocuses danced in the light breeze. She watched dog-walkers and couples strolling hand in hand around the lake. She breathed in the air and exhaled before washing down the worktops and switching the kettle on.

Nell opened the kitchen door and smiled at her mum. 'The brownies and sausage rolls are baked, over there on the trays, ready to display in the counter. More scones are in the oven, cream meringues on the side and Alan from the butcher's has dropped off some sausage and bacon for the lunchtime trade which is in the fresh drawer of the fridge. Oh, and I've had a little spring clean.'

'You have been busy and flowers as well.'

Gilly had even ventured out the back and picked some of the crocuses and dotted them in jam jars all around the kitchen.

'Kettle's boiled, let me make you both a drink,' Gilly said, tossing a tea-bag in each mug.

'Superstar!' Bea exclaimed, casting her eyes around the kitchen, 'Look at this place, it's spotless. Why didn't I employ you sooner?'

'I keep asking myself the very same question,' Gilly chuckled, handing a mug of tea to the pair of them. Bea and Nell sighed as they heard the door to the deli open, 'I'll go. You two take a breather for a minute,' Gilly insisted, disappearing through the kitchen door towards the deli counter.

Alan Webster from the butcher's, who was built like a string bean and had the hair of a mad professor, beamed over the counter at Gilly and handed her a tray of bread buns.

'Second time today,' he chuckled, 'We need to stop meeting like this.'

'You daft thing,' Gilly said, swiping his arm.

He grinned, 'These were delivered next door by mistake. One of the staff signed for them but then we've realised they were for you.'

'Don't worry,' Gilly said, taking the tray from him. 'Thanks for bringing them over.' He swiftly disappeared as Gilly took the tray into the kitchen.

The Cosy Canal Boat Dream

'What have you there?' asked Bea, as she sidled up to the tray of buns and scanned the advice slip.

'Alan popped them in. They were delivered there by mistake.'

'Damn,' Bea murmured, taking the tray from Gilly, 'I've only gone and ordered double. That'll be the baby brain already kicking in. What the heck are we going to do with all of these?'

'We've already prepared the sandwiches for the lunchtime rush on the granary and bloomer bread. We can't keep these until tomorrow, they'll go stale,' Nell added.

'Bacon baps?' Gilly suggested, 'Everyone loves a bacon sandwich.'

'Right, good idea! Gilly, you update the blackboard and Nell, you start grilling the bacon.'

Nell saluted 'Yes, chef!'

Bea threw a box of chalk towards Gilly, 'Price one pound. Let's get these shifted.'

Gilly disappeared on to the shop floor and promptly peered back round the kitchen door. 'There's a couple of customers sitting at the tables inside waiting to be served.'

Bea took a swig of her drink and clutched her pen and notepad, 'I'm on it,' she said, painting a wide smile on her face and hurrying back out into the deli.

Bea's eyes flitted between the two customers; there was a man sitting in the corner perusing the menu, mid-sixties, dressed in a flat cap, waterproof trousers and green wellington boots. He unravelled his scarf and placed it on the empty chair next to him. His cheeks were rosy and his glasses were perched on the end of his nose. He spotted Bea and gave her a warm smile. The lady sitting on the other table was busily scribbling away on a notepad. Her blonde hair fell below her shoulders, her chiselled cheekbones were streaked with blusher and she looked very business-like sitting there in a blue pinstriped suit with heels. Bea guessed she was early thirties and was definitely not passing through on a narrowboat.

Bea's mouth suddenly went dry and her palms began to sweat, this woman oozed best delicatessen judge all over.

'Keep your cool, keep your cool,' she muttered under her breath.

'Did you say something?' Bea met the woman's icy stare.

She shook her head and took a breath. 'Hi, I'm Bea, welcome to my deli. It's a lovely day out there isn't it? At least the rain has stopped. Have you come far?' What the heck was she doing? She'd never rambled on so much to a customer before.

The woman glowered at her, 'Can I just give you my order please,' she said, in a very abrupt tone.

'Yes, of course, sorry. What can I get for you?' Bea asked, poised with her pen on the pad.

The unfriendly woman reeled of a long list of food while Bea scribbled quickly on her pad.

'Are you expecting company?' Bea asked politely, thinking it was an awful lot of food for one person to manage.

The woman stared at Bea, 'No, I'm assuming you can bring me what I've ordered.'

Bea's voice faltered, 'Of course, madam. It'll be right with you.'

Just as Bea turned away, the woman spoke again. 'Oh and a coffee please and I don't mean any of that instant rubbish.'

The Cosy Canal Boat Dream

Bea bit down on her lip and met the woman's glare, 'Certainly, madam,' she said, giving her the sweetest smile she could muster. Bea felt sick to her stomach, remembering the coffee machine was still broken and the engineer wasn't coming out until this afternoon to fix it. 'We won't keep you long,' Bea said, before walking over to the elderly gentleman sitting in the corner.

'Hello, are you ready to order?' Bea asked, smiling brightly at the man.

'Good morning, what a lovely day it is today, very spring-like.' The man was jolly and smiled warmly back at Bea.

'It's beautiful out there today,' she said. 'What can I get for you?'

'Full English with all the trimmings, granary toast and a mug of coffee,' he said, then lowered his voice to a whisper, 'And I don't mind any of that instant rubbish,' he winked at Bea, who smiled at him. 'And a scone to take home for my lovely lady. She likes a good scone.'

'Certainly sir,' she said, opening his napkin and laying it on his lap for him.

Bea hurried back to the kitchen, 'Shoot!' she exclaimed, as soon as she was safely on the other side of the door.

'What's up with you? You look flustered.'

'It's her,' Bea whispered, but she didn't know why she was whispering, it wasn't as though the snooty woman could even hear her in the kitchen.

'It's who?' Nell asked perplexed.

'The judge from the competition, she's even dressed like a judge, keeps writing things down then shutting her notebook.

She's ordered anything and everything off the menu and hasn't cracked a smile or been polite since she got here.'

Quickly Nell got up and peered around the kitchen door into the deli, 'Oh yes, it's definitely her. No one passes through the marina dressed like that. Look at that suit, very Ted Bakerish, and are those Jimmy Choos?' she gave a low whistle. 'I was hoping for someone friendly like Mary Berry,' she said, spotting Gilly coming back through the deli door.

'What are you two whispering about?' Gilly looked amused as she placed the chalk box back on the kitchen shelf. 'You two are acting very cloak and dagger.'

'That's the judge,' mouthed Bea, pointing in the direction of the kitchen door.

Gilly raised her eyebrows, 'The snooty one?'

Both Bea and Nell nodded.

'Why do you say that?' Nell asked in wonderment.

'She's just made a flippant comment about a greasy spoon café after she spotted the sign I'd just written on the specials board about the bacon butties.'

'Oh God, we are doomed!' Bea exclaimed.

'Don't panic! We have everything she's ordered. Except for the coffee,' Nell assured her friend.

'We have coffee,' Gilly waggled the jar of instant by the kettle.

She specifically said, 'None of that instant rubbish.'

Nell rolled her eyes, 'Mum, sneak out the back door and run over to The Waterfront and bring back a coffee.'

'I'm on it,' she said, thrusting her arms into her coat and scooting out the back way towards the pub.

The Cosy Canal Boat Dream

'Is that cheating?' Nell asked, shrugging her shoulders.

'Needs must. We have everything else. And here's the order for the gentleman in the opposite corner,' said Bea, placing the ticket on the counter, 'He would like a full English, granary toast and a scone to take home for his wife.'

'Aw how lovely. What's she ordered?' Nell asked, casting her eyes over the order pad.

'A champagne breakfast, dessert, a fresh strawberry tarte, and speciality cheese and biscuits.'

Nell raised her eyebrows, 'Jeez! Where is she going to put all that?'

'That's exactly what I thought and asked her if she was expecting company.'

'Oh God, you didn't?'

'I did and the poor man in the corner was chuckling under his breath.'

Nell fell about laughing and Bea swiped her arm playfully, 'Never mind laughing, is the champagne cold?'

'Yes, it's in the bottom of the fridge along with the salmon.'

'Phew.'

Gilly promptly appeared and placed the coffee on the worktop.

Nell quickly poured it into one of their mugs, 'Mum, take this through to her with the biggest smile you have.'

'Will do,' she said, planting a wide smile on her face and walking out of the kitchen door.

'Let's get this show on the road,' Nell said, swiping her hands together.

Bea's expression suddenly hardened as she began to concentrate on preparing the fresh food. For the next ten minutes, Nell and Bea worked in silence while Gilly served behind the front counter.

Nell exhaled sharply and caught Bea's eye, 'I think we're ready.'

Bea nodded, picking up the plate and the champagne flute before she walked into the deli.

'Enjoy your breakfast,' Bea said politely, with a smile, as she placed the food down on the table alongside the glass. The woman tapped away on her mobile phone and didn't even make eye contact with her.

How rude, Bea thought to herself, before turning to the man in the corner who was reading his magazine, 'Your order is just coming,' Bea said, warmly, as the man gave her a smile.

'Excuse me,' the woman clicked her fingers. Immediately Bea spun round. 'My glass appears to be empty.'

'I'm just bringing the champagne for you now,' Bea forced a smile and did everything in her power not to curtsey.

A frantic Bea returned to the kitchen.

'You need to go and pour the champagne and the full English is now ready for table five, along with his coffee. I'm just toasting the bread.'

'Who does she think she is?' Bea's face was like thunder.

'Take deep breaths, it will soon be over. We've dealt with worse.'

'Have we, when?' Bea questioned, taking the bottle out of the fridge.

'Actually, I don't think we have! But on the plus side, it's character-building.'

The Cosy Canal Boat Dream

'I don't need my character building. Manners cost nothing.'

'Very true. Do you want me to go and serve her?' Nell suggested.

Bea shook her head, 'No way, she's not getting the better of me.'

'Good girl, now stay calm for the baby's sake.'

'And smile,' Bea winked at Nell as she walked back through the door in an entirely professional manner.

After pouring the champagne, she returned to the kitchen and grabbed the man's breakfast and coffee. 'Enjoy your breakfast. I've put you an extra sausage and piece of bacon on for you and your toast is just coming.'

'Very kind of you and this ...' he said taking a sip of his drink, 'is a very nice cup of coffee.'

'Thank you,' Bea answered, thinking what a lovely man he was.

When Bea returned to the kitchen once more, Nell was spying around the door, 'Get in there,' Bea laughed, shooing her back into the kitchen.

'Toast is ready.'

'My cheeks are actually aching from all this smiling!' Bea said, taking the toast from Nell, who thrust her hands in the sink and began to wash the pots.

'The strawberry tart and cheese and biscuits are all under the glass dome when she's ready.'

'Thanks, Nell. What would I do without you?'

'Hang on in there, she'll be gone in twenty minutes or so,' she said, looking up, her face brightening. 'I've already prepared her bill so we don't get flustered at the till.'

'You're simply the best.'

While Bea and Nell busied themselves in the kitchen, Gilly served a steady stream of customers and for the next ten minutes the boaters got wind of bacon barms for a pound and they were flying out of the deli.

'Good morning, Fred,' Gilly said cheerfully when he walked into the deli.

He tilted his cap.

'What can I get for you?'

'The board outside, bacon baps, any left?'

'There is, just the one?'

'Two please,' he answered, 'and brown sauce on both.'

'To take out?'

He nodded.

'Coming right up,' Gilly smiled, popping back into the kitchen.

The woman in the corner of the deli, who was sipping her champagne, glanced over and gave Fred a look of disdain as he slapped a two-pound coin on the counter and shuffled his feet while he waited.

The moment Fred left the shop the woman clicked her fingers again. This time Gilly slipped over towards her. 'Can I have the bill please?'

'Certainly, madam, but what about the rest of the food you ordered?'

'Box it up for me.'

'Of course, right away,' she said, turning back into the kitchen.

The Cosy Canal Boat Dream

Within five minutes, all three of them stood in the deli window and scrutinised the woman as she tottered up the towpath on her Jimmy Choos, clutching her notepad.

'Don't hurry back,' Nell muttered under breath.

'How do you think we've done?'

'I've no idea, but she's going to catch pneumonia from that icy persona of hers if she doesn't watch out.'

They all chuckled.

'Shall I put the kettle on?' Gilly asked. 'I think we could do with a cuppa.'

'You read my mind,' Nell said flinging a tea towel over her shoulder.

'I'll go and check on the gentleman in the corner,' Bea said, relieved that the woman had finally gone.

'How was your breakfast?' she asked as the man laid down his knife and fork on the empty plate.

'That's the best fry-up I've had in a long time, but don't tell the missus!' he grinned, wrapping his scarf around his neck. 'I'm meant to be watching the cholesterol levels.'

'I promise,' Bea said brightly, warming towards the old man. 'Can I get you anything else?'

'Only the bill please.'

If only more customers were like him, Bea thought to herself, as she gathered up the empty plates and disappeared back into the kitchen.

When she returned with the man's bill he was waiting by the counter with his boating magazine tucked under his arm as he grappled with his money.

'Here's the scone for your wife,' she said, placing the paper bag on to the counter. 'Would you like some clotted cream and jam to go with it?'

'Strawberry is her favourite, thank you, very kind. And you, my dear girl, deserve a medal.'

'What for?' Bea asked holding his gaze.

'That woman. She would test the patience of a saint.'

Bea smiled and handed over his change. 'You have a lovely day.'

He nodded and walked out of the door.

As soon as the door closed behind him, all three of them heaved a huge sigh of relief.

'Urgh! What a horrible woman she was.' Bea stated, 'I think I need a drink – an alcoholic drink.'

'You can't, you're pregnant! But you can have this,' Nell laughed, handing her a mug of tea.

Suddenly, there was a loud knocking on the window and all of them jumped out of their skin. They spun round to see Guy standing there, beaming back at them.

He opened the door and Sam waited patiently outside, his tail thumping on the ground. 'What's up with you ladies? You look frazzled. Bad morning?!'

'Yes!' All three replied in agreement.

'We've just had the judge from hell,' Nell rolled her eyes.

'Come again?'

'The Melting Pot has been entered for Delicatessen of the Year and the judge has just darkened our day, but this one did amazing,' she added, rubbing Bea's arm.

'Oh, interesting! So, I take it you all charmed the socks off her?'

The Cosy Canal Boat Dream

'Jimmy Choos, more like! It's safe to say she had a heart of ice, but fingers crossed,' Bea answered.

Guy crossed his fingers too.

'And what can we do for you?'

He glanced back over his shoulder towards the chalk board outside, 'That sign has tickled my taste buds. Any chance of a couple of those bacon baps? I'm starving! And a coffee?'

'But none of that instant rubbish,' both Nell and Bea said together, then laughed.

Guy raised his eyebrows, 'Eh?'

'In joke, don't worry about it! Gilly you take a break. I'll get the bacon baps and the coffee.' Bea and Gilly slid past Nell into the kitchen.

Nell stood on the other side of the counter and caught a whiff of an inherently spicy masculine fragrance, Guy's aftershave. It was a lot stronger than Ollie ever wore, but it suited him. For a brief moment she closed her eyes and inhaled.

His face flickered with amusement, 'You okay?'

'Sorry,' she said, feeling a little embarrassed. Pull yourself together, Nell, were the words whirling around in her head.

'No need to be sorry. There's another reason. I've nipped in.'

'Oh! Which is?' she asked, thankful he'd changed the subject so quickly.

'I've put together a financial plan for you, outlining the potential costs of the picture house. Let me cook you dinner tonight and I'll go through it with you.'

'Cook?' she said, 'Tonight? That sounds lovely. What time?'

'Say seven?' his eyes twinkled as he held her gaze.

'Perfect.' Nell's lips twitched with a smile. 'Shall I bring a bottle?'

'Sounds like an excellent plan.'

As soon as the door to the deli closed behind Guy, Nell felt a warm fuzzy feeling inside. She folded her arms, leant on the counter and stared around the room. She could remember how excited Bea had been when she'd opened up The Melting Pot for the very first time. She'd worked so hard transforming the place and Nell had been with her every step of the way. Working here for the past two years had given Nell the confidence and experience she needed to run her own business: everything from stock-taking, working the till and customer service. Nell knew if she was successful in winning the auction, she would make the Old Picture House a success.

Chapter 18

'Damn, blast.' Guy shouted, flustered. Why the heck had he uttered those words 'I'll cook for you, Nell.'

The last hour had been a complete disaster for Guy. He'd decided to prepare the meal for Nell in Ed's kitchen, instead of the annexe, for two reasons; one it was bigger, and two he could chat away to Ed at the same time. As plans went it wasn't the best one he'd ever come up with. He hadn't spoken two words to Ed in the last half an hour who was lying on the settee listening to the slamming of cupboard doors and the banging of pans coming from the kitchen. Even Sam had vacated the kitchen and was now curled up on the floor in front of the fire.

'Ouch, that's hot. Oh God.' Guy felt his cheeks flush. The kitchen had gone from an average temperature of seventeen degrees to boiling as Guy threw open the kitchen window and was thankful for the blast of cool air. Smoke from the sizzling venison had activated the smoke alarm and Sam had begun to howl at the high-pitched din.

'What the hell are you doing in there, mate?' Ed asked, from the comfort of his settee as he reached for a biscuit from the plate on the coffee table.

'Just teething problems,' Guy answered frowning and wiping his brow with a tea towel while trying to follow the recipe on YouTube. How do they make it look so easy? They aren't sweating cobs or swiping tea towels at the smoke detector. They look cool, calm and collected, unlike Guy who'd just caught a glimpse of himself in the mirror. He was losing the will to live.

He took a deep breath and tried to compose himself. The woman, who was called Gloria, cracked open two eggs and dropped them into the mixing bowl. Guy mirrored her actions only to witness half the broken eggshell sliding into his bowl. Damn again. As he was trying to scrape the shell from the bowl without any success, Gloria was already measuring out the flour.

'Slow down, you are going too fast,' he bellowed at her, but she just smiled back at him. 'And your smile is beginning to get on my nerves.'

'Who are you talking to?' Ed shouted towards the kitchen, but there was no answer.

Guy decided to leave the shell. What's a bit of eggshell between friends? 'No harm done,' he muttered to himself. He followed the next instruction, only to find when he tore open the bag of flour it mushroomed out into a huge snowstorm in front of his face, split all the way to the bottom and spilt out on to the table.

'Right that's it, I've had enough,' he cried, switching off his iPad and cringing at his pathetic attempt to make venison pie. He made a mental note never to offer to cook for anyone again. He wasn't cut for out for this.

The Cosy Canal Boat Dream

There was a slam of the fridge door and Guy marched into the living room muttering. His face was flushed and his t-shirt covered in flour. He raked a hand through his hair and took a huge gulp of his beer.

Ed tried to hide his smile by avoiding his glare.

'You don't have to go to all this trouble for my sake. A simple omelette or a pizza would have done.' Ed looked up at his brother, 'Actually, anything is welcome after that hospital food. I never want to see another creamed potato as long as I live,' he chuckled to himself.

Guy sighed, 'It wasn't for you. I can still make you an omelette,' Guy stopped in his tracks, 'Oh actually, I can't. I've just used the last of the eggs.'

Ed had never seen his brother looking so stressed before. 'Joking apart, I'd help you out but, you know, I'm convalescing.'

Before Guy could say anything there was a knock on the annexe door.

'What's the time?' Guy asked, quickly checking his phone.

'Just before seven.'

Guy groaned, 'That'll be Nell and look at the state of me.'

Ed's eyes narrowed at Guy, 'You aren't by any chance trying to impress the lovely Nell, are you?'

Guy felt Ed eyeing him with uncertainty. 'You do know Nell is not only lovely but really lovely and has been through a very difficult time. Look, all I'm saying is ...' There was another knock on the door. 'Tread carefully. Does she know why you are here?'

Guy shook his head, 'She knows half the reason. I'm here to look after you.'

Christie Barlow

'You need to be straight with her, she's worth her weight in gold that one.' Ed's tone was firm, 'Go and answer the door. Don't leave the poor lass waiting on the step.'

Guy didn't need to be told twice, but panic hit him as he hurried to open it. Ed was right, he needed to be straight with Nell about why he was really here, and sooner rather than later. He should have been straight with her from the start and felt bad about lying to her but if he told her the truth now he wasn't sure if it would ruin everything.

Guy took a deep breath and swung open the door, 'Hi.'

Nell's face broke into a grin, 'Hi yourself,' she eyed him up and down, 'You appear to be covered in ...'

'Flour, don't ask.'

'Okay! I won't!' she answered holding a bottle of wine up in front of him, 'I thought if you were cooking then it was only polite to bring the wine. What are we having?' laughed Nell nervously.

'It's a surprise,' he said, opening the door, and it really was. He had no idea what he was going to feed her now. Nell slid past him and hung her coat on the hook in the hallway

'Ed's through there. Go through, he'd love to see you. I'm just going to clean myself up.'

Nell walked into the living room. Sam lifted his head and thumped his tail on the floor. 'Am I not worth getting up for, Sam?' Nell joked, 'And hello to you, Ed, how are you?' she settled in the armchair after placing the bottle of wine on the coffee table.

'I mustn't grumble, they treated me well in hospital but I have to admit I like my home comforts.'

The Cosy Canal Boat Dream

'I can imagine.'

'And how are you? What have I missed?' asked Ed.

'All good here. It's been fairly quiet,' Nell answered, wondering where to start, 'I was knocked over by a red setter and met a man called Guy whose dog decided to swim across the marina to a narrowboat on the other side. Then there was the rescue of Sam, followed by the Old Picture House going up for sale, the deli has been nominated for Deli of the Year, Sam decided to swim back out to the same boat and rescue a man who'd collapsed, then we've had the judge from hell and ...'

'Whoah! Stop there! It's been a quiet time, then?' Ed laughed, 'I'd best not go away again!'

'You best not! Oh,' Nell took a breath, 'Has Guy mentioned to you that I'm thinking about bidding in the auction for the Old Picture House?'

'He did, very exciting stuff. It would be great to see that place thriving again.'

Nell bent down and whipped out some rolled-up papers from her bag, 'I've been busy! My head is so full of all these ideas I can barely sleep. Look I've even drawn up some plans – well, as plans go with my lack of talent for drawing.' She laid them out on the table.

'Let me get you a drink and I'll have a look over them. I don't know where that brother of mine has disappeared to.'

'Don't you dare move. I'll get us one.' Nell stood up. 'Peruse all you want,' she nodded towards the plans.

'Kitchen's through there. There's beer and wine in the fridge. Beer for me, please.'

Nell patted Ed's sleeve as she passed and then stood opened mouthed in the kitchen doorway. Her eyes followed the devastation around the room.

'Goodness me,' gasped Nell.

'What's the matter?' Ed swung his head towards her.

'Ed, I don't know how to tell you this,' Nell swallowed, 'But are you aware there seems to have been some sort of nuclear explosion in your kitchen?'

'I daren't look,' Ed rolled his eyes.

'Whatever the hell's happened?'

'From what I can gather, a woman called Gloria, a YouTube recipe and my brother's failed attempt at cooking venison pie from scratch,' Ed chuckled from the settee.

Nell gave a small laugh, 'Please tell me this wasn't all for my benefit?'

'I'm saying nothing!'

'Oh God!'

Quickly, she handed Ed a beer. He was looking over the drawings that Nell had brought and she busied herself tidying up in the kitchen, wiping down the worktops and loading the dishwasher.

Guy appeared in the next five minutes, 'What are you doing?'

Nell spun round to see him standing in the doorway, every nerve in her body tingled as she flicked her eyes over his toned body. Nell wanted to run her hands over the contours of his strong arms, the desire almost too much to bear. He was showered and not a speck of flour in sight.

'Apparently, cleaning up after your liaison with some woman

The Cosy Canal Boat Dream

called Gloria,' grinned Nell, throwing the dishcloth into the sink and picking up her wine glass.

Guy shook his head, 'Not one of my finest moments, but hopefully I can redeem myself,' his eyes sparkled.

'Hopefully you can,' Nell teased, feeling a rush of warmth towards him. 'Was all this for my benefit?'

'Hmm, I'm saying nothing. Come on, let's go next door to the annexe,' He said touching her arm gently. Nell felt her pulse quicken as she felt a sudden intense heat radiating from his touch. She wondered if he felt that too.

'What about Ed?'

'Don't mind me,' Ed said, overhearing the conversation. 'I've got the remote control, and a take-away menu.'

'Are you sure?' Nell asked, 'I don't like leaving you on your own.'

Everyone was startled by Sam's sudden bark, 'See, I'm not on my own. Sam can stay with me,' Ed laughed, 'I'll shout if I need anything.'

Guy and Nell disappeared towards the annexe, 'Just one question, Guy?'

'Anything.'

'What are we having for tea?'

'Guy Cornish's signature dish!'

Chapter 19

'Wow, look at this. You have been busy.'
Guy had laid the table in the annexe and pulled out a seat for Nell.

'You even have flowers,' Nell admired the pink carnations in the vase in the middle of the table as Guy opened a napkin and placed it on her lap before switching on his iPod for some background music. 'Picked by my own fair hands just for you. Now don't move a muscle, just sit and relax. Dinner will be served in five minutes,' he smiled, tapping his watch.

'I won't be going anywhere,' Nell said, amused, looking forward to Guy's signature dish, whatever that might be.

'That's good to hear.'

'I feel like we need a drumroll or something.'

'Maybe a little bit over the top, but you know I'll go with the flow,' he grinned, disappearing back towards the kitchen.

'I don't have to clean up in there too, do I?' she shouted after him.

His head appeared back around the door and he winked, 'Cheeky! Now, close your eyes tight and no peeping.'

'Are you serious?'

The Cosy Canal Boat Dream

'Yep!'

Nell squeezed her eyes shut, 'Okay, if you insist. Ready when you are!'

She heard Guy's footsteps behind her and two plates being placed on the table. He then sat down opposite her.

'You can open your eyes now,' said Guy, his chin resting on his hand as his eyes sparkled at Nell.

Nell looked down at the plate with amusement and bit down on her lip then laughed heartily. 'Beans on toast – I love your way of thinking!'

'I'm not sure whether this goes better with red wine or white. It's your choice!'

'I have no idea! I may just have a glass of both.'

'Go for it!' he joked. 'It's the only thing I can cook without burning.'

Nell chuckled, 'You are so funny!'

'I aim to please and I didn't even have to watch a YouTube video to prepare this,' he said proudly.

'Eat your heart out MasterChef!' said Nell, picking up her knife and fork and grinning like a Cheshire cat. She began to scoop up the beans with her fork, 'Mmm, cooked to perfection.'

He picked up his knife and fork and paused.

'Aren't you eating?' Asked Nell.

'I'm sorry, I did want it to be perfect, but Gloria got the better of me.'

'You don't have to apologise, it is perfect.' Nell met Guy's gaze. 'I mean it. I'm having a wonderful evening.'

'I feel like I've let you down.'

'Any particular reason why?' asked Nell, puzzled.

Guy hesitated, 'Because I wanted to cook you something special and ...' he took a breath, 'I really enjoy your company,' he said softly. 'I hope we can do more of this ... but without the beans.'

Nell felt the corners of her mouth lifting and her heart beat a little faster. Nell felt the same. She wanted to spend more time with Guy, 'Beans or no beans, Guy Cornish, shall I let you into a little secret?'

'Go on.'

'Beans on toast is my favourite meal ever.'

'Is that right, Nell Andrews?'

'Most definitely,' she giggled, 'but do you have any brown sauce?'

'Don't move a muscle.'

Nell had no intention of going anywhere.

Chapter 20

Twenty minutes later, Nell and Guy had finished eating and made themselves comfortable on the rug in front of the fire with a bottle of wine.

'I see you've come prepared' said Guy, unfolding the plans and ideas that Nell had gathered together.

'You sound like a boy scout,' she teased.

Nell watched Guy as he looked over the plans.

'So, what do you think?' urged Nell, impatiently waiting for an answer. 'I've opened up the back of the foyer and got rid of that ramp, the box office would go here,' she pointed at the drawing, 'and the popcorn machine here, with maybe a small bar here, serving refreshments. There will be a seating area here, which can be enjoyed by everyone. I was thinking on a Wednesday afternoon there could be reduced rates for the senior citizens with maybe a free drink with each ticket and film nights for the kids on a Friday at a special family rate. I want everyone flocking in here – a feel-good community atmosphere bringing all the generations back together. Ollie would have loved that. Come on ... tell me what you think, for heaven's sake.'

'Did Jacob draw these plans?' asked Guy with a grin, jokingly putting his arm around her shoulder and giving it a squeeze.

'You what?' giggled Nell, 'I have many talents you know ... well actually, drawing obviously isn't one of them, looking at these!'

'Many talents, you say? I hope to find out very soon,' he peered up under his dark eyelashes and brushed his fingertips against hers. She looked straight into his eyes, his gaze was still fixed on her. She lowered her eyes to his perfect lips, the gentle lift of his mouth was mesmerising. Guy leant forward and kissed the tip of her nose lightly. Nell felt her heart hammering against her chest and a smile etched all over her face. Even though she barely knew Guy she knew she'd clicked with him. He was so easy to be around and, not to mention, drop-dead gorgeous.

Nell clapped her hands in excitement, 'Come on, let's have a look at your figures, then,' she said, grabbing the spreadsheet from beside Guy.

'Figures, you say. All is looking good from here,' he nudged her and gave her a mischievous grin.

'Money figures,' she said, mindful she'd turned a bright shade of crimson.

Nell was finding it hard to concentrate but she forced her eyes over the sheet of paper.

'So, what do you think?' asked Guy.

Nell didn't answer. After digesting the information, her mind was whirling. She couldn't quite believe what she was seeing. Taking another gulp of wine, she pondered.

The Cosy Canal Boat Dream

He noticed the shift in mood, 'Hey, you okay? You've suddenly gone very quiet, not to mention white.'

Take a deep breath, Nell.

Nell's smile had suddenly plunged into despair, her heart sank to a new level, her stomach churned and reality had hit, 'Jeez, that's an awful lot of money,' she said slowly, taking in the proposal and digesting all the information. 'I think I need more wine.'

Guy smiled and promptly filled up her glass.

'It's an awful lot of money, but remember, this is worst-case scenario, and I'm sure it won't come to that.'

Thoughts of letting Ollie down filtered through her mind.

'I'm kidding myself, aren't I?' she sighed heavily and stared towards the fire, her eyes threatening tears. Had her mum been right after all? Was this one of those 'told you so' moments? Nell looked at Guy incredulously and exhaled. 'I'm not sure I can afford this ...'

'Oh Nell, I don't know what to say to you. I've been as honest as I can be with the maths. The last thing I want is for you to get into any sort of financial difficulty.'

'I know and I'm thankful, really I am,' she leant over and squeezed his knee, 'But it just doesn't leave much money left over, if any,' she rested her head on his shoulder.

'It really does have to be thought about carefully.'

She nodded, 'You know, when Ollie died, my whole world stood still. Recently, it's felt as though I was getting a little bit of me back, something to work towards and look forward to. I've got that horribly gut-wrenching feeling in the pit of my stomach again. What if it is all too much for me?' Her chest tightened and her eyes glazed over.

Guy instinctively turned towards her, tucking a stray hair behind her ear and wiping away a tear. She smiled a sad smile at him.

'Come here. It's natural to have doubts,' he said, taking her into his arms. She snuggled into his chest and the pair of them sat in a contemplative silence while Nell blinked away more tears and swallowed a lump in her throat. Could she do this? Could she actually do this? She made herself take a breath.

Her eyes flickered up towards him, 'What am I going to do?'

'Only you know the answer to that one,' he said softly.

'If only it was that simple.'

'It's a huge task, but if anyone can pull this off you can. From what I've seen so far, Nell Andrews, you are an amazing woman. I mean look at all this,' he gestured to the plans and the ideas she'd drawn up. 'Take the spreadsheet home and sleep on it. The auction isn't for a while yet – there's ample time to make your mind up.'

'Look at me stumbling at the first hurdle.'

'Don't panic, no one is stumbling, because I'd catch you,' he smiled warmly. He hesitated slightly before moving his lips closer to hers. Her stomach fluttered with a hundred fireflies. She wanted him to move closer, she wanted to feel his lips on her and taste his kiss. The intensity of his gaze made her shiver in anticipation and a warm feeling that had been missing for far too long flooded through her body. He finally

The Cosy Canal Boat Dream

lowered his head and kissed her tenderly on the lips, leaving her wanting more.

'That made me feel a little better,' she smiled, resting her head against his.

'Only slightly? We'll have to see what we can do about that,' he whispered softly.

'Please do, and Guy – thank you,' she said softly.

'What for?'

'Just this, helping me out.'

'Believe me, the pleasure is all mine,'

He hugged her, his grip was firm, then kissed her gently on the top of her head. 'What do you want to do now?'

'The options being?' asked Nell, casting her eyes upwards.

'I can either walk you home or we can open that other bottle of wine.' He tilted her chin towards his gaze and his eyes didn't leave hers. Nell's heart skipped a beat at the thought of spending more time in Guy's company and she reminded herself to breathe normally. It felt so good being with him and she pressed her lips together to try and hide the delight that was about to burst out at any second. Nell was a strong believer in fate. Things happened for a reason, in her book, and she was thrilled Guy had come into her life when he had.

'Second bottle sounds good to me.'

'Me too.'

Chapter 21

The following morning Nell looked out of the window of the 'Nollie'. Little Rock Marina was still bright on such a grey day, but now she longed for the warm summer days to arrive. The towpath was already busy with dog-walkers and joggers and Nell noticed the blackboard was already standing outside the deli. Bea must have been up with the larks, she thought to herself. Cracking open her boiled egg, she glanced over the figures on the spreadsheet that Guy had prepared. Luckily, she'd slept well, despite her going to bed with the uncertainty hanging over her, but having slept on it, she'd woken up more determined than ever to win that auction.

'No more dithering,' she muttered to herself. After finishing her breakfast and washing the pots, she glanced at her watch.

There was still an hour before she was due at the deli. Quickly grabbing her coat and a flask of tea, she locked the 'Nollie' behind her and stepped out into the crisp morning air. Most of the boats still lay in darkness as she strolled up the path towards the lake.

Her feet echoed over the wooden bridge and she snuggled deep inside her coat before perching on the edge of the bench

The Cosy Canal Boat Dream

under the willow tree. There were a couple of swans gliding through the water with such grace, and a mallard with its brown speckled plumage bobbed its head under the water.

'Morning Ollie. I know it's early,' she said out loud, taking a sip of her tea, 'And you're not one for early mornings, but I have news.' She felt comfort as a robin flew and landed on the arm of the bench next to her. 'Big news that I'm so excited about! You know we always talked about undertaking a project, something for the community? Well the Old Picture House has come up for sale and I'm thinking of restoring it to its former glory. Actually, not just thinking about it, I'm going to do it. What do you reckon?'

She stared out across the tranquil lake and had a sudden flashback to a conversation she'd had with Ollie when he had been umming and aah-ing about buying the yard. They'd been sitting outside The Waterfront sipping on a cool beer on a red-hot summer's day when Ollie had shown Nell the property details of a business yard on the edge of Heron's Reach. Nell could see the excitement in his eyes and the fire in his belly as he told her that he was thinking of buying it.

'Let's flip a coin: heads we buy it, tails we don't,' Ollie had suggested. Of course the coin had landed on heads.

'Best of three,' Nell chipped in, flipping a further two heads. They'd bought the yard and it had been a good decision. Ollie had been very happy there.

'Maybe that's it – let fate decide for me,' said Nell, peering up at the sky.

She dug deep into her coat pocket and pulled out a ten-pence piece.

Christie Barlow

'Heads or tails?'

As she flipped the coin in the air, 'Heads,' she said, catching the money and placing it on the back of her hand.

For a brief moment, she closed her eyes, not daring to look. Slowing removing her hand, 'Heads,' she murmured, 'Best of three.' She flipped the coin twice more and both landed on heads.

She heaved a huge sigh of relief, 'Thanks, Ollie, decision made. I knew you'd come good. There's something else too.' She paused and took a deep breath. 'He's called Guy. We've become friends. You'd like him.' Nell knew she was waffling but felt that she needed to say the words out loud. 'I think I really like him.'

Suddenly, Nell was surprised by the intensity of the presence she felt. He was here, listening to her and comforting her, 'You really are here, aren't you?' she whispered.

'Whoa!' Nell jumped out of her skin as she felt a hand on her shoulder. She flew off the bench and spun round.

'Sorry ... sorry. I didn't mean to startle you.'

Guy's eyes locked with an alarmed Nell, 'Jeez, you frightened the life out of me,' she said, her heart pounding.

'I'm so sorry, I didn't mean to scare you.'

Nell exhaled and held her hand to her chest, 'I'm surprised you didn't give me a heart attack.'

'Well, I'm glad I didn't!'

'Honestly, for a moment there, I thought ... oh don't worry, it's my fault I never heard you. I was lost in my own thoughts. What are you doing down here?' she asked, forcing herself to breath normally.

The Cosy Canal Boat Dream

'Walking Sam before we open up the yard.' He was currently ferreting around by the water's edge. 'Why are you here?'

Nell felt her thumping heart settle, 'Now you'll think I've lost the plot, but I was sharing my news with Ollie.' Nell stared straight at him, trying to gauge his reaction.

'News?'

'Having slept on it, I'm definitely going to bid for the Old Picture House.'

'Nell, that's great. All systems go, then?'

'All systems go,' she smiled.

'And I don't think you've lost the plot. I talk to my granddad all the time,' he smiled, warmly towards Nell, 'Shall we walk back? Are you ready?'

She nodded and stood up, 'I am.' Giving a last, fleeting glance towards the lake Nell felt a sense of calmness, the decision was made. She was going to do this.

Nell linked her arm through Guy's and they ambled back over the bridge in silence towards the towpath. Sam ran up ahead, nose to the ground, running in and out of the bushes.

'So the sleep did you good, then?'

'Yes, but my head's a whirl with builders, plumbers, electricians ... the list is endless.'

'You have to win the auction first,' Guy grinned at her enthusiasm.

'Pah! That's the easy bit, the hard work comes after.' With a spring in her step Nell sounded ridiculously hopeful and she was pinning all her hopes on winning that auction. 'And the flip of the coin never lets me down.'

Guy looked at her, confused.

'When in doubt, flip a coin, best of three.'
'Seriously.'
'Yes seriously!'
'You are a mad one, I'll give you that!'
'Heads I bid, tails I didn't and heads it was, so I'm bidding,' Nell said, beaming from ear to ear. The only slight niggle in the back of her mind was Gilly, but she'd made the conscious decision to go and talk to her mum about it as soon as possible and put whatever worries she had to bed.

Guy stopped walking and stared at her. He took both of her hands, his gaze bore deep into her eyes, 'In my book everything happens for reason and I think it will be a huge success with the amazing Nell Andrews in charge.'

'So you think I'm amazing, do you?'

Nell pressed her lips together with a secret smile.

He closed the distance between them and wrapped his arms around her, then squeezed her hand reassuringly. 'I do indeed, amazing, gorgeous, funny ...' his words were soft in her ear and her whole body tingled in anticipation. He stroked her hair, then traced his finger along the side of her chin, finally tilting her lips towards his.

'You're not so bad yourself, Guy Cornish. Are you going to kiss me?'

'I am,' giving her a sheepish grin. He didn't need to be asked twice.

'You are just perfect,' he said, lowering his lips to hers. Nell couldn't wait any longer, she grasped his hair and their lips locked, gently at first, but then harder. She closed her eyes and basked in the pleasure of his touch. Her heart

The Cosy Canal Boat Dream

constricted at how gorgeous he was and swelled with happiness for the first time in ages. In such a short space of time, she was falling hook, line and sinker for Guy Cornish.

Chapter 22

An hour later Nell walked into the deli to find Bea dancing around the kitchen and miming to the radio. She stopped in mid-flow and clapped her hands when she spotted Nell, 'Let's get this deli open for business.'

'You're in a good mood!' Nell exclaimed, raising her eyebrows while draping her coat over the back of the chair.

'I've had a cream meringue for my breakfast and at this precise moment I don't feel sick, which is a good start to the day.'

Nell heard her phone beeping from her coat pocket and quickly glanced at the message before tying on her apron. She flicked her hair over her shoulder, chewed her lip and smiled to herself before sliding the phone back into her pocket. Bea watched in amusement.

'Mmm ... what's going on with you? You look different, kind of rested, happy, in fact absolutely glowing,' she mused, 'Anything you want to tell me?'

'Me? No, I've got absolutely nothing to tell.'

Bea tutted, 'You so have. I know that look! How was your dinner date last night?'

The Cosy Canal Boat Dream

'Dinner date?' said Nell, acting coyly.

'Yes, the dinner date with the gorgeous Guy.'

'It wasn't a dinner date,' Nell avoided Bea's inquisitive stare as she piled the freshly baked scones on to a tray and tried not to smile.

'Did he cook you dinner?'

Nell smiled remembering the state of the kitchen and Guy's attempt at muddling together the venison pie.

'He did,' Nell carried the scones over to the counter and slid them into the glass cabinet, 'They smell delicious. Have those ones got chocolate chips melted into them?'

'They have and stop trying to change the subject,' Bea said, switching the deli sign to open.

'I wasn't.'

A flash of annoyance passed over Bea's face, 'You are trying to avoid my questions.'

Nell suppressed a smile, 'I'm not,' she answered as her whole body tingled remembering the kiss she'd shared with Guy.

'There's more to this than meets the eye.'

'There isn't!' Nell was reluctant to share how she felt – she didn't want to tempt fate and it was all very new for her.

'I've seen the way he looks at you!' Bea insisted.

'What do you mean?' Nell asked her.

'You like him as much as he likes you.'

'Maybe.'

'I knew it, I knew it!' squealed Bea.

'Or maybe we are just friends?' Nell teased.

'Just friends? No man and woman are ever just friends.

Name a man who you are just friends with?' Bea stuck her hands on her hips and waited for Nell to answer.

There was silence for a couple of seconds.

'See you can't!'

Nell racked her brains then wagged her finger at Bea in jest, 'A-ha! Yes I can ... Nathan!' Nell stuck out her tongue at Bea and looked smug with her answer.

'He doesn't count, I'm married to him!' Bea laughed and smacked Nell's arm playfully. 'So, what did Guy cook you?'

'Beans on toast.'

'Don't be ridiculous!'

Nell laughed heartily, 'I swear it's the truth, the whole truth and nothing but the truth!'

Bea rolled her eyes, 'What time did you get home?'

'Eleven ... ish.'

'How many bottles of wine did you drink?'

'Two and a bit.'

'Did he walk you home?'

'Yes.' Nell could feel herself blushing. Guy had insisted he walked her back to the 'Nollie'. They'd walked side by side along the towpath when Nell had stumbled slightly. Guy had simply stretched out his hand and grasped hers and they had carried on walking. They'd paused by the railings just outside the picture house and stared up at the stars in the clear night sky.

'Quite something, isn't it?' said Guy, pulling Nell in close, his arm draped around her shoulder as he pointed out the different star constellations in the sky.

'Yes', Nell had whispered back, feeling the first flush of love.

The Cosy Canal Boat Dream

'Let's get you home,' he'd said, and when they'd arrive at the 'Nollie', he'd kissed her and watched her climb safely on to the boat. Once her head had hit the pillow she'd fallen into a contented sleep.

'Have you kissed him?' Bea carried on with her questions.

'Bea, I feel like a teenager answering to my mother!' Nell objected.

'Have you kissed him?'

Nell rolled her eyes, laughing.

'I knew it! I knew it! I'm so pleased for you. It's about time you put a smile back on that face of yours.'

'You know nothing, we talked figures ...'

'Oh, I bet you did!' chuckled Bea.

'Bea! Stop it! Figures as in costs for the Old Picture House.'

'Ha, I'm only teasing you. I'm just jealous. I spent the night browsing through the Mothercare website looking at prams, which was mind-boggling.'

'I know you're teasing,' Nell paused, 'Talking of mothers, where's mine?'

Gilly was already half an hour late, which wasn't like her and Nell wandered over to the door and peered up the towpath.

'Here she is, cycling up the towpath now,' Nell said relieved. She heard her mum ring the bell on her bike and wave at Guy, who was talking to a man outside the boatyard.

'You're late,' Nell jokingly tapped her watch.

Gilly pulled on her brakes and climbed off her bike.

'You look awful,' Nell said, her heart pounding with anticipation. 'Is everything all right?'

'I need a good strong cuppa,' she said, 'It's not been the best morning so far.'

Gilly leant against the counter and took a deep breath, 'I know there was nothing I could do, but when I checked on the kittens this morning, I found Rosie dead in the basket.'

'The mother?' Nell swallowed her own sadness, 'That's awful.'

'Oh God, I feel a bit emotional, what an absolute shame,' Bea said, standing beside Gilly and Nell. 'The poor thing.'

'What are you going to do now?'

'That's why I'm late. I've just cycled over to the vet's to ask for advice.'

'And?' Nell asked.

'He said I need to keep the orphaned kittens warm, make a nest in a small box and line it with towels to help them conserve their body heat. I've left them mewing in a box, which I've placed at the foot of the Aga.'

Nell nodded, 'Good idea.'

'Then he's given me some kitten formula and syringes. I have to feed them that way until they can go on to solids next week some time, which isn't that long now.'

'Is that when I can take one off your hands?' Bea asked, picking up the deli phone, which was ringing.

'If you're sure, Bea?'

She covered the mouthpiece, 'Yes, very sure.'

'Anyway, there's nothing I can do now except my best.' Nell gave her mum a hug and an offer to help in any way she could.

'Right, let's get my coat hung up,' Gilly said, throwing it over her arm and walking around the back of the counter.

The Cosy Canal Boat Dream

They both looked up towards Bea, who'd placed the receiver back down and was now staring towards Gilly and Nell.

'You okay?' Nell asked, noticing that Bea had turned a ghastly white colour.

She hesitated, 'That was my sister.'

'Fern? Have you spoken to her since that night?' Nell said, stopping in her tracks.

Bea shook her head, 'Over four years ago now.'

'What does she want?'

'It's my mother, she's dying ...' Bea took a breath, 'She's asking to see me one last time.'

Nell knew everything about that night four years ago. Bea and Nathan had been so distressed, especially when they'd made the decision to never speak to either Fern or her mum again. Nell knew Bea would be feeling apprehensive but knew she wouldn't forgive herself if she didn't see her mum one last time, even if this did mean crossing paths with Fern once again.

'Whatever you decide, I'll be here for you,' said Nell. And if you need to take some time off, I can keep this place afloat in the meantime.'

'Thanks, Nell. I don't know what I'd do without you.'

For a moment, Nell felt a pang of guilt. Here she was getting excited about fulfilling her own dreams and hopefully renovating the Old Picture House just as Bea needed her support. Nell knew the next few weeks were going to be a strain for all of them.

Chapter 23

Jacob stood rooted to the spot on the jetty and stared up at 'The Old Geezer'. Fred Bramley was sitting on a blue-check deckchair on the deck of his boat, his rod cast in the water while his hands were cupped tightly around a mug of tea.

Jacob's watchful eyes followed Fred's every move as he reeled in his line and leant forward to examine the hook.

'Have you caught anything?' Jacob shouted towards Fred, who spun round and locked eyes with the little boy.

He tweaked his cap from over his eyes, 'Not this time,' he grumbled, casting the line back in the water. 'These fish must be still sleeping under those river banks.'

Jacob chuckled.

'Shouldn't you be at school, young lad?'

Jacob shook his head, 'I've been poorly.'

'You best get yourself inside then, lad, keep yourself warm.'

Fred noticed Nathan talking to Guy outside the boatyard and watched for a split second as Jacob clomped back towards his dad, who was now walking towards him. He grasped his hand and they pushed the door open to the deli and disap-

The Cosy Canal Boat Dream

peared inside. Jacob hovered in the deli window and waved at Fred, who tipped his flat cap once more in acknowledgement.

'What are you doing here?' Bea was amazed to see Nathan and Jacob up and out so early. Immediately she pressed a hand to his forehead, 'Oh, you do feel a little better.'

'What's up, little man?' asked Nell.

Nathan and Jacob followed them into the kitchen.

'I'm poorly, Aunty Nellie. I feel hot, but Daddy wanted an English breakfast muffin and promised me a doughnut for later.'

'Oh, he did now, did he?' Nell laughed, reaching for the grill pan, 'I'll get to work on that in a moment.'

'Cup of tea too?' asked Gilly, holding up the kettle.

'You read my mind,' he smiled.

'Jacob, go and sit at the desk. Do you think you can manage some toast?' asked Bea, retrieving the emergency colouring book and pencils from the desk drawer and putting them down in front of him. 'Here, do some colouring.' Jacob nodded and sat down quietly while Gilly, Nell and Bea congregated in the middle of the kitchen.

'Are you okay? You look a little upset,' Nathan narrowed his eyes towards his wife.

'I was going to give you a quick ring mid-morning when it had quietened down.'

'Why what's up?'

She took a breath. 'Fern rang.'

Immediately Bea could see the look on Nathan's face change, 'What does she want?'

Bea hesitated and shuffled Nathan to the other side of the

kitchen away from Jacob, 'It's Mum,' she took a deep breath, 'She's dying and wants to see me one last time.'

Nathan raised his eyebrows, 'How are you feeling about that?'

'I don't actually know,' she said, staring into Nathan's eyes.

Nell tapped Bea on the arm, 'I'll go and help Gilly in the front.'

'Thanks, Nell.'

Bea turned back towards Nathan.

'I have to admit I wasn't expecting that,' he said.

'Me neither.'

'How did she sound?'

'Very matter of fact and straight to the point. Mum's at home.'

Bea wrapped her arms around Nathan's waist and he hugged her tight, kissing the top of her head.

'I remember that night like it was yesterday.'

'I do too. I vowed I would never speak to her again.'

'Is she still with Pete?'

'I've no idea, I never asked. It took me by surprise just hearing her voice again.'

'How long has your mum got? I'm assuming it's cancer.'

Bea nodded and wiped away a tear.

'Hey don't cry, none of this is your fault.' Nathan reached inside his pocket and handed Bea a tissue.

'I know, I just wish it could have been different. I always thought Mum becoming a grandmother might have mellowed her a little. If Dad was still here I think he would have seen sense about this whole situation.'

The Cosy Canal Boat Dream

'But he's not and we made the decision not to speak to either your mum or Fern again after that night. We made that choice together.'

'I know,' Bea sighed. 'But she's only got days left to live, Nathan. She's deteriorating by the second, Fern said.'

'Then you need to make a decision sooner rather than later, then if you want to see her one last time you've still got the chance. Whatever you decide, I'll stand by you. You know that, don't you?'

Bea gazed into her husband's eyes, 'I couldn't imagine life without you.' She kissed him tenderly on the lips.

'It's a good job you don't have to, then, isn't it?' he said warmly.

'Come on, I'd best help the girls. I'll mull it over and make a decision tonight.'

'Okay, now keep that chin up.'

'I will, I promise,' said Bea, turning back towards Jacob.

'Where's he gone? Where's Jacob?'

Bea's eyes spun around the room but Jacob was nowhere to be seen.

'He'll be out the front with Nell and Gilly. Come on, let's check. Oh and I never did get my breakfast muffin,' he said, looking longingly towards the grill pan.

'Always thinking of your stomach,' she said grinning, swiping the tea towel in his direction.

They pushed open the kitchen door and saw Gilly and Nell standing behind the counter, 'That was a mad five minutes, already the pasties and Danish pastries are dwindling.'

Christie Barlow

Nathan looked around the shop, 'Where's Jacob?'

'In the back with you,' Nell answered, chucking some money in the till.

Nathan met Bea's worried stare, 'He's not wandered out here?'

'I've not seen him,' Gilly answered, 'Is everything okay?'

'I'm not sure, I'll check the toilet,' said Bea, hurrying towards them. 'He's not in here,' Bea's urgent tone rang out.

Everything seemed to stand still for a moment.

Gilly shot Nell a quizzical look, 'Where is he?'

Nell shrugged but was determined not to panic, 'He can't have gone far,' she said in a calm voice. As much as Nell sounded in control, nothing was going to calm Bea's thumping heart.

'I've not got a good feeling about this,' said Bea, exhaling a shaky breath, her eyes brimmed with unshed tears, her mouth had gone bone dry, 'Where is he?'

Nathan cleared his throat, 'Like Nell said, he can't have gone far.' He moved towards the door and everyone followed him. 'I'll stay here in case he comes back,' Gilly said, hovering by the counter.

Bea, Nathan and Nell spilled out of the deli on to the path. They all scanned the wharf in every direction but there was no sign of him. There were a few shoppers milling about and people cleaning the decks of their boats. 'Hey, have you seen a boy – about this big?' Nathan stopped a passer-by. They shook their head, 'Sorry no.'

A huge dollop of fear descended all around them.

Nathan raked his hand through his hair, the anxious expression written all over his face.

The Cosy Canal Boat Dream

'Hey, where's the fire?' Guy shouted over, leaning against the doors of the boatyard.

'It's Jacob ... he's missing.' Nell bellowed back.

Guy stared at her for a split second before quickly locking the doors to the yard and bounding towards them with Sam speedily following behind. 'I'll help you look. How long has he been gone?' he asked, standing by Nell's side.

'Five minutes max, maybe?'

Tears were pricking Bea's eyes, 'He was here one minute and gone the next. It's my stupid fault, I was so engrossed in talking to Nathan.'

'It's no one's fault,' replied Nell in a sympathetic tone, rubbing her arm, 'He can't have gone far.' Thankfully she sounded a lot calmer than she felt and her voice didn't falter.

'What if he's fallen into the water?'

They rushed towards the railings and each and every one of them scanned the water, but they couldn't see anything. 'Or worse, someone's snatched him.'

'Think rationally. He was in the kitchen, no one enticed him out,' said Nathan. 'Let's split up.'

'Good plan,' Guy answered.

'Guy can you check the shower block, mate? Nell, you check the laundry room, Bea ...' he grabbed both her arms, 'I promise you, he'll be okay.'

'How can you promise me that? If anyone has hurt him,' she pulled away from Nathan's hold. The fear stabbing in the pit of her stomach.

'You check up and down the jetty and knock on the boats, see if anyone's spotted him.'

While Nathan was organising the party, Gilly had checked every inch of The Melting Pot. She popped her head out of the door, 'He's definitely not playing hide and seek in here.'

Bea's knees began to tremble as she stumbled towards the furthest jetty and began to search. 'Jacob,' she wailed, her heart pounding.

They all hurried in different directions.

Nell heard Guy shouting in the shower block, but there was no sign of him. Nell darted towards the laundry room and frantically turned over every basket of washing and checked inside every washing machine, which she knew, deep down, was daft, but what if he was just playing hide and seek?

'Are you in here, Jacob?' But there was no answer.

'Nothing,' said Nell grimly, looking at Guy as they met back up on the towpath. 'There's no sign of him anywhere.'

'We need to phone the police,' Guy said with authority, 'We can't leave it any longer.'

Nell sobbed, she knew Guy was right and took her mobile phone from her pocket.

'I wouldn't wish this on my worst enemy,' she wept.

'Is everything okay?'

Guy and Nell spun round and locked eyes with a wizened face which was staring back at them both. His face was a map of wrinkles, his blue eyes framed by thick white busy eyebrows and his stubble chin sprouted white whiskers. The old man was dressed in a flamboyant purple suit, sporting a bright-red checked cravat and was leaning on a cane.

'My apologies, I recognise you ... but I'm not sure where from?' Guy racked his brains, but nothing.

The Cosy Canal Boat Dream

'I believe, young man, you saved my life,' his tone was soft and friendly, 'I can't thank you both enough.' He stretched out his hand, 'Lloyd.'

Guy hurriedly shook his hand, 'Lloyd, please, forgive us, I don't mean to be rude but I'm just about to ring the police, a child has gone missing.'

'Would that be a little boy in a pair of bright-yellow wellies?'

All eyes locked on Lloyd.

'Yes, yes, it would. I'm Nell,' she said, shaking his hand, 'I was there with Guy, on your boat, when the paramedics arrived. Have you seen him ... Jacob?'

'I saw a little boy about this high,' he gestured with his cane, 'jumped on to that boat about five minutes ago.'

Nell and Guy swung towards 'The Old Geezer,' and there were Jacob's wellies strewn on the mat on the deck of Fred Bramley's boat.

'Look! Are they Jacob's?'

'Yes,' Nell's heart thumped, 'Bea, here, Nathan,' she yelled as loudly as she could.

Nathan and Bea's footsteps came thundering up the wharf. 'You got him?'

'Thank you so much,' Nell enthused, relief flowing through her body as she smiled up at Lloyd.

'No problem at all, young lady. You go and get the boy.' With that Lloyd waggled his cane in the air, turned and walked away.

'Thanks again,' Guy shouted after him.

Just at that moment the deli swung open, Gilly was clutching the phone, 'It's Fred. He's with him, on his boat. He's just phoned me.'

'Yes, Lloyd spotted him,' shouted Nell as Bea and Nathan pounded the jetty and jumped on to the narrowboat, quickly followed by Nell and Guy, leaving Gilly staring at the man who'd walked off up the wharf and disappeared around the side of the boatyard. Fred opened the door and there was Jacob beaming back at them, wearing Fred's fishing cap and holding his rod.

Bea's heart soared with love for her little boy, the relief was written all over her face as she scooped him up and pressed her lips against his cheek, then hugged him so tight he could barely breathe. 'Don't you ever do that to me again,' she sobbed, her voice wobbly.

'What's the matter, Mummy?'

Bea swallowed and brushed away her tears.

'You disappeared without a word. I've never been so scared.'

'I saw Mr Bramley fishing and wanted to know if he'd caught anything. He thinks I'd make a very good fisherman, especially with my bright-yellow wellies.'

'That you would, without a doubt,' she said smiling at her little boy.

'I telephoned the moment he stepped foot on the boat.'

Nathan touched his arm, 'Thanks Fred.'

Nell crouched down in front of Jacob, 'You had Aunty Nellie worried there for a moment. Promise me you'll always tell someone where you're going.'

'I promise, Aunty Nellie.'

She cupped her hands around his face and kissed him on his forehead.

'Here lad, you take these,' Fred handed him a pile of fishing

The Cosy Canal Boat Dream

magazines, 'You have a look through the pictures and learn all about the fish in our waters.'

'Yes, Mr Bramley. Will you show me how to fish one day?'

'I know a better man for the job,' Fred tipped a wink towards Nathan. 'I think you need to take your son fishing,' Fred said, slapping Nathan on his back.

'Can we, Daddy? Please.' Jacob's eyes were wide with excitement.

'We sure can, son, we sure can.'

Chapter 24

'Well, that was an afternoon and a half,' exclaimed Guy, locking up the yard and turning towards Nell.

'Oh no! You're all teary – come here,' he said.

'I can't stop feeling emotional. I know Jacob's safe but I've never felt panic like that in my life. Goodness knows how Bea must have felt. I was so afraid.' Nell's voice faltered.

Guy clutched at her elbows and could feel her shaking. He moved closer and grasped her hand, 'It's the shock. Let's get you back to the Nollie.'

'I'm thinking we should row across and see Lloyd.' Nell gazed towards the narrowboat on the other side of the marina, 'I felt a bit rude cutting him short like that before, especially when he came to thank us.'

'I know what you mean, but he'll understand ... does that mean you want me getting in that boat again?' Guy looked towards the boat bobbing about in the water.

Nell smiled towards him, 'Let's go and see him.'

Guy sighed, 'The things I do for you, Andrews!'

'I'll make a sailor out of you yet! Shall we take Sam?'

The Cosy Canal Boat Dream

'Best had, he's the real hero here. Come on then ... but let me borrow the life jacket again.'

'I best check with Fred that's it's okay to borrow his boat first. Meet you back here in five.'

As the little rowing boat set sail towards the other side of the marina Nell looked at Guy with amusement, 'See, it's not that bad. Your knuckles aren't as white as last time.'

'You're not funny,' he grinned, watching the oars glide gently through the water. In no time at all the little rowing boat bumped against the narrowboat and Nell tied up the rope on to the wrought-iron ring, to stop them from floating away.

Sam bounded out of the boat on to the deck, leaving Nell steadying Guy as his nerves sprang back into action by the rocking motion.

So much for being the macho man, Guy thought to himself.

'See, you're in one piece,' smiled Nell.

'Just about – like I said before, the things I do for you.'

Nell rapped on the door and within seconds Lloyd opened the door.

'Sorry,' apologised Nell, 'I hope we aren't disturbing you?'

'No, not at all, come in ... come in,' he said in a jolly manner, 'You are the first visitors to the boat, except for the paramedics, that is. Let me get you both a drink and some water for the dog.'

'This is Sam, the real hero of the hour.'

Lloyd turned round and patted Sam on the head, 'I can't thank you all enough. Have a seat, cup of tea?'

'Only if you have time,' said Guy.

'I have all the time in the world.'

Lloyd placed the kettle on the gas and took the mugs out of the cupboard.

'We've not seen you around these parts before,' said Nell, distracted by all the film posters pinned to the wall of the boat.

'I'm here on business, just for a few weeks.'

'It's a very interesting boat you have here,' said Guy, intrigued.

'Ah-ha, the posters. I'm a huge fan of the film industry.'

'And the photographs,' Guy pointed towards the wall.

'My wife, she was an actress, starred in the West End.'

'How fabulous,' said Nell, 'Is that her there?'

Lloyd flicked a glance towards the photo that Nell was pointing at.

'Yes it is.'

'She's beautiful.'

'Does she still perform?' asked Guy.

'Unfortunately not. Annie passed away nearly thirty years ago but I couldn't bear to part with any of her possessions.' Lloyd slid two mugs of tea towards Nell and Guy before placing a bowl of water next to Sam, who'd flopped down under the table.

'Have you always lived on this boat? It's got a very theatrical name.'

'No, I've lived abroad for a while, but always kept this little thing ticking over. A friend of mine has been looking after it, but when I knew I was coming back home, me and my boat

The Cosy Canal Boat Dream

had to be reunited, and then I go collapsing, worrying the locals.' Lloyd rolled his eyes, 'I'm so sorry about that, I didn't mean to frighten you.'

'We're just glad you are alright.'

'I am indeed,' he said, loosening his cravat from around his neck. 'So where are you from, lad?' he directed his question at Guy, 'You don't sound very local to me.'

'Ireland, I'm here for a short visit. It's my brother Ed who owns the boatyard, but Nell here, she's a proper local!'

'Yes Little Rock Marina, born and bred,' she smiled towards Lloyd. 'I work in the deli – my friend Bea owns it. And I live on the Nollie, jetty number ten.'

'Interesting name for a boat.'

'Nell and Ollie put together. My husband Ollie passed away.'

'I'm sorry to hear that, lass.'

Nell smiled towards him, 'Thank you.'

'I know you said you were here on business, but were you originally from around these parts?' asked Guy.

'I was,' smiled Lloyd, 'Many moons ago.'

'Nell here is thinking of bidding on the Old Picture House.'

'The one in the marina.' Lloyd sat up with interest.

'That's the one,' answered Nell, sipping her drink.

'Not to bulldoze, surely,' Lloyd narrowed his eyes at her.

'Of course not! It holds some great memories for me and I want to restore it in my husband's memory – maybe make it a place for the community to share.'

'Well, I wish you all the luck in the world. That sounds like a wonderful idea, a great community project, something all generations can enjoy.'

Christie Barlow

'That's my thoughts exactly.'

'And if you ever need any contacts in the film industry I still have a few I could put you in touch with. They could help with the décor of the place, it's the least I can do.'

'That would be brilliant, thank you. Fingers crossed I win first.'

'Fingers crossed,' Lloyd crossed his fingers and smiled towards Nell.

'I could sit and talk for hours, but we mustn't keep you,' said Nell, not wanting to outstay her welcome.

Lloyd got up and shook both of their hands, 'It was great to meet you both and thanks again for calling the emergency services.'

'I'd say anytime, but let's hope it doesn't happen again,' grinned Guy.

Lloyd cupped his hands around Guy's and shook his hand heartily.

As they climbed back on to the boat, Lloyd waved them off.

'What a character,' exclaimed Guy, saluting Lloyd as he sat down on the slats inside the boat.

'And what a lovely offer of help for the Old Picture House – if I win of course.'

Within a few minutes they bumped lightly into the jetty on the other side of the marina. Nell climbed out and steadied the boat for Guy.

'Where have you two been?'

Nell spun round to see Gilly poised on her bike staring at them.

The Cosy Canal Boat Dream

'We've been to visit Lloyd – you know, the man who Guy found collapsed.'

At the mere mention of his name, Gilly stiffened.

'I thought I said it was best not to disturb him.'

'There's nothing wrong with introducing ourselves and making sure he's okay.'

'You can't go bothering folk.'

'Mum, there's nothing to worry about, he was glad of the company. His wife used to be an actress and the boat is packed with all photographs of her way back in the day, not to mention the film posters. He's offered his help if I win the Old Picture House. He still has contacts in the industry.'

'You're not still toying with that idea, are you?'

Nell bit her lip, frustration battling through her body, 'What's up with you, Mum?' she asked defensively, still not understanding why her mum was so dead against the idea.

'Nothing,' she mumbled, putting her foot on the pedal of her bike, 'I must get back to the kittens.'

Nell and Guy watched Gilly ride off up the wharf.

'It's not just my imagination, is it? She's definitely against this auction,' Nell turned towards Guy.

'Maybe she's just worried you are biting off more than you can chew.' He put his hand in the small of her back and guided her through the railings.

'I'm not convinced,' she answered, watching Gilly disappear out of sight. 'I'm not convinced at all.'

Chapter 25

After Jacob was found safe and sound the only thing that was preying on Bea's mind was the phone call with Fern. She'd spent the whole time mulling over the situation and was still no nearer to making a decision. She lay in bed with the early-morning sunlight poking through the gap in the curtains and sighed.

'That's a big sigh,' Nathan said, popping her a cup of tea on the bedside table.

'I'm just torn.'

'I know,' he sat on the edge of the bed next to her and gently pushed her hair out of her eyes, 'You tossed and turned all night.'

Bea sat up, pulled her knees to her chest and cupped her hands around her drink.

'Why is life so complicated?' she paused, 'We were trundling along quite nicely and then, wham, another drama.'

'Blooming families, eh? Just think, we've managed without them for the past two years,' said Nathan softly.

'I'll never forgive Fern, never.' Bea's eyes were full of turmoil.

The Cosy Canal Boat Dream

'Neither of us will. It's us now. It's this family that means the world to me.'

'Me too, but I think I need to see Mum one last time. I'm not sure I'd forgive myself if I didn't.'

Nathan nodded. He'd had a feeling that would be the case. 'So, the question is when, and do you want me to come with you?'

'Do you mind?'

'Of course I don't mind.'

'I'm sure Nell will look after Jacob for us.'

'I'm sure she will. Are you going to let Fern know you're going?'

Bea shook her head, 'No, I don't want to increase my chances of bumping into her.'

'When do you want to go?'

'Tonight, after work, get it over and done with.'

Nathan kissed his wife lightly on the top of her head before standing up, 'I'll ring Nell now and ask her if she's free.'

'Thanks, Nat,' she said, as she watched him disappear out of the bedroom.

Bea sunk back under the duvet and exhaled. Her stomach was already twisting in a thousand knots and she felt anxious about even setting foot in that house again.

She brushed away a tear from her face. Bea was the younger of the two sisters and Fern had always been the golden child in her parents' eyes. A straight-A student with plans to go to Oxford University.

Bea's relationship with her mum had always been a challenging one. Bea's talent lay in a passion for cooking, but her parents frowned upon her career choice, her mother's words still rang in her ears, 'You want to go to catering college? Don't be ridiculous. When has cooking ever paid the bills? You need to get yourself an office job, something in admin. That would pay you a decent wage.'

Bea had pretended to land a job in an office but had actually attended catering college for two years while supporting herself with a bar job in the evening.

Bea had hoped that once her father had died and Jacob was born that her mother might have mellowed a little, but she never had. Bea could never do anything right in her eyes.

It had all come to a head four years ago, a night she'd tried to block from her mind.

Nathan interrupted her thoughts, 'Yes, Nell can look after Jacob, she said it would be her pleasure,' he said popping his head around the door and giving Bea a smile. 'Come on, you need to get up.'

'I know,' she said, finally throwing back the duvet and heaving herself out of bed.

'How you feeling? Any sickness?'

She shook her head, 'None, I'm actually feeling quite human this morning.'

'That's good to hear. You jump in the shower and I'll make Jacob his breakfast.'

'Thank you.'

'And Bea, don't worry about tonight, just say goodbye, do what you have to do and tomorrow we can put all this behind us once more.'

Nathan put his arms out and Bea fell into them.

The Cosy Canal Boat Dream

'Just for the record, Bea Green, no one will ever hurt my family again.'

'And just for the record, Nathan Green, I love you more than life itself.'

'You too, now best foot forward and pin a smile on that beautiful face. We have each other and that's all that matters.'

Chapter 26

Standing on the driveway and looking up at 1970s semi-detached house on the corner of Heath Road, Bea felt as if she'd never lived there, her life had moved on so much. Nathan put his arm around his wife's shoulder and squeezed her tight, 'You ready?'

She nodded and pushed open the garden gate. 'I think so,' she said, her voice shaky. The upstairs curtains were drawn, but Bea spotted a movement in the downstairs living room. Taking a deep breath she knocked on the door and waited. Her heart was pounding as she heard footsteps echoing down the hallway.

They were greeted by a nurse, 'Hello, can I help you?' she asked politely.

'Hi,' Bea said, swallowing down a lump, 'I'm Bea, Dot's daughter.' The nurse dipped her head in acknowledgement and opened the door wide. 'And I'm Claudia. Pleased to meet you.'

Nathan and Bea stepped into the hallway.

'How is she?' Bea asked.

'There's not much time left,' answered Claudia softly. 'She's becoming weaker by the second.'

The Cosy Canal Boat Dream

'Is anyone else here?' Bea asked, glancing towards the living room.

The nurse shook her head, 'No, just me. Your sister normally arrives just after seven,' she replied, glancing at her watch, 'There's another half hour or so until she's due.'

The relief surged through Bea's body.

'Do you want to go up and see her?' Claudia hovered at the bottom of the stairs and Bea locked eyes with Nathan.

'Do you want me to come with you?' asked Nathan.

'Will you wait outside the room and give me five minutes?'

'Of course,' he nodded.

Bea wearily climbed the stairs, grasped the door handle and kissed Nathan on the cheek before slowly pushing it open. The curtains were drawn and the lighting was low. Bea gazed at her mother lying in the bed. She looked so frail, so old, a shell of the person she remembered. Her breathing was laboured, the rasp echoing around the room. The pungent smell hit Bea as she perched on the chair at the side of her bed. Her mother lay still, her mouth opened and closed but her eyes were shut.

Claudia appeared behind her, 'The yawning is usual. It's a natural response to draw in more oxygen.'

Bea nodded, she hadn't known what to expect. She watched as Claudia checked her pulse and wiped her brow.

'Hold her hand, talk to her, she'll know you are here.'

She said softly, resting her hand on Bea's shoulder. 'Can I get you anything?'

Bea shook her head, her eyes brimming with tears. How had it ever come to this?

'Keep her lips moist,' she said, handing Bea a damp cloth, 'She may feel a little cold too.'

Bea nodded and gently grasped her mother's hand, the tears now gently rolling down her cheeks.

'I'll leave you for a moment.'

'Thank you,' replied Bea, her voice barely a whisper. She watched as Claudia left the room.

'Mum it's me, Bea,' her voice wavered.

Bea thought she felt a slight squeeze of her hand. 'Can you hear me?'

Suddenly, Bea was alarmed by the rattling noise in the back of her throat. She clasped both hands around her mum's, 'I do love you, you know,' she said softly, following Claudia's lead and dabbing her lips with the damp cloth.

'Nat, are you there?'

'Yes,' he answered, walking into the room and crouching by Bea's side.

'I can feel her slipping away.' Bea sobbed quietly. 'Will you go and bring Claudia?'

He squeezed his wife's shoulder and left the room.

Bea held her mother's hand tightly as she gave a long out-breath followed by another intake of breath a few seconds later.

'No, don't go,' wept Bea, 'Please don't go.'

Bea looked up to see Claudia and Nathan hurrying back into the room.

'I think she's gone.'

Claudia checked her pulse, 'I'm so sorry.'

The tears continued to fall down Bea's cheeks as Nathan wrapped his arms around his wife.

Chapter 27

Nell sat huddled on the 'Nollie', playing a game of snakes and ladders with Jacob.

'Whoosh, down the ladder again, Aunty Nellie!' Jacob giggled once more.

'It's not my day today, is it?' she grinned, as Jacob threw a six and landed on the final square.

'I've won! I've won!'

Nell ruffled his hair, 'You certainly have. How about a jammy dodger to celebrate?'

'Yes please!'

Nell heard a soft laugh behind her. She spun round to see Guy standing in the doorway, 'What's all the commotion?' he smiled.

'Jacob here, has beaten me at snakes and ladders ... again!'

'Well done! Can I come in?'

'Of course,' Nell smiled, 'No Sam?'

Guy shook his head, 'He's keeping Ed company. I left my phone at work and just nipped back to get it.'

'Cup of tea?' Nell asked, filling up the kettle.

'If you have time?'

Nell smiled, 'Oh and a jammy dodger,' she said, sliding the plate of biscuits on to the table.

Guy sat down next to Jacob, while he was already chomping through his first biscuit.

'I've just seen Lloyd,' Guy said, taking a mug of tea from Nell. 'He was standing outside the Old Picture House.'

'Did you speak to him?'

Guy shook his head, 'No, he didn't see me.'

'I was thinking about having another chat with him about his contacts. I'm quite intrigued by his wife being an actress and his links to this place. He didn't actually say why he was back in the area.'

'Good idea. How does he get to his side of the marina?'

'I noticed a small boat floating at the back of his boat or he could walk the long way round.'

Guy nodded.

'Was that nice?' Nell turned her attention back to Jacob, whose hand was hovering over the biscuit plate once more.

'I think I need another one, Aunty Nellie, so I can make my mind up!'

The two of them exchanged mischievous grins.

'You, Jacob Green, are a little rascal,' she wagged her finger at him in jest.

'What do you think, Guy? Is he allowed another one?'

'I think so, he's a growing boy,' grinned Guy, while Jacob high-fived him. 'So, what are you doing here, little man?' Guy asked him as he moved the counters on the board back to the beginning.

'Just spending time with his Aunty Nellie,' Nell answered,

The Cosy Canal Boat Dream

while checking the message that had just landed on her phone.

Nell stared at the screen and Guy noticed she looked a little alarmed.

'You okay?'

She nodded, then looked towards Guy,

'Jacob, would you nip into the bedroom?' she asked 'And fetch my handbag?'

He saluted and trundled off in the direction of the bedroom.

'What's up?'

'It's Bea's mum,' said Nell, keeping her voice to a whisper, 'She's passed away this evening.'

'I'm sorry to hear that.'

'They haven't spoken for a few years, but it's hard for her. Jacob doesn't know, but she's on her way over to collect him and I think she's in need of a strong drink ... only she's pregnant.'

'Would it help if I take him over to the yard for half an hour? Give you some space?'

'Would you mind?' asked Nell, feeling thankful that Guy had offered.

Guy shook his head, 'Not at all, I've even spotted a couple of fishing rods in the office at the yard. We can have a look at those.'

'Thanks Guy,' she touched his arm affectionately.

'Right, young man, would you like to go and check out a couple of fishing rods at the yard with Guy for twenty minutes?'

Jacob's eyes grew wide, 'Would I ever!' he squealed, grabbing his coat and stuffing another jammy dodger in his pocket.

'I saw that, Jacob Green!'

Nell watched them stride up the wharf and out of view. She thought to herself how quickly Guy had slotted into her life and how much she loved his company. Offering to look after Jacob was such a kind thing to do and she trusted him implicitly. She switched the kettle back on and ten minutes later she heard footsteps echoing up the jetty.

Nell looked up to see a tear-stained face peering around the door.

'Oh Bea, I am so sorry.' Nell flung out her arms and wrapped them around her friend.

'I never thought my day would turn out like this,' she forced a smile through her tears and sat down.

'You okay, Nathan?' asked Nell, pressing a swift kiss to his cheek. He slid off his coat and scooted on to the bench next to Bea.

'Yes, I'm fine,' he said softly.

'Cuppa?'

They both nodded, 'Where's Jacob?' asked Bea, spinning her head around the 'Nollie'.

'Guy's showing him a couple of fishing rods over at the yard. Hope that's alright?'

Bea nodded, 'I've no idea what to tell him.' Her lips began to wobble and she stared at her handbag, twisting the strap, then sighed.

Nell's heart went out to her.

The Cosy Canal Boat Dream

'Do you want to talk about it?'

Bea paused for a second and Nathan slid his arm around his wife's shoulders and squeezed her.

She took a deep breath and met Nell's gaze, 'Oh, Nell, it was awful, it was so sad.'

Her eyes brimmed with tears.

Nell placed a cup of tea in front of them both and sat down next to them.

'I'll be honest, I don't know what I was expecting.' She took a breath. Bea sniffled and Nell passed her a tissue.

'Our relationship was always challenging, but it didn't mean I didn't love her. We just didn't have that close a relationship.'

Nell felt sorry for Bea. Her own relationship with her mum was one of friendship, they enjoyed shopping trips and lunches together but she knew Bea had always longed for the same, but it just wasn't there.

Nathan squeezed his wife's hand, 'But you were there at the end.'

'I was – we were.'

'Did she know you were there?' Nell asked tentatively.

Bea look up at Nathan, 'I think so, but it was hard to tell. I thought she'd squeezed my hand, but she couldn't speak or open her eyes.'

'I'm sure she would have known.'

Bea nodded, 'I am glad I was there – it was just difficult. I never got to say what I really wanted to say or try and put the situation right.'

'You did put it right – you went to say your goodbyes. Did you see Fern?'

Bea shook her head, 'The nurse said she was due any moment, but I didn't want to hang around. The last time I saw her she was ...' Bea winced, 'She was bawling at us through the window all those years ago. I knew we shouldn't have gone out that night. I didn't want to go out that night,' she turned towards Nathan.

'I know, but it's done now,' he said, 'We can't turn back time.'

'That night still seems so surreal,' Bea said as she wiped a tear from her eyes.

'I'm not sure how anyone could leave a child like that to cry, let alone her own nephew' Nell said softly, remembering how distraught Bea had been at the time.

'I think we all felt the same,' replied Nathan. 'It was one thing leaving Jacob to cry like she did, but for Fern's boyfriend to bawl after us like that. He's a bastard child because we weren't married. And Fern did nothing!'

Bea shuddered, 'And for Mum to stand there and do nothing too. He was a child, for God's sake. He wasn't being naughty, he just needed a cuddle. I trusted them to look after Jacob. How could I have ever left him with them again, if that's what they thought of him?' Bea blurted, the hurt still visible on her face.

'We couldn't, we made the right decision to walk away from them.'

For a moment everyone was silent and sipped their tea, 'What about the funeral? Are you going to go?' asked Nell.

Bea flicked her eyes between the pair of them, 'I've no idea. I've not given it a second thought yet or what are we are going to tell Jacob. Do we even need to tell him?'

The Cosy Canal Boat Dream

Nell glanced through the window and spotted Guy and Jacob strolling up the wharf hand in hand. Jacob was hanging on every word Guy was saying, with a huge smile on his face. Guy looked a natural with him. He oozed charisma, his manner was gentle and he would definitely make a good father one day, Nell thought to herself.

'They're coming now,' Nell nodded towards the porthole as Nathan and Bea peered through it.

'I'll nip to the bathroom and clean up my face.' Bea swiftly stood up and disappeared towards the bathroom.

'Let's not say anything in front of Jacob.'

Nell nodded, acknowledging Nathan's request.

'Daddy,' Jacob burst through the door, 'I've had the best time.'

'Glad to hear it.'

'What have you been up to?' Bea reappeared from the bathroom.

'I beat Aunty Nellie at snakes and ladders and then Guy showed me the fishing rods at the yard. They were taller than me!'

Guy clapped Jacob on his back, 'I've got a feeling this one is going to be a natural fisherman one day,' he grinned.

'I think Guy may be right,' laughed Nathan, 'Looks like I might need to get myself a pair of wellies.'

Nell took a moment and watched the banter between her friends. Nell had no idea how anyone could ever think of hurting Jacob – it was unforgiveable as far as she was concerned.

Guy sat down at the table and Jacob slid on to his knee. Guy looked up and caught Nell's eye.

'You alright?' he mouthed at her.

'More than,' she replied warmly.

'Glad to hear it.' His eyes sparkled at her and suddenly Nell felt a huge rush of affection towards him. Without question Guy had stepped up the mark tonight and Nell couldn't thank him enough. Guy was becoming a huge part of her life, in fact it was safe to say she didn't want him going back to Ireland any day soon, if at all.

'Right, Jacob Green, I think it's time to get you home and bathed before bed.'

'Aww,' he protested and wrapped his arms around Nell's neck.

'I'll see you very soon,' she said, before turning towards Bea, 'And you ring me if you need anything.'

'I will, I promise, and thanks for having Jacob and thank you Guy. We'll miss you when you leave us.'

'Leave you?'

'When you go back to Ireland.'

'I might just stick around. I'm getting used to this place, it certainly has its attractions,' he smiled at Nell, who felt herself blush a little.

'That's good to hear.' she said.

Two minutes later, Nell and Guy watched Nathan and Bea walking up the towpath, swinging Jacob between them.

'What a lovely family,' Guy said.

'They are indeed,' replied Nell, placing the empty plates and mugs into the sink.

'Have you ever thought about having a family?' Guy looked up at her.

The Cosy Canal Boat Dream

'I always thought I'd have a couple of kids by now, but then when Ollie passed it just wasn't an option.'

'And now?'

'And now I've realised that time moves on and one day I'd love to be a mother.' She sat down next to Guy.

'I've seen how you are with Jacob and you, Nell Andrews, will make the most fantastic mother one day.'

'What about you? I saw the way you were with Jacob too, such a natural.'

'I've always wanted a family, kids, grandkids, and the more the merrier. I'll always cherish the relationship I have with my parents and grandparents,' Guy answered quite honestly.

'You, without a doubt, would make a fantastic dad.'

'Why, thank you,' Guy leant forward and kissed the tip of Nell's nose. He felt a pang of guilt inside, knowing he hadn't been quite honest with Nell, but as their relationship grew he was finding it harder to tell her the truth. If only he'd been honest with her from the start.

'Do you need to get back?' asked Nell, hoping he would stay.

Guy shook his head, 'No, not at all. No plans whatsoever.'

'Cuppa or a glass of wine?'

'Could murder a glass of red.'

'Me too,' Nell answered happily.

Chapter 28

It was Friday night and Nell watched through the porthole of the 'Nollie' a steady stream of people wandering towards The Waterfront as she blow-dried her hair.

She applied the finishing touches to her make-up and with a swish of black mascara, which complemented her nude shiny lip gloss, she squirted on her perfume and declared herself ready.

Nell waited at the end of the towpath for Bea and two minutes later spotted her walking up the wharf with a huge smile etched on her face.

'You're beginning to waddle,' Nell grinned as Bea approached her.

'Oi, cheeky, I'm not,' she declared, smiling, bringing her hand up to her heart in mock outrage before linking it through Nell's arm.

'I'm only joking! But I'm sure it won't be long!' Nell grinned.

Moments later they pushed open the doors of the pub and were hit by the deafening noise of chatter and the band playing in the corner. It was already jam-packed with thirsty revellers

The Cosy Canal Boat Dream

and they began to nudge their way through the crowds when Bea spotted a table.

'You go and sit down,' Nell insisted, 'I'll bring the drinks over.'

'Just an orange juice for me,' said Bea, throwing her coat over the back of the chair and sitting down at a nearby table while she waited for Nell to return.

Two minutes later Nell placed the drinks down on the table, 'Gosh, I feel warm,' she said, unzipping her coat and unravelling her scarf.

'I was thinking the same,' answered Bea, taking a sip of her drink. 'I wish I was allowed a couple of beers,' grinned Bea.

'It'll soon be over and then you will be too tired to even think about alcohol.'

'Ha! You are absolutely right,' Bea chuckled, remembering that even after Jacob was born she didn't touch a drop until she'd finished breast-feeding.

'I was meaning to ask, have you heard anything about the deli competition yet?'

Bea shook her head, 'No, not a thing.'

'I'm sure you will hear something soon.'

The pair of them listened to the band while they played their next song. Then Nell glanced around the pub and her heart lifted when she spotted Guy and Ed walk through the double swinging doors. Guy stopped as he caught Nell's eye, and his face broke into a warm smile as she waved at him. Nell nudged Bea with her knee under the table.

'They're coming over,' Bea whispered in Nell's ear as they both watched Guy and Ed weave their way through the crowd of drinkers towards their table.

'Hi,' said Guy, leaning across and kissing Nell on the cheek. 'Fancy seeing you here!'

'Fancy indeed,' she replied, inhaling his woody scent, which immediately made her go weak at the knees.

'Have a seat,' Bea gestured to the empty chairs opposite, 'How are you Ed? Feeling okay?'

'Right as rain, a few twinges, but nothing to worry about. Can we get you ladies another drink before we sit down?'

Bea and Nell glanced down at their glasses, 'I'm actually alright for a minute,' answered Bea, 'I need to pace myself. There's only so much orange juice a girl can drink.'

Everyone laughed.

'You poor thing,' Nell squeezed her arm and smiled.

'No Nathan?' Guy asked scanning the room.

'No, boy's night in, which I think consists of building the biggest Lego tower ever.'

'You look lovely,' Guy said, leaning over and giving Nell another quick peck on the cheek.

'Thank you,' she answered, as a swarm of fireflies erupted in her stomach and she took a sip of her drink to disguise her blushes.

He glanced towards the band and watched them for a moment as they struck up the next song.

Nell gave him a sideways glance and studied his face. His jaw was strong and his dark hair fell across his eyes, which flashed instant warmth.

'Do you remember this song, Guy?' Ed patted Guy on the back and handed him his beer.

Guy didn't answer, just rolled his eyes at his brother.

The Cosy Canal Boat Dream

'Sounds like there's a story behind it?' questioned Nell, flicking a grin towards Guy.

'This one here used to play the guitar in a band. He was once a wannabe rock star,' winked Ed.

Guy squirmed in his seat, 'That's a bit of an exaggeration,' he grinned, taking a swig of his beer.

Ed chuckled to himself.

Nell and Bea looked on in amusement.

'I know exactly what you're laughing at.' Guy gave Ed a playful stare.

'This song is by a band called "The Mystic Chairs".' Ed said, 'Ever heard of them?' He turned towards Bea and Nell.

Nell thought for a second, 'Yes, wasn't that the band whose lead singer wore tight-leather pants and half his hair was shaved and the other half bright red?' said Nell.

'Oh, I remember them!' Bea mused, 'Did you like them back in the day, then, Ed?'

'Mmm, let's just say *I* wasn't their biggest fan,' he chuckled.

They both swiftly turned towards an embarrassed Guy, who was shaking his head towards his brother.

'Okay ... I have to admit I was a teeny bit obsessed with the lead singer,' admitted Guy, sitting back in his seat and throwing his hands in the air.

'That much so, he borrowed the dog's hair clippers to shave off half his hair and used his pocket money to buy an auburn red hair dye from the local chemist. Not only did he end up dyeing his hair, which looked ridiculous, I may add, but half the white bathroom suite looked like it had caught the measles, it was covered in red sloshes, much to Mum's delight!'

There was an outburst of laughter from Nell and Bea. 'What I want to know is, is there any photographic evidence of this?' asked Nell, nudging Guy with her arm playfully.

'That's not the half of it,' Ed added grinning.

'Oh God! No!' Guy protested, knowing full well his brother was about to divulge all.

At the same time both Nell and Bea leant forward and placed their elbows on the table. Their eyes didn't leave Ed.

'Wannabe rock star here took himself down to the local market and purchased a pair of the tightest leather pants you'd ever set eyes on.'

Nell and Bea swung round to look at Guy, who was shaking his head in embarrassment.

'Except they weren't leather, more like plastic, I'd say,' said Guy.

'Ooo I used to have a pair of plastic leather-look trousers,' Bea chipped in.

'A-ha that's right!' smiled Nell.

'Well, this one here spent nearly two hours in his bedroom trying to wriggle into them, but by the end of the night he'd sweated in those pants that much that they clung to his skin. Mum literally had to lie him on the kitchen floor and cut them off with a pair of scissors. Then we discovered he was covered in a rash!'

'OMG!' Nell exclaimed, 'How old were you?'

'Seventeen,' Guy answered, shaking his head in embarrassment. 'I thought I looked very cool!'

'I hope you have no plans for dyeing your hair red again?' asked Nell.

The Cosy Canal Boat Dream

'Not one,' grinned Guy, swigging his pint.

'Every cloud,' teased Nell, giving him a cheeky wink. Guy squeezed her knee under the table then entwined his fingers around hers.

'Did you have any aspirations to become a rock star, Ed.'

'None whatsoever. I was always dismantling things I shouldn't, once a tinkerer always a tinkerer. I love it at the boatyard, I'm my own boss, work in the outdoors, wouldn't change it for the world.'

'When are you back at work, Ed? asked Bea.

'Hopefully one day next week,' he replied as Bea tucked her arm through Nell's.

'That soon?'

'I feel ready and that's good enough for me.'

'So what happens to you, then?' asked Bea, her eyes diverting quickly towards Guy.

'Me? That means I'm redundant,' he joked. 'He's packing me back off to Ireland.'

At the sound of those words, Nell's heart plummeted to somewhere near her knees. She felt like the bottom had just fallen out of her world.

'Hey, he does like me really,' Guy joked, noticing the look on Nell's face.

'Does that really mean you're going back to Ireland?' she queried, uncertain whether he was actually joking or not.

Guy met the concerned look in her eyes, 'At some point I'll have to go back home, but I'm not sure when yet.'

All Nell could manage was a nod, her mood suddenly

dampened by the thought of Guy no longer milling around the marina.

'But don't worry I'll be around for a little while longer yet.'

'That's good to hear,' she said, smiling weakly, knowing she had fallen for Guy. In the last few minutes Nell felt sombre, she didn't want Guy being around for a little while longer, she wanted him around full stop.

'What's the latest on the Old Picture House, Nell? Are you attending the auction? I think it will be good for the marina to get that place up and running again,' said Ed.

Nell nodded in agreement, 'I'm going to give it my best shot and hopefully it'll be within my budget.'

The next couple of hours flew by, the four of them chatting about everything and anything while drinking and listening to the band play.

'Last song in a minute,' said Bea, her eyes drooping, 'I'm not sure I can last much longer. Sorry, I'm yawning!'

'One last drink for the road?' Guy asked.

'Not for me. I'm dead on my feet but I've had a fantastic evening,' smiled Bea.

'Me too,' Ed chipped in, swilling down the last of his beer. 'If you two want one for the road, I can walk Bea back home, it's on the way?'

Nell looked across at Bea to gauge her reaction.

'That'll be perfect, thanks, Ed,' she said, before turning back towards Nell and Guy. 'You two stay. Enjoy yourselves.'

'Only if you're sure?'

'I'm sure,' she said, leaning over and popping a swift kiss to Nell's cheek.

The Cosy Canal Boat Dream

'Ready?' Ed asked, pushing his chair under the table.
'I'm ready.'
Ed helped Bea to her feet like a true gentleman and held her coat open while she slipped her arms inside. They said their goodbyes and Nell and Guy watched them both make their way to the entrance through the dwindling crowd.

'Another drink?' Guy asked, reaching inside his jeans pocket for his wallet.

Nell hesitated for a second, 'How about a drink back at mine?'

'I'm up for that, if that's okay with you?'

She nodded, 'I'm not quite ready for bed, but want to wind down a little.'

'Sounds like a plan,' he answered.

Nell stood up, slipped on her coat and grabbed her bag. They weaved their way to the entrance and stood outside. Nell snuggled down inside her coat and Guy dug his hands in his pocket to shield himself from the cold night air. His shoulders were hunched up as they walked quickly towards the 'Nollie'.

Once inside, Nell switched on the lamp and threw some coal on the fire.

'Glass of red?' she asked, beginning to pour the wine.

'Perfect,' he answered. She noticed his eyes sparkling in the dim light as they settled on the rug in front of the fire.

Since the conversation had turned to Ed returning to work earlier on in the evening there'd been a question burning inside Nell, and now was the time to ask it.

'Guy,' she murmured, looking into his eyes.

'Yes.'

'Are you really going to go back to Ireland?'

He hesitated, 'I will have to at some point. My job is there. It's where I live.'

Nell took a deep breath, 'I've kind of got used to you being here.' She blinked the teary mist away from her eyes, 'My, I'm getting all emotional, what's wrong with me?'

'It's allowed,' he answered softly. 'I kind of feel a bit like that too. Come here.'

He opened his arms wide and Nell slipped inside them, resting her head against his chest. She could hear the constant thud of his heartbeat and they both stared into the dancing flames of the fire. They sat like that in silence for a couple of minutes. Guy began to stroke Nell's hair gently and, for the first time in a long time Nell felt content and happy. She snuggled in closer, then Guy tilted her head towards his. Studying her face closely, he met her beautiful eyes. They held each other's gaze and Guy brushed his finger across her lips. She held her breath. She wanted to kiss him; she wanted him to kiss her. He tipped his head forward and pressed his lips on the top of her head lightly before she nestled back into his arms. Neither of them spoke. Nell's head was a whirl. His arms were wrapped tightly around her body.

'You need to get some sleep soon,' he whispered, 'I don't want to keep you up.'

She pressed her lips into a smile, 'Do I have a say in the matter?' Her eyes held his. 'I'm not sure I want you to go home, I kind of ...'

The Cosy Canal Boat Dream

'Kind of what?' Guy interrupted softly, entwining his fingers around Nell's.

She forced herself to breathe calmly. 'What if? ...' she paused.

'What if? ...' he murmured. Their eyes never left each other.

'What if I want you to keep me up?'

There, she'd said it and there was no taking it back.

'Is that what you really want?'

Nell couldn't deny these feelings any longer. The more time she spent in Guy's company the more she'd begun to realise she didn't want just his friendship, she wanted him full stop.

'It is. Stay?' she answered, her voice barely a whisper. Raw emotion began to run through her body and she blinked away a tear.

'Hey, don't cry.'

'I'm not, it's just ...'

'Just what?'

With a slight hesitation Nell spoke, 'I never thought I'd ever have these types of feelings again.' For a second Nell's mind drifted towards Ollie. Her head began to fight her heart. Ollie was gone; there was no bringing him back. She wanted Guy to hold her; she wanted his lips on hers. She glanced nervously into his eyes and took a deep breath. Her heart was clattering and she could barely breathe. She took the lead and moved her face closer to his. Her pulse was racing; his smell, his touch, the spark was explosive. Guy traced his finger under her chin, then tilted it towards him. She could feel the breath on her face, her heart was beating so fast she thought she was going to explode. The hairs on the back of Nell's neck prickled as she murmured, 'Kiss me.'

Their eyes stayed locked and neither of them faltered. Nell grasped at the back of his head and pulled him closer, their lips met. They kissed slowly at first, the tingle in Nell's body immense. She pulled away, 'Come on,' she said, taking his hand.

Guy hesitated for a second.

'Are you okay?'

'Nell ...'

'Shh, don't say anything,' she said leading him to the cabin. She lay down on the bed and Guy was above her. Nell ran her hands over his strong arms then his toned torso. He kissed her neck as she began to unbutton his jeans pushing them slowly down. Her hands explored every inch of his body. He lifted up her blouse and unhooked her bra, every nerve in her body tingled.

'You are perfect,' he said tenderly.

She kissed him passionately then he rose above her, his strong arms either side of her body.

'Are you sure?'

Nell nodded. 'I've never been more sure about anything in my life. I want you, Guy,' she kissed him, knowing that she had fallen badly for him.

Chapter 29

The next morning, Nell woke up with sunshine bursting through the curtains. Within a split second thoughts of last night came flooding back to her and her heart swelled as she remembered being curled up in the strong arms of Guy all night. She smiled to herself, feeling content and turned over to face him, but the bed was empty. She listened for a moment, but there was deadly silence in the cabin – all she could hear was the chugging of the boat engines outside. She ran her hand over the rumpled duvet, then sat up straight in the bed. His scent still lingered on the duvet as she pulled it tightly around her body. Last night, Guy had made her feel like the only girl in the world. He had devoured her body with such passion, making her gasp at every touch and now he was gone. Feeling confused, she hugged her knees, tears brimming her eyes.

She sat there for a while longer, then locked eyes with the photograph sitting on her bedside table, a photo of her and Ollie on their wedding day. She stared at the photo and suddenly her heart plummeted as a flash of guilt ran through her body. Had she made a mistake? Why would someone disappear in the early hours? This was the first time she'd felt close to anyone in a long time and now she was smothered in feelings of abandonment.

She wiped the tears with the back of her hand, fleeting images ran through her mind from last night and suddenly she felt confused and empty. Where was Guy? Did he regret last night?

She threw back the duvet, swung her legs to the floor and walked gingerly into the bathroom. She climbed into the shower and let the water cascade over her body while she grappled with her conscience. She raked her hands through her hair, her mind whirling. Why did she feel so guilty, so sad?

Fifteen minutes later she was hugging a mug of tea, gazing wistfully out of the window while trying to cope with her own feelings. She spotted Guy in the boatyard, Ed and Sam by his side as they tinkered away with a boat engine.

She watched them for a couple of minutes. Guy looked happy enough, throwing a ball for Sam while handing Ed some tools. She noticed him delve into his pocket and take out his mobile phone. He punched something into the keypad. Two seconds later Nell's phone vibrated and she looked at the screen to see a text message from Guy.

Good morning, I didn't want to wake you. I'm in work, last night was perfect, text me when you're up. x

Relief ran through her body, he hadn't regretted last night, he was just up early to open the boatyard and no doubt needed

The Cosy Canal Boat Dream

to walk Sam. She ran her finger over the message and bit down on her lip, unsure what to text to back.

She glanced back over towards him. His sleeves were pushed up over his arms, his forearms were lean and his dark hair fell in his eyes. She closed her eyes for a moment, remembering his touch and his lips on hers. She knew she wanted more, but with him returning to Ireland was she setting herself up for more heartache?

Quickly she thrust her feet into her boots and grabbed her coat and found herself standing on the jetty outside the 'Nollie'. She was thankful Guy and Ed were deep in conversation as she slipped up the towpath without being seen.

In no time at all she found herself standing on the wooden bridge gazing over the lake. The sky glowed soft blue and the naked branches of the trees swayed in the gentle breeze. She stopped and listened to the sound of the birds chirping. There was a calmness about this place that she loved.

She wandered over the bridge and walked towards the water's edge. She took a deep breath before speaking, 'Morning, Ollie,' she whispered, perching on the edge of the bench and tilting her face towards the warm sun. She closed her eyes.

Suddenly, she felt a shadow cast over her and opened her eyes to see her mum sitting down next to her.

'I thought it was you, penny for them.'

'You don't want to know,' replied Nell.

'A problem shared and all that,' said Gilly, casting an eye over the lake.

Nell took a moment, 'Mum, I feel terrible,' her voice quivered.

Christie Barlow

Gilly turned towards her daughter and met her grief-stricken eyes, 'Whatever it is, it can't be that bad.'

'I've ... Guy.' Nell couldn't bring herself to say the words and her voice petered off, leaving Gilly to fill in the gaps.

'You're getting close to Guy?'

Nell nodded.

'And you're feeling guilty?'

'A little, actually a lot.'

'It's understandable, Nell. Ollie was your life, but don't feel guilty about moving on. Life for you is becoming bearable again and I'm sure that's got a lot to do with Guy.'

Nell smiled thinking of Guy, 'It's easy being around him. I feel alive again.'

'And that's nothing to feel bad about at all, it's the most natural thing in the world.'

'So why do I feel like I've betrayed Ollie, then?'

'Maybe because you never thought you'd could be happy with anyone else other than Ollie. Nell, all these feelings are natural. Ollie was one in a million, one of the good guys. We'll never forget him and if he were here, things would be different, but he isn't here and he wouldn't want you spending the rest of your days on your own. And if you think this Guy is good enough for you then I'm sure that's good enough for Ollie too.'

Nell locked eyes with her mum and brushed away a lonely tear that was rolling down her cheek.

'But then there's the issue with Guy.'

'What do you mean?'

'I don't think he's staying around.'

The Cosy Canal Boat Dream

'Why?' Gilly pulled her daughter in close and placed her arm around her shoulder.

'His home, his job is in Ireland,' sighed Nell. 'And now I think I'm just going to get hurt and I really can't cope with any more pain,' the tears began to roll down her cheeks.

'Have you asked him how he feels?' asked Gilly calmly.

She shook her head, 'Given everything I've been through, I'm not sure I can cope if the answer is something I don't want to hear.'

'Oh, Nell.' Gilly hugged her daughter tightly.

'How can I have fallen for someone so quickly, Mum?'

'Because people come into your life for a reason. Life is definitely not easy sometimes,' said Gilly cautiously, pulling away from the hug and not meeting Nell's eye.

'There's one thing I do know for certain. I don't relish the thought of him going back to Ireland.'

Gilly patted her daughter affectionately, 'Then you need to tell him how you feel.'

'He texted me this morning.'

'And?'

'I haven't answered.'

'Then do it. I'm sure the poor man will be checking his phone every two minutes waiting for your message.'

'Do you think?'

She gave Nell a knowing nod, 'Text him.'

'I will and thanks, Mum' said Nell, smiling through her tears.

'Anytime.'

'What are you doing up and out so early anyway?'

'Just running a few errands and I nearly always walk this way round,' she said, squeezing Nell's hand before ambling over the bridge and out of sight.

Nell stood up and took one last look up at the sky, 'I will always love you,' she said, scarcely breathing.

When Nell crossed back over the bridge, she took her mobile phone out of her bag and opened up Guy's message.

She tapped back, *I had a good night too. x*

Almost immediately she received a reply, 'Fancy dinner tonight?'

Feeling more positive, the slumping sensation of the early morning lifted as she smiled at the message. He hadn't run out on her, he'd replied instantly. She bit down on her lip and typed a message back, 'That would be perfect, look forward to it.' she answered, knowing Guy had definitely come into her life for a reason.

Chapter 30

Two weeks later...

Guy hummed his way through his shower and let the water cascade over his body. The past two weeks had been dreamlike. Every spare minute he'd spent with Nell and they'd grown extremely close. He grabbed the towel off the rail and jumped out of the shower before quickly throwing on a pair of jeans and a t-shirt. Sam was barking at the front door, his tail thumping on the wooden floor.

'What is it boy, is someone at the door?'

Sam's feet danced as Guy glanced at the clock and twisted the key.

Nell was forty-five minutes early but he didn't mind, he couldn't wait to see her. She'd spent most of the week researching suppliers, builders and even discovered an internet site for all film memorabilia, which Lloyd had kindly recommended. With the auction taking place tomorrow, Nell was like an excitable puppy. Everything was in place, researched to the max, every scenario accounted for and tonight they were going through the figures one last time. Guy had already

Christie Barlow

set the property details out on the table, uncorked a bottle of red and a beef casserole was simmering nicely.

With a huge beam on his face, Guy swung opened the front door, 'You're early, but I don't mind.'

He stopped dead in his tracks. His eyes travelled upwards and his smile disappeared. He blinked straight at her, his mouth dry.

'Pleased to see me?'

Guy was speechless as he stared at the woman in front of him ... his wife.

Kate was dressed in her usual attire, a power suit with high heels and no doubt another new handbag, which she'd purchased from a last-minute Paris trip with her latest fancy man.

'What are you doing here?' Guy demanded, his tone less than friendly.

'What sort of welcome is that?' she said, leaning forward, kissing him on his cheek and taking him by surprise.

He bristled and squared his shoulders.

'Aren't you going to ask me in?' Kate said with a sweet, sickly smile. 'I bet you didn't expect to see me.'

'I was hoping I didn't have to see you again,' he said, meaning every word.

'Ah, don't be like that,' she waltzed past him straight into the hallway.

He had no idea why she was here. All he knew was whatever she wanted, he needed to get rid of her quickly, before Nell arrived.

'Come on in, why don't you?' he said, with a hint of sarcasm in his voice, and gestured towards the kitchen.

The Cosy Canal Boat Dream

'It's a bit poky in here,' she said, flitting her eyes over the place.

'Homely, I'd call it.'

There was a lull in conversation as Guy hovered around the table and stared at Kate. He took a deep breath. 'So you didn't answer my question, what exactly are you doing here?'

'Well, that's a nice welcome,' she said, her eyes glinting towards him.

He kept his poker face.

'I've come a long way, you know. Aren't you happy to see me?'

'I'm not sure Ireland is classed as a long way or I'm assuming that's not where you've come from?'

'Oh Guy, you need to loosen up. You always seem so tense. It's not good for you, you know.'

'I'll ask you again, what are you doing here?' He said glancing at his watch.

'Am I keeping you from anything?' she trilled, trying to hold his gaze.

'I'm on my way out,' he answered bluntly, but knowing that wasn't strictly true.

'Surely you can make time for your wife?'

He opened his mouth to speak but words failed him.

Kate took a step towards him and ran her finger over his chest.

'Mmm,' she uttered seductively.

He could feel her breath on his face and she moved closer. His skin prickled at her touch and he grabbed her hand. His eyes hardened, 'What do you think you are doing?'

'Making up for lost time.'

Guy could feel his temples beginning to throb as the anger rose inside him.

'Making up for lost time? You didn't want to make up for lost when I discovered your affair, let's just remind ourselves ... with my boss, of all people.'

'It's not what you think,' she said softly, giving him that look that once he would have fallen for, but not now.

Guy shook his head in disbelief.

'Shall we talk about your trip to Paris?' Guy stared straight into her eyes. 'I'm not stupid, you know. I found the emails, the receipts. On a residential training course, you said.'

'Like I said, it's not what you think,' repeated Kate unconvincingly, shifting from one foot to the other.

'Really ... the best you can come up with is that old cliché. What you probably actually mean is your sugar daddy blew you out, so you thought you'd come crawling back ... for what exactly?' Guy could feel his anger beginning to reach boiling point.

'We can work through this.'

Guy shook his head, 'You are deluded, everything about you is false,' Guy was on a roll now and couldn't stop himself, 'Everything that comes out of your mouth is a lie.'

'Don't say that, we had a good life together, we *have* a good life together.'

'Did we? Which part? I gave up everything for you, even working with my Granddad because you wanted a man in a suit on your arm; a builder's labourer just wasn't good enough. I was an embarrassment to you, to your friends – admit it.'

The Cosy Canal Boat Dream

'We needed the money, you were bringing in a pittance and Daddy pulled some strings to get you that job.'

It grated on Guy the way she still called her father 'daddy' at her age.

'No, we didn't need the money, the mortgage was paid for each month, with enough left for a few nights out.'

Money didn't matter to Guy, unlike Kate. He wasn't materialistic in the slightest. He'd worn the same pair of comfy converse and Levi's for as long as he could remember and had no inclination to change them any day soon.

'It doesn't hurt to want nice things and holidays too.'

'Something your sugar daddy can obviously provide.'

'Listen to me, we can't just throw all these years away.'

'Can't we?' he answered, knowing he had no intention of saving his marriage, he'd already moved on.

'You don't mean that, I know you.' Kate blinked at him then sat down at the table.

'You have no clue who I even am,' said Guy in despair.

'Come home, Guy, we've had some time apart and I've missed you.'

Guy was lost for words at Kate's attitude. He raked his hand through his hair and let out an exasperating sigh.

'The least you can do is offer me a drink,' she added, stalling for time, hoping to bring him around.

Against his better judgement Guy began to get Kate a drink, hoping to get rid of her quickly. But he turned back round he noticed Kate was perusing the property details of the Old Picture House.

She folded her arms and looked at him. 'What's this?' She

asked, scanning back through the property details of the Old Picture House that Guy had left on the table.

Damn.

'I hope you're not thinking of investing our money in something I don't know about.'

'So this is what this is all about ... money, the house? You can have the house, Kate, I'm really past caring.'

Kate ignored his comment, 'Is this for you?'

'Not that it's any of your business but I'm looking over a project for a friend, the auction is tomorrow,'

'Tomorrow? Looks like a good investment. They could soon flatten that and build a few houses. Quick cash turn-a-round.'

Guy could have kicked himself for providing the information to Kate, knowing she worked for a property developer. He leant forward and took the details from her hand and gathered up the loose papers on the table, placing them in a pile on the worktop.

'Kate, look.'

'No, let me speak,' she interrupted, 'I can see I've taken you by surprise, but surely you must have been thinking about us.'

Actually, Guy hadn't given Kate a second thought since he'd left Ireland. The only person who *had* been on his mind was Nell and right at this very moment he didn't want her turning up and running into Kate.

'I'm hoping you will fly back to Ireland with me.'

He exhaled sharply, rubbed a hand over his face and sat down opposite her.

'Why would I do that?'

The Cosy Canal Boat Dream

'Because that's where you belong, you are my husband.'

For the past couple of weeks Guy had begun to think less about Ireland and was contemplating making a fresh start here in England. He looked away from Kate's stare.

'All marriages go through difficult times, Guy.'

He sighed, 'Kate, it wasn't just your latest affair ... I know about all your other men too.'

Guy had suspected more than several misdemeanours in the past but now it was time to hold her gaze and watch her squirm.

'Okay, if we are going to make a fresh start, I need to be honest with you.'

Guy knew exactly what she was going to say before the words even left her mouth.

'What girl doesn't like a bit flirting? They didn't mean anything, it was just drinks.'

'Drinks? How stupid do you think I am? Actually, don't even answer that, it doesn't matter.'

'I didn't connect with these people mentally.'

'So that makes it all right, then?'

'But you were so distant towards me! You changed, Guy.'

'How many others were there, Kate?'

Kate shrugged, 'There weren't many.'

'How many?' He demanded.

She paused, and Guy wondered whether she was actually doing a mental calculation in her head, 'Maybe seven or eight.'

Guy couldn't believe she was being so blasé about it. His pulse had doubled, his palms sweating. He banged his hand on the table and straightened up his body to catch his breath.

'Seven or eight? Kate, you are mistaken if you think we are getting back together. It's not happening, not now, not ever.'

'We can work through this, Guy, I know we can. I love you.'

'You don't know the meaning of the word. For as long as I can remember I've lived half a life. Always doing want you wanted me to do. You never loved me for who I was. This needs to stop now. Since we split up I've begun to enjoy life again.' Guy knew he was nearly shouting now.

'You can't make a decent living from being a builder's labourer! I did it for you, Guy. I wanted you to make more of yourself, realise your own self-worth.'

'Bollocks ...' he took a breath, 'Maybe I don't care about mortgages, maybe I don't care if I live in a cardboard box on the street corner, how would you know? You've never asked me or listened to what I wanted. All you have ever done is told me what to do. It's always been about you.'

'That's not true. We wanted to start a family.'

'Don't even get me started on that,' he jabbed his finger towards her.

Guy had noticed Kate's eyes begin to fill with tears. 'Oh brilliant and now comes the waterworks. You know what, Kate, I was mad to even get involved with you in the first place. I don't know what I ever saw in you. You are manipulative, false and, quite frankly ...' he paused,

'Is there someone else?' Her eyes locked with his.

Thoughts of Nell flooded his mind; gorgeous Nell, who was beautiful on the inside and out. He looked away from her stare.

'There is, isn't there?' Kate slumped back in her chair. Guy

The Cosy Canal Boat Dream

noticed a flash of anger in her eyes. Her mouth fell open and she folded her arms, waiting for him to answer.

'And quite frankly ...' he repeated himself, 'I want a divorce.'

Just as the words left his mouth there was a knock on the annexe door.

Guy and Kate just stared at each other.

'Aren't you going to get rid of whoever that is?'

Guy felt the colour drain from his face, knowing Nell would be standing on the other side of the door.

'Is that her? Is that her now?' Kate stood up.

'Kate no,' Guy pleaded.

She narrowed her eyes at Guy, 'Does she even know you're married? She doesn't, does she?'

'Kate, no, not like this.'

'And here you are accusing me of being a liar, kettle ... pot ... black, springs to mind. I think she needs to know, oh, and there's another thing she needs to know too,' she shouted.

'What are you talking about now?'

Kate pursed her lips, 'She needs to know I'm carrying your baby. That's why I'm here, Guy.'

Guy's jaw fell somewhere below his knees and he felt his whole world crashing down around him.

It took a couple of seconds for the words to register.

'Don't be ridiculous, it's not possible, we haven't slept together for months.'

'The opening night of the town hall project. You came back to the house, we had sex.'

Guy vaguely remembered that night. He'd been a little bit worse for wear and the whole night had been a blur, thanks to the free bar. But he had remembered spending the night with Kate and he could kick himself now

'I don't believe you.'

'What, that we had sex?'

'No, that you are pregnant.'

Kate flounced towards the front door.

Guy watched in horror. 'Kate NO!'

But it was too late. Kate flung the door open to see innocent Nell standing there, smiling up at her.

'Oh, hello,' Nell said, instantly she recognised the woman standing before her, 'I think we've met before.'

'I don't think so,' Kate replied rather abruptly.

Nell noticed Guy standing behind the woman – he was visibly shaking.

'Yes, we have, the deli competition – you were the mystery shopper, the judge?'

Kate stared at Nell, 'I've no idea what you are talking about,

'You came into the deli.'

'You've been here recently?' Guy asked puzzled.

'I wanted to see where you'd run off too, there's no crime in that is there?'

'Have you been spying on me?'

Nell clearly had no idea what was going on.

Guy felt devastated that she was about to be dragged into this unholy mess. His pulse was throbbing on the side of his head and his heart was thumping.

If only he'd told Nell about Kate before.

Kate turned towards Nell, 'Let me introduce myself, I'm Kate, Guy's wife, and I hope you're going to be the first to

The Cosy Canal Boat Dream

congratulate him on becoming a father,' she announced, before pushing past Nell and storming off up the path. She quickly disappeared out of sight, leaving Guy lost for words.

Nell swallowed as dread rose through her body. She stumbled backwards and reached out for the fence as the words rang loud and clear in Nell's ears ... WIFE. She met Guy's stare and shuddered as panic rose through her whole body.

'What did she just say?' her eyes filled with tears.

Guy didn't want to repeat it. He didn't want to believe it himself. He could see the hurt in Nell's eyes and was aware he could hear his own breathing.

'I'm sorry, Nell,' the colour drained from his face.

Nell felt as if she'd been kicked in the stomach.

She stared at him as the hurt stabbed her entire body. She felt sick and wanted to scream and shout, thump his chest.

He had a wife, who was pregnant.

Nell edged backwards, clutching her heart.

'Nell, please wait. Please.'

'Don't you ever come near me again.'

'Please let me explain,' said Guy desperately.

But it was too late. Nell's legs were already powering her out of sight. She didn't look back.

Chapter 31

As Nell's legs pounded up the wharf, the tears blurred her eyes and the pain gripped her stomach. She felt as if she was riding an emotional rollercoaster, a feeling she'd never wanted to experience again as long as she lived. How could he do this to her?

Turning the corner by the side of the boatyard, Nell bumped slap-bang into Lloyd, who was ambling along, stretching his legs.

'Whoa! Slow down, where's the fire?' he asked, straightening his cravat, then waggling his cane in the air.

It took Nell a moment to steady herself, 'I'm so sorry, I should have been looking where I was going,' she said, forcing a smile and wiping away the tears with the back of her hand.

Lloyd ushered her towards the railing, suddenly noticing the distressed look on her face.

'Lean against this for a moment, catch your breath,' he didn't take his eyes off her. 'That's your boat, isn't it?'

Nell nodded, 'Yes,' she could feel her lips beginning to tremble again and the tears cascaded down her cheeks again.

The Cosy Canal Boat Dream

'Let me walk you home.' He touched her lightly on her arm and she didn't object when he linked his arm through hers. He pointed his cane towards the colourful narrowboat. 'Nearly there,'

Nell snagged a look towards the sky. What a fool she'd been, trusting Guy. Ollie had never hurt her or lied to her like this. How could Guy do this to her? What was he playing at? She'd let him into her life and he'd made her world come crashing down around her once again.

Arriving at the edge of the jetty, Nell dabbed her nose with a tissue, 'Thank you, I'll be okay.'

'If you don't mind me saying, you don't look okay. Is there anyone you'd like me to call?'

Nell shook her head and the tears began to run down Nell's cheeks once more, 'I'm sorry, I don't mean to cry on you,'

'Come on, at least let me see you through the door,'

His voice was soft and his eyes were kind. 'I don't like to see anyone upset.'

'Thank you, I can stretch to a cuppa and a slice of Victoria sponge?'

'That, m'dear, sounds like an excellent invitation,' he smiled kindly. 'Are you sure?'

Nell nodded.

Once inside, Nell passed Lloyd a drink and a slice of cake. She settled down at the table opposite him.

'Sometimes, you know, things are never as bad as they seem,' he said wisely.

'I wish I could believe that,' Nell swallowed down a lump in her throat and wished with all her heart that she didn't have any feelings for Guy, but the pain hammering against her chest was telling her otherwise.

'In my experience, cake as delicious as this always makes things a little better,' Lloyd wiped the sugar from around his mouth, 'This is actually damn good.'

'Thanks, it's baked by my friend, Bea, from the deli.'

'A jolly fine baker.

'The best,' agreed Nell.

'Do you want to tell me what's upset you?'

Nell really didn't feel like spilling her worldly worries to Lloyd and as much as she was hurting she didn't want to tell tales on Guy either. The only thing she needed to do was stay out of Guy's way and concentrate on winning that auction and moving on with her life. A completely fresh start. But both were easier said than done.

'It's safe to say someone I trusted has let me down,' Nell said, not giving any more away.

'I'm sorry to hear that. Do they know they've let you down?'

'I think the answer to that would definitely be a yes.'

'Then let them come to you and apologise. Anything is solvable if both parties are willing to forgive and forget.'

'I'm not sure I can do either at this moment in time,' said Nell, pushing her plate away. She'd completely lost her appetite.

'Give it time.'

'Maybe.' She felt herself sigh and her shoulders sag.

They exchanged looks. Nell folded her arms and leant on the table. 'I was looking forward to life again, then it's all

The Cosy Canal Boat Dream

changed in a blink of an eye, but now I'm going to concentrate on what's important.'

'Which is?'

'Winning that auction tomorrow.'

Lloyd turned his head towards the porthole and stared out towards the Old Picture House.

'I have a good feeling about that place,' he gave Nell a nod.

'Do you want to see my plans?'

'That would be grand! Now that's dedication – plans before you've won.'

Nell smiled at his old-fashioned way of talking as she retrieved the plans from the cupboard and rolled them out on the table in front of him.

Lloyd took a sip of his tea, 'This, young lady, looks fantastic. Talk me through it.'

Nell slid next to him and was grateful of the chance to be distracted. She talked Lloyd through her plans, her vision of bringing all the generations in the community back together. 'I've kept all the original features inside the Old Picture House too,' she said proudly, 'And I can't wait to get started and co-ordinate it all. This is just what I need, something for my future.'

'This is just what this place needs. It will be the icing on the cake, so to speak,' he chuckled, finishing off his slice of cake.

For a split second Nell beamed, forgetting all of her troubles.

'I think so. As well as something for the community, it will be a memorial to Ollie. I'm doing it in his honour.'

'Very commendable and these plans look perfect. It's a jolly good idea. You are an amazing young lady.'

'It's a shame my mum doesn't think so, she seems quite opposed to the idea.'

'Your mum?'

'Yes, I think it's because I've never undertaken anything like this before. Have you been into the deli? She works in there too – Gilly.'

Suddenly there seemed a strange tension in the air and Lloyd took a breath.

'I think she thinks I'll end up in some sort of financial mess. I suppose she just worries about me,' Nell quickly added, not wanting to appear disloyal to her mum.

The pair of them looked up towards the window as they both heard footsteps drumming along the jetty. Nell spotted Bea jumping on to the deck of the 'Nollie' and the door flung open.

Lloyd stood up and grabbed his cane, 'My cue to disappear and leave you youngsters to it,' he raised his eyebrows towards the plans lain on the table, 'Mark my words, go for it. Do you and your Ollie proud.'

'I will and thanks for bringing me home.'

He nodded towards Bea and was soon on his way, walking up the wharf.

'Was that the man who collapsed?'

'Yes, he's rather an eccentric old thing but adorable.'

'Looks like an old movie star the way he dresses, and anyway, what's going on? I've just read your text but it was rambled,' Bea's eyes were wide as she unbuttoned her coat and sat down next to Nell, 'I didn't quite understand it.'

The Cosy Canal Boat Dream

'I don't quite understand it either,' Nell took a deep breath, 'Guy has a wife ...' She watched Bea's face change as the words registered.

'He's got a what?'

'And not only has he got a wife, she's pregnant.'

Chapter 32

Nell and Bea were now sitting on the bench on the deck of the 'Nollie', with a blanket wrapped around their shoulders. Nell brushed away the tears with the back of her hand before glancing up at her friend.

'Oh Bea, I've been so stupid' she snuffled, looking at the brown substance in the glass.

'What's in this, by the way?'

'Nathan's whisky, drink it,' Bea insisted, squeezing her friend's hand, 'It will help with the shock.'

'I'm not sure anything will help with the shock.'

Nell took a swig and felt the burn in the back of her throat, 'I thought my life was about to change. I thought Guy was different …' she sobbed into her tissue.

'I'm still trying to take it all in. Why would he not mention he'd got a wife?'

Nell shrugged, 'I even asked him outright and he said he was single.'

'Why in God's name did he feel the need to lie? It's not as though at some point you wouldn't find out.'

Nell's shoulders drooped, 'Maybe I wouldn't have. Maybe

The Cosy Canal Boat Dream

I was just a so-called holiday fling, something to keep him occupied while he was here. He could have disappeared back at any time and I would have been none the wiser where or who he'd gone back to.'

'I've no words, Nell, I really haven't.'

Nell turned towards Bea, 'Wait until you find out who she is.'

Bea sat upright and locked eyes with Nell, 'You mean I know her?'

Nell took a deep breath before speaking, 'In a kind of roundabout way ... you know the snooty woman, the judge, the mystery shopper for the deli competition – well she's not the judge.'

Bea looked confused, wondering where Nell was going with this, 'The power-suit woman wearing the Jimmy Choos? How do you know she wasn't the judge?'

'Because that woman is Kate Cornish, Guy's wife.'

'Whoa! Really? I wasn't expecting that,' Bea exclaimed taken by surprise. 'I wouldn't have put them together in a million years, he's so ...'

'Nice,' Nell said, finishing off Bea's sentence. 'Or so we thought up until this moment.'

'And she's so ...'

'Up her own arse,' Nell finished off,

Bea could see the sadness in Nell's eyes.

'Maybe they're separated.'

'Separated enough to get her pregnant?'

'Fair point.'

'But that's not all,'

Bea's eyes widened, 'Go on.'

Nell took a deep breath, 'We've been sleeping together.'

Bea locked eyes with her friend, then tipped the glass towards her mouth, 'Drink some more.'

Nell didn't hesitate and did as she was told.

'Why Bea? He was so lovely to me, genuine, I trusted him; the first man I'd let get close to me since Ollie. He made me feel loved again, special.' Her whole body drooped, 'And now he'll be going back to Ireland to play happy families.'

The tone of her voice broke Bea's heart, 'Oh Nell.'

She held out her arms and Nell fell into them.

'What am I going to do, Bea?' Nell asked, hoping her best friend had the answer.

'There isn't anything you can do, except hold that head up high and get on with it like a trooper. Concentrate on this week. You are still going to the auction aren't you?'

'Yes, of course, that's not changed. I'm doing this for me and Ollie, the man who never let me down.'

'Good girl, let's just focus on the positives and soon Guy Cornish will become a distant memory.'

'Why does it hurt so much in here?' asked Nell, clutching at her chest.

'Even at our age, a broken heart doesn't get any easier.'

Bea glanced at her watch, 'It's getting late now, try and get some sleep,' Bea stood up and Nell followed her inside the Nollie. 'Tomorrow is a new day and a big day for you and when you are the proud owner of The Old Picture House then we will celebrate in style ... maybe with a takeaway.'

The Cosy Canal Boat Dream

'We know how to enjoy ourselves,' Nell said, attempting a weak smile.

Bea noticed a shadow cast over the porthole, then there was a gentle rap on the door. They both looked up, startled to see Guy standing on the other side.

He sheepishly pushed the door open, 'Can I come in?'

Nell's heart was pounding and immediately tears sprung to her eyes, 'It's okay, come aboard.'

'I'll leave you to it. Ring me if you need me,' said Bea, standing up and glaring at Guy.

Bea left and Guy hovered nervously in the kitchen.

'Why are you here? Shouldn't you be looking after your pregnant wife?' Nell knew she sounded bitter and childish, but she couldn't help herself.

'Can I sit?'

'If you must.'

He slid in the seat next to Nell and leant on the table, clasping his hands together.

'How are you?'

She closed her eyes and forced back the tears. Nell was afraid if she opened her mouth she'd throw up. She felt that sick about Guy's lies.

'Silly question, I know,' he said softly.

'How the hell do you think I'm doing?'

'It's not what it seems,' he said, raking a hand through his hair.

'So, she's not your wife and she's not pregnant?' She was praying it was all some terrible nightmare and that she'd wake up any minute.

She stole a furtive glance at Guy while she waited for the answer.

'No, she is definitely my wife and, according to her, she is pregnant.'

Nell's voice cracked, 'Why did you lie to me, Guy? How did I get this so wrong?'

Silence.

'You can't even explain yourself,' Nell shook her head in disbelief. 'Do you know how much this hurts, after everything? I feel such a fool.'

A tear ran down Guy's cheek and he brushed it away with the cuff of his jumper, 'It really isn't what it seems, Nell.'

'Is this the *"my wife doesn't understand me"* speech? Because if it is, please don't bother. I don't want to hear it.'

'I promise you it's not,' his hand crept towards Nell's, but immediately she moved hers away.

He paused for a moment and cleared his throat and took in a deep breath, filling his lungs with air before he began talking. 'I met Kate on a job. She's a property developer and her father's company employed my granddad's business to construct a handful of new-builds on the edge of town. It was a huge contract and provided work for nearly twelve months. Once we started work on the site, she seemed to find more and more excuses to visit. Granddad put me in charge of the project so I was always her first point of contact. She was vibrant and full of fun and began to text or ring me most days. The lads told me to stay clear, she already had a reputation.'

'A reputation for what?' Nell chipped in.

The Cosy Canal Boat Dream

'For being a bit of a player, putting it about a bit. It didn't bother me. I was young and wasn't looking for anything serious. I was one of the lads, enjoying my Friday nights playing pool, drinking beer and ending up in the curry house. Life was simple. Then she started turning up wherever I was. The lads used to joke she'd had me tracked. But I liked it. She wasn't like anyone I'd ever been out with before, she dressed in the latest designer gear, drove a BMW convertible. She reeled me in hook, line and sinker. We married after six months, a whirlwind romance. Everyone said it was too soon. My granddad warned me against it ...'

'But you think you know best at that age.'

He nodded. 'As soon as we were married, she seemed to change overnight.'

'In what way?' asked Nell.

'She was pushing, all the time, for me to ask my grandfather for the business, but I wasn't going to do that. I was happy with the job I was doing. Like I said, I was young, one of the lads, I didn't want to become their boss. My mates down the pub were down to earth, but hers were different to mine. I never felt comfortable around them. And she couldn't ever bring herself to say I was a builder's labourer. I was proud of my granddad and what he'd achieved but she did nothing except ridicule him. Then, one day, she came home holding up a designer suit. She'd set up an interview for me to go and work in her dad's office. We argued about it, but she convinced me it was the right thing to do if we wanted to start a family, and the extra money would come in handy. It makes me sound weak, I know, but at the time I'd fallen in love with her and would have done anything for her. I went for the job, got it and hated every minute of it. I missed working with Granddad, missed working with the lads. Then around six months after that it all came to a head.'

'What happened?'

'My gut feeling was telling me she was having an affair. She of course denied it, but the tell-tale signs were there. And every time she convinced me it was all in my head. I was mentally exhausted with it but however hard I tried ... it just didn't work out.'

'What do you mean?'

'I just couldn't stand it anymore. I gave it, gave *her*, my best shot, but when I discovered she was having an affair with my boss that was the final nail in the coffin. I'd put up with her antics for years and years, enough was enough. I moved out three months ago and told her it was over. It was Mum who suggested I take some time away and when Ed said he needed help while he was recovering from his operation, I jumped at the chance.'

'Oh Guy, but why did you tell me you were single? You could have told me the truth, you know.'

'I know, I'm sorry, Nell,' His voice faltered and he took her hands in his. 'I was so ashamed. I always thought I could make my marriage work, be as happy as my granddad and granny were for all those years but it just never happened. I felt such a failure.'

'But what I don't understand is if you've been separated for a few months how far pregnant is she?'

He sighed and took a deep breath, 'I hadn't slept with her

The Cosy Canal Boat Dream

for nearly seven months. Then just before I came to England we ended up at the same place one night and I was drunk. I'm not proud of it and the second I woke up the next morning I regretted every minute of it. This is the first time I've seen her since then. When she turned up on the doorstep I was shocked. It was the first I knew about her pregnancy. I've messed everything up haven't I?' He locked eyes with Nell.

Nell couldn't find any more words.

What a mess.

'I'm so sorry, Nell, I really am. I just wanted to move on, forget about my failed marriage and I thought that telling you I had a wife, with everything you've been through, would ruin things between us, but now I can see I was wrong to keep it from you. I've been an idiot. I should have been straight with you from the start.'

'Yes, you should,' said Nell.

'I'm feeling pretty ashamed.'

Nell pulled him gently towards her and he didn't object. She grasped at his jumper. 'You know I never thought I would have feelings for anyone else again.' She sobbed quietly. Guy kissed the top of her head and stroked her hair softly.

'You know I feel the same, Nell ...'

'But ...' Nell pulled away, her blurry eyes locking with his. She was conscious her heart was pounding and a feeling of trepidation ran through her entire body.

'But?' he pressed.

'This can't happen; there's a bigger picture now. Divorce I could deal with, but now you have a baby who needs a father.' Her voice was shaky. 'The baby has to come first.'

Nell stood up, the tears rolling down her cheeks. 'This is too difficult, Guy. I think you just need to leave, my heart is breaking enough.'

Guy shook his head, 'I don't want to leave.'

'You have to do the right thing,' she said, looking up through her tears.

'But I feel like we are only just beginning and it's been snatched away from us. You are beautiful, warm and funny and I never dreamt you would look at someone like me.' He brushed her hair out of her face.

'Someone like you? Guy, I've fallen for you, more than you will ever know.'

'I know,' he said kissing her gently on the lips, 'And I feel the same, believe me I do. We can make this work, Nell. I know we can.'

Nell shook her head, 'Your main priority is your family. I can't do it Guy. I can't have you hopping between countries or staying here with me, knowing I'm keeping you away from your child. I'd feel too guilty. As long as I win that auction, I'll be okay. I'll throw myself wholeheartedly into the Old Picture House. I'll get over you – I've done it before.'

The silence echoed all around.

There was nothing more to say. She could see it in his eyes he was hurting as much as her.

'Another lifetime, hey?'

'Another lifetime,' he echoed.

'Damn that timing,' she whispered.

He wiped away his tears and kissed her tenderly, not wanting to pull away. He took her hands in his. 'I've never

The Cosy Canal Boat Dream

felt so much alive and have loved every second I've spent with you.'

They both stood up and Nell walked him to the door. Guy held her hand and he pulled her in close and they wrapped their arms around each other one last time.

They both reluctantly let go.

'Good luck with the auction.'

'Thank you.'

'And remember to stay calm and don't get lost in the moment.'

'The story of my life – joke, joke,' she said, trying to lighten the mood a little.

He smiled at her, 'Just stick to your budget. Don't go over it.'

'I won't.' she promised.

'Night, Nell.'

'Night.'

She took a shuddering breath as she watched Guy with his head bent low, turn and walk up the jetty, out of her life. She closed the door, lay down on her bed and wrapped the duvet around her body. The tears fell on to her pillow, her heart breaking once more.

Chapter 33

Nell tossed and turned all night, until she finally drifted off to sleep somewhere around 5.30a.m., only to be woken by the alarm clock an hour later. She stretched out her arm to shut off the constant beeping, then snuggled back down under the duvet. She was exhausted.

She lay there for a second, thinking about the day ahead – auction day –, and hopefully the start of the rest of her life. She had no idea how it was all going to pan out, but there were a couple of things she knew for certain: by the end of the day she was either going to be the new proud owner of the Old Picture House or she wasn't, and soon Guy would be on his way back to Ireland. Bea and Gilly had to work in the deli today, but Nathan had offered to be by her side, every step of the way...

She reached for the bedside lamp and switched it on, the light dazzling her eyes for a split second before she stood up and stumbled towards the kitchen still half asleep. After grabbing a quick cuppa, Nell sat down at the table and opened the brochure and browsed through the properties that were being auctioned off today – the Old Picture House was lot

The Cosy Canal Boat Dream

number five. She glanced across at the figures that Guy had prepared – she knew her financial limits and needed to make sure she didn't carried away. She lay down the paperwork on the table and reached across to the photograph of her and Ollie. She traced his face with her finger, 'Wish me luck,' she murmured.

Hearing a gentle rap on the door, she looked up to see her mum standing on the deck of the 'Nollie' and by the look on her face, Nell knew she certainly had something on her mind.

'You look as bad as me. What's up?' asked Nell, unlocking the door and standing to one side as her mum came on board.

'Why, what's up with you?' quizzed Gilly, automatically filling the kettle up with water.

Nell sighed, 'Me and Guy, it's over before it began.'

Gilly's eyes widened, 'Why, what's happened?'

'He forgot to mention he had a wife ... oh and he found out yesterday she's also pregnant.'

'What?' exclaimed Gilly, alarmed.

'Apparently they'd separated, but it appears they had a drunken one-night stand just before he came here, and hey presto, she's pregnant.'

'Oh Nell, I'm so sorry,' Nell felt her mum's reassuring touch as she squeezed her hand.

'Not as sorry as me. He's going back to Ireland in the next couple of days or so.' Nell could feel the emotion rising inside, her breath caught in her throat, 'He's doing the right thing, he'll make an amazing father.' Her eyes blurred as the words left her mouth. 'Anyway, I'm trying not to think about it.

Today I want to concentrate of winning that Old Picture House for me and for Ollie.'

'That's why I'm here.'

'Why?' Nell asked, making her mum a cup of tea and sliding it in front of her. 'I don't understand.'

'Please don't do this,' said Gilly. 'Don't go to the auction.' Once the words were out there was no taking that back.

For a second no one said a thing and the air felt tense.

'Why wouldn't I go to the auction?' Nell narrowed her eyes at her mum. 'Why are you so against me doing this?'

Gilly's face turned white and she dropped her gaze to the ground, 'I just have a feeling it's not the right thing to do.'

'Based on?' Nell asked, feeling a little annoyed.

'Please just trust me on this one,' Gilly's face was flushed and her tone was borderline manic. 'It's a waste of Ollie's money. He wouldn't want you to put yourself in that position.'

'Whoa! Stop there! That's a low blow. I've worked out my finances and I think I would know more than you what Ollie would or wouldn't want me to do.'

Gilly's face looked defeated.

'So unless you're going to give me a valid reason ...'

Gilly looked as if she was going to say something, but clamped her mouth shut.

Determined not to lose her temper, Nell said calmly, 'Mum, this is silly, it's my money. I'm a big girl and it's most definitely not something to fall out over,' as she leaned across and grasped her mum's hand. 'I know you're only worried about me, but honestly there's no need.'

Gilly just nodded.

The Cosy Canal Boat Dream

Hearing another rap on the door, they both looked up to see Bea smiling back at them.

Nell gestured for her to come in.

'Have I interrupted something?' asked Bea, detecting a somewhat chilly atmosphere.

Nell left it to Gilly to rescue the situation, 'No, not at all. I'm just off. I'll see you in work in an hour.' She stood up and walked towards the door.

'Aren't you going to wish me luck?' shouted Nell after her, but she was already walking down the jetty.

'What was all that about?' Bea asked.

'Honestly I've no idea. For whatever reason, she's acting all weird and doesn't want me to go to the auction today.'

'Why?' Bea asked puzzled.

'Your guess is as good as mine,' Nell answered, not having a clue why her mum was so against it. 'I simply have no idea.'

'Strange, that's not like Gilly, usually she's very supportive,' replied Bea, shrugging her shoulders, 'She hasn't said anything to me.'

'Me neither, except Ollie wouldn't want me to do this,' she raised her eyebrows, 'but I know Ollie would support me in this.'

'And how are you feeling, after everything?'

'All over the place. Sad that it didn't work out with Guy, but excited that I may win the auction.'

'Nathan will pick you up just before 8a.m. Don't be nervous.'

'I'll try my hardest.'

'Right, I'd best get back to baking and make sure you text me when you know one way or the other.'

'I will, I promise.'

'And good luck. If it's meant to be, it's meant to be!'

A while later Nell walked along the wharf towards the main road. She waved at Ed, who was pottering about inside the yard and Sam was at his heels, but Guy was nowhere to be seen. She waited by the roadside and spotted Nathan's blue BMW driving towards her. He pulled over and she climbed inside, clutching her bag, which contained all the paperwork for today.

Once inside the car Nell let out a sigh.

'That's a big sigh.'

'Yes, I think the nerves are kicking in now.'

Nell focused on the road ahead. She hadn't been to a house auction before and didn't know what to expect.

'Bea told me about Guy.' Nathan gave Nell a quick sidelong glance as he changed gear. 'I'm sorry.'

'Me too,' Nell said, still staring at the road ahead.

They drove in silence for a couple of minutes before Nell spoke, 'How's Bea doing after Dot's death? She hasn't really mentioned it.'

'She hasn't spoken to me much about it either. I think it's had a massive effect on her but she's keeping it all bottled up.'

'Has she seen or heard from Fern again.'

Nathan kept his eyes on the road but shook his head. 'No, thankfully, and I'm hoping it stays that way. The less stress she has in her life the better, especially with the baby.'

The road into town was already busy and they began to

The Cosy Canal Boat Dream

crawl towards the town centre. Nell glanced out of the side window of the car, 'Whoa! Look at that crowd of people already gathering outside the auction room.'

'There's a fair few here, but, remember, there are an awful lot of properties up for auction today. They aren't all going to be there for the Old Picture House.'

'Yes you're right. I'm just beginning to feel the nerves. Look, I'm shaking,' said Nell, holding up her wobbly hand.

'Don't be nervous, just go with the flow,' said Nathan, manoeuvring the car into an empty space a stone's throw away from the auction house. As they climbed out of the car there seemed to be a frenzy of people.

Nell heard her name being hollered from the other side of the street. She turned round to see Lloyd standing on the other side of the road, dressed in his usual flamboyant style, waving his cane in her direction. Nell smiled as they crossed the road towards him.

'Good morning, Lloyd, what are you doing here?' asked Nell as they began to walk along the pavement together.

'Just some early morning banking. And yourself?'

'I'm here for the auction, for the Old Picture House.' She held up her crossed fingers and smiled.

'I hope you win and beat all those pesky developers. It'll be good for the marina.'

'Thanks, I'll let you know.'

'You make sure you do.'

He saluted and ambled up the road, tapping his cane as he walked.

'He's quite something, looks like a right character.'

'He does, doesn't he? Come on, let's get inside.'

'Are you ready to do this?' asked Nathan, 'I'm feeling nervous for you!'

Nell stood still and fumbled inside her coat pocket, grabbing a coin, 'Let's ask Ollie, 'Best of three ... Heads!' she called flipping the coin in the air and catching it.

'Heads.'

'Heads.'

'Heads.'

Nathan grinned, 'You and your coin! But it looks like he's on your side!'

They joined the back of the queue and filed into the auction room, which was already packed to the rafters.

There were clumps of people huddled together flicking through folders and comparing notes, and the noise was deafening. The place seemed to be dominated by men. In fact as Nell scanned the room she only saw another couple of females and one of those was the estate agent who had accompanied her and Guy on the viewing of the Old Picture House.

'The noise, it's so loud, is this normal?' Nell enquired with concern, following Nathan through the crowd of people.

'Yes, once the auction starts you'll be able to hear a pin drop,' Nathan answered. The room was laid out with rows and rows of chairs and they managed to grab two spare seats near the front.

'Oh God, my heart is actually racing. It feels like it's going to burst out of my chest at any minute,' said Nell, fidgeting in her seat.

'Just relax, take some deep breaths,' ordered Nathan,

The Cosy Canal Boat Dream

looking over towards the podium, where the auctioneer was standing skimming through the brochure.

'Not long to go now, he's getting ready.'

There was a buzz of excitement in the room as the auctioneer blew into the microphone and just like Nathan had said, the whole room fell silent.

Immediately, everyone sat down in their chair.

'Jeez,' Nell whispered. 'I feel like I've gone deaf.'

'I told you!'

Nell gazed towards the front of the room. The auctioneer introduced the first lot and began to spout words so fast that Nell couldn't keep up. Everyone's head synchronised between the bidders and the auctioneer. Hands were raised, heads were nodding and then the entire room turned towards the front, 'Going once, going twice ... sold.' The hammer thudded and within a matter of seconds the first lot was sold.

'That was quick,' Nell muttered, amazed.

'Soon be your turn,' Nathan whispered.

The two of them watched while the next three lots passed. One didn't reach the reserve price but the other two went way beyond.

'What if the Old Picture House goes way beyond my budget, too?'

'You can't speculate but any second now we are about to find out,' replied Nathan, squeezing her arm. 'Are you ready?'

'Ready as I'll ever be. Oh God.'

Nell spun her head around the room and then spotted a colourful figure standing right at the back of the room ... Lloyd.

He tipped his head and waved his cane in the air.

Nell smiled nervously back at him.

'What's he doing here?'

'Probably intrigued to see if you win. Here we go,' Nathan chimed.

Nell listened intently as the auctioneer's voice bellowed out the details.

Nell clutched the edge of her chair and kept her eyes firmly on the auctioneer.

'Lot number five, The Old Picture House, Little Rock Marina.'

Nell took a deep breath. Thoughts of her mum suddenly flashed through her mind, 'Don't do this, Nell, you'll have bitten off more than you can chew.' This was the first time she'd doubted herself. But Nell didn't have time to dwell on it any longer because immediately the reserve was met due to the internet bids. The tension ricocheted through the room and Nell had never felt tension like it.

Within seconds a hand was raised at the side of Nell.

'When do I bid?' She whispered to Nathan – her heart was pounding.

'Not yet, hold off, you don't want to show your hand too early. We don't want to push the price up if we don't need to. I'll tell you when.'

She nodded.

'Bid here at the front,' the auctioneer pointed straight at Nell.

Nathan's eyes widened, 'I told you to hang fire,' he said, amused, seeing the shock written all over Nell's face.

The Cosy Canal Boat Dream

Nell could have kicked herself, 'I was answering you,' she whispered.

Nathan gave a hearty laugh, 'Keep your head still. Take note. Do not move until I say.'

Nell was outbid from a gentleman at the back of the room and then by someone else to the side. When she swung round to have a look, that's when she noticed him standing next to Lloyd. Her heart hammered against her chest even harder, if that was at all possible, as Guy smiled back at her. He'd come to support her in his own way. As much as he'd made a mess of things, he was still rooting for her. She gave him a nod of appreciation and he smiled back. She turned back towards the auctioneer.

'Any advance on £65,000?' The auctioneer looked towards the man at the back of the room, who shook his head.

'Any more bids, any more bids.' The rapid combination of numbers took Nell by surprise.

'Going once ...'

'It's still within budget. Now!' ordered Nathan.

Catapulting her arm in the arm, 'I'm going to have a heart attack in a minute,' she uttered under her breath.

The auctioneer shifted his gaze back towards Nell.

'Lady at the front here.'

Nell nodded and was now the highest bidder.

'It's in the bag,' Nathan said, 'It's better than the horse racing, this is.'

The auctioneer's head swivelled around the room, 'Last shout out for the Old Picture House, Little Rock Marina, going once, he lifted his hammer, going twice ...'

Nell squealed and clapped her hands together.

'New bidder at the back of the room. The auctioneer pointed.'

'What?' exclaimed Nell.

The pair of them spun around.

'Who's bid?'

Nell snagged the eye of a woman standing at the back of the room and met the stony-faced stare from Kate. Her stomach churned.

'What's she doing here?' Nell hissed towards Nathan. Who is she?'

'Guy's wife, she's a property developer.'

Nell locked eyes with Kate, who gave her a smug smile.

'She's going to have more funds than me.' Nell could feel the anger rising inside her.

'Keep bidding,' Nathan encouraged, 'but do not go over your budget.'

'Any more takers?' The auctioneer bellowed. In a manic flurry Nell thrust her arm in the air and her bid was noted.

Kate nodded towards the auctioneer with a haughty look on her face.

They were now in direct competition.

Nell had never been more determined in her life. Her hand was firmly in the air.

She turned round and stared at Kate, then noticed Guy swiftly weaving towards her through the crowd, but Kate didn't take her eyes off Nell and raised her arm again.

Within a couple of seconds he was at Kate's side and Nell could see a heated discussion going on between them.

The Cosy Canal Boat Dream

Guy could have kicked himself for leaving the property details on the table, and was furious that Kate had dared to show up today. How did she think this was going to help their relationship?

'What the hell are you doing here?' he hissed.

'Bidding on a property, that's what us property developers usually do,' she uttered sarcastically.

'Don't do this,' ordered Guy, thinking of Nell, who'd put so much preparation into making this happen.

'But Guy, this one has so much potential.'

'Going once ...'

'Don't you dare,' ordered Guy furiously, before grabbing her elbow and escorting her out of the building.

'What do you think you are doing?' she spat, her lips were pursed.

He rolled his eyes and let go of her arm as a couple walked past them staring.

He lowered his voice, 'Never mind me. For God's sake, what the hell do you think you are doing? You know I was looking at this property for a friend.'

'Not just any friend, it seems. She doesn't look the sort to me who'd want to build houses. I could easily throw up a couple of apartments on that plot and make a quick profit.'

'And that's exactly what she doesn't want to happen.'

Kate tilted her head to one side, 'Romantic notions never made profit,' she said, giving a self-deprecating laugh then rubbing her elbow with a hurt expression on her face.

'Oh please, stop the drama, I didn't grab you that hard,' claimed Guy, as he noticed people beginning to file out the

Christie Barlow

back of the auction house. 'Just go back to the hotel, will you.'

Kate opened her mouth to protest but thought better of it. His eyes blazed at her as he watched her turn and storm off up the market place. He didn't follow but spun round as he recognised the excited chatter behind him.

Lloyd was congratulating Nell, and Nathan was standing by her side, beaming like a Cheshire cat.

'You will be the making of that place,' he touched her arm. 'I have every faith.'

'Please come to the opening night ... even though it will be a while off yet.'

Lloyd nodded his appreciation before crossing over the road and disappearing amongst the crowd of shoppers.

'Does this mean you won?' asked Guy nervously.

Nell grinned and the relief was written all over her face. 'I'm so pleased for you, Nell, you deserve this,' Guy went to hug her but then held back. He didn't want to make this any harder than it already was.

Nell sensed his hesitation, 'Come here, give me a hug and thank you for everything, looking over my plans, talking me through the finances.' Her heart began to beat in double time and every nerve in her body tingled as she inhaled his aroma for one last time.

'Take care, Guy, and be happy.'

He forced a smile but the sadness in his eyes told a different story. 'You too, Nell. Take care.'

Nell and Nathan watched Guy walk through the square until he disappeared.

'You alright?' Nathan asked tentatively.

The Cosy Canal Boat Dream

'Yes, even though I thought it was all over, thanks to Kate, until Guy escorted her out of the room.'

'Well, don't worry about that now – onwards and upwards.' He leaned towards her and picked her up and spun her around like a little child, 'Ollie would be so proud of you and even prouder when that old place is up and running again.'

'Yes, he would be and I can't wait to get started! Eek! I'm actually the proud owner of the Old Picture House. Pinch me, Nathan, I can't quite believe it.'

Nathan pinched her arm.

'Ouch! I didn't mean it!' she laughed.

'You need to go back in and fill in the legal stuff, tell them your solicitor's details and all that stuff.'

'That shouldn't take too long – and, to celebrate, how about I treat you to lunch at the deli?'

'Sounds like an excellent plan, especially if it includes seeing my beautiful wife – then I am always up for that.'

'I can't wait to spill the news!' grinned Nell, linking her arms with his, 'and I think we both deserve no less than a whole bottle of champers!'

Chapter 34

A sudden surge of emotion flooded through Nell as she opened the deli door and met the gaze of her mum and Bea.

Nell took a deep breath and exhaled. She'd intended to stay poker-faced and kid them along that she'd been pipped at the post, but to their utter relief Nell's face broke into a huge smile.

'OMG! OMG! You did it! You did do it, didn't you?' exclaimed Bea, weaving around the counter towards Nell.

Nathan stood behind her like a proud parent, 'She did it indeed!' he beamed, patting her on her back.

Gilly looked sheepish as she tucked her tea towel under her belt and walked towards Nell. 'Congratulations,' she said half-heartedly, kissing her on both cheeks.

'Have you signed all the legal stuff?'

'I've given them all my solicitor's details. Now, please stop worrying about me. Nothing will go wrong, I've got this.'

Gilly wasn't exactly brimming with enthusiasm and busied herself back behind the counter. Bea shrugged her shoulders at Nell, then went to hug her one more time.

The Cosy Canal Boat Dream

'Look at that sparkle in your eyes. I'm so proud of you! And I know Ollie would be too. What happens now?'

Nell cast her eyes around the deli, 'Let's grab that table over there and a pot of tea,' Nell said jokingly.

'Tea? Tea,' Bea screwed her face up, 'More like a glass of the good stuff for you lot. Gilly, there's a bottle in the bottom of the fridge. I'll have my usual orange juice!'

'Glass of the good stuff, that sounds more like it,' said Nathan, before kissing Bea on the cheek, 'and how are you feeling, my lovely wife?'

'I was feeling all anxious this morning, waiting to see what happened.'

'It was touch and go for a minute,' Nathan kept his voice low.

'What do you mean?'

'Guy's wife ...'

'Kate?'

'Only turned up and began to bid against Nell. They went head to head.'

'You're joking?'

'No,' he shook his head.

'And Lloyd was there.' Nell chipped in.

'Lloyd?' Gilly asked cautiously, appearing by the side of the table.

'Yes. He walked me home last night and came in for a cuppa and I told him all about the auction. Actually, he was very supportive,' Nell looked towards her mother, 'He thought it was a great idea to bring the community back together by re-opening the old place.'

Gilly's eyes widened and her face paled, 'He was on your boat? Oh, Nell, you need to be careful, you can't go entertaining strangers on the boat.'

Nell chuckled, 'Stop being overdramatic, he was lovely. What do you think he's going to do, hit me over the head with his walking cane and rob my Cath Kidston bunting?'

'Stop being facetious.'

Nell stared at her mum, noticing again the strange tension in the air whenever the Old Picture House was mentioned.

'Never mind all that, you've gone and done it! Let's celebrate,' said Bea, smiling.

Nathan disappeared behind the counter and returned holding four champagne flutes. 'It's time to make a toast,' insisted Bea, clearing her throat.

'Oh God, I hope this isn't going to be like our wedding.' Nathan laughed.

Bea rolled her eyes at him, 'I'll have you know, speeches don't always have to be done by the best man, there are best women in the world too!' She put her arm around Nell and smiled as Gilly popped the cork and filled up their glasses with fizz.

Bea cleared her throat, 'Ha hum ...' her eyes were tearful as she caught Nell's gaze. She took a deep breath. 'Today, I think you'll all agree, not that we are biased or anything ... we are super- proud of you, Nell, and we wish you all the success with your new business venture.'

'Oh stop, you're going to make me cry!'

'It has to be said,' Bea blinked away her own tears. 'We all miss Ollie and we all wish things were different but I know,

The Cosy Canal Boat Dream

you all know, he would be so proud of you.' They all raised their glasses, 'Here's to Nell, the Old Picture House and, of course, to Ollie.'

They all echoed Bea's words.

'The development of the Old Picture House will bring a new lease of life to Little Rock Marina, that's for sure,' chipped in Nathan, 'And I can't wait to be sitting in those plush-velvet red bucket seats once more, eating popcorn on a Friday night. I'm assuming it is free popcorn for friends,' he winked at Nell.

'Without a doubt!'

They all raised their glass once more.

'To Nell,' they chorused.

They all clinked their glasses and took a sip.

'What's next? When do you get your hands on the actual keys?' Bea asked, sliding into the seat next to Nell.

'There's a fourteen-day completion rule, but once the money is transferred it could potentially be sooner, depending on my solicitor. Then I can get to work.' Nell rubbed her hands together in enthusiasm. 'So, soon it will be all systems go. I've got the builder in place and can give Mike the heads-up, he'll organise the clearance of the site and the builders accordingly.'

'You sound like a proper property developer,' grinned Nathan.

'Is it just as easy as that?' asked Bea, amazed at how quickly it all could get moving.

'I'm hoping it all runs smoothly, but before the clearance can start I need to go back inside and make a list of everything I want to keep, especially the room where all the films and equipment were kept.'

'I'd love to have a peek inside before the clearance begins.'

'Of course. I'm sure the estate agent will give me the keys for a couple of hours so we can have a quick look around.'

Nell knew the next six months were going to be sheer hard work, but she was ready for it, 'And once it's all finished, I want you all walking down that red carpet with me on opening night,' she chuckled, 'We'll be like proper famous movie stars.'

They could all hear the happiness in Nell's voice.

'You bet. Any excuse for a new dress,' giggled Bea.

'I knew somehow it would end up costing me money,' Nathan kissed the top of his wife's head.

Suddenly everyone noticed Nell had gone very quiet.

'You okay?' mouthed Bea.

'Red Carpet,' answered Nell.

'You've lost me.' Bea arched an eyebrow.

'The Red Carpet Cinema. Wouldn't that be a fantastic name for the Old Picture House? What do you think?' Nell asked, flicking a glance between them all.

Bea mulled it over for a second, then a fleeting smile played across her lips, 'You know what? I actually quite like that.' She held up her glass, 'Here's to the Red Carpet Cinema.'

'The Red Carpet Cinema,' everyone clinked their glasses together.

Chapter 35

The warmer days were coming; the sky was an alluring blue with a few clouds dotted around and Nell, Bea and Gilly stood in front of the Old Picture House. Nell shook with a mixture of pleasure and fear as she jangled the keys in the air.

'The estate agent has let us borrow the keys for a couple of hours max.'

'That's really kind of them,' said Bea, clapping her hands together in excitement.

'I know, I just wanted to have a look at the stuff that I might be able to salvage before the completion goes through.'

'Good idea.'

'I feel like I'm about to burst,' grinned Nell, 'Are we ready?'

Bea hovered behind her, waiting for her to open the door, 'Come on, hurry up!'

'And Mum ... I've no idea why you've bought a pile of cleaning products with you. The whole place is going to be gutted as soon as the money has been deposited in the account and the builder sends his men in.'

'Always be prepared,' claimed Gilly, 'You never know what we might need.'

Christie Barlow

As Nell twisted the key in the lock she swallowed down an excited squeal and wrapped her fingers around the door handle. She took a deep breath and pushed opened the heavy door with a flourish.

'Ta-dah! Welcome to the Red Carpet Cinema,' she said tremulously, her heart clattering with anticipation.

All three of them stood in the magnificent foyer and took in their surroundings. The sunlight poured through the broken glass windows and specks of dust danced about before their eyes.

'Look at this place, it's just how I remembered it,' said Bea in awe. Gilly placed the box of cleaning products on the floor and they all spun round, taking in the view.

'I can just imagine crowds of people queuing up here for their tickets, then over there for their ice-creams.'

'How are you feeling?' asked Bea, tentatively.

Tears pricked Nell's eyes, 'Ollie would have loved this so much.'

Ollie.

She was doing this for Ollie, his memory.

'He would.' Gilly squeezed her arm, for the first time showing her support for the project.

Wiping the tears with the back of her hand, she gave out a tiny laugh, 'I'm not sad, just emotional,' she admitted. 'I'm feeling good.'

Today was the start of Nell's future.

She sighed happily, 'Come on, let's sort out what we need to keep.'

'Anyone there?' the door opened and Nathan strolled in.

The Cosy Canal Boat Dream

'What have you done with Jacob?'

'He's gone to his friends for tea and I couldn't miss this,' he said, 'I hope you don't mind me gate-crashing.'

'Not at all, come on in.'

'I was expecting a pile of rubble inside,' he admitted, 'It's quite spectacular, isn't it?'

'It's something else,' agreed Nell, 'But when we go through to the cinema rooms it may be a little dark, the electricity wasn't working when I first came to view the place.'

'I can have a look at that,' Nathan suggested, 'You go ahead. I'll catch you up.'

They watched Nathan wander over to the cloakroom area before Bea and Gilly followed Nell down the ramp towards the smaller screen.

'Oh my memories, memories, memories,' said Gilly.

'It seems a little strange we are in here and it's soon to be mine.' Nell met her mum's gaze. 'Here, I remembered to bring a torch,' she said, fishing around in her handbag and handing one to her mum.

Shining the beam towards the chairs, 'What do you think? Are they salvageable? I know they smell damp and a few of them are ripped, but do you reckon they could be saved with a deep clean?'

Gilly ran her hand over one, 'Yes, definitely feels damp,' she said, bending over and wriggling her nose, 'and pongs a little, too, but they are not in bad condition at all, considering.'

Nell walked up each row, checking the condition of each chair, when suddenly the whole place burst with light.

'Whoa! Electricity!' exclaimed Nell, trying to focus as dots danced before her eyes.

The door swung open and Nathan swiped his hands together, 'All fixed, the electricity had tripped at the mains, probably due to the rain seeping in, who knows.'

'Thanks, Nathan! At least we can give everywhere a thorough inspection now.'

Thirty minutes later, all three of them were up in the projector room. It was an emporium of treasures. Reels and reels of films, posters, ice-cream trays and clapperboards.

'All this stuff should belong in a museum. It's funny to think that even after technology has evolved so much they still used the old methods to show the films in this cinema,' Gilly mused while blowing the dust off a couple of reels. 'Do you think you are going to go all digital on us, Nell?'

Nell stood and thought about it for a moment, 'I have no idea, but wouldn't it be fantastic to keep at least one of the cinemas with this set-up? Playing the old films from the past using the old-fashioned methods. I mean, look at all this ...'

She chewed her lip while deliberating what to do about the old projector. 'It's an amazing piece of equipment. I wonder if it still works?'

'There's only one way to find out,' said Nathan, bending down at the side of the machine and scrunching up his face with concentration.

He flicked a switch and a cloud of dust spluttered into the air. He coughed as the machine began to whir, then he flicked a lever. They watched in amazement as the empty reel holder began to turn. Nell twisted the lens caps and pulled. A bright

The Cosy Canal Boat Dream

beam of light shone straight through the small window in front of them towards the heavy-duty curtains in the cinema below.

'Well, just look at that!' Nell clapped her hands together in excitement.

'I can't believe it's still working,' Gilly answered.

Nell raised her eyebrows and held out her hand, 'Wait there!'

They all watched Nell run out of the room, her footsteps echoed towards the main foyer, then they finally petered out, but soon they heard Nell holler, 'Down here.'

Bea rushed towards the window and saw Nell standing below in the auditorium, madly waving her arms at them.

'What are you doing?' she shouted.

'Watch!'

They all stood and watched as Nell fumbled around with a switch panel at the side of the room and suddenly there was a loud creaking noise.

Gilly gasped and grabbed Bea's hand, 'My gosh, look.'

The curtains began to part slowly until, finally, the old cinema screen was revealed.

Nell gave them the thumbs-up and within a couple of seconds was standing back in the projector room. 'How magical was that?' said Nell, glancing through the window towards the cinema below.

'Like some grand unveiling,' Gilly said, smiling at her daughter's excitement.

Nell spun round to them both, 'This is a crazy idea but ...' Nell's voice rose an octave.

'You look mischievous,' grinned Bea.

'Pick a reel,' Nell insisted, her eyes sparkled as she playfully pushed Bea towards the boxes on the shelf. 'And don't look which one it is.'

Bea reached to a high shelf and pulled down a box.

'Pass it to Nathan.'

He held out his hands, not having a clue what Nell was up to.

'Do you think you can hook it up to the projector?'

'I'll give it my best shot,' he said, staring at her, then towards the black contraption.

'Come on,' she said, grabbing her mum's and Bea's hands, 'Let's go. Take a seat and watch a film!' Nell's heart skipped with happiness as they hurried towards the cinema screen.

Within five minutes the auditorium burst into life, the sound boomed out, 'OMG its "Asteroid"! Now we are in a proper cinema!' Nell squealed, conducting the theme tune and humming loudly.

'Got to love a bit of Pearl and Dean,' Nathan grinned sliding into the seat next to them.

'I feel like a kid in a sweetshop,' grinned Nell,

'It's just a shame we haven't got any popcorn.' Gilly slid into the chair, making herself comfy.

'I've got a packet of fruit pastilles, but quite honestly I'm not sure how long they've been festering away in my jacket pocket, but I'm more than happy to share.' Nathan reached inside his pocket.

'I think on this occasion I'll pass,' chuckled Nell.

'It's about to start.'

The Cosy Canal Boat Dream

'Shh! Keep your voice down,' Nell whispered, widening her eyes towards Bea and everyone giggled like a group of school kids.

Bea leant across and slapped her knee playfully. They all settled down in their chairs and watched the title roll.

'I don't think I'm familiar with this one.' Nell crossed her legs, trying to get comfy, 'Do you know it, Mum?'

Gilly didn't answer – she was too busy staring at the screen.

'She's watching the film,' Bea whispered in Nell's ear, 'Stop yattering!'

Nell squeezed her knee.

Bea rested her head on Nathan's shoulder and he tilted his head towards and smiled, 'I feel like a teenager again!'

'You've got a good memory, then!'

No one spoke for the next twenty minutes as they watched the film, until suddenly Nell bolted upright and stared at the screen.

'What's up with you?' whispered Bea, but wasn't sure why she was actually whispering as there was only the four of them there. It wasn't as though she was interrupting the film for anyone else.

'Surely not,' she muttered.

'Surely not what?' queried Bea, looking at the screen, then back towards Nell.

'I thought I recognised him, but I couldn't quite think where from. Then it hit me. He's so much younger there and without his beard.' Nell shifted in her seat and scrutinised the screen. 'Yes, it's him.'

'Who's him?' asked Nathan, intrigued.

'That man. Look at him closely, admittedly he's a lot younger.'

'Where am I even meant to be recognising him from?'

'It's Lloyd, the man on the boat, you know ... the one that Guy rescued. He was at the auction with us.'

Nathan scrutinised the screen, 'I think you're right.'

'But he told me that his wife was an actress. He never mentioned anything about him being an actor, too!'

'And his boat is called Much Ado About Nothing.'

'He was at the auction with you?' Gilly suddenly chipped in.

'Not exactly with us, with us. We bumped into him outside and then I noticed him standing at the back of the auction room.'

'You know what, Nell, it's definitely him.' Nathan was still looking at the screen. Do you know him, Gilly? Is he an actor from way back?'

They all swivelled their heads towards Gilly.

'I'm not familiar with him at all,' she answered, her voice shaky.

'Well I never. I can't wait to ask him,' Nell slumped back in her chair and tucked her feet underneath her.

Once the film had come to an end, they all sat forward in their seats and watched the credits begin to whizz up the screen.

'Yes! It's him, Look!' She pointed towards the screen.

'Lloyd Keaton! Well, fancy that!' exclaimed Nell.

'You must mention it to him next time you see him; the first film you watched in your cinema was with him in it,' said Bea.

The Cosy Canal Boat Dream

'I'm almost tempted to go across now. We have our very own film star mooring at our marina.'

'I'll switch the lights on,' Nathan bounded over to the panel and flicked the switch. Immediately the room lit up.

'How brilliant is that? Everything actually all still works, so apart from new windows, carpets, curtains and a lick of paint, if we deep-clean these seats we could be up and running within six months. What do you all think? Would that be realistic?'

'Possibly, but you really do need to check out the wiring, plumbing and all that. It will certainly be full on. Maybe it's worth thinking about keeping one of the cinema rooms for all the old films like this, and setting up a digital one for the latest releases,' suggested Nathan.

She nodded, 'What do you think, Mum?' They all turned towards Gilly, who hadn't joined in any of the conversation. She'd turned a ghastly white colour and all of sudden didn't look well.

'You okay, Gilly?' asked Bea, raising her eyebrows at Nell, who looked at her mum with concern.

'Mum?'

'You've looked like you've seen a ghost.' Nathan touched her arm.

Gilly roused herself, but it was clear she was having difficulty speaking, 'I'm just feeling a little unwell. I think I'm getting one of my headaches, it's been a while. I need to go.'

And with that she got up and hurried out of the auditorium.

'What was that all about?' asked Bea

'I've simply no idea but I'm going to find out,' Nell said, dumbfounded, watching the cinema door swing shut after her mum. 'I'm genuinely worried about her. She doesn't seem herself lately at all, especially where this place is concerned.'

'No it's not like Gilly at all.'

Chapter 36

The next day, Nathan pulled the car into an empty space in the hospital car park and smiled towards his wife. It was the afternoon of their first scan. He'd already picked Jacob up from school and dropped him at the deli, armed with the latest Lego magazine. Nell was looking after him until closing time.

'You've got that look about you now,' Nathan said, smiling warmly at his wife, before switching off the car engine.

'What look?'

'That sexy glow to your cheeks kind of look.'

'I really don't feel like I'm glowing, more like I'm burning. This one in here has it's very own central heating system,' she said, patting her tummy.

He leant over and kissed Bea on the cheek before climbing out of the car and walking round to her side.

'I can barely climb out of the car,' she puffed, 'It's embarrassing. I feel like I've already put on loads of weight.'

'Craving for scones with butter doesn't help,' he teased, 'If you carry on eating four of those a day you will be waddling sooner than normal.'

She playfully hit his arm before holding his hand and strolling towards the main entrance of the hospital.

Once inside, they followed the blue arrows on the signs up the squeaky-clean corridors towards the ante-natal clinic.

'It only seems like two minutes since we were here last,' Bea said, handing the appointment letter over to the receptionist, who told them to take a seat in the waiting room. They sat down on the uncomfortable plastic chairs and Bea thumbed through an ancient magazine.

'Why is it these places always make me feel nervous?' Bea said. Glancing up towards the TV screen that was airing repeats of the Jeremy Kyle Show, 'And that's something I won't be doing whilst on maternity leave,' she rolled her eyes.

'What's that?' Nathan asked.

'Watching brain-numbing TV. That's enough to drive anyone back to work.'

'What are your plans for maternity leave?'

'I've not really thought about it yet. I'll see how I feel, but maybe it's best if I start to look for more help, especially now Nell will be busy with the cinema.'

Nathan agreed, 'I think that a good idea.'

'Blimey! She's got her hands full,' Bea exclaimed, flickering her eyes towards a heavily pregnant woman who sat down on the other side of the artificial plant. She was pushing a double buggy and grasping the hand of a toddler.

'Beatrice Green,' they heard a voice shout.

'Urghh, I hate that name,' Bea muttered under her breath.

Nathan smiled at his wife in amusement. 'There's nothing wrong with your name. It's beautiful and suits you.'

The Cosy Canal Boat Dream

They followed the nurse to a room at the end of the corridor.

'Hi, my name is Natalie. I'm your sonographer,' she gave Bea a reassuring smile. 'How are you feeling?'

'Yes good, the sickness has become a little more bearable.'

'That's good to hear. If you slip your shoes off and make yourself comfy on the couch ... and Mr Green?'

Nathan looked at Natalie. 'Take a seat next to your wife,' she gestured to the seat beside Bea.

Natalie lowered the table and Bea climbed on.

Nathan leant across and held her hand.

'Okay, I can see from your notes that you've done this before, but I'll just recap what is going to happen.' Natalie switched on the monitor and typed some details into the computer before turning back towards Bea and Nathan. She smiled. 'At this twelve-week scan this is the first in-depth look at your baby. We look and listen for the heartbeat, measure the size of the embryo to check the due date of the pregnancy. It allows us to assess the early developments of your baby. Do you have any questions before we start?'

Bea shook her head and looked at Nathan, 'No I think we are good,' he answered.

'Great, let's make a start, then. I'm going to put some gel on your tummy. It may feel a little cold,' Natalie informed Bea, squeezing the gel on to her tummy and tucking tissue paper around her to protect her clothing. 'You may feel a little pressure, but it shouldn't be painful.' She began to slide the hand-held transducer over Bea's skin.

At first the monitor was facing Natalie. Intently she watched the screen then turned to face Bea and Nathan.

Christie Barlow

'Is everything okay?' Bea asked, a little worried.

Natalie swung the monitor towards them both and beamed. Nathan and Bea stared at the black and white image on the screen.

'They are both doing absolutely fine,' Natalie answered.

Bea's mind boggled, 'What do you mean, they are both doing fine?'

'Healthy heartbeat number one, healthy heartbeat number two,' she pointed at the monitor, 'Congratulations Mr and Mrs Green, you are expecting twins.'

Startled, Bea swung round towards Nathan, her jaw had dropped to the floor and she was so overwhelmed her eyes filled with tears.

'Twins?' Nathan questioned, 'Are you absolutely sure?'

'I'm absolutely sure,' Natalie confirmed. 'Any twins in the family?'

'My mum's a twin,' piped up Nathan.

'Well, there you go,' smiled Natalie, taking the measurements of each baby and recording them on the screen.

'Twins,' Bea squealed, not quite believing what was happening.

They watched the two hearts pulsating as the nurse talked them through the position of the babies.

As soon as the scan was over and the excess gel wiped off Bea's tummy she stood up and hugged her husband.

'You know what this means don't you?'

'Double crying, no sleep whatsoever, double washing, and double projectile vomiting!' he grinned.

'Double love! I can't wait to tell Jacob and Nell.'

The Cosy Canal Boat Dream

The next scan appointment was booked and once outside the hospital building, Bea couldn't wait a moment longer, she was bursting to share her news as she punched in Nell's number.

'Hi Bea, my godson is only on his second cupcake, nothing to worry about at this end.' Bea could hear Jacob giggle, 'Aunty Nellie, that was our secret!'

'Anyway, how did the scan go?'

Bea paused for a second.'

'Bea are you okay?'

'Are you sat down?' Bea teased in quite a serious tone.

'You're worrying me now, yes I'm sat down.'

'There isn't going to be one baby Green, there's going to be two! I'm expecting twins!'

Nell shrieked down the phone so loudly that Bea held the phone away from her ear and Nathan laughed.

'Eek! Double the cuddles, I am so excited for you.'

'I'm glad about that because, Aunty Nellie, you are going to have your work cut out on double babysitting duties!'

'The pleasure will be all mine!'

Chapter 37

It was the early hours of Wednesday morning and Nell couldn't sleep. She made herself a cup of tea and curled up next to the warm glow of the fire. All of a sudden she felt sad and let out a weary sigh.

Last week she'd been on a high, winning the auction, but now there was no denying she felt at an all-time low. She'd tried to talk to Gilly about her quick exit from the Old Picture House but she'd just reiterated that she'd come over all queasy and had been off work ever since with a sickness bug and with Guy heading back to Ireland today she just wanted to hide herself away from the world.

'Deep breaths,' Nell told herself. If it wasn't meant to be, it wasn't meant to be. Even though Ireland wasn't a million miles away from Little Rock Marina, it still felt like the other side of the world to her.

She knew it was for the best that he was putting his child first and she wouldn't have it any other way, but that still didn't stop her from hurting or wanting things to be different.

Startled, she heard a rap on the door. Nell raised her eyes and came face to face with Guy. Her face lit up briefly when

The Cosy Canal Boat Dream

she saw him, but then her heart plummeted. She knew this was goodbye.

She rose to her feet and unlocked the door, 'Hi.'

He dropped his hood back from his coat and smiled, 'It's quite fresh out there,' he said, rubbing his hands together.

'I'm sure it is at this time in the morning.'

'I didn't know if you'd be up.'

'I couldn't sleep, a bit of a restless night. Come on in, don't stand in the doorway.'

'Me too,' he admitted, stooping his head and walking inside the 'Nollie'. 'I'm leaving in an hour, and I couldn't go without saying goodbye.'

'Ed told me you were leaving today,' Nell could already feel herself trembling. She bit down on her lip to stop the tears escaping, 'Where's Sam?' she asked, trying to steer the conversation in any other direction – she wasn't ready to say goodbye.

'He's staying here for the time being, with Ed. I think he likes the company and he's got used to the yard. It was Ed's idea.'

'You'll miss him,' she said, her voice barely a whisper, 'At least there's a little part of you that's staying behind.'

'You make sure you give him lots of cuddles from me.'

'I will,' promised Nell.

'I'm going to miss you,' he said softly, touching her hand lightly before holding out his arms wide. She met his eyes and took a tiny step towards him, her shoulders drooped and she stepped into his arms. Neither of them said a word as they hugged, their cheeks pressed together. Nell's tear dropped on to his shoulder.

'I'm glad our paths crossed, even if it was for a short time,' he said softly.

Nell couldn't trust herself to speak – she could only manage a nod. They clung to each other before finally pulling apart.

'I feel like someone's died,' she swallowed down a lump in her throat.

'I know what you mean.' He looked at her grief-stricken face and brushed away a stray hair, hooking it around her ear and stroked her chin softly. 'Listen to me, you are going to be brilliant at bringing that picture house back to life and I'm sure Ed will keep me up to date with all developments.'

She nodded.

'If only things were different,' he whispered.

'I know, it's complicated.'

Nell's heart sank and she closed her eyes, 'This is it, isn't it? I'm never going to see you again.'

'You will, don't say that. I promise you'll see me again.'

'One day,' she thumped his chest, 'You know what, Guy Cornish, you'll make the most fantastic dad and junior will be very lucky to have you. Promise you'll send me lots of pictures when the baby is born.'

Guy's eyes glistened with tears. 'I will.' He squeezed her hands tightly, his heart pounding against his chest.

'I've got to go, Ed's giving me a lift to the airport.' He took a deep breath and tilted her chin towards him, 'I'm so glad I met you, Nell Andrews.'

'Me too, obviously I mean you, not me,' Nell forced a laugh through her tears, trying to make light of the situation.

The Cosy Canal Boat Dream

He lowered his head and kissed her. Neither of them wanted to pull apart.

'Go, just go,' she whispered, the tears flowing freely down her cheeks.

'I miss you already.' He kissed her lightly one last time before he hesitantly turned and walked away, his heart was breaking too.

Nell wrapped her arms around her body and hugged herself tightly. She watched him through the porthole of the 'Nollie'. Nell breathed deeply before saying to herself,

'I don't want you to go.'

Within seconds, he'd walked up the towpath and disappeared out of sight.

She caught her breath and slumped on to the chair, her heart had only just begun to mend and now it had smashed into thousands of tiny pieces once more.

Chapter 38

Nell spent the rest of the day in a daze. After she'd finished work at the deli she wanted to clear her head and walked along the towpath, nodding at dog-walkers and boat-owners until a couple of hours later she found herself standing on the steps of Bluebell Cottage. The cottage looked beautiful at this time of year; the daffodils bloomed and danced at the edge of the path leading towards the old front door and clusters of crocuses had burst into bloom and encircled the foot of the old oak tree. Everywhere Nell looked, it teemed with life. She loved everything about Bluebell Cottage, her childhood home full of wonderful memories. Nell's thoughts switched to her dad, Benny. They'd shared a real father and daughter bond and he had been kind and considerate and had always encouraged Nell to be the best at what she did, however hard she struggled. She smiled, remembering the time her dad had taught her to tie her shoelaces. She must have been about seven, and it hadn't been an instant success, instead taking her numerous attempts over many weeks. But he'd had the patience of a saint where Nell was concerned, and finally, when Nell had mastered the art, he'd simply smiled

The Cosy Canal Boat Dream

and said he'd known she'd get there in the end. She was lucky to have shared such precious time with her dad.

As she knocked on the front door of the cottage she wondered what her dad would have made of her buying the Old Picture House. She glanced to the side of the cottage and noticed that her mum's bike was missing. Usually it was propped up underneath the window.

She cupped her hand around her eyes and peered through the kitchen window, but there were no signs of life.

Rummaging in her bag, she fished out her keys and opened the door. 'Mum, are you here?' Nell called out.

There was silence, except for a thud on the ceiling above. 'Mum, is that you?'

There was no answer and, as she peered up the stairs, she was startled to see three pairs of eyes staring back at her.

'Phew, you gave me a fright, I forgot you were here,' she said, heaving a sigh of relief.

The kittens padded down the stairs towards her and one of them arched his back, brushing his black and white body against her, 'My you've grown, Oreo,' she said, scooping him up into her arms. He snuggled into her neck and began to purr contentedly before she placed him back on the floor.

Nell wandered into the kitchen. She loved this room; it had a homely feel about it, with a round pine table in the middle and four chairs tucked underneath, a Belfast sink at one end and a sofa and coffee table at the other. This really was the hub of the house. Nell wriggled her nose, the aroma of freshly baked cake led her straight towards the cake tin. 'Yum,' she said, picking up a knife and immediately tucking into a slice of ginger cake. Switching on the kettle, she made herself a cuppa and texted her mum.

'Where are you?' she pressed send. Instantly, she heard her mum's phone beep – it had been left on the kitchen table. Wherever she was, she'd left her phone behind.

Nell pulled out a chair and sat down, moving an old shoebox out of the way. She didn't have a clue where her mum was, but she'd drink her tea and leave her a quick note to let her know she'd been. Glancing up at the kitchen clock she felt sad. She knew Guy would be well and truly back at home in Ireland by now, with Kate. She sipped on her drink and turned her attentions back to the old battered shoebox on the table. Nell didn't recognise the box and as curiosity got the better of her, she pulled it towards her, lifting the lid.

Inside was a handful of theatre and cinema stubs, old programmes from the theatre shows and tickets to the old theatre in the next city.

What was all this stuff?

Puzzled, she sat for a moment and stared at the box before tipping the contents on to the kitchen table and rummaging amongst it.

'It must be Mum's old memory box,' Nell said out loud. She couldn't believe her mum had kept it all these years. Some of this stuff dated back twenty years or so. Her eyes darted over the contents of the box and as she began to look at everything closely, Nell's mind whirled. There was one thing every memory in this box had in common ... Lloyd Keaton.

Nell was mystified. What was going on? This didn't make any sense.

The Cosy Canal Boat Dream

Why hadn't her mum said anything the other day when his name was mentioned? They'd even sat through a whole film together and she still claimed she didn't know who he was. Then Nell remembered her speedy exit from the auditorium.

According to this box of treasures, it looked as if her mum had followed Lloyd Keaton's career for years; actually, not followed, more like stalked. Nell thumbed through newspaper cuttings, magazine articles and could see that Lloyd Keaton was definitely a handsome pin-up in his day. Girls must have swooned over him.

Nell spotted a pile of envelopes bound together with ribbon. She counted over fifteen letters altogether, each one addressed to Lloyd Keaton and each one had been returned to sender, Gilly Harper...

She pulled on the ribbon, but noticed that each one of the envelopes was still sealed shut. None of it made any sense. This had certainly been some infatuation.

For a couple of seconds, Nell battled with her own conscience. Had these letters got anything to do with her mum's odd behaviour? Her hands were sweating as she grabbed a knife from the drawer and placed it under the lip of the envelope. Why was her mum writing to Lloyd and why were there so many letters? It just didn't make any logical sense.

Nell's heart was pounding and she was just about to open one of the letters when she heard a thud against the window and recognised the sound of her mum propping up her bike. Panic rose inside, her fingers fumbling as she quickly scooped everything else back into the box. She closed the lid and stood up at the kitchen sink just as her mum walked into the kitchen.

'Gosh, you frightened me then,' said Gilly, bringing her hand up to her chest. 'What are you doing here?'

'I've come to see how you are. Feeling better?'

'Better? ... Oh, yes, loads better, thank you. How long have you been here?' Nell noticed her mum's fleeting glance towards the shoebox.

'Long enough to make myself a drink and pinch a slice of that delicious cake. Where've you been?'

'I'd been pottering about in the garden so I cut some flowers and popped them on your dad's grave.'

Nell watched as her mum placed the cake tin on the kitchen table and swiftly picked up the shoebox.

'What've you got there?' queried Nell.

'Ooo, you are full of questions this morning aren't you? Where've you been? What's in there? Are you sure you're not the mum here?' answered Gilly, completely swerving the question.

Nell narrowed her eyes and observed her mum. She seemed a little agitated as she put the box on the worktop in the utility room and firmly closed the door behind her.

'More cake?' she asked, smiling at her daughter.

'Go on, then,' answered Nell, not taking her eyes off her mum for a second.

Gilly slid a couple of plates on to the table, 'You look tired today.'

Nell sighed, 'I didn't get much sleep.'

'Any reason why?'

The Cosy Canal Boat Dream

'Guy flew back to Ireland this morning.'

'How do you feel about that?' asked Gilly, sitting down at the table.

'Heartbroken, again.'

'Sometimes life deals a card for a reason. We just don't know what it is yet, but you'll be alright,' she promised.

He'd only been gone a matter of hours and Nell's heart was already aching. She could picture the warmth of his eyes, the feel of his touch, 'Well, I wish life would stop dealing these cards because it's confusing the hell out of me at the minute.'

'Would he have gone back to Ireland if it wasn't for the baby?'

Nell shook her head, 'I don't think he would have. From what he said, his marriage was long over, but now there's a child ...'

'That's a recipe for disaster, mark my words. No marriage can survive without love or mutual respect and it sounds like there's neither. Sometimes parents are better to be apart. It doesn't mean they love the child any less. He'll be back,' she said reassuringly, 'Trust me, I'm your mum.' Gilly gave Nell a knowing look.

'All I know is he's gone and I feel like I've lost my best friend.'

'Oh Nell,' Gilly squeezed her hand, 'You need to keep yourself occupied.'

'Yes, exactly, and the Old Picture House project will be good for me. Oh, and talking of the project ...' it was now or never, 'I was meaning to ask ...'

'About?'

Christie Barlow

Nell took a deep breath, her eyes turned towards her mum.

'Lloyd Keaton' she said out loud

Was it her imagination or did her mum just shiver at the sound of his name?

'Who?' Gilly stood up and avoided all eye contact with Nell. She placed the empty plates in the sink and wiped her hands on the tea towel before hooking it on the cupboard door.

'Lloyd Keaton,' Nell repeated.

Her mum's pupils dilated, but she stayed composed.

'The actor in that film. Are you sure you've never heard of him? He must have been around in your day.'

'Listen to you ... in my day ... You need to remember, we didn't have all this social media back then.' That was the only explanation forthcoming.

Now Nell knew her mum was definitely hiding something. She just had to work out how to get to the bottom of it. She had a feeling that the answer was in those letters. But how could she find out the truth without it looking as if she'd been snooping amongst her mum's personal belongings.

'Oh, guess who I bumped into this evening too?' prompted Gilly, quickly changing the subject.

'I've no idea, who?' answered Nell, going with the flow, but her mind still firmly thinking about the contents of the old shoebox.

'Nathan, he was taking Jacob to the park and he told me the news!'

'Twins! I know, who'd have thought?'

'They are going to have their work cut out,' Gilly said. 'It was hard enough with one.'

The Cosy Canal Boat Dream

'Did you never want any other children apart from me?' A question Nell had never asked before but had often thought about.

They stared at each other for a split second. Nell noticed her mum bite down on her lip, something she did when she felt anxious or uncomfortable.

'I was content with just you and couldn't ever imagine sharing my love. You were perfect.'

'What about Dad?'

'He felt exactly the same. We were over the moon to have one beautiful daughter. Now, what are your plans for the rest of the evening? I want to finish up in the garden. Do you want to help?'

There she goes again changing the subject, Nell noticed, shaking her head, 'I think I'm going to take advantage of the good weather and hose down the deck of the Nollie.'

'Good idea,' Gilly said, sliding her feet into her gardening shoes and grabbing her gloves from the windowsill.

Nell stood up and pressed a swift kiss to her mum's cheek, 'I'll see you in the morning at the deli.'

'Bright and early,' Gilly answered, waving a hand above her head and wandering down to the bottom of the garden.

Nell watched her for a moment before leaving Bluebell Cottage and strolling towards the towpath. She knew her mum was hiding something, she just knew she needed to get to the bottom of it.

The canal was busy for this time of year, the waters now dotted with brightly coloured narrowboats, chugging along.

She watched a tawny mallard guide her six fluffy ducklings away from the oncoming boats into the safety of the bank and she smiled at a standard poodle sitting by his master's side as he stood at the helm, guiding the boat through the calm water. The man saluted at Nell, who waved back as she climbed over the stile that led her back to Little Rock Marina.

Walking towards the moored boats, she squinted and noticed Ed in the yard, Sam was lying nearby on the flagstones, fast asleep. There were hordes of children, clutching balloons and party bags, who had wandered off the 'Mugtug', a barge for painting crockery, and pub-dwellers were beginning to frequent the tables outside the Waterfront pub.

Nell smiled at Fred, who was fishing off the side of his boat. He had a portable radio blaring out the latest horse race and then Fred punched the air with his fist.

'Did you win?' Nell shouted, smiling at his enthusiasm.

Fred spun round, 'Aye, I did, lass. Makes a change. Glad to see you're smiling. You seem in a better mood than your mum this afternoon.'

'My mum?' Nell was a little taken aback, 'I've just been up to the cottage.'

'I don't mind people taking my boat, but a little common courtesy doesn't go amiss,' he grumbled.

'You've lost me, Fred?'

'This afternoon your mum swung by and took my boat.'

Nell was taken by surprise, 'Are you sure it was Mum? I didn't even know she knew how to row.'

'Usually such a polite lady, too. She was definitely in a

The Cosy Canal Boat Dream

hurry.' Fred rolled his eyes. 'I asked her where the fire was and she blanked me. I wouldn't mind, but it's my boat.'

'She didn't even say where she was going?'

'No, she tied up the boat a good hour and half later and didn't even say thank you.'

Nell was bewildered. That didn't sound like her mum at all.

'Did you see where she went?'

'Aye, she rowed straight over to the far jetty.' He enlightened Nell by tipping his cap in the general direction.

She cast her eyes over the water, 'She got off over there?'

'Yes and straight on to that barge.'

She exhaled, 'Much Ado About Nothing, Lloyd Keaton's boat,' she uttered under breath.

Nell swung to face Fred, her eyes wide, 'Are you absolutely sure?'

'Yes, absolutely sure.'

'Enjoy your evening, Fred.' She smiled and jumped on the deck of the 'Nollie'. She thrust her hands in her pocket and stood at the rear of the boat. Her heart thumped as she stared towards the narrowboat on the other side of the marina.

What was it with Lloyd Keaton and what was her mum hiding? Nell had no idea, but she had a burning desire to get to the bottom of it.

Chapter 39

Thud. Thud. Thud.

Bea bolted upright in bed, 'What's that noise?' She shook Nathan, who was still fast asleep. 'Wake up, you'll sleep through anything, you will,' she said in a disgruntled manner.

'Huh,' he answered, rubbing his eyes, 'It's Sunday. Where's the fire?'

'I'm not sure, listen.'

They both listened.

Absolute silence.

'You're dreaming.'

'I'm not,' Bea insisted, but was beginning to wonder whether Nathan was actually right.

Thud. Thud. Thud.

'See,' she said, jumping out of bed and grabbing her dressing gown from the back of the door.

'That's the front door,' Nathan claimed, sliding into a pair of tracksuit bottoms and throwing a t-shirt over his head.

'I hope Jacob doesn't wake up,' Bea said, bounding downstairs and grasping the front-door keys from the hall table.

'Let me go first. Think of the babies.'

The Cosy Canal Boat Dream

'I'm quite capable,' Bea grappled with the lock and flung open the door, while Nathan peered over her shoulder.

Standing in front of her was Fern, her eyes were dark and she was visibly shaking.

'She had to die in your arms, didn't she,' the venom in her voice sent a shiver down Bea's spine and she could feel her own cheeks burning as she locked eyes with Fern.

'What are you doing, shouting the odds at this time in the morning? Are you drunk?' Nathan asked, his eyes narrowing at her.

'Drunk? You have the audacity to call me drunk?' she bellowed. Her eyes were red and bulging.

'What exactly are you doing here?' Bea said, her tone direct.

'This, this is what I am doing here,' she spat, rustling in her bag and pulling out an envelope.

Bea and Nathan stood rooted to the spot. 'What's that?'

'Here, take it,' she said, thrusting it into Bea's hand.

'Give it to me,' Nathan said, taking a moment to digest the information inside the envelope.

'What is it?' Bea asked, trying to read over his shoulder.

'It appears to look like your mum's will and from what I can see ... she's left everything in a trust for Jacob, until he's eighteen.'

'That about sums it up,' Fern said, fuming. 'Where have you been for the last few years while I've nursed her, fed her and bathed her?' She jabbed her finger towards Bea.

Bea had to admit, she was a little taken back by her mum's decision. It wasn't what she was expecting in a million years and she could see why Fern would be a little rattled by her decision.

'This was my inheritance, *mine*, and you've snatched this away from me. This was my chance to ...' Fern stopped in her tracks.

'Your chance to do what? Come on, to do what?' Bea probed, seeing for the first time the anguish in Fern's eyes.

Fern didn't answer.

'Maybe it's time you left,' said Nathan, trying to usher Bea back into the house. 'We don't need to get into slanging matches at this ungodly hour on the doorstep.'

'Is that all you've got to say?' Fern's face was flushed and she was staring straight at Nathan.

'Look, Fern, I can't change this decision and please don't come around here again shouting the odds.'

Fern raked her hand through her hair, the unshed tears glistened in her eyes. 'You don't understand,' she snatched the letter out of Nathan's hand, 'I needed this, I was relying on this,' She said, waving it in the air.

Bea narrowed her eyes at her sister. 'Why do you need the money so badly, are you in trouble?'

'What would you care if I was?'

'Try me.'

'I need a fresh start, away from here before it's too late, that's all.'

'Always a drama queen,' Nathan rolled his eyes.

Bea flicked a stare between the pair of them, 'Make a fresh start from what?' she asked, not letting the subject drop. 'I think you'd better come in,' Bea said, as she stared at her sister.

The Cosy Canal Boat Dream

'Are you serious?' Nathan questioned his wife, who shot him a warning look, and he was immediately silenced.

Fern stepped into the hallway, much to Nathan's displeasure, and followed Bea into the living room.

'Have a seat,' Bea gestured towards the settee while she sat in the chair opposite and Nathan hovered near the fireplace.

Bea stared at Fern, who looked visibly uncomfortable sitting there, but there was something telling Bea there was more going on here. She had a gut-wrenching feeling in the pit of her tummy.

'Why do you need the money that badly?' Bea asked tentatively, trying to coax her sister to talk.

'You aren't going to believe me if I told you.' Fern's voice faltered and her face crumpled. She bit down on her lip and blinked back the tears.

Bea handed her a tissue from the box on the table and Fern dabbed the corner of her eyes.

'I know you've lost mum and I do understand your grieving,' Bea spoke softly.

'It's not that.'

'Well, what is it? It can't be that bad that it can't be fixed. Are you in debt?' Is that why you need the money?'

Fern shook her head, 'It'll be easier if I just show you.'

Bea's mouth became dry and her palms sweaty as she watched Fern slip her arms from her coat. Bea and Nathan watched, both wondering what the hell was going on.

Fern rolled up the sleeves of her jumper and Bea and Nathan looked horrified. 'What are they ... burns?' stammered Bea.

Fern nodded, 'He does this to me, he twists my wrists and stubs his cigarettes out on me.' Fern stared towards the ground then swept her fringe to one side before flicking her teary eyes towards Bea.

'I needed that money to escape from him. I couldn't do it before. I couldn't leave Mum, but I knew once she was gone it was my chance, it was my chance to make a run for it. Start afresh somewhere else, where no one knows me and where he could never find me.'

Bea got up and sat herself down next to her sister on the settee, 'Why the hell haven't you told us before?'

'How could I?' she paused, 'After that night you cut me out of your life, and I don't blame you, I would have done the same in the circumstances, but I couldn't stand up to him, I was crying inside.'

She lifted up her jumper to reveal bruising to her ribs, 'This is what happens if I stand up to him or look at him in the wrong way.'

Bea gasped and stared, devastated at the hurt and pain that her sister had endured. 'Oh Fern.'

'That night, the night you came to pick up Jacob,' said Fern, 'I didn't mean to just stand there, I really didn't. I felt so ashamed, I wanted to scream at him for calling Jacob what he did. I wanted to scream that *he* was a heartless bastard. When Jacob was crying in his cot, he wouldn't let me pick him up or comfort him. Pete said he needed to learn that just because he cried didn't mean I would go to him and comfort him. But please believe me when I say, I knew he was safe in his cot, I knew he couldn't go anywhere and if I did try and

The Cosy Canal Boat Dream

go to him, I was frightened he would harm him too. I'm so sorry, I really am.'

Fern could barely breathe as Bea put her arms around her sister and pulled her in close. 'You're safe now,' she whispered. 'Nathan put the kettle on.' Bea glanced over her sister's shoulder towards him.

He nodded and immediately disappeared into the kitchen without saying a word.

'Two days before that night ...' Fern wept, 'I lost my own baby and couldn't tell a soul. I didn't even tell him I was pregnant. I was scared witless.' Fern was shaking and wept into Bea's arms.

'I just don't know what to say,' Bea whispered, 'Except, no one is treating you like this again, do you hear me?'

Fern barely managed a nod.

Bea's heart was thumping, 'How long has this been going on?'

Fern sat back and hugged a cushion to her chest. In a trancelike state she began to talk. 'For the first six months everything was okay. Pete treated me like a princess and I felt a million dollars. He wined and dined me, bought me the most lavish gifts and I fell in love with him, but when I got my promotion at work things began to change, slowly at first. He'd been made redundant and began to drop me off at work in the morning and he was always there picking me up in the evening, even though I'd insisted on numerous occasions I wanted to take the bus. It gave me a bit of me time, time for my own thoughts on the way to and from work.'

Bea nodded.

'Then one evening, he just lost it. He'd arrived early and spotted me talking to my boss Dan outside the building. Pete went berserk, accusing me of having an affair and all sorts. When we got home, he pushed me to the floor and I hit my head against the corner of the coffee table. I remember feeling a warm, throbbing sensation and realised I was bleeding. It was the first time he'd laid a finger on me. He was sorry, of course. In fact he went into complete meltdown, blaming it on being at home with no job, feeling worthless and threatening to leave me because I deserved better. I honestly thought he was depressed and that it was just a one-off. But over time he became more possessive. He didn't like me going out with my friends, or work colleagues, he'd get jealous of me even talking to anyone else and the abuse became more frequent. I was too ashamed to ask for help,' Fern sobbed.

Bea slumped forward with her head in his hands. 'This is just awful,' her voice barely a whisper.

'Here, take this,' Nathan said, perching on the edge of the coffee table and handing them both a cup of tea.

'When Mum became ill it gave me the perfect excuse to spend a couple of hours away from him. I could just sit by the side of her bed and everything was calm, well, for a short while, at least, and then when she died ...' Fern broke down.

'You didn't have that escape. Come here,' Bea took the mug from her hands and held Fern as she wept into her arms.

'I don't even have a job now. He made it so difficult for me to go to work. He's made it so I only have him to rely on. That's why ... that's why I needed this money. I was going to run away from it all.'

'I promise you, you'll never be scared again, don't we, Nathan?'

'Of course,' replied Nathan, 'You're safe now. Move into the spare room until the twins are here.'

'Twins? You're pregnant?'

Bea smiled, 'Yes, we are expecting twins.'

'That's fantastic news, congratulations to you both.'

'Thank you, honestly we won't take no for an answer, move in and we can sort out a more permanent plan later.'

'I can't do that,' sobbed Fern.

'You can. This will be the last place he will look. No one is ever hurting you again,' said Bea, giving Nathan a warm smile for suggesting it.

'Thank you, thank you both so much.'

'You don't need to thank me, that's what sisters are for.'

Chapter 40

Nell stepped from the cold of the pavement into the warm entrance of the garden centre. It was Sunday afternoon and she'd received a garbled message from Bea asking her to meet her there at two o'clock sharp. She glanced at her watch before noticing Bea's car pulling into the car park. Nathan was driving and Bea was sitting in the passenger seat. She saw Jacob's face pressed up against the window. His face beamed when he spotted Nell and he waved madly. Then Nell noticed a figure sitting next to him, she squinted and realisation struck home.

'Fern,' she said, under her breath, 'Surely not.' Bea jumped out of the car and Nathan beeped as he pulled off.

'Close your mouth or you'll swallow flies.' Bea's lips twisted in lopsided smile.

'I thought I was seeing things for a moment. I could have sworn that was Fern in the back of the car.'

Bea slipped her arm through Nell's, and they headed towards the café in search of a coffee and a bite to eat.

'It was, what a morning.'

Nell scrutinised her face, 'Have you been crying?'

The Cosy Canal Boat Dream

'A little, let's grab a drink and I'll tell you all about it.'

A couple of minutes later, they were huddled in the corner of the café, hugging a mug of coffee.

'It's awful,' said Bea tearfully, swallowing down a lump in her throat. She paused and brushed a strand of hair from her face.

Nell reached across the table and squeezed her friend's hand, 'Whatever's happened?' Nell studied her eyes and knew that whatever Bea was about to tell her must have been major for her to even contemplating speaking to Fern again.

Bea took a deep breath, her lips quivered. 'We were woken up this morning by hammering on the front door and when we opened it, we were faced with a very angry Fern clutching a letter. Cutting a long story short, my mum has left all her money and house, in fact everything, to Jacob, in a trust fund ...'

'And Fern wasn't happy?' interrupted Nell.

'Yes, but not for the reasons we may have thought.' Bea took a sip of her coffee. 'She was banking on the money being left to her, she needed it.'

'What for?'

'To escape.'

'Escape?' asked Nell perplexed.

'You remember Pete?'

Nell rolled her eyes, 'Do I ever? There was something about him. I never felt comfortable in his company. Shifty eyes in my opinion.'

'Well, you're a good judge of character.'

'What do you mean?'

Bea lowered her voice and leaned over the table, 'He's not only been mentally abusing her for years, but physically too.' Bea's face crumpled as the words tumbled from her mouth.

Nell could see the hurt visible on Bea's face, 'Oh, Bea, I don't know what to say.'

'He's basically isolated her, stripped her of her self-confidence, self-worth and made her reliant on him for money and food.'

'I thought she'd a job?' Nell lowered her mug and placed it on the table.

Bea shook her head, 'From what I can gather he made life so difficult for her she went off with depression and never went back. When Mum became ill it gave her some relief from the situation.'

'This is terrible.'

'And now she's died, she's back to being with him twenty-four seven.' Bea squeezed her eyes shut, blinking away the tears. 'She needed Mum's money to leave without a trace in the middle of the night. She didn't have Mum to look after any more and I'd cut her out of our family.' Bea rummaged in her bag – grabbing a tissue, she dabbed her eyes.

'What sort of sister have I been? I've completely let her down.' Bea looked up briefly, before staring down into her mug.

'Now, you listen to me,' said Nell in a kind voice, tapping her hand, 'You haven't, you can only react to the circumstances you know about.'

Bea looked up through her fringe.

'As far as you were concerned, she stood by Pete when he

The Cosy Canal Boat Dream

called Jacob a bastard and they left him to cry in his cot when they were babysitting him that night.'

'She had no choice,' said Bea, taking a deep breath. Her shoulders were shaking and she squeezed her eyes shut. 'Fern was protecting Jacob. Yes, he was crying, but in the past every time Fern stood up to Pete, or even looked at him the wrong way, he would make her pay. I've seen the bruises,' Bea flinched just thinking about it. 'He told her she couldn't go to Jacob, and she knew if she went to his cot it would trigger his temper even more. She was afraid he would hurt Jacob too – she was actually guarding him from Pete's erratic behaviour.'

Nell slumped back in her chair, 'Did she ever tell your mum?'

Bea shook her head, 'I think she's been too scared. The only way out that she could see was the money from the will, and as soon as she found out it was left to Jacob, she thought her life was over.'

Nell felt a pang of sadness, 'I don't know what to say. Nobody has any idea what is really going on in someone else's life, do they?'

They sat in silence for a moment, lost in their own thoughts, before Nell spoke. 'What happens now?'

'I know I've not always seen eye to eye with Fern in the past but I can't stand by and let her suffer any more. She's moving in with us until the twins are born.'

Nell sat up in her chair, 'Okay, I can really understand where you are coming from but what if, and I'm only throwing this out there because I'm worried about you, but what if Pete doesn't like that? What if he comes after you?'

'He won't think she's with us and if he does come anywhere near, the first people I will be phoning is the police.'

Nell nodded and heaved a sigh of relief, 'And when the twins are born?'

'I've no idea, but we've got a few months to come up with a plan.'

Bea's phone beeped and she swiped the message, 'That's Nathan now. He's dropped Fern at home and Jacob off at a party. He's got a couple of errands to run and then he'll pick her up. I can't leave her there any longer. She's going to throw some essentials into a suitcase and move in today.'

Nell took the last swig of her coffee, 'Come on, it's walking distance to Fern's house from here, let's walk over and help her pack.'

Bea nodded, 'How would you feel if I offered her a job at the deli?'

'I think that is just what is needed, it'll give Fern something positive to focus on and build her confidence too. Ask her. See how she feels about it.' Nell also felt relieved, not only would this be the perfect solution for Bea and Fern, it meant it would free Nell up to work on the Old Picture House knowing Bea was in safe hands.

They grabbed their coats and bags and began to amble towards Fern's house.

'I was meaning to ask,' Bea turned towards Nell, 'What's been going on with you this week? Don't think I haven't noticed you are very quiet. Is it Guy leaving?'

'That and my mother.'

'What's Gilly been up to now?'

The Cosy Canal Boat Dream

Nell looked at Bea, 'I'm not entirely sure, but something is niggling away at me.'

Bea raised her eyebrows.

Nell linked arms with Bea, 'Let's walk and talk and I'll tell you all about the secrets of the shoebox.'

'The secrets of the shoebox, this sounds ominous.'

'It does, indeed. It also involves a film actor and a secret stash of letters.'

'Any film actor in particular?'

'Lloyd Keaton,' answered Nell.

'Get talking, Andrews.'

Chapter 41

Nell stared down at the white oblong cardboard box. It was five-thirty on Monday morning and for the second time this week she'd woken up with a bout of nausea.

'No time like the present,' she muttered to herself as she went to the bathroom and stared at her own reflection. 'This isn't how it was meant to be.' She felt tired and rubbed her eyes. She'd always dreamed of having kids with Ollie, a proper family, but she'd never even considered it as a single mother.

She was hoping the sickness would subside soon because this morning she'd been summoned to the solicitor's to go through the final paperwork for the Old Picture House. Everything was finally moving forward.

Nell splashed cold water on her face, took a deep breath and perched on the edge of the bath. She held the plastic wand in her hand, then took the plunge.

For a full two minutes she sat tight, forcing herself to breath calmly. Deep down, she already knew the result. There was a strange sensation inside her body, one she didn't recognise, her breasts were tender, a metal taste in her mouth and not forgetting the major give-a-way sign, there was no period.

The Cosy Canal Boat Dream

She took a deep breath and raked her hand through her unruly morning hair. She clutched the no-question-about-it-I-am-pregnant stick as the two bold blue lines glared back at her.

'Shit,' she said out loud, throwing the test into the bin and running the water for the shower.

The timing couldn't be any worse.

Climbing into the shower, she let the warm water cascade over her face and sighed. Wasn't the moment you found out you were pregnant for the very first time meant to be a joyous occasion? And what the hell was she going to do about Guy – he already had one baby on the way with his wife! And then there was the restoration project, not to mention the deli. What if the morning sickness began to take its toll and she left Bea in the lurch earlier than expected? It was all such a mess.

Twenty minutes later, Nell was dressed, tucking into a bowl of cornflakes and staring out of the porthole. Her thoughts were all over the place as she spotted Bea walking up the towpath, swinging a bunch of keys and looking down at her phone.

Nell quickly typed her a text, 'Pop in before work.'

Immediately Bea glanced towards the 'Nollie' and saw Nell's face through the porthole. She waved and diverted towards the jetty.

'Morning,' she said cheerily, stooping through the door.

Nell looked up, 'Morning.'

'Mmm, I know that look!'

'What look?'

'That look of panic on your face means you're either mulling something over or you have no idea what to do about something.'

'That's what I like about you, Bea Green, you know me so well.'

'Come on then, spill the beans,' she unbuttoned her coat and slid into the seat next to her.

Nell took a deep breath and scrunched up her face, 'What would you say if I said ...' She stopped in her tracks and twisted her wedding ring around her finger. Even though Ollie was gone, she'd never felt the time was right to take it off. Now, all of sudden, she felt so guilty, which was silly as she hadn't been unfaithful.

'What would I say if ...?' Bea prompted.

'If I said I was pregnant too.'

Bea gave a nervous laugh while she studied Nell's face, 'Okay, now I can't make up my mind whether you're actually joking or not.'

'That would be not joking.'

Bea's eyes widened and her jaw dropped open.

'Nell, I don't know what to say. I'm stunned.'

'Not as stunned as me. We'll be able to open up our own nursery at this rate.'

'Maybe that's what we should do,' she said, still trying to take it all in. 'So, what's the plan of action?'

'Get fat?' Nell said with a light-hearted laugh. 'Isn't that what usually happens?'

'You've still got your sense of humour, so that's a good start!'

The Cosy Canal Boat Dream

'The timing couldn't be worse.' Nell gave a brief smile.

'It's not the best,' agreed Bea, 'But things happen for a reason. What does Gilly say?'

'I've not told her. I've only just done the test.'

They sat in silence for a couple of moments.

'I've got so much to cope with at the moment.'

'Any more thoughts on asking your mum about the shoebox?'

Nell shook her head,

'It's been whirling around in my mind. I've got a few choices, tell her straight I've snooped in the box, tell her Fred told me she'd taken his boat or I could ask Lloyd straight out if he knows my mother. Whichever one it is, it's on my list to delve further this week.'

'Yikes, no offence, I'm glad I'm not in your shoes this week, however, if you need a right hand woman, I can be Cagney to your Lacey.'

'I'll bear that in mind,' smiled Nell, not relishing any of the choices.

'He'd come back you know, if he knew you were pregnant.' Bea threw it out there and the words hung in the air.

Nell shook her head, 'We don't know that for certain and anyhow how can I put him in that position? I can't make him choose between two unborn babies.' 'It's a tricky one, I have to admit, but Nell, and I know I can say this to you, but don't you think that's his decision to make?'

'I've not had much time to think about anything, it's been ...' she glances at her watch, 'about half an hour since I've found out.'

'It'll be hard on your own, single mum. No one to hand the baby over to for a rest. Every cry, every night feed will have to be done by you.'

'But what choice do I have? He's actually married to someone else, lives in Ireland, and is having a baby with her. I was stupid, it was a spur of the moment thing. I stopped taking the pill a little while back as there was no point and it didn't cross my mind about contraception.'

'Caught up in the moment, you aren't the first and you won't be the last.'

'I'll manage, I'll have to manage, there's no other choice.'

'There's always a choice.'

Nell shook her head and sighed, 'Maybe this has happened for a reason, a sign to start afresh, my own little family, just for me.' Her voice trailed off.

'Just don't be overdoing it with the Old Picture House and everything.'

'I won't, I promise, and for the time being, can we just keep this between ourselves?'

'Of course,' Bea smiled.

'And I know I shouldn't ask you this, but I mean, from Nathan too.'

'I promise, it's your news, not mine to tell.' She squeezed her arm in reassurance.'

I just need some space to get everything worked out in my head.'

'I understand.'

'And that includes Mum. It's early days. I'll wait until the first scan until I make it public knowledge.'

The Cosy Canal Boat Dream

Bea nodded.

'How's Fern? Has she settled in okay?' asked Nell, changing the subject.

'She was very quiet at first.'

'That's understandable.'

'I've had a chat with her about working in the deli. I think it'll be good for her to interact with people again, build up her self-confidence and, of course, she'll have me, you and Gilly to look out for her and support her.'

'What did she say?'

'At first she didn't want to be a burden, thought I was offering her a job out of pity until I put her straight. I know you'll be leaving soon and with the twins on the way I will need someone to take over and run the place. I'd already asked Gilly if she wanted the responsibility, but she preferred just to do an honest day's work with no added pressure of ordering, accounts and banking.'

'Yes, that sounds like Mum. And what about Fern? Did you convince her it wasn't about feeling sorry for her?'

'Yes, I think so. This week she's going to take it easy. She has personal stuff to do, opening a bank account, change of address and all that stuff. So we agreed she would start next week, maybe mornings at first, and when she feels up to it and finds her feet, she can build up her hours.'

'That sounds like an excellent plan.'

'I best go and start the baking. Are you okay if I get off?' asked Bea, standing up and zipping up her coat.

'Yes, and thanks for being there for me.'

'You don't have to thank me, that's what best friends are for.'

Nell smiled warmly towards Bea. 'Actually, I know I'm abusing my position here, but I was already taking an hour out later this morning to tie things up at the solicitor's and collect the keys, but can I just come in after that? I could do with just trying to get my head together.'

'No problem. You put your feet up for an hour. We'll see you in a little while and make sure the first thing you do when you arrive is put the kettle on!'

'Yes, boss!' saluted Nell as Bea disappeared through the door of the 'Nollie' towards the melting pot.

Nell had a pang of guilt after Bea had left because she had no intention of putting her feet up for an hour. In fact, she had something more pressing on her mind, something that had been niggling away at her ... her mum's shoebox.

Chapter 42

Halfway up the towpath Nell spotted her mum pedalling towards her on her bike and her stomach flipped a double somersault. Gilly was humming away to herself and rang her bell at a passing narrowboat. Nervous butterflies began to flutter around her stomach at a rate of knots as she quickly hid behind the gnarled trunk of an old oak tree.

'What are you doing?' Nell muttered to herself, stealing a furtive glance around the tree towards her mum. She then breathed in and prayed she wouldn't be spotted and, much to her relief, Gilly sailed past without knowing she was there. She waited until her mum was out of sight before stepping out from behind the tree and striding up the path towards Bluebell Cottage.

Nell fished out the keys from her bag and heaved a huge sigh of relief once she was on the other side of the closed front door. She headed straight to the kitchen and popped her bag and the keys on top of the table.

Her mum's dirty breakfast dishes were still in the sink and a crossword puzzle lay open on the table. The only thing Nell could hear was the noisy hum of the refrigerator.

She spotted the kittens curled up in their basket next to the Aga. One peered out of a sleepy eye, but the other two didn't move a muscle. The adrenalin began to run through Nell's body as she swung open the door to the utility room. She peered inside, but the shoebox was gone. She opened every cupboard door but still there wasn't a shoebox to be found.

'Okay,' she said out loud, 'Mum's bedroom.'

Just at that moment the letterbox clanged and she froze.

The post fell on to the mat.

'Jeez!' said Nell out loud, her heart pounding.

She dithered for a moment, making sure the postman had gone, before taking a deep breath and climbing the creaky stairs.

Her mum's bedroom was pretty, oak beams ran across the ceiling and the room had such a relaxing feel about it with its beautiful Laura Ashley floral duvet and shabby-chic furniture. The window looked out over the half acre of back garden, which was now in bloom with the daffodils dancing and the tulips swaying from side to side in the light breeze. Wisteria clung to the beams of the wooden summerhouse and beyond the garden the view stretched for miles and miles. Old oak trees flanked the edge of the farmer's field, where ponies grazed and sheep were dotted alongside them.

Taking a deep breath, she opened her mum's wardrobe. Her clothes were hung in a neat fashion and her shoes stacked up in a row at the bottom. She stood on her tiptoes and peered on to the shelf above the rail. There was the old box of photo-

The Cosy Canal Boat Dream

graphs that had been stored there for years next to a pile of neatly folded sheets. Nell felt around with her hand but couldn't feel or see anything else.

She quickly grabbed the dressing-table stool and balanced on top of it while she took a better look. There it was, pushed right to the back of the wardrobe, the shoebox. Her hands were shaking as she reached forward and grasped it. She climbed down carefully and settled on her mum's bed with the box on her lap. 'The little shoebox of secrets,' she said softly, lifting the lid. Everything was still the same, the theatre ticket stubs, the newspaper articles and the letters tied up with the ribbon. As she pulled on the ribbon, Nell was fighting with her conscience.

Open the letters, don't open the letters.

Nell knew that the moment she opened one there was no going back. She flicked through the envelopes, looking at the date stamps on the postmarks. The letters had been stacked in order, the top letter being the first one that was ever sent and returned.

She ran her finger over the address and turned over the envelope.

Why had so many been sent and why had so many been returned? The address on the front was a flat in Stratford upon Avon. That was about an hour's drive away from Bluebell Cottage. Nell knew it was famous for being the birthplace of William Shakespeare and had fond memories of visiting the quaint town as a child. She remembered eating an ice-cream while sitting on a wooden bench next to the river Avon alongside her parents.

Suddenly, one of the kittens jumped on to the bed and startled Nell, 'We need to find proper names for you guys,' she said, stroking the soft fur as the kitten arched his back then padded the duvet cover with its paws before curling up in a ball next to her.

'Okay, little thing,' she said to the kitten, 'It's now or never.'

Taking a deep breath, she carefully slit open the first envelope. She knew she was over-stepping the mark, trespassing inside her mum's life, but even though her head was telling her it was wrong to open the letters, her heart was singing from a different hymn sheet altogether.

Her heart was racing as she peered inside. She had no idea what she was about to discover. Her hands began to sweat as she pulled out the letter inside. She unfolded the cream paper and a picture fell on to her lap.

She looked down and gently picked it up. She stared at a photo of a new-born baby wrapped up in blanket, sleeping in a cot. Her mind went into overdrive. It didn't make any sense to Nell whatsoever. Why would there be a picture of a baby in the envelope. She placed it carefully on her knee and her eyes skimmed over the letter.

Dear Lloyd,
 I hope this letter finds you well.
 Please find enclosed a picture of the baby, she is beautiful.
 I miss you,
 G x

The Cosy Canal Boat Dream

Staring at the words in the letter, Nell was absolutely mystified. It didn't make any sense to her. Why would her mum be sending pictures of a baby to Lloyd Keaton? And why did she miss him? The letter didn't go into any more detail and Nell was left feeling as confused as she was before.

Next, Nell began to read through the newspaper clippings and she became so engrossed that she jumped out of her skin when her phone beeped. Quickly, she rummaged inside her bag and saw a text message from Bea flashing on the screen.

'Good luck at the solicitor's. Let me know when those keys are firmly in your hands.'

Nell's return message was upbeat, even though guilt swept through her at riffling through her mum's private life. Deep down, she wanted to open the rest of the letters but Bea knew she must leave now to make it to the solicitor's on time.

She stared at the letters in her hand before quickly stuffing them inside her coat pocket and then carefully returned the shoebox to where she'd found it.

Twenty minutes later, Nell climbed off the number 54 bus in town and walked along the high street towards the solicitor's.

On arrival, the receptionist asked her to take a seat in a battered old leather chair outside Mr Forster's office.

'He's just on another call, he won't keep you much longer.'

Nell nodded and waited a further five minutes until his office door swung open.

Mr Forster was a man in his mid-sixties with a portly face and wearing a tweed suit. He looked over his round spectacles and then smiled towards Nell, 'Come in, Mrs Andrews, and take a seat.'

Nell followed him into his office and watched as he shuffled through some papers, before loosening his tie. She noticed a bead of sweat on both his temples.

He cleared his throat and fixed an intense stare in her direction.

'Have the estate agents spoken to you in the last twenty-four hours at all?'

Nell shook her head.

'I was just wondering whether you had any indication of what I'm about to tell you,' he probed.

Nell shifted self-consciously in her seat.

'No one has spoken to me about anything,' Nell felt confused, 'Is there a problem?'

He shuffled again through his papers and Nell was beginning to feel increasingly unsettled.

'I must warn you that what I'm about to say next is not the norm when purchasing a property by auction. In fact, I've never come across this before in my time of being a solicitor.'

Nell gulped away a lump in her throat. She was praying she hadn't lost the Old Picture House. She didn't think she could cope with any more surprises today.

'I've been instructed by the vendor of the Old Picture House to return your money to you.'

Nell was aware of the rising panic inside her, 'Why? Is it no longer for sale?'

Mr Forster looked over the top of his glasses again, 'Mrs

The Cosy Canal Boat Dream

Andrews, they have instructed me to hand back the sum you've bid because they are gifting the property to you.'

Nell's eyes widened, 'Gifting the property to me? Are you sure? Why would someone do that? I don't understand,' she said, feeling perplexed.

'Yes, I'm sure. The current owner is giving you the property and all the monies have been returned to your bank account.'

Nell shook her head in disbelief. 'Are you saying I'm still the owner but I don't have to pay for it?' Nell was utterly confused by the whole conversation.

'That is correct, Mrs Andrews, the property is all yours and you are free to pick the keys up from the estate agents in your own time.'

'Why would someone do that? Who would do that?' Nell couldn't take it all in.

Mr Forster thrust a sheet of paper over the desk, with a pen, 'Sign on that bottom line by the cross.'

Nell quickly scanned the documents and, as Mr Forster had informed her, the property had indeed been gifted to her.

'Unfortunately the vendor, at this time, wishes to remain anonymous.'

'So you're telling me I don't even know who has given this to me.'

'That is correct.'

Shakily, Nell picked up the pen and signed on the dotted line.

'Thank you, Mrs Andrews, that is all for now.'

Nell stood up and shook Mr Forster's hand. She was too

shocked to say a word as she began to walk towards the estate agents to collect the keys.

An hour later, after Nell had picked up the keys to the Old Picture House, she'd caught the bus back to Heron's Reach and was now walking in a daze up to the crest of the hill towards the old church. She pushed open the wrought-iron gates to the graveyard and made her way towards her father's stone.

In loving memory of Benny Harper

Nell ran her fingers along the chiselled stone as the emotion surged through her body.
'What's going on, Dad?' she asked, wiping away tears of frustration. 'Who would give me a property and why?' Her heart was thudding loudly against her chest. What did it all mean? She crouched before her dad's grave and pulled out her mobile phone, quickly typing a message to Bea.
'Please can you meet me back at the Nollie in half an hour and don't say anything to Mum.'
Almost instantly, Bea replied, 'Of course.'

Chapter 43

Nell's pulse throbbed in the side of her head as she clutched her mum's letters in her pocket and bounded on to jetty number ten before jumping on to the deck of the 'Nollie'.

Once inside, she slid her arms out of her coat and made herself a cuppa before sitting down at the table. She moved the mug to one side and laid all the letters out in date order. She stared at them, then reached for the first envelope and removed the first letter and the baby picture and placed it on top of the envelope.

She took a deep breath and reached for letter number two.

Carefully, she opened it. Again it contained a short letter written on exactly the same kind of paper with yet another photograph enclosed. Her heart was pounding as she swallowed and squinted at the picture of a baby kicking its legs on a crochet mat on the floor.

Even though the photograph wasn't the best quality, there was no mistaking that the picture had been taken in Nell's parents' living room. She immediately recognised the carpet and the fireplace. Turning over the photograph, she gasped: Nell Harper, six months old.

Her jaw hit the floor. With her hands shaking, she placed the photo on the table and read the letter.

Dear Lloyd,
   Please find enclosed a photo of Nell, 6 months old.
   All my love,
   G x

Just like the first letter, short and sweet.

For the next thirty minutes, Nell opened every letter and placed them in order, on top of each envelope. She sporadically wiped away escaping tears of puzzlement, she was so confused by it all. Each one contained a very brief letter and a picture of her, including her first day at school, sports day, when she won an award for a writing competition and not forgetting photographs from secondary school.

Bleary eyed, she looked up to see Bea standing in the doorway.

'What's going on, Nell?'

'I'm not actually sure, Bea,' Nell said, as she gazed wearily at her friend, then back towards the table.

'What's all this? It looks like a jigsaw puzzle.'

'It's a giant puzzle, all right,' Nell's voice cracked.

'But you'll never guess what's happened at the solicitor's. That just adds to the mystery.'

'Go on,' Bea slid off her jacket and slipped into the seat next to Nell.

'The solicitor has handed me my money back for the sale of the Old Picture House.'

The Cosy Canal Boat Dream

'What? Does that mean it's fallen through?' Bea's eyes were wide.

Nell shook her head, 'Far from it. The person who owned the Picture House has given it to me.'

'Come again. They've given it to you?' the look of puzzlement on Bea's face said it all.

'Yes.'

'So the question is who?' Bea couldn't take her eyes off Nell.

'Well ... that's a mystery too. I wish I knew, but apparently they want to stay anonymous.'

'Jeez, who gives that much and wants to keep it quiet?'

'I really have no idea, but before I went to the solicitor's I went somewhere else.'

Nell could see the concerned look in Bea's eyes. 'I didn't mean to keep it from you, but I'd no idea what I was going to discover and I was already feeling guilty about where I was.' Nell hesitated for a second, 'I'm not proud of my actions but ...'

'But ...'

'But I knew Mum was hiding something.'

'The shoebox?'

Nell nodded, 'I found it strange that Mum would deny knowing someone. What reason would she have to lie?'

Bea shrugged.

'The same evening I found the shoebox I also bumped into Fred. He'd told me Mum had taken his rowing boat with no explanation and was rather rude towards him.'

'That doesn't sound like Gilly.'

'I know, but it was when he said where she'd rowed to that my mind went into overdrive.'

'Why, where'd she gone?'

'Over to the boat, "Much Ado About Nothing", Lloyd Keaton's boat.'

Bea raised her eyebrows.

'But she said she didn't know who he was when we were watching the film.'

'Oh I know, so we are agreed she's covering something up?'

Bea nodded, 'It appears that way. What are all these?' She gazed towards the handwritten letters, 'These are in Gilly's handwriting, even I can see that.'

Taking a deep breath, Nell explained. 'This morning, I sneaked back to Bluebell Cottage. Something was niggling inside me. Mum had hidden the box on the top shelf inside the wardrobe. All these letters were tied up in there.'

Bea looked towards the table.

'Each one unopened and marked returned to sender.'

'Your mum?'

Nell nodded.

Bea picked up the first letter. She glanced at the letter and the baby picture, 'Who's this?'

The emotion was running through Nell's body, 'It's me, there's one of me inside all the other letters.'

'A photograph in every one?'

'Yes, from being in my cot until the last day of school, when I was sixteen.'

'So she wrote to him once a year, for all that time? Why?'

The Cosy Canal Boat Dream

'I've no idea, there are fifteen letters altogether: each one, like I said, returned unopened.'

'So why keep writing them if they just keep coming back?'

'Your guess is as good as mine.'

Nell could only see one logical explanation, 'The gut-wrenching feeling in the pit of my stomach is telling me I know what all this means. You know what I'm thinking, don't you?' said Nell.

'I think I do,' said Bea, regretfully.

Nell bit down on her lip and her eyes brimmed with tears as her world came crashing down around her once more.

'He's my father, isn't he?' were the only words she could muster up.

Bea put her arm around Nell's shoulders and squeezed her gently.

'We don't know that for sure yet.'

The tears were now free-falling down Nell's cheeks.

'It's the only explanation.'

Bea passed her a tissue from the box on the table.

'Is everything I've ever known a complete lie?'

Nell could see the concern in Bea's eyes.

'It can't be true. Please tell me it's not true?'

'We don't know anything yet.'

Nell could hear the hesitation in Bea's voice.

'It seems way too much of a coincidence. He's suddenly turned up at Little Rock, Mum is refusing to admit she knows him, then the letters and her rowing over to his boat.' Nell reeled off a list. 'But what I don't understand is why she didn't want me to win that auction and who the hell has given the Picture House to me.'

'When you put it like that.'

Both of them were quiet for a second.

'What are you going to do about it now?'

'There's only one thing I can do. I'm going to ask her.'

'Are you sure you want to do this, Nell? Because once you've admitted you've seen these letters, it's out in the open, there's no going back.'

There was a burning desire inside Nell to know the truth, 'What choice have I got? I need to do this.'

'Will you promise me something? Don't go in all guns blazing. Sleep on it – make sure it's straight in your mind.'

All Nell could do was manage a nod.

'And don't forget, whatever happens, I'm here for you.'

'I know.'

Chapter 44

The sunshine streamed through the gap in the curtains when Nell woke the next morning. She'd dozed in and out of sleep and she'd made the decision to tackle her mum after work tonight. She needed answers to the questions whirling around in her head.

By the time Nell arrived at the deli, it was already a hive of activity. Gilly was running through the ropes with Fern behind the shop counter. Nell couldn't even bring herself to look at her mum, she just knew she needed to get through today before she tackled her. But whatever she'd discovered, she knew she was about to open a right can of worms.

'All the speciality cheeses and pâté's are in this counter, freshly baked crusty bread in the baskets, and drinks over in the chilled cabinet next to the fresh cream cakes,' chimed Gilly happily.

'How does anyone keep their weight under control working in a place like this? Everything looks so scrumptious.' Fern hummed as she laid the freshly made sandwiches inside the counter.

'They don't,' Gilly joked, 'It's impossible!'

They looked up to see Nell standing in the doorway.

'Bea, Nell's here,' Fern squealed, taking Nell completely by surprise.

'Good morning,' grinned Gilly.

Nell's face was solemn, 'Morning,' she said, forcing herself to be as polite as she could.

Gilly raised her eyebrows at her, 'Has someone got out of bed the wrong side this morning?'

Nell didn't answer.

Just at that second, Bea came trundling through the kitchen door, her face lifted into a smile as soon as she saw Nell.

'Is something going on? You look like you are about to burst.'

'Something is definitely going on!' Bea had the biggest grin planted firmly on her face.

'Oh God, don't tell me they've got the scan wrong and you're expecting triplets,' joked Nell.

Bea raised her eyebrows.

'OMG, am I right?'

'Ha no! Thankfully!'

Nell rolled her eyes while Bea turned and grabbed a letter that was propped up on the front of the till. 'Here, take a look.' She thrust the letter into Nell's hand, while Gilly and Fern hovered, grinning by her side.

Nell opened the envelope and quickly skimmed over the words, her eyes widened and her mood lifted a little, 'Wow Bea! This is brilliant and extremely well deserved,' Nell exclaimed. 'I'm so proud of you, my clever friend.'

'I know! I couldn't believe my eyes when I opened it.

The Cosy Canal Boat Dream

'Beatrice Green, owner of The Melting Pot has been awarded Deli of the Year,' she said, in a very posh voice.

Nell leant towards her best friend and planted a huge kiss on her cheek, 'It couldn't have happened to a nicer person!'

'Aww thanks, shame we can't have a glass of champers to celebrate.'

'You can have sparkling water!'

'Don't I just live such a rock 'n' roll lifestyle?'

Everyone laughed.

'What happens next?'

'Some sort of presentation, but in the meantime, chop chop, let's get this deli open and back to work!'

'Wins an award and she becomes all bossy!' laughed Fern, teasing her sister.

'You better believe it!'

'Can I just say, while we are all gathered here, thank you all for making me feel so welcome.'

'You don't need to thank us,' said Nell, making her way into the kitchen. 'Can I hide out with you in here today, Bea?'

She gave Nell a knowing nod.

'What's up with you?' asked Gilly touching her arm, 'You seem a little tense.'

'Nothing,' replied Nell, giving her mum a stern look before turning and flouncing into the kitchen.

Bea walked out of the kitchen and both Gilly and Fern inhaled the delicious aroma of the freshly baked loaf. She popped a rustic breadboard on top of the counter and Gilly and Fern stared at the ripped-up chunks of crusty bread and the pot of extra-virgin olive oil.

'That looks so good,' murmured Fern, her tastebuds watering.

'It's not for you, it's for the customers,' smiled Bea, swiping Fern's hand with a tea towel, 'I've got my eyes on you two.'

'Bea, can I just ask, is everything okay with Nell? She seems kind of het up?' Gilly asked, her voice low.

'I've not noticed,' she replied, knowing that wasn't strictly true.

Gilly watched Bea disappear back through the kitchen door. Maybe Nell was just tired, she did have a lot on her plate at the minute, she thought to herself.

'Has she gone?' chuckled Fern, dunking a piece of warm bread into the oil and popping it into her mouth.

'Mmm, heaven,' she uttered.

Suddenly, the kitchen door swung open and Bea stared at them both with her hands on her hips before wagging her finger at Fern.

Fern had guilt written all over her face.

'No more. It's for the customers not you!'

Fern giggled, catching the crumbs with her hand after Bea disappeared back inside the kitchen.

At that moment, the deli door opened and Gilly and Fern looked up and to meet Ed's beaming smile. Sam was waiting patiently on the other side of the window, his tail thumping on the ground and his nose pressed to the glass watching Ed's every move.

'Good morning, lovely ladies, and where is she this morning? I've just been into the butcher's and Alan's just told me the news.'

The Cosy Canal Boat Dream

'Bea, you've got a visitor,' shouted Gilly.

Two seconds later, Bea appeared, swiping the flour from her hands.

'There she is, Miss Deli of the Year. Congratulations! Come here!' Ed pecked a kiss to her cheek, 'Well deserved.'

'Aww thank you,' she blushed at all the sudden praise.

'Famous at last,' Nell chipped in from around the kitchen door, 'People will be coming from far and wide to sample the delights of The Melting Pot,' she grinned, before disappearing back inside the kitchen.

'I hope you'll still have time to make your favourite boatyard man a sausage and egg muffin.'

'Absolutely, our best customers will always get priority,' Bea winked at Ed. 'Is it your usual now?'

'Oh go on … you've twisted my arm,' he winked, leaning against the counter. 'I may as well while I'm here.'

'Fern …'

Fern swung her head towards Bea.

'Ed is your very first customer and would like his usual.'

'Which is?' Fern flicked her eyes between all of them.

'A sausage and egg muffin and a mug of coffee,' Bea and Gilly sang in unison.

Fern's eyes widened, 'I've got a confession to make.'

'Which is?' Bea asked.

'When I make coffee it looks like thick tar and I can't believe that I've got to this age without knowing how to cook an egg,' she confessed with a gulp.

Gilly's face flickered with amusement and Bea gave a hearty laugh.

Fern felt a blush creep from her neck up to her ears and she remained silent.

'I don't think she's joking,' exclaimed Ed, trying to hide his smile by shoving a piece of crusty bread in his mouth from the top of the counter.

'Really?' asked Bea.

'Really,' answered Fern.

'Well, there's only one thing for it. Nell!' Bea bellowed towards the kitchen.

Nell peered around the door, 'Where's the fire?'

'Could you possibly teach Fern how to make a sausage and egg muffin?'

Nell looked between Bea and Fern in wonderment, 'You're winding me up, aren't you?'

Everyone shook their head, even Ed.

'You just can't get the staff these days,' joked Nell, ushering Fern into the kitchen, but not before she pinched another piece of crusty bread from the counter as soon as Bea's back was turned. 'Come on.'

'How are you feeling, Ed?' asked Gilly.

'Fully recovered, but I have to say ...' Ed lowered his voice and looked towards the kitchen door, 'And do not repeat this, but I'm missing him.'

'Guy?'

Ed nodded, 'Sam is excellent company around the yard but he doesn't quite have the same banter.'

Gilly smiled, 'Nell is like a bear with a sore head at the minute. I'm assuming she is missing him too.'

The Cosy Canal Boat Dream

'I'm sorry about all that business.'

'You don't need to apologise. It's not your fault he's gone back to Ireland.'

'His wife isn't a patch on Nell, you know.'

Gilly gave him a smile, just as Fern came bursting through the door with a huge beam on her face. She was carrying a wrapped-up muffin and a polystyrene cup of coffee.

'One sausage and egg muffin and one coffee that actually looks like coffee.' She handed them over the counter. 'Made with my own fair hands,' she said triumphantly.

'Well, who's a clever girl?' teased Gilly.

Fern rolled her eyes at Gilly's quip but took it in her stride, 'Brown or red sauce?'

'Brown please,' Ed replied.

She passed over a couple of sachets as he grappled with the loose change in his pocket and paid before saluting and heading back towards the boatyard with Sam trotting at his side.

'You're getting the hang of this already, the customers love you!'

Fern smiled, 'One customer!'

'There'll be plenty more.'

They both looked up to see an array of people walking down the wharf.

For the next forty minutes, Gilly and Fern served a steady stream of customers while Nell and Bea prepared the food in the kitchen for the customers at the tables.

'I officially declare it's tea-break time,' said Bea, eventually placing a drink on to the counter for Gilly and Fern once there was a lull in customers. 'How's she doing?' Bea turned towards Gilly.

'Fern? ... Like a duck to water.'

'Excellent.'

'Where's Nell? She's rarely appeared this morning.' Gilly sipped her drink, giving a fleeting glance towards the kitchen door.

'She's coming now,' answered Bea.

Nell appeared a couple of seconds later and walked straight past Gilly and stood in the deli window, looking out over the marina.

'I'm going to catch five minutes in the sun; a little fresh air is needed,' said Nell, over her shoulder, taking her mug of tea and sitting at the table outside. She knew she was acting abruptly, but the questions inside her were festering and she just needed to stay out of Gilly's way until she had the chance to confront her later. Stretching out her legs, she tilted her face towards the sun and closed her eyes. She'd been on her feet all morning and was feeling a little tired, but thankfully, at the minute, it was just about manageable.

Nell sipped her tea and watched the boats chugging out of the marina. Then suddenly something caught her eye.

She squinted towards the opposite side of the marina. There standing on the boat, 'Much Ado About Nothing', was Lloyd Keaton.

Nell sat upright in the chair and stared at him. Her heart was thumping. What was he really doing here? 'You okay?'

The Cosy Canal Boat Dream

asked Gilly, standing on the towpath just outside the deli door. 'You seem very standoffish today.'

'I'm fine,' answered Nell, closing her eyes and avoiding all eye contact with her mum, knowing everything was far from fine.

'You don't sound fine, if you don't mind me saying.' Even though Nell's eyes were shut she could feel her mum watching her.

'You would tell me if something was wrong, wouldn't you?'

Nell opened her eyes, and looked towards the shop. Fern and Bea were laughing inside. This wasn't the best time to reveal what actually was bugging her. Nell sat up straight, took a deep breath and looked out over the water.

'I'm just enjoying the sunshine.'

'It's beautiful, isn't it?'

'Little Rock Marina is always beautiful. And there's Lloyd. Nice man. I'll have to introduce you.' Nell was testing the water. She carefully watched her mum's reaction as she glanced over towards his boat, but she didn't answer.

'Do you think he'd come to the opening night of the Old Picture House once it's up and running?'

Nell watched her mum's reaction closely.

'He'll have probably moved on by then,' answered Gilly.

'Huh,' Nell huffed under her breath but still loud enough for Gilly to hear.

'What's got into you today? Why are you being so snappy?' Gilly glared at Nell, who didn't answer.

'Anyway, I'd best get back inside. I'm teaching Fern how to

make bread next. She is missing some very basic life skills, that one.'

Nell watched her mum quickly disappear back inside before looking back towards Lloyd Keaton.

Whatever was going on, she was determined to find out the truth.

Chapter 45

It was 6.30pm and Nell and Bea stared at the letters one last time. They were all laid out in chronological order, with the photographs placed on top. Nell was meeting her mum in just forty minutes.

Bea folded her arms and leant on to the table, 'It's times like this I could murder a glass of wine. That one's cute,' smiled Bea, staring at one of the photographs of Nell on sports day.

Nell rolled her eyes.

'Sorry, I couldn't resist, so before you go round there ...'

'Which I'm not relishing in the slightest, especially when she discovers I've been snooping through her personal things ...'

'Yes, I see where you are coming from with that one, but there's a bigger picture here.'

Facing the fear from her mum was one thing, but Nell was dreading uncovering what all this was actually about.

They both slumped back in their seats until Nell exhaled deeply, her eyes brimmed with tears. 'In my heart I know what I'm about to discover.' Her voice cracked.

There was a pause.

Bea put her arm around her shoulder.

'She's had an affair.'

'You put these letters away and I'll make you a strong cuppa.' Bea re-filled the kettle.

Bleary eyed, Nell reached for the first letter and placed it back inside the envelope.

'Where's your laptop?' asked Bea, looking around the boat.

'Over there, why?'

'To search the web, to see if we can find out anything about Lloyd's background.'

'I'd never thought of that,' Nell reached for the laptop and switched it on.

Two minutes later, Bea cast her eye over the computer screen while Nell looked over her shoulder and watched while Bea typed the name Lloyd Keaton into Google.

It took a second to load before she clicked on a link.

Bea read out loud.

Lloyd Keaton was born in Staffordshire, England.
An English actor, film director ranked alongside Robert Redford and Clint Eastwood.
Spouse Annie Clayton.

'Is that it?' Nell asked.

'Pretty much so. There's a list of all the films and plays he's performed in. Shakespeare too. He's had a very successful career, according to this, and even directed films.'

The Cosy Canal Boat Dream

'The address on all the letters are Stratford, though, look,' Nell let out a long sigh and met Bea's gaze.'

She took a deep breath, her face looked anxious as she spoke, 'I'm going to go now.'

'Over to Bluebell Cottage?'

Nell nodded and managed a nervous smile. She took the last gulp of her tea and stood up.

'Do you want me to come with you?'

Nell shook her head, 'This is something I need to do on my own, but please be on the end of that phone.'

'I promise.'

Bea followed Nell on to the deck of the 'Nollie'. Nell's heart was thumping so loudly she was convinced that Bea would be able to hear it. For a moment they stared out over the marina before turning and walking down the jetty. Fred was still fishing off the side of his boat.

'Good evening,' shouted Bea over to him.

He looked up and tipped his cap in his usual acknowledgement.

He turned his gaze to Nell, 'Evening, hope you're well.'

'All good here, Fred, thank you.'

'She's taken the boat again, you know. She's becoming quite a regular over there. Off again about ten minutes ago, she was.'

Both Nell and Bea glanced towards the narrowboat moored over on the far jetty. The little rowing boat was tied up and bobbing away in the water alongside Lloyd Keaton's boat.

Nell's heartbeat quickened, 'I'm going over. I need the canoe from the boatyard.' She swung under the rail of the jetty and powered her legs towards the boatyard. Bea quickly followed her.

Two minutes later, Nell was clutching the oars and manoeuvring the canoe towards the water.

'Wait,' shouted Bea, finally catching her up.

Nell looked up, tears were threatening to spill over. 'I think she did have an affair and ...' her voice quivered, 'I think there's only one reason why she's been sending him photos of me. He's my dad and now I'll have the pair of them in the same place.'

'Please, stay calm until you know all the facts.'

'I can feel it here,' Nell thumped her chest. I knew the moment I set eyes on that little shoebox that she was hiding something.'

'I'll be waiting here for you,' Bea gave her a reassuring smile as she watched Nell launch herself into the canoe. She pulled the oars and began to glide effortlessly through the water towards the narrowboat. She was about to get some answers...

Chapter 46

With adrenalin pumping through her veins, Nell tied up the canoe and stumbled on to the deck of the boat.

She snagged a look inside as she took in a deep breath. There, sitting at the table inside the boat was her mum and Lloyd, deep in conversation.

Whatever her mum was hiding, she was about to find out the truth. Bursting through the door, both Gilly and Lloyd looked up, startled. Nell's eyes glanced between the pair of them, her heart thumping. Then she spotted the shoebox in the middle of the table.

'What are you doing here?' Gilly's voice was shaky and the colour instantly drained from her face.

There was silence.

With a trembling hand, Nell reached inside her pocket and lay all the opened letters on the table. 'I could ask you the same question. Looking for these, by any chance?' she stared at her mum, willing her to speak. Nell's throat became tight and she felt that at any second her legs were going to buckle underneath her.

Lloyd stood up, 'Please sit down,' his voice was soft.

'I'm fine standing.'

'Please sit down, Nell. We were just on our way to see you.'

Nell stared at her mum.

'Please believe me, we were. That's why I'm here. I knew the letters were missing.'

'I know what went on,' Nell spat, testing the water, 'How could you do this to my dad? How could you?' Her body was visibly shaking.

'Oh, Nell. It's not what you think, please sit down.'

Nell stared at Lloyd with hatred before slumping into the chair. 'What do you know? Or what do you think you know?' asked Gilly, sounding more calm than she felt.

Lloyd sat back down. Nell noticed he looked anxious.

'There's no point in lying to me any more. I've seen what's in all these. Why else would you be sending letters and photos of me to him?'

'You had no right snooping through my personal stuff.'

'I think me snooping through your stuff is the least of everyone's worries, don't you?'

Gilly and Nell stared at each other. There was a strange tension in the air.

'So why all the lies, claiming you didn't know him?' Nell couldn't even bring herself to say his name. 'When obviously you do.'

Lloyd leant forward and picked up one of the envelopes. 'You kept these all these years?'

Gilly swallowed down a lump and nodded.

'I couldn't open them. I knew if I did, I'd come back.' His voice was barely a whisper.

The Cosy Canal Boat Dream

'I know, you don't need to explain yourself.'

'Someone clearly needs to explain themselves,' Nell stared straight at her mum. She couldn't hold in the question that was burning inside her any longer. She took a deep breath, 'Did my dad know I wasn't his?'

Gilly closed her eyes and nodded.

Nell gasped.

'But it's not what you think.'

'Well, tell me what I think, then. Are you my father?' Nell turned her attention to Lloyd. 'Is my mum sending you letters with photos of me, because you are my father?

Lloyd placed his head in his hands. He was clearly distraught.

He looked up at Nell, 'Yes, I'm your father.'

Nell's lips were trembling, her whole body ached with pain. She exhaled.

'Nell, you have to listen to me.'

'I don't think I want to listen to any more of your lies.' Nell's breathing became erratic and she had to force herself to breath calmly. The tears were free-falling and she wiped them away with the back of hand. She felt drained and battered.

Gilly took her hand, 'Okay, You weren't meant to find out this way.'

'Were you ever going to tell me?'

Chapter 47

'Please listen to me.' Gilly knew that what she was about to tell Nell could change her life forever too.

Nell remained silent, her heart was beating in double time, waiting to hear what her mum was about to say.

'This is Lloyd Keaton.'

'Yes, I know who he is. What was it? A one-night stand? You couldn't resist someone famous. Let me guess, you met at the theatre, you were a groupie.'

'Nell, stop it now.' Gilly took a breath.

'We didn't meet at the theatre, far from it.' Lloyd added softly. 'We met at 41 Church Lane.'

It took a second for the address to register, 'My grandparents' house? They knew about the affair?' Nell's eyes darkened.

'There was no affair. This is Lloyd Taylor.'

Nell listened to her mum's words, 'But that's your maiden name. I don't understand.'

'My brother,' said Gilly simply, 'Lloyd is my brother.'

Nell eyes widened and she let out a cry, 'Someone really needs to be telling me what I should be thinking right now.'

The Cosy Canal Boat Dream

'You are brother and sister? This is so wrong.' Nell buried her head in her hands.

'Nell, this isn't what you think, please listen,' said Gilly as the emotion gripped her and the tears burst through.

Lloyd grasped her hand and squeezed it tight. 'Here, take this,' he offered her a tissue, 'Let me explain.'

'My stage name is Keaton. It was changed when I landed my first film role. It was during the filming that I met and fell in love with my beautiful wife Annie, Annie Clayton. She too was an actress.'

'Such a wonderful person,' Gilly said, dabbing her eyes with a tissue.

'The day she told me the news we were expecting our first child was the happiest day of my life. I was over the moon, everyone was, but I knew it was never going to be easy as we were both working up and down the country and both on different film sets for long periods of time.'

He took a deep breath, 'Everything was going well. We bought a little house not far from Mum and Dad and Annie gave up the stage a couple of months before the baby was due.'

'Lloyd was working away in Stratford when Annie's waters broke,' Gilly chipped in. 'We telephoned the theatre, but he was already in the middle of his performance.'

'They passed the message on in between scenes and I knew there was a possibility I'd manage to catch the last train back if I hurried after the play.' Lloyd wiped away a tear and paused.

'It was too late, when Lloyd arrived ...'

'There'd been complications,' he said. 'And my darling Annie passed away during childbirth. I never even got chance to say goodbye.'

Lloyd took a deep breath. He looked so sad and rubbed his hands over his face, 'When I arrived at the hospital ...' Lloyd couldn't finish his sentence. He stood up and placed both his hands on the sink and bowed his head.

Gilly took over, 'When Lloyd arrived at the hospital, he found me and your dad cradling you.'

'Me?'

'Yes. Nell, you were the baby.'

Nell felt as if she'd been hit by a high-speed train. Her head was whirling trying to take everything in. Nausea had taken over her body and the tears fell.

'Nell, I know this is a huge shock for you.'

She looked up and met Gilly's eyes, 'You're not my mother?'

Gilly bit down on her lip and shook her head. 'I'm not your biological mother, but I will always be your mother. Me and your dad loved you like you were our own. You are our own, you were so special to us and Lloyd knew we'd love you with all our hearts.'

'Why didn't you want me?' Nell's voice faltered, her heart was breaking and she didn't attempt to wipe away the tears.

'The circumstances were tragic,' Lloyd turned back to face her. He stretched over the table and took Gilly's hand, 'When Gilly and Benny found out they couldn't have any children of their own they were devastated, we were all devastated. They had so much to offer. When Annie passed, and believe me it was the hardest thing I've ever done in my life, I gave them you, the most special gift of all. They could give you a

The Cosy Canal Boat Dream

happy, stable home; they could give you roots. They gave their lives to you, which makes them very special people. I love them dearly. With me you would have been passed from pillar to post, with childminders, never making friends because you'd never stay in one place long enough. It seemed the best solution. Annie had passed away and your mum and dad had you, a child they never thought they'd ever have.' Lloyd wiped away his own tears.

Nell's heart was shattered, 'Why didn't you open any of these?' she pointed to the letters on the table.

'I couldn't. My heart was broken letting you go and I knew I had to have a clean break for Benny and Gilly's sake. If I saw a picture of you, I'd want to come back and I couldn't do that to them or you. You were theirs now, but my love for you never diminished,' he managed a weak smile, 'You have to believe me.'

'Lloyd never knew your name until he was sitting on your boat. He put two and two together when you mentioned my name and that I worked in the deli.'

The knots in Nell's stomach took her breath away, 'You never knew my name?'

He shook his head.

For a second everyone was lost in their own thoughts until Nell spoke, 'Why now? Why come back now?'

'I had business in the area. I thought I could keep a low profile, living on the boat until the transaction went through.'

'Transaction?'

'The Old Picture House.'

Nell gasped, 'You owned the Old Picture House?'

Lloyd nodded, 'I couldn't believe it when you told me you wanted to buy it and renovate it in Ollie's honour.' Lloyd's voice became shaky.

'Is that why you didn't want me to buy it?' Nell turned towards her mum.

'I panicked. I was scared that somehow your paths would cross. I know it was daft. You have a different surname to me and Lloyd didn't even know your name. I just couldn't cope with the thought of what might happen. You've been through so much heartache recently and I suppose I was trying to protect you as much as I could.'

Nell turned towards Lloyd, 'It was you. You gave me that place.'

Now it was Gilly's turn to look surprised. 'What's all this?'

'I was called into the solicitor's office to be told my funds had been returned to my bank account but I was still the owner of the Old Picture House.'

Lloyd took a breath, 'When I discovered who you were and why you wanted to re-open that place, it was the least I could do. You are my daughter. I was proud of the reasons you wanted to save it. That place is special to me. I used to date Annie there. I bought it after it closed its doors for the last time because I couldn't bear it being demolished to make way for houses. There were too many memories there. I retired abroad but came back because,' He paused and glanced at Gilly. She nodded, giving him the approval to carry on.

'Because my health isn't the best.'

'I don't understand,' Nell said.

Gilly took a breath, 'Lloyd has cancer, Nell. He came back

The Cosy Canal Boat Dream

to say goodbye. He hired this boat for a short time to be close to us and to sell the Old Picture House. He wanted to see us one last time.'

Nell had no words and broke down, the tears cascaded down her face as she sobbed. Gilly wrapped her arms around her daughter and hugged her tight.

'How long have you got?' Nell whimpered.

'Months.' Lloyd looked down at his hands unable to make eye contact.

The three of them sat in silence, lost in their own thoughts, until Lloyd spoke, softly.

'I've lost a lifetime every day I existed without you. You have to believe me when I say I thought about you every day. I just managed to carry on and now ...' He wiped away his tears, 'And now I'm hoping to get to know you in the little time I have left.'

Nell met Lloyd's gaze; his eyes were hopeful.

'I've missed my brother too,' she squeezed his hand across the table before turning to Nell.

'As far as I'm concerned, nothing changes. You are *my* daughter and I love you with all my heart, your dad loved you with all his heart too.' The tears were now cascading down Gilly's cheek, 'I'm so sorry you had to find out like this, but there never seemed a right time to tell you and I never knew whether I would ever see Lloyd again.' Gilly let out a long, shuddering breath.

Nell nodded. She knew, deep down, everyone had been trying to protect her.

'We can't change the past but hopefully we can all spend

some time together in the future,' said Gilly, standing up and opening her arms wide to them both, Lloyd followed her lead and opened his too. Nell stumbled to her feet and fell into both of them as they all hugged each other tight.

Finally Nell pulled out of their arms and sat back down while Lloyd reached for a bottle of whiskey from the kitchen cupboard and poured three glasses, 'I think we need one of these,' he said, sliding a glass each towards Nell and Gilly.

'I think we all need something for the shock,' said Gilly softly.

'Actually, I can't,' said Nell, sliding the glass away. 'You two aren't the only ones with a secret.'

All eyes were on Nell. Even though it's early days, it seemed the right time to get it out in the open, 'I can't drink it ... I'm pregnant.'

'You're pregnant?'

Gilly was bewildered, 'How?'

'I don't think I need to tell you how,' smiled Nell, 'And I know this isn't in the best circumstances, being on my own, and I'm hoping you two will help as much as you can.'

They both smiled fondly at Nell.

'That goes without saying,' beamed Gilly.

'I will love this little one like I've never loved anyone before,' declared Nell.

'I'm in no doubt,' Gilly smiled proudly at her daughter.

'You are going to be a granddad Lloyd,' Nell turned towards him. Lloyd was lost for words as the tears of joy streamed down his face.

Chapter 48

The next morning after breakfast, Nell washed all the dishes and put the pots back in their rightful places before swinging open the doors of the 'Nollie' and stepping out on to the deck. There wasn't a cloud in the sky and even though it was early morning, there were already boats gliding through the water. Nell sat down on the bench and stared out towards Lloyd's boat. She had no idea what it would have been like walking in his shoes for nearly the best part of thirty years, losing the woman he loved and handing his child over to his sister. Nell didn't feel any bitterness towards him. So many things in her life had changed in such a short space of time, and she needed to take the positives from the situation. She knew Lloyd had suffered enough and understood his reasons perfectly for giving her to Gilly and Benny.

Hearing footsteps behind her, she swung round to find Bea standing on the boat, 'Come here,' she said, 'I wanted to come over last night but knew you needed space.' She sat down next her friend and squeezed her knee.

Nell had texted Bea late last night and told her not to worry and that she would explain everything before work.

'Well, it's true. Lloyd is my father.'

Bea widened her eyes, 'I don't know what to say,' she said softly.

'I kind of worked that bit out for myself, but it's the next part that shook me to the core.'

'Go on.'

'Lloyd Keaton is actually my mum's brother.'

Nell saw the shock on Bea's face as the words registered. 'Which means my mum isn't my biological mum,' Nell added.

'Whoa, I wasn't expecting that either.'

'It's been a huge shock for all of us.' Nell quickly filled Bea in on everything she had learned last night.

'Oh, Nell, this is all so heart-breaking.'

'There's more,' she locked eyes with Bea and took a breath, 'He came back for two reasons …'

'The first?' asked Bea.

'To sell the Old Picture House. It was his.'

'So he was the one who gave it to you?' Bea clasped her hand over her mouth, 'Wow.'

Nell nodded. 'Yes, once he found out who I was, but now for the sad part.' Nell's eyes were bleary, 'He's selling the Old Picture House because he has cancer and only a matter of months to live.'

'Oh no, how sad, come here.' Bea slid her hand around Nell's shoulders and hugged her friend. 'How are you feeling about it all?'

'At least it's all out in the open and no more secrets. I can't change any of it and it's very strange discovering that my parents aren't really my biological parents, but I'll never think

The Cosy Canal Boat Dream

of them any differently. They made me who I am, nurtured and cared for me and loved me with all their hearts.'

'And that's why I love you, Nell Andrews, for who you are. They did a wonderful job.'

'Giving me to them must have seemed like the simple solution at the time. They couldn't have children and Lloyd was also grieving. They kept me in the family.'

'Do you forgive Lloyd?'

'I have no bitterness towards Lloyd whatsoever. How must he have felt every birthday, every Christmas? My birthday is the day his wife died – so heart-breaking for everyone.'

'Where do you all go from here?' asked Bea tentatively.

'I'm going to make the most of the time I have left with Lloyd. He's an old man and I can't wait to get to know him better.'

'And your mum?'

'I love her with all my heart, that'll never change.'

Nell's eyes met Bea's, 'I told them about the baby.'

'How did they take it?'

'On the whole it couldn't have gone better. They are delighted to become grandparents. Now my only dilemma is what I do about Guy.'

'You mean, do you tell him?'

Nell nodded, 'It's still very early days. I've got enough time to figure that one out yet.'

Bea smiled at her friend, 'You know, no matter what, I'm here for you.'

'I couldn't have got through any of the last few years without you and Nathan and that gorgeous godson of mine.'

'Onwards and upwards,' Bea smiled, 'Are you up for working in the deli today?'

'Of course. I'll follow you across in a minute and it's a big week for you too.'

'Yes, I've got Fern and Gilly sprucing up the shop for the presentation on Friday.'

'Deli of the Year. You so deserve it, my gorgeous friend,' Nell popped a swift kiss on Bea's cheek, 'We must make a night of it after the presentation – a meal at The Waterfront.'

'Excellent plan,' said Bea, standing up, 'I'll see you in a minute.'

'I won't be long,' said Nell, watching her friend walk down the jetty and disappear inside the deli.

Nell took a moment to reflect on the last twenty-four hours. She felt shattered, emotionally drained but relieved that all the secrets were out. She knew she couldn't change any of the past. Benny and Gilly had been her rock growing up and in her eyes would always be her parents. That would never change. Nell was loved by both of them and throughout her whole life she'd wanted for nothing. She was going to make her mum proud and get on with her life. As Bea had said, onwards and upwards was the only way to go.

Chapter 49

It was fast approaching eleven o'clock when Nell, Gilly and Fern stood behind the counter of the deli hugging skinny lattes and admiring their handywork.

The floral bunting draped the windows, jam jars of daffodils were dotted on top of the counter and scented tea lights flickered on each tabletop. The front of the counter revealed an array of scrumptious-looking cakes on glass-domed stands and the aroma from the coffee and freshly baked bread was simply delicious.

'Deli of the Year,' said Nell, and they all clinked their mugs together.

'I can remember mother saying when we were teenagers she'd never make a living from catering, and now look at what she's achieved.'

'You have to do a job you love, otherwise every day of your life would be miserable,' said Gilly, 'The funny thing is, I was one of those people who never knew what they wanted to do in life and I still don't.'

'But you're happy,' Fern chipped in.

'I'm happy because I was surrounded by the love of good

people, Benny and Nell, everything just worked, and now Lloyd is back in my life too.'

'I never wanted to be an accountant,' Fern suddenly piped up, her face saddened.

Nell swung round towards Fern, 'I thought that was always what you wanted to do?'

She shook her head, 'Parental expectations. I was bright, straight-A student, top of the class in maths. If the truth be told, I hated maths.'

'No way! I wasn't expecting that,' said Nell, astounded.

'Bea was the feisty one. She stood up for what she believed in. I towed the line, mainly for an easy life. I wish I'd been more like her. Goodness knows where my path would have taken me.' Fern's eyes were teary, 'Look at me getting all emotional.' She flapped her hand in front of her face.

Gilly touched her arm affectionately. 'What did you want to do?' Gilly asked tentatively?

'I always wanted to be an artist.'

'An artist?' Nell echoed her words. 'Did you ever tell them that's what you wanted to do?' queried Nell.

She shook her head, 'I used to store a set of paints and brushes in the back of the garage and wait for Saturdays, when Mum and Dad were out doing the big shop, because it usually gave me a couple of hours.'

'It's never too late to follow your heart. You're still only young. Why not give it ago?' suggested Gilly, taking a sip of her coffee.

Fern hesitated for a second, 'You know when Mum was dying and bed-ridden?'

The Cosy Canal Boat Dream

'Yes,' answered Nell.

'I began to paint again. I couldn't tell Pete what I was doing. He would have just ridiculed me ...' she took a breath, 'So it was my little secret, something just for me. I set up a painting studio in Mum's back living room. It was an ideal place to store my paints, canvas and easel and when she was sleeping I began to paint again.'

'Fern, that's amazing. What've have you done with the artwork?'

'It's all at Mum's. I've even painted a picture of the deli.'

'The deli?' Nell's eyes widened as she placed her mug on top of the counter.

Fern nodded, 'Yes, I missed Bea so much that I sneaked up here a few times when Pete was in the pub on a Sunday. I took some photos on my phone and then went to my easel. I painted the shop, the marina and even the Nollie is on there.'

'Wow, what are you going to do with it?'

'I'm not sure.'

Nell beamed, 'How about giving it to her as a present today. The timing couldn't be better.'

'Now there's a plan,' Fern smiled, 'Have I got time to nip back for it now?'

'Look,' said Gilly, and they all swung round towards the window, 'Apart from the fact you'll get soaked, the rain doesn't look like it's going to let up anytime soon and Nathan's car has just pulled up at the side of the deli.'

'We can keep an eye on the weather and maybe nip out after the presentation. I'm sure we could rope Nathan into giving us a quick lift later.'

Just at that minute, the deli door swung open and Bea walked in, hunched over with her coat held over her head to shield her from the rain.

Nell, Gilly and Fern began to clap, 'Here she is, Miss Melting Pot herself.'

She lowered the coat and met their eyes and beamed, 'What a welcome and just look at this place, you've all worked so hard,' she beamed, sniffing the daffodils and admiring the floral bunting across the windows.'

'You're welcome,' Nell said, smiling, taking the soggy coat from her, 'I think this torrential rain is keeping all the customers away.'

'I know,' Bea sighed, glancing over her shoulder to see the rain hammering against the window. 'And look at those boats bobbing on the water. Even Fred has battened down the hatches.

'I think the weather has put everyone off,' Bea exhaled.

'We are all here and that's all that matters,' Nathan kissed his wife lightly on the head.

'Ooo, who's this? That's a posh car!' Gilly interrupted, pointing outside. Everyone swung round.

It was unusual to see vehicles this far up the wharf, except the butcher's lorry delivering the meat to the shop.

They watched a man open the passenger's door, He held an umbrella above her head to shield her from the rain as she stepped from the vehicle.

'I feel so nervous,' Bea whispered to Nathan, 'Which is daft when all I have to say is thank you. I've got some right flutterings going on in my stomach.'

The Cosy Canal Boat Dream

Nathan quickly placed his hand on his wife's tummy, 'Are you sure that's nerves and not the babies moving?' He quickly placed his hand on her stomach.

Bea's eyes sprang towards Nathan, 'Yes, Bea, I felt that.' He beamed at his wife and swiftly placed her hand onto her stomach. For a couple of seconds, Bea waited and nothing, then 'OMG! Yes, yes I felt them move too.'

Everyone in the deli cheered as the door sprung open, 'Hi, I'm looking for Beatrice Green,' the woman beamed.

'I'm Bea,' she answered, shaking her hand.

'Pleased to meet you. I'm Tasha Miller and here to present you with your award on behalf of the DSA and this is …'

Tasha turned round and gestured to the gentleman standing at the side of her, 'Alf Kemp.'

Instantly, Bea recognised the gentleman, but couldn't quite place him.

'Have we met before? I seem to know you from somewhere.'

'Sorry to interrupt, but can I get you both a drink?' Nathan asked politely.

'A cup of tea would be great, thank you,' said Tasha.

'And a coffee for me … Alf paused, 'But none of that instant rubbish.'

As soon as the words left his mouth Bea noticed the twinkle in his eye.

'It's you, it's you!'

He grinned, 'The last time you saw me I was wearing false spectacles, a flat cap, waterproof trousers and green wellington boots.'

'And you took a scone home for your lovely wife.' Bea grinned widely.

'You have a very good memory.'

'I thought you were a boater,' Nell exclaimed.

'That was the idea.'

'And I thought the woman opposite you was the judge.'

'Can I commend you on the way you dealt with that awkward customer? I'm not sure I would have been that patient,' he gave a little chuckle and extended his hand, which Bea promptly shook. 'Pleased to meet you, Bea. Your food was outstanding and your service impeccable.'

Bea blushed and introduced them to the rest of the staff before they moved over to the café part of the deli.

'Look at this rain,' Tasha gazed out over the marina.'

'I know,' Bea sighed. I was hoping there'd be a few regulars in to see me awarded with the plaque, but I can understand why no one's here.'

Nathan rubbed his wife's back and she kissed him on his cheek.

Just at that minute, the deli door burst open. Bea looked up and saw Alan giving Gilly the thumbs-up behind the counter. Following him were all the staff from his shop, the pub, boutique owners and right at the back of the long queue were Ed and Lloyd. Bea chuckled when she spotted Sam loping at Ed's side – he looked dapper with a huge bow tied around his neck.

'Surprise!' Alan bellowed. 'You didn't think we'd abandoned you, did you? This rain wouldn't keep us away.'

'I can't believe that all these people turned up out of the

The Cosy Canal Boat Dream

blue. I was beginning to feel a little disappointed,' Bea said, smiling happily.

'You can thank Mum for that. She was on the phone to Alan first thing this morning organising the troops because of the weather,' Nell replied.

Bea smiled, 'Thanks so much, everyone. I'm honestly thrilled and feeling a little giddy.'

'And so you should.'

After Nell said hello to Lloyd and Ed, everyone began to gather around the tables at the back of the deli and Gilly and Fern were pushing through the crowd, carrying a tray of champagne flutes full to the brim.

Fern handed one to Bea, 'This one is lemonade, but it still looks the same.'

'Thanks, Fern.'

'Here's the press now,' Tasha glanced over towards the door. In walked a tall man with a camera dangling around his neck. He pushed to the back of the deli and introduced himself to Bea.

He manoeuvred her next to Tasha and snapped a few shots before Alf clinked his glass with a spoon and the whole deli fell silent. All eyes were on Bea. 'Today we are here to present Beatrice Green with the most prestigious award we offer.'

Both Nathan and Nell stifled a giggle as they saw Bea squirm at the mention of her name, 'I don't know why she doesn't like her name, it suits her,' Nell whispered to Nathan.

'Here at the DSA,' Tasha continued, 'The Deli Standards Association, the Michelin stars of all delis and coffee shops, me and Alf have what I consider to be the best job in the world. We travel up and down the country tasting the most delicious food, granted it's not good for the waistline,' she patted her stomach and everyone chuckled, 'However, when you discover a place like this,' she swept her arms outwards, 'It makes it all worthwhile. The Melting Pot is not only exceptional in terms of customer service and ambience but it attracts a wide range of customers, from people living on barges to local families. The standard of food is excellent, reasonably priced and it gives me great pleasure to present the award of Deli of the Year to Beatrice Green of The Melting Pot.' Tasha handed over the plaque and Bea shook hands with both her and Alf. The photographer snapped away while everyone else erupted in cheers and clapped. And not forgetting Sam, who thumped his tail on the floor.

Once the photographer had finished taking photographs, Nell moved forward and threw her arms around her best friend while she blinked back the tears.

'Congratulations you!'

'Thank you,' Bea was grinning like the Cheshire Cat, 'I couldn't have done any of this without you.'

'The dream team!' Nell high-fived Bea and they both chuckled.

'I have to ask, was it you?'

'Was what me?' Nell asked.

'Who nominated me? Come on, you can tell me now.'

Nell shook her head, 'Honestly, it wasn't me. I'd told you before, I'd tell you if it was.'

'Well, who was it then?' Bea asked, perplexed, turning towards Alf, who was chatting with Nathan beside them.

The Cosy Canal Boat Dream

'Sorry to interrupt, but Alf, could I ask, and I'm not sure you can tell me, but who nominated me?'

Alf glanced towards Tasha before flicking back through some papers in his hand. His eyes scanned the page and he ran his finger across it.

'You were nominated by a Dot and Fern Watson.'

Bea gasped.

'Your mum and sister,' Nell nodded, her approving eye ran over the names on the page before squeezing Bea's arm, 'See, she was proud of you.'

Bea swallowed a lump and bit down on her lip, trying to keep the tears from falling, but the emotion was too raw.

She turned towards Fern, who was chatting behind her with Alan and Lloyd, 'It was you.'

She smiled warmly, 'More like Mum. I just filled in the form. She spotted an article in a magazine and said you would be the perfect nomination and she was right.'

'You don't know how much this means to me,' sobbed Bea, smiling through the tears.

'I think I do, come on, group hug.'

Fern extended her arms and Bea, Nathan and Nell fell into them. Tears a-plenty.

Chapter 50

Despite the torrential rain everyone had a fantastic afternoon. Tasha and Alf left soon after the presentation, but not before Bea had put together a small food hamper for them both and Alf promised next time he was in the area with his wife he would visit for a cream tea.

The mood was jovial and after Nathan shushed the remaining guests he erected the plaque in the middle of the wall behind the counter and they all stood and admired it.

'My face is actually aching. I don't think I've smiled this much in ages,' Bea laughed, pinching her cheeks with her fingers.

'You must be tired,' Nathan grabbed a chair, 'Take that weight off your feet.'

'Are you saying I'm fat?'

Everyone chuckled.

Finally, after a couple of hours the rain had begun to ease a little and Fern ushered Nell into the kitchen.

'It will only take me fifteen minutes or so to nip back to Mum's and grab the painting. But what's the story if Bea asks where I'm going?'

The Cosy Canal Boat Dream

Nell paused for a minute, 'I've no idea, but I've got to nip to the Old Picture House in the next half an hour. The builder is meeting there to discuss something about the re-wiring.'

'Sounds riveting,' Fern laughed, snatching her coat from the back of the office chair.

'It's been a fantastic afternoon, hasn't it?'

Nell agreed, 'Yes, and made even more special knowing you and your mum nominated Bea for the award. That was definitely the icing on the cake.'

Fern smiled and touched Nell's arm, 'I'll see you in a little while. I'm going to sneak out the back door.'

'Good idea.'

Nell locked the door behind Fern and wandered back into the deli. Everyone was huddled around laughing and chatting. Gilly was standing with Lloyd in the corner and Sam was sitting at his side.

'Looks like you've made a new friend there,' Nell bent down and ruffled Sam's fur.

'What a fantastic day,' Gilly turned towards Nell, 'Will it be alright if Lloyd joins us at the pub for Bea's celebratory meal this evening.'

'Of course. I'm sure Bea won't mind and neither do I. The more the merrier.'

'Come and join us, you three. Don't stand in the corner, grab a chair,' Bea hollered, 'And where's that sister of mine disappeared to?'

Nell pulled up a chair alongside her friend, 'She'll be back in a minute. She's just nipped out for a second.'

'Where to?'

'I didn't ask and anyway where's that lovely godson of mine? He must have finished school by now.' Nell changed the subject, steering the conversation away from Fern.

'He's at a friend's house for tea. That's why we are taking advantage of some adult time in the pub for tea, which will finish off the day perfectly.'

'Gushing-friend moment coming up,' Nell warned Bea, 'I'm so proud of what you've achieved here.'

'Thank you.'

'I've just got to nip out for a short while. I'm meeting the builder at the Old Picture House anytime now,' she glanced at her watch, 'I'll see you in the pub when I've finished. It shouldn't take too long.'

'Make sure you do.'

Nell stood up and slipped her arms inside her coat before hurrying up the wharf towards the Old Picture House. Nell took a moment outside and smiled at the huge yellow skip outside, which was packed to the brim with rubble. She still had to pinch herself. She couldn't quite believe this place was hers and already it was beginning to be transformed into something special. She willed the day to hurry when she could open the doors to the public and, with everything running so smoothly, hopefully it would soon.

Nell turned the key in the lock and pushed open the door to the Old Picture House. She stood proudly inside the foyer. Already she could imagine how everything was going to look. The builders were already doing a fantastic job, the wallpaper had been stripped and the worn carpet ripped away. The

The Cosy Canal Boat Dream

windows were being replaced in the next few weeks and everything was on track. She knew, even though it was still a fair few months off completion, that it would all come together in the end and look magnificent.

Nell wandered around the place, the ladies' and gents' were an empty shell waiting to be tiled and painted, then the new toilets could be installed. This coming week the cinema chairs were going to be deep-cleaned and the new heavy red-velvet curtains that were to hang in each auditorium in front of the screen were on order.

She climbed the stairs to the projection room. The shelves of films had already been transferred to plastic boxes and labelled in alphabetical order. The walls had been painted in magnolia, which gave it a more airy, clean feel.

She sat on one of the chairs and glanced at her mobile. The builder was already fifteen minutes late. She sent a text asking how long he was going to be, knowing that he'd probably been caught up at another job.

Almost immediately the phone beeped and she swiped the screen.

'Just caught in traffic. I'll be there in ten minutes.'

Nell walked back down the magnificent staircase towards the foyer. She stood still for a second thinking she'd heard a door creak at the end of the hallway towards the small cinema room.

'Don't be daft,' she murmured to herself, 'It'll just be the wind.' For a second she loitered at the bottom of the stairs, when she heard it again. Her heart was thumping as she swung her head round and stared towards the door at the bottom of the hallway.

She hollered, 'Hello, who's there?'

But there was no answer.

She felt uneasy as she tiptoed along the floor and pressed her hand to the door. She took a deep breath and pushed it open.

The room was in complete darkness.

'Stupid woman,' she uttered, rolled her eyes and heaved a sigh of relief. 'It'll be a draught somewhere.'

She turned round and squealed. Placing her hand on her heart, Nell forced herself to breathe calmly.

Guy beamed back at her. 'Fancy seeing you here.' Nell stared in amazement, 'You nearly gave me a heart attack! What the heck are you doing here?'

He looked gorgeous standing there in his ever-faithful Levi's and converse. He nervously swept his fringe away from his eye, allowing his hazel eyes to lock with Nell's.

'You're shaking.'

'No bloody wonder, I thought there was an intruder.

Guy, you frightened the life out of me.'

'It's good to see you,' his eyes sparkled at her.

Nell had to admit, it was good to see him too.

'Any chance of a hug?' he tilted his head to one side and slowly opened his arms.

'Go on, then, if I must.'

He wrapped his arms around her and Nell almost melted, it felt so good.

After a few seconds Nell pulled away, 'I'm meeting the builder in a minute. He wants to have a chat about the re-wiring. But what exactly are you doing here, Guy?'

The Cosy Canal Boat Dream

'There is no builder. I telephoned Mike and asked him to arrange the meeting.'

'No meeting? It was you?'

'Yes! I wanted to surprise you!'

'Well, you did that all right!'

He smiled at her and Nell swiped his chest playfully, 'Look at this place. It looks different already. You've worked really hard bringing everything together.'

'I'm actually quite proud of myself, even if I do say so myself,' she beamed.

He grabbed hold of her hand and pulled her in close once more, wrapping his arms around her and rested his chin on top of her head, 'I have missed you, Nell Andrews.'

She closed her eyes, her heart clattered at his touch and he smelt divine. She'd missed him too but he wasn't hers to miss. 'Me too, but it's too complicated. We shouldn't be talking like this,' her voice was barely a whisper.

'We need to talk,' he said firmly, pulling away and gripping her hand. 'Back to the Nollie and I'm not taking no for an answer.'

Chapter 51

Guy was standing behind Nell while she fumbled with the keys in the lock to the 'Nollie'. 'You're making me nervous,' she laughed over her shoulder.

'Is that a good thing?'

'I'm not entirely sure.' She finally held the door open so he could step inside.

'I believe Bea's had a good day,' he said, slipping out of his coat and settling at the table, he folded his arms and shifted his gaze to Nell, who was standing smiling at him.

'What are you smiling at?'

'Nothing whatsoever, make yourself at home,' she chuckled, 'It's like you've never been away. Drink?'

'Cup of tea would be great.'

Nell made them both a drink and slipped on the seat next to him.

'Bea was delighted with the award. Despite the weather, Alan rallied all the troops and the place was packed. I know I'm biased but it was well-deserved. She works hard.'

'And I believe Sam looked dapper in his bow tie.'

Nell chuckled, 'How do you know about any of this?'

The Cosy Canal Boat Dream

'Because when I dropped off my suitcase at Ed's I wanted to know why my dog was suddenly sporting a bow tie.'

Nell had only focused on one word in that sentence, 'Suitcase? Are you back for a while, then?' she felt a nervous flutter in her stomach waiting for his answer.

'Hopefully, Ed has offered me a job at the yard and I can stay in the annexe until the new lodgers move in.'

It took Nell a moment for all this to register, 'You're really back?'

'Back for good.'

'But, I don't understand, what's happened?'

She saw a sadness wash over him and he took a sip of his tea before turning towards her. He rested his face on his hands and exhaled.

'Me and Kate, it was never going to work, was it? I'd lost all respect for her a long time ago and as far as love went ...' he paused and exhaled.

Waiting in anticipation, Nell came over all emotional, 'She's lost the baby, hasn't she?'

Their eyes locked, 'Not quite,' he finally said, swallowing down a lump. He raked his hands through his hair and clearly looked distressed.

'The only reason I went back was for the baby, you do know that don't you.'

Nell nodded, 'I believe you. You don't have to explain yourself. You were putting your baby first. It takes a special kind of person to do that,' she said softly.

'When I got back to Ireland, it didn't feel like home. I wanted to be anywhere but there. I felt so lonely, unhappy and I missed you dreadfully.' He shifted his gaze to Nell, his expression was earnest.

'I know it sounds overdramatic but all I thought about was you. I dreamt of this place. My dreams were so vivid I'd wake up and then reality hit, I wasn't here. Kate and I barely spoke, everything felt forced and false. I went back to work and I hated every minute of it. My heart wasn't in it. I didn't want to be with Kate, there was no love there any more. Well, not from me, anyway. The more I thought about it, the more I resented being there. What life would it be for a child to be brought up in those circumstances?'

'A difficult one,' admitted Nell.

He nodded. 'So I wrote my letter of resignation and they accepted it. Even though it hurt to go back, I had to give it a try, otherwise I would have always been wondering what if.' Guy was now wearing his heart on his sleeve.

'Especially for the baby's sake.'

'But I knew the moment I left you here, it was never going to work.'

Nell blushed. Guy was staring deep into her eyes. She leant forward and kissed him lightly on the cheek. He smiled warmly at her and took a deep breath.

'I decided to tell Kate I was coming back to England and if she made it difficult for me I'd fight for custody if I had to.'

'How did she take that?'

'She laughed in my face.'

Nell's eyes widened. 'Why would she do that?'

He took a deep breath, 'She laughed because there is no baby.'

The Cosy Canal Boat Dream

Nell sat up straight and stared at Guy. 'No baby? What do you mean?'

'There was never a baby. She made it up, said it out of spite, probably because she knew I'd feelings for you. It was a control thing, she just wanted me back in Ireland.'

Nell took a moment to digest the information. 'She knows you are a decent guy and would do the right thing.'

'Possibly so.'

'But what a thing to do.'

'What she did was unforgivable.'

They both sat quietly for a moment until Nell broke the silence.

'You deserve so much more than that. I'm so sorry.' Nell's stomach lurched and she felt sickened by such a lie, 'It's such a terrible thing to lie about. What did she think was going to happen in seven to eight months' time?'

'I really have no idea.' Guy took a moment to collect his thoughts, his body was trembling with anger and his eyes were bleary with tears.

'After I packed my suitcase I gave her a few choice words and told her I was filing for divorce.'

Nell squeezed his hands tight. 'I always admired you for putting your baby first. How do you feel now you know there isn't one?'

'Sad and relieved, if that makes any sense. Sad, I suppose, because I think I'd be a good dad and I love children and I'm relieved that I'm not tied to Kate for a lifetime. I want a family with someone I love, someone I respect, who feels the same about me. I know one day that could possibly happen.'

'Any ideas who that person could possibly be?'

Guy turned towards her, 'I'm not the best with all this sloppy stuff ...'

'You're doing alright so far,' her fingers entwined around his.

'I've never missed anyone like I've missed you. I mean I really missed you. I want to be happy with you ...' he hooked a strand of hair around Nell's ear then tilted her chin towards his face, 'I love you, Nell Andrews, you make me happy and I feel alive again.'

Nell's heart thumped faster hearing those words.

'I love you too, Guy Cornish, but there's something you need to know.' Nell could feel the emotion rising inside her. She had to tell Guy that she was carrying his baby. He stroked her hair gently, 'What is it?'

'There have been quite a few changes since you left.'

'Changes? What sort of changes,' he had no clue what Nell was about to tell him.

'I don't really know where to start, so I'll blurt it out quickly and make of it all what you will.'

'Okay, I'm ready.'

'Lloyd Keaton, the guy you rescued on the boat, is an actor, in fact a famous actor, but his real name is actually Lloyd Taylor.'

'I've no idea where you are going with this,' interrupted Guy, puzzled.

'He's my mum's brother.'

'How did you not know he was your uncle?' Guy was even more confused now.

The Cosy Canal Boat Dream

'He's not my uncle, he's my father.'

Guy's eyes widened and he sat upright. 'You've definitely lost me now.'

Nell filled him in on everything that had happened while he'd been away.

'I think I need a drink,' Guy looked over to the wine rack.

'There is so much more to tell you, but I should be meeting Bea in The Waterfront,' she glanced at her watch.

'I leave you for a second and you've been on a roller-coaster of a ride.'

'Welcome back to Little Rock Marina!' she smiled.

'Surely we need a quick toast to welcome me back?'

It was now or never, 'You can have one but I can't ... Guy there's more to tell you and I'm not even sure how to tell you.'

Guy stared at Nell, who suddenly looked anxious, 'You know you can tell me anything,' he squeezed her hand reassuringly.

Nell felt nervous. She had no idea how Guy was going to react to the news. She took a deep breath, 'I'm pregnant and I know the timing isn't great and ...'

Nell didn't finish her sentence before Guy pulled her to feet and lifted her off the ground and spun her round.'

'Stop spinning me, you'll make me sick,' she giggled.

'Sorry, sorry,' he tilted her upwards and they locked eyes. 'You're pregnant, you're actually pregnant?'

'I am. What do you think?'

'What do I think? I think it's fantastic!'

Guy stood still and looked at Nell, 'What do you think?'

'I can't wait to bring this little one into the world.'

'Phew! I think the timing is more than great. In fact, it's perfect. I can get myself established at the boatyard, there are so many plans to make ... where will we live?'

'Whoa! Slow down! All I need to know is this is what you want? Me and the baby.'

The grin on Guy's face said it all, 'Nell Andrews, you have made me the happiest man on the earth. I'm not going anywhere ... ever!'

'Good, I'm glad to hear that.'

'I can't believe it, I am going to be a father.'

'You are and a brilliant one at that,' she leant up and kissed him, every nerve in her body tingled.

'I love you,' he whispered.

'I love you more. Now come on, let's get to the pub before Bea sends out a search party.'

Chapter 52

Guy had a barrage of questions he wanted to ask Nell, but they would just have to wait until they got back from the pub.

'I'll fill you in as much as I can en route.

'I can't wait! Will they mind if I tag along tonight and gatecrash the party?'

'Mind? Not at all. Lloyd is joining us too. The more the merrier, as far as I'm concerned,' she said leaning in and kissing him on his mouth.

'Do we have to go out?'

'We do but ...' she said, brushing his lips with her finger, 'I can't wait for later.' She replied with a sparkle in her eye.

'What time can we make our excuses?'

'Guy, behave,' she grinned, pushing him out on to the deck of the 'Nollie'.

Within a couple of minutes Nell and Guy joined everyone in the pub. They were all standing around the table in the far corner admiring Fern's painting.

Bea looked up and spotted Nell walking towards them.

'Here she is, what's been keeping you?' She tapped her

watch, 'That must have been a hell of meeting about re-wiring.' She pretended to yawn, before noticing Guy standing at the side of Nell.

'I believe congratulations are in order,' Guy leant in and gave Bea a peck on the cheek.

'OMG you're back!' she snagged a quick look at her best friend, who was grinning from ear to ear. 'How, when, why?' she exclaimed.

'So many questions,' laughed Nell, putting her bag down on the table.

'Are you here for a while?'

'I hope so,' Guy beamed, squeezing Nell's hand.

'That's good to hear! And Nell look at this,' she insisted, turning Fern's painting towards them.

'Wow! That's amazing, look at the detail and oh my, the Nollie is on there. You have an amazing talent, Fern.'

'Thank you,' she blushed.

'Maybe you should paint some pictures to decorate the deli walls, we could even see if you could sell a few,' Bea suggested, propping the picture up against the wall.

'I'd love that.'

'And please forgive my manners. Can I introduce you to Guy? This is my sister Fern.'

Guy shook her hand and gave her a huge smile, 'Pleased to meet you.'

'Likewise.'

Nathan patted him on his back, 'Welcome back, mate.'

'Thanks,' he said, giving him a friendly handshake.

Bea stared in Nell's direction and mouthed, 'Does he know?'

The Cosy Canal Boat Dream

Nell grinned widely, 'Yes, he knows.'

Bea did her best to suppress her squeal. As soon as Guy and Nathan were out of earshot, Bea leant in towards Nell. 'That's a turn up for the books. What's going on? There's never a dull moment around here?'

'You wouldn't believe me if I told you.' Nell kept her voice to a whisper. 'You know he only went back to Ireland to try and make it work for the baby's sake?'

'So what happened?' Bea's eyes locked with Nell's.

She took a deep breath, 'Because there is no baby, just a big fat lie.'

Bea sat back in her chair still staring at Nell. 'Whoa! Are you telling me she wasn't pregnant?'

'That's exactly what I'm telling you. It appears she made it up to lure Guy back to Ireland.'

'But what did he say about your baby?'

'I'll fill you in later, but I think everything is going to be alright!'

'That's brilliant, you do make a lovely couple and it's great to see that twinkle back in your eye.'

There was no denying Nell shimmered with happiness. 'I can't believe he's actually back. I literally had a heart attack when I saw him.' Her smile turned into a huge grin.

'He is quite delicious,' Bea pretended to fan her face whispering, 'Hot, hot, hot' under her breath.

'Stop! Seriously, just stop, he'll hear you,' Nell stifled a giggle and swiped Bea's leg under the table. Nell looked up at Guy, her eyes sparkled as he settled in the seat next to her and looped his arm through hers. In the last few hours her life had changed once more in such a short space of time: Guy was back and everything was feeling fresh and exciting again.

'We need a photo,' Nell suddenly declared.

Everyone groaned jokingly.

'She makes no apologies,' Guy said in a heavily accented Irish accent.

Both Nell and Bea swooned, 'That accent,' Nell placed her hand on her heart.

'There's something about that voice,' Bea laughed, batting her eyelashes.

'Behave,' Guy grinned, picking up his pint glass.

Nell whipped out her phone from her bag,

'I don't mind taking the photo of you all.' They looked up to see Lloyd standing at the side of the table.

'You will not, you need to be in the picture,' Nell declared, giving the phone to the passing waiter.

'Come on, everyone. Lloyd, you sit next to Mum.' Everyone snuggled in close and smiled. Once the photos were taken, Nell picked up her glass and declared a toast.

'Today has been a very special day.'

Nathan gave his wife a proud look of affection while Fern squeezed her hand.

'Not only is Bea a truly special individual and my best friend, but she without a doubt owns the best deli in the country, and we know that as of today it became official. It's an absolute pleasure to be part of the team and a huge thank you to Bea for taking me under her wing when I needed looking after the most.'

The Cosy Canal Boat Dream

Bea's eyes brimmed with tears, 'You'd do the same for me.'

'Not only has Bea been awarded with Deli of the Year, Fern has learnt to cook an egg ...'

Everyone chuckled.

'I absolutely love working alongside you all, we are the dream team,' chipped in Fern.

'Guy is back,' Nell smiled towards him,

'For good,' he added.

'And Mum has been reunited with her brother. I think that's enough drama for Little Rock Marina this week!'

Everyone laughed.

Nell raised her glass, 'To Bea and The Melting Pot.'

'To Bea,' everyone echoed.

'And to Nell, my best friend,' Bea raised her glass once more, 'Here's to happy ever after.'

Bea took a sip of her drink then suddenly sadness flashed across her face and her shoulders slumped.

Nell met Bea's eyes, 'What's the matter?' She placed her glass on the table.

'Nothing, I'm just being daft.'

'Go on, we're amongst friends.'

Her eyes briefly slid from Nell's, 'Because, it's all about to change.'

Nell grabbed her hand, 'Don't get all morose. This is your day.'

'I said I was being daft, but we're all embarking on new adventures: me with the twins and you with the Old Picture House and the baby.'

'Adventures that no doubt will be bringing us closer together, especially when the boys are on babysitting duties and we are out on the town,' winked Nell.

'That sounds like a great idea,' smiled Bea.

'Not to me, it doesn't,' laughed Nathan.

'And Gilly and I will be working hard in The Melting Pot to keep things ticking over, especially now I can boil eggs, fry eggs and poach eggs! I'll be giving Jamie Oliver a run for his money yet.' Fern smiled at her sister.

'Don't get too carried away,' she teased.

Fern brought her hand up to her chest in mock outrage and grinned.

For the next hour everyone sat and chatted about anything and everything. Lloyd mesmerised them with stories from his past, from how he got his first acting break to having lunch with Frank Sinatra. Everyone was in awe. It was such a wonderful evening.

'You know when you don't want an evening to end, well, that's me right now.' Everyone looked towards Bea, 'but I'm beginning to feel tired.'

'I'll get the bill,' Nathan stopped the passing waiter and put his bank card down on the table.

'I've had the best night,' Nell squeezed her friend's hand.

'I think we all have,' agreed Fern.

'Nathan can you carry the painting to the car for me? And thanks again, Fern, I absolute love it.'

'Of course.'

Gilly and Lloyd rose to their feet, 'Lloyd's going to walk me home,' said Gilly, 'Thanks again everyone for such a wonderful evening.' Nell rose to her feet and kissed them both on their cheeks and waved to everyone as they left the pub.

'And then there were two,' Nell turned towards Guy, holding on tightly to her smile.

'Two indeed, another drink?'

Nell scrunched up her face, 'It's not much fun when you can't drink.'

'Ha, yes, sorry! Any other suggestions, then?' he grinned his handsome smile and swept his fringe from his eyes.

'I have a few, now grab your coat.'

'Okay, captain,' he saluted, before following Nell through the crowded bar.

As they opened the double doors and stepped outside the pub they stopped and stared up at the stars, 'Are you happy?' Guy asked Nell, linking his arm through hers.

'More than you'll ever know, Guy Cornish, more than you'll ever know.

Chapter 53

Nine months later

Guy was standing in the kitchen of the 'Nollie' sizzling sausages when Nell slipped her arms around his waist and snuggled into his neck.

'Good morning, sleepy head,' he said, turning and kissing the tip of her nose. 'I didn't like to wake you.'

'Not like that little madam, at one o'clock, two o'clock, three o'clock,'

'I get the picture,' Guy grinned at Nell, 'Where is our gorgeous daughter?'

'Can you believe, she's still fast asleep?'

'Good, because that gives me a little time to spoil you. Now you sit yourself down and breakfast will be served in a minute. There's some tea in the pot too.'

Nell cast a glance over her shoulder before sinking into the settee and pulling a grey woollen throw over her lap.

Nell glanced at the photograph on the side, a photo of her, Guy and Annie the day their daughter was born. Both Lloyd and Gilly had been over the moon when they'd

The Cosy Canal Boat Dream

announced they were going to call the baby Annie after Lloyd's wife and Nell's biological mum. Both of them were as proud as punch and were certainly the doting grandparents.

Everything was going from strength to strength. Guy had moved into the 'Nollie' and Ed had offered him a partnership at the yard. Nell couldn't wish for anything more; she was truly happy and burst with love for Guy and Annie.

'What time have you been up since? This looks all very grand. I could get used to this,' she smiled and poured herself a mug of tea.

Guy took the plates out of the oven and popped them down in front of her.

'Have you warmed the plates too? I'm very impressed,' she smiled.

'I have indeed, now help yourself, there's sausages, bacon, mushrooms, tomatoes – the full works,' he said placing the steaming food on to the table. 'How are you feeling?'

'I can't believe the day is finally here! I'm excited, nervous and can't wait to cut that ribbon and open the doors to The Red Carpet Cinema for the very first time.'

'I'm so proud of you, you know and Ollie would have been too.'

Nell tucked into her breakfast, 'I know and thank you for everything. I couldn't have done any of it without you.'

'When Annie wakes up, I'll bath her, get her dressed and fed – you just worry about yourself this morning.'

'Everyone should have a Guy Cornish in their life – you are simply the best.'

Christie Barlow

'And don't you forget it,' he smiled lovingly towards Nell and her heart soared with love for him.

She watched as he stood up and buttered the toast. 'Have you seen outside this morning?' asked Guy, staring out of the porthole of the 'Nollie'.

'No why?'

'Close your eyes,' he ordered.

'What?'

'Just do it!'

Nell closed her eyes and he took her by her hand. He led her carefully on to the deck of the 'Nollie'.

'Open them.'

Nell gasped, 'The whole marina appeared silent, except for the snow falling lightly on the roofs on the boats. The frost had polished the boathouse, the deli and there stood The Old Picture House glistening in silver sheen.

'Oh Guy, this is just perfect.'

He pulled her in close, wrapping his arms around her body, while they looked up at the flakes falling.

'That's not all. I have another little surprise.'

Nell followed him to the front of the boat, 'I know we haven't got much room for a Christmas tree inside the Nollie so, ta-dah!'

There on the bow of the boat was a small pine Christmas tree with its lights twinkling away.'

'It's so magical, I love you.'

'I love you too. Come on, let's eat, then I'll clear up and get our daughter ready.'

Nell stood for a moment watching the flakes fall, her heart

The Cosy Canal Boat Dream

bursting with happiness, she stood and thought about everything that had happened in the last twelve months, and how her life had changed. She smiled, even though Ollie wasn't around she was now on a different path and he'd never be forgotten. He'd always be part of her life. She hoped somehow he knew that he would always hold that special place in her heart.

'Hey, what are you doing standing out here? You'll catch your death,' Nell swung round to see Nathan pushing the double buggy up the wharf.

'We are admiring our new tree. How are Alice and Arthur this morning?' They both smiled down at the twins, wrapped up tightly in their woven blankets and pink and blue hats.

'Had us up every hour on the hour – if it wasn't one, it was the other. The joys of parenthood,' he grinned.

'But look at those bundles of cuteness,' oozed Nell, 'Utterly gorgeous.'

Nathan looked adoringly towards his children, 'Yes, I wouldn't swap them for the world. Bea is having an hour to herself, hence the reason I'm out for an early morning walk in the snow and Jacob is still asleep.'

'It's alright for some,' Guy smiled.

'I'll leave you to it and we'll see you later for the grand opening!'

'Can't wait,' beamed Nell, sliding her arm around Guy's waist.

Nathan manoeuvred the buggy through the slushy snow and waved his hand above his head as he disappeared along the towpath.

Christie Barlow

'Come on, let's get you inside and eat our breakfast before it goes cold.

They stamped the snow off their slippers and Guy leant forward and wiped a snowflake from the tip of Nell's nose, then kissed her gently.

Just as they sat down, Annie began to murmur from the Moses basket at the side of their bed. 'I'm sure she knows the minute we are going to eat,' Nell shook her head smiling, 'It's like she has a built-in radar.'

'I'll get her, you eat.'

'Thank you,' Nell poured herself another cup of tea and dipped her toast in her egg and thought about the day ahead. In a couple of hours' time she was opening the door to The Red Carpet Cinema for the very first time. Everyone was going to be there and she couldn't wait. She'd worked hard to bring it altogether and with the help of Lloyd and his contacts within the film industry the décor inside was truly magnificent.

'Hey, you're all teary,' said Guy, juggling Annie with one hand and kissing Nell on top of her head.

'Just emotional but happy,' she smiled up at Guy and her daughter, who was gurgling away. 'I can't believe how things have turned out, you, this little one, I truly couldn't be any happier. I love you both so much that I can't even describe it.'

'I love you too.' he said kissing Nell on the lips. 'You two are my life and I wouldn't change it for the world.'

Two hours later Nell and Guy left the 'Nollie' with Annie fast asleep in the baby sling attached to Guy's chest. 'It feels like

The Cosy Canal Boat Dream

we packed supplies for a year and we're only leaving the boat for a couple of hours,' he laughed, slinging the packed rucksack over his shoulder. Guy took Nell's hand as they walked towards the Old Picture House.

Nell's heart thumped with excitement and she took in a breath when she saw the building and stopped in her tracks. 'Did you do this?' she gasped and turned towards Guy, 'Just look at this place.'

He smiled at Nell, 'I might have had something to do with it.'

A red carpet trailed all the way up the stone steps, and to the left of the entrance an enormous Christmas tree towered, the lights sparkling like a thousand diamonds.

People had already started to form a queue, 'I've even got customers. I can't believe it.'

'You better believe it.'

Nathan appeared around the side of the building and spotted Guy, who gave him a nod of the head and a thumbs-up.

'What's going on now?'

Just at that moment, the local church choir and brass band struck up a chord. Nell gasped, she blinked hard trying to hold back the tears. They were all wrapped up in their winter woollies, swinging lanterns as they walked around the corner and stood on the steps of the Old Picture House singing 'Silent Night'.

'I'm not sure I can take much more,' said Nell, already wiping her blurry eyes.

Guy put his arm around her, 'Enjoy it. This is your day.'

Bea appeared at her side with the twins in their pushchair, along with Gilly, Lloyd, Ed and Sam. 'This is fantastic, Nell. I'm so proud of you,' Gilly's eyes brimmed with unshed tears.

Nell was too emotional to speak and just hugged her mum before turning to Lloyd.

'Annie would have loved to be here on a day like today,' he squeezed Nell's hand, 'You have done everyone proud,' he said, his voice faltered.

'Thank you, I can't believe the turnout, it's truly magnificent.'

All of them stood huddled together listening to the choir, goose bumps prickled every inch of Nell's body.

'Aunty Nellie, Aunty Nellie.' Nell spun round to see Jacob holding Fern's hand clomping towards her in his bright-yellow wellies.

'Hello my bestest godson.'

'Auntie Nellie, you always say that and I'm your only godson!'

Nell crouched down and hugged him, 'Still the bestest one though! Surely those wellies don't still fit you?'

'Just about.' Jacob grinned.

'Where's your dad? He's disappeared.'

'I'm not allowed to say.'

Nell tickled his tummy, 'You can tell me anything, Jacob Green.'

'Not this time,' he zipped his mouth and grinned.

Nell looked towards Bea and Guy. 'Come on, what's going on? I know that look.'

Suddenly, the choir stopped singing and the only sound

The Cosy Canal Boat Dream

Nell could hear was the massive roar of an engine. The excited chatter all around began to peter out as heads turned. Nell peered over Bea's shoulder and watched the crowd part to see a beast of a motorbike drive slowly up the wharf towards her with a huge red-velvet ribbon tied around each of the handlebars. It stopped in front of Nell and she brought her hands up to her face when Nathan took off his helmet and grinned.

'This is it, isn't it?' Nell gasped, staring at the bike.

'It sure is and what a beauty!'

'Ollie's motorbike and it actually works!'

'We built this from scratch with our own bare hands and, thanks to Guy who tracked down the missing parts, we managed to finish it.'

Nell's eyes shone, 'Thank you so much, both of you, you really don't know how much this means to me.'

Nell hugged them both.

'Aunty Nellie,' Nell felt a small hand slip into hers, 'I was sworn to secrecy. Dad said if I didn't tell you what they were up to, then I could have a year's supply of free popcorn.'

Everyone laughed, 'And I promise you, you can have free popcorn for a lifetime.'

Jacobs's eyes sparkled, 'You are the best Aunty Nellie anyone could ever have.'

Bea looked at Nell, 'It's time, are you ready?'

Guy squeezed her hand reassuringly, 'I love you.'

She kissed him, then the top of Annie's head, before moving towards the stone steps. The whole crowd erupted in cheers. She paused at the top of the steps in front of the red ribbon and took in the view. She stared out over the crowd. She couldn't believe so many people had turned out to come to the opening of the Old Picture House. Her eyes glistened with happy tears. Everyone gathered at the bottom on the steps, all smiling proudly up at Nell.

Nell swallowed down the lump in her throat as a photographer from the local paper handed her a pair of scissors. He took a few snaps while Nell took a deep breath.

The crowd suddenly fell silent and all eyes were on Nell.

Her whole body trembled, her throat dry, 'Firstly, thank you all for coming today,' she was thankful her voice sounded a lot calmer than she actually felt. 'Nearly three years ago my life changed dramatically overnight when I lost my husband in a tragic accident.' She could feel herself getting emotional, which was understandable. 'We'd often talked about doing something together, taking on a project that would benefit the community, bringing all generations back together. So when this place came up for sale I knew I had to do everything in my power to buy it. This place, in particular, holds special memories for me. Most Sundays when I was a child, my dad brought me here and this was where I first dated my husband all those years ago.' Nell felt her voice wobble. She glanced towards Guy, who beamed back at her.

'I couldn't have undertaken this project without the backing and support of some special people in my life. Firstly to my partner, Guy, and my daughter, Annie, you are both my world. My mum, Gilly, and Lloyd,' Nell glanced towards them; both were tearful. 'My best friend, Bea, and husband, Nathan, and all of their beautiful children, I thank you from the bottom

The Cosy Canal Boat Dream

of my heart.' Nell stood to the side and pulled on the gold cord, unveiling the plaque on the wall, 'In loving memory of Ollie Andrews – always in our hearts.' Nell composed herself while everyone burst into a rapturous applause.

'And finally ...' the crowd quietened down. 'I declare the new Red Carpet Cinema open and please enjoy the film,' Nell cut the ribbon and everyone cheered. She pushed the doors open and all her family and friends joined her at the top of her steps.

'You did great,' Guy hugged her tight.

'I'm so proud of you, Nell,' Gilly kissed her daughter before Nell fell into Lloyd's arms. 'You did fantastic.'

'Thank you,' she said, dabbing away the tears. 'Are you all ready to come inside?' smiled Nell.

'You better believe it,' Bea beamed, linking her arm through Nell's as they stepped into the lavish foyer.

'Wow! Just look at this place. It looks amazing,' exclaimed Bea, 'Ollie would be so proud of you.'

'I know, he'll always hold that special place in my heart, but I know he'd be happy that I've found love again with Guy.'

'He most certainly would.'

They all stood in awe, the crystal chandelier hung from the high ceiling and the red majestic carpet stretched for what seemed miles towards the regally arching staircase and the place was alive with staff.

'I see you put up the posters of our favourite films,' Bea said, pointing to *Bridget Jones*, *Top Gun* and *Back to the Future*.

'Absolutely thanks to Lloyd, he's got some brilliant contacts!'

The popcorn machine was in place in the corner and the

ice-cream sellers were ready and waiting as the crowd began to spill in to purchase their tickets. Nell had approached the local council and sourced all her employees from teenagers and the elderly who were struggling to get jobs, bringing the whole community together, just like she'd talked about with Ollie.

'Where are Gilly and Lloyd?' asked Bea.

'Over there in the popcorn queue with Jacob and Fern,' grinned Nell.

'He's a little monkey! And how are you feeling?'

'Honestly, like I've just won the lottery. I'm on such a high and I can't thank you both enough for all you've done – the band, the red carpet and the motorbike.' She squeezed Bea and pecked a kiss on Guy and Nathan's cheek.

'Don't be daft, we are just glad it's a huge success.'

'Sorry to interrupt, Mrs Andrews,' Jason, the manager, looked at Nell, 'The press are waiting. Is it possible to borrow you for five minutes for a quick interview?'

Nell looked at Guy, 'You go. This one is still asleep, thankfully, but not sure how much longer for.'

Nell felt like a film star as an abundance of photographers shouted 'smile', the cameras began to flash and she was enjoying every minute of it.

Guy and Bea helped themselves to a glass of mulled wine from the refreshment area, 'The girl did well didn't she? Look at all these people, this place will be booming,' Bea exclaimed in admiration.

'She's done amazing.'

The crowd began to disperse into the main auditorium

The Cosy Canal Boat Dream

once they purchased their tickets and the excited chatter began to peter out. Nell appeared back at Guy's side joined by Gilly.

'I'm going to take this little one home while you enjoy the film,' they all smiled at Annie, who was still fast asleep against Guy's chest.

'Are you sure?'

'Absolutely, you enjoy your time today.'

'Thanks, Mum, what about Lloyd?'

'He's staying, he wouldn't miss the first showing for the world.'

'That's great,' Guy carefully untied the sling and passed a sleeping Annie carefully over to Gilly.

'Can I join you with the twins?' Fern asked, 'I don't mind looking after them while Bea and Nathan watch the film.'

'Yes, of course. I'll see you across at the Nollie.'

'Perfect,' replied Fern, 'I'll catch up with you in a minute.

While everyone settled inside the auditorium, Guy and Nell climbed the stairs to the projection room.

He put his arms around Nell's waist as they glanced through the window into the room below. Everyone was sitting down.

'Look at them all, how does that feel' he asked.

'Honestly? Amazing, I never in a million years thought I'd pull this off.'

He beamed at her, 'Right are you ready?'

'I'm ready.' Nell pressed a button and the lights dimmed in the auditorium below and as the red- velvet curtains began to open, everyone cheered.

'Now the projector.' Guy moved out of the way and Nell

switched on the machine. It kicked into action and began to whirl.

'What is the first film that you'll be showing in the cinema?' Guy asked, looking towards the screen below.

'The film Ollie and I watched on our very first date when we were seventeen – *Shrek the Third*! I thought Jacob might like it too.'

'Good choice!'

'Guy, I know we've mentioned Ollie a lot today, but I really couldn't have done this without you. He'll always have a place in my heart, but it's you I love. So much.'

He tilted Nell's head to his and kissed her on the lips.

'I love you, too, Nell. Now, come on, otherwise we will miss the film.' He grabbed Nell's hand and they began to run towards the auditorium.

Nell's heart swelled with happiness. Finally all her dreams had come true.

Acknowledgements

Squeal! It's been quite a journey and I really can't believe my sixth novel is here and published! There's a long list of truly fabulous folk I need to thank, who have been instrumental in supporting me and crafting this novel into one I am truly proud of.

Mum, Dad, Chris, Emily, Jack, Ruby and Tilly, my beautiful nutty funny gang, who inspire me every day. I couldn't do the job I love so much without the support of you all, thank you.

Woody, my man, my mad crazy cocker spaniel, who is always by my side and unquestionably the best company ever.

The clever people at HarperImpulse, Charlotte Ledger and Kimberley Young. Both of course who are utterly fabulous. They have helped, encouraged and believed in me right from the start. I thank you from the bottom of my heart for turning my story into a book and creating the dreamiest of covers. My editor the wickedly smart and humorous Emily Ruston who, in the most awesome way made this book the best it could possibly be.

Christie Barlow

A special mention to Jenny Oliver because without her, I would never have been introduced to the wonderful publishing team above!

For making me a happier human – Anita Redfern, can't fault her ... my best friend in the world ever!

Team Barlow! Big love to my merry band of supporters and friends, Nicola Rickus, Louise Speight, Sarah Lees, Catherine Snook, Alison Smithies, Caroline Shotton, Sue Miller, Emma Cox and Sharon Pillinger who provide oodles of laughs, cake and gift bags full of chocolate when I'm locked away in the writing cave for hours on end. Writing fiction can be a lonely job but your texts, tweets and emails along the way always make me smile on a daily basis. I am truly grateful for such consistent support and friendship.

Paula Jackson, for letting me bombard her with numerous research questions when I discovered she lived on a narrowboat! I hope you enjoy the story!

Finally high fives to everyone who enjoys, reads and reviews my books especially book bloggers Claire Knight, Lorraine Rugman, Sarah Hardy, Noelle Holten, Annette Hannah, Joanne Robertson and Petra Quelch. Your constant sharing of posts has never gone unnoticed and your support for my writing is truly appreciated.

Last but not least, *The Cosy Canal Boat Dream* wouldn't have been written if it wasn't for my daily walks around Barton Marina in Barton-under-Needwood, this spectacular place of tranquillity provided that little spark of inspiration behind this story.

I have without a doubt enjoyed writing every second of

this book and I really hope you enjoy hanging out with Nell Andrews and Guy Cornish. Please do let me know!
  Christie xx

Printed in Great Britain
by Amazon